THREE GREAT LIES

VANESSA MACLELLAN

HADLEY
RILLE
BOOKS

THREE GREAT LIES

    Cover art © Tom Vandenberg
    Map at end of book © Ginger Prewitt
    Edited by Eric T. Reynolds

    ISBN-13   978-0-9892631-4-6
    Published simultaneously in the United States of America and the
    United Kingdom by
    Hadley Rille Books
    PO Box 25466
    Overland Park, KS 66225 USA

    www.hrbpress.com
    contact@hadleyrillebooks.com

To my Mother

and

All the Smiling Dogs

Part 1: The Montu Bull

Come in Peace to the Beautiful West

Chapter 1

WITH NO WARNING, the teen jerked the motorcycle off the main road onto a washboard gravel path. Dust erupted from the tires' grind. Jeannette Walker scrambled for a handhold she knew wasn't there, her sweaty fingers slipping against the interior surfaces of the sidecar certainly older than the Second World War. Just an hour ago she'd been bored, pacing through market stalls erected in plywood, cloth and corrugated steel at the heart of old town El-Balyana, killing time on her fifth of a seven day tour of Egypt—her first trip beyond the States. Then the boy had called out to her. Dazzled her with the promise of "New tomb just opened. No other tourists there."

The actual ancient sites she'd visited had been somehow diminished by the swarms of tourists and press of locals selling plastic mummies and miniature Giza pyramids manufactured in China. How could she refuse "No other tourists there"?

They dipped down into a valley protected between two low mounds, and drove for another jaw-cracking ten minutes. Jeannette tried to blink the grit from her eyes. About a half mile up on the western side of the hill a rough stone mastaba had been partially unearthed. A remnant of the Old Kingdom, five thousand years ago.

When the teen had waved at Jeannette from the market crowd, arms frantically slicing the air, all elbows and knees, she judged him to be maybe fifteen. His body, entirely in motion, buzzed with the electrical energy of the young, or maybe he'd just downed three cups of Turkish coffee. Skin deeply browned, it was darker than the other city inhabitants', enhanced by eyes that rich chocolate she so admired, unlike her own generic gray-blue. Perpetually beaming, he radiated good-natured mirth.

She studied him, just waiting for the lie. Life had taught her many things; she had her eyes out for lies.

Instead, out of his mouth danced the promise, "No other tourists there," and the dreaded haggle.

"I make you good deal. Give me one-hundred forty pounds for my excellent tour of tomb, just opened. I promise you best tour in great land of pharaohs." He'd opened his arms wide, encompassing the entire country with his gesture. Jeannette faltered. Sky high tour price—and she'd already toured the Great Pyramids plus the Valley of the Kings and

5

other minor tombs. But honestly, she'd had enough of that gaggle of blue-hairs and walker jockeys for the rest of her trip. Plus, her best friend Gabby would do it.

Something newly opened... something fresh. "For my sick mother," the kid wheedled, reaching a hand out to her, giving her the biggest brown eyes full of pitiable need.

She knew there had to be a sick someone in the fine print. It was practically required.

But to see something new, something that didn't have a small village of tourist stalls speckling the grounds like gopher mounds, that had its appeal. To visit a tomb where she might be one-of-a-few instead of one-of-five-hundred, that was what she dreamed of. That embodied the true heart of Egypt she'd longed to explore: the draw of the pharaohs and the pyramids, the magic of the mummified dead.

It took a certain turn of a blind eye to trust the kid's driving skill. With her 'life experience' calculator Jeannette thought about it. Really thought about it. It wasn't like Egypt was a quick trip across the ocean. Gabby boasted about her adventures with the gift of gab; in Malaysia she'd taken a bike tour with a geezer older than her grandfather and showed Jeannette the pictures of her and the old man. Jeannette doubted the kid had plans to kidnap her, smuggling her off to some terrorist training camp; she had a sense about these things. The 6 pm tour bus would be here to take her back to Luxor and her luxurious, yet whitewashed, hotel. There was time.

Her young tour guide handed her a skull cap helmet scratched so much the gleam of metal streaked the black paint. After examining the inside for crawling things and finding nothing, Jeannette yanked the rubber band off her ponytail and pulled the helmet onto her head, cinching the chinstrap as tight as she could. With backpack pressed into her lap, she settled the arms of her sunglasses under the chinstrap, trapping the loose strands of her brown hair against her head. The boy had no helmet. Perhaps she should have acted the adult and returned the helmet to him, made sure the child was safe; then she remembered that this was Egypt and this boy was no longer a child.

Like dime store thieves, they'd burst from the town. As the determined bike chewed up and spat out miles of highway, the traffic evaporated from a deluge to a trickle until long spans passed where they were alone on the road. Cavities the size of pit traps spotted the surface, but the boy avoided them with micro-adjustments to his steering, and under engine speeds chugging to keep them upright, they crested a hill.

From the ridge she had a perfect view of the valley of the River Nile. The river flowed in lazy coils, losing itself in the horizon, lined by a civilization so ancient that it could count millennia. Her imagination struggled to comprehend it. Her entire country could practically count its years on fingers and toes, and Washington State was a spit in the sea. A ribbon of cities and green lined each bank. Sailing boats passed below the tall palm trees that stood sentry along the river. And from here the river looked blue, and she could imagine the respect the ancient people once had for it, a respect that had lost its place in this modern age.

Beyond the river unfolded the desert, stark and dry—a sustaining dry that kept mummies and papyrus preserved for thousands of years. A person could get lost out there in the endless nothing, lost forever and nobody would ever know.

During the ride she prayed—though not to a god she no longer believed in—hoping the kid would prove true to his promise. Enough people had already failed her. She'd woolgathered with a sour dread that he would park her next to a rickety pile of stones and declare them a national treasure.

Which he didn't. He was true to his word.

No other tourists here.

Anticipation returned, bumping the second-guessing devil off her shoulder. They arrived at the bi-leveled tomb and her guide killed the engine. The silence hummed in her ears. She struggled out of the sidecar, feeling like a newly hatched chick for the weakness in her limbs.

They were alone. Well, not completely alone. A dog sat next to the entrance.

The dog was smiling at her.

It was one of those mongrels that had the breed bred right out of him from generations of back alley affairs. They all looked the same: mid-sized, brown kinky fur with a curly tail and intelligent eyes. Jeannette guessed all the dumb ones had gotten run over by the locals three days after gaining their walking legs. She'd seen a few of the sad victims already: flat and desiccated by the thirsty wind, a cold reminder of life's delicate constitution and the maniac impatience of Egyptian cabbies.

Casualties of an indifferent life.

The boy pointed to the mastaba's rectangular opening; it stood dark and forbidding, the mouth of a desert demon. He still wore his smile, though this time it took on the quality of pride.

THREE GREAT LIES

"Here it is. Just uncovered," he said.

Jeannette unbuckled the helmet and perched her sunglasses on top of her damp head to better examine the structure, still half hidden under a tidal wave of sand. The mid-day sun had baked her brain within the black helmet, and sweat lacquered the sides of her face, behind her ears and the lids her eyes. She'd been cured, like a Christmas ham.

"Is it legal that I'm even here?" she asked, pulling a handkerchief from her pack to scrub down her face, dabbing water from her water bottle onto the fabric. Her nostrils felt encrusted by half the Sahara.

"Oh yes, this is my uncle Akil's land." The boy dismounted and the bike creaked in sudden relief. "Come, I show you." He waved his arm at her, and she watched him stride toward the tomb entrance, obviously having no trouble walking after the long ride. Jeannette lurched after him, muttering about the young. The dog lay down, forelegs stretched straight ahead in the fine, dry soil. Its tongue hung long from its mouth.

Layered along an inward slant, mud bricks formed a corner and one wall of what she'd learned was an Old Kingdom, rectangular burial chamber. At the center of the western side of the mastaba, two tall stones supported a small opening. A stout board propped up the left support, and a jumble of equipment lay in a pile outside: picks, brushes, wooden pallet-crates.

Only a few steadfast footprints impressed in the fine dirt revealed that anyone had been here in days. The air was still, somehow hollow. This was it, really it. A new discovery, the untrod path.

Jeannette tugged a small pouch containing a digital camera from her pack and hung it around her neck. She slung the backpack over her shoulders and lumbered over to where the boy stood by the entrance, the contents on her back shifting against her stiff gait. She tightened the straps as the boy offered her a flashlight with his eager grin. Taking it in hand, she grinned back. Jiggling the flashlight to get a firm grip, the battery rattled within.

She squinted through the entrance—the sun's light barely breached the darkness. "Whose tomb is this?" She bet Gabby had never seen anything like this.

The boy's eyes widened and he glanced up over Jeannette's shoulder into the sky. "Usurped prince of Egypt. He would not fight crocodile for his honor. He was killed and buried here."

"Was crocodile fighting common in Kemet?" she asked, using the traditional name for Egypt, and wondered what new tale the boy could devise on the spot, or perhaps he'd memorized this story and could recite it by rote.

"Yes, yes." He nodded at her, amusement glittering in his gaze. "Many men and princes had to fight crocodile with just spear." His voice grew high as he told the tale and his hands began dancing through the air. "The boys go to river edge in morning, waiting for crocodile to come from water. They wait for crocodile bird sitting in his mouth, picking out bad meat." The boy opened his mouth into a huge yawn, his tongue pressed against his bottom lip. "Then," he continued, "they sneak on great beast and fling mud at his eyes." He pretended to throw mud at an invisible crocodile in the sand. "When blind, the boys stab it with spears." He leapt through the air and poked his imaginary weapon at his blinded foe. The dog sat upright and barked once. When the boy completed the destruction of his enemy, he stood tall and turned to Jeannette, chest puffed out. "When boy kills first crocodile, it is great honor."

"Did all the cities do this?" she asked, aiming her light into the dark mouth of the tomb and glancing in. Dust motes danced in the beam of light.

"No. Some cities eat crocodile. Have no respect." He spat. "We go inside?" He flipped on his own flashlight and nodded at her.

A buzz of excitement tightened the skin at the back of her neck and with a final glance at the dog, she followed the boy.

The temperature drop as she entered the darkened passage chilled her, like crossing the barrier that separated the land of the living from that of the dead. Perhaps ghouls had crossed over her grave, or ghosts passed through her corporeal being, but as the shiver ran up her spine, she felt misplaced. Even with the flashlight, the contrast from the bright afternoon outside to the dull black caused an unsettling blindness. She waited, blinking repeatedly until her eyes acclimated, and then she discovered that she was alone. The boy must have already moved ahead.

"Hello?" she called out.

"Here!" he called back, his voice sounding somehow buried. She stepped deeper into the dim.

The soft light of the flashlight revealed dust everywhere, filtered through seams between the stones to add minute layer upon layer until everything wore a hefty coat of it. Certainly nothing so grand as a pharaoh or prince's tomb, no matter what the boy had said, it was, however, interesting and new. It was real. Something unattainable from library books or sanitized tours. A minefield of rubble and ankle-twisters made up the floor of the first chamber. A glance at the ceiling to see if any loose stones might fall upon her head proved nothing. It looked safe enough. The boy had run ahead—his fresh footprints conquering others in the dirt—so she guessed it wasn't too dangerous.

Her progress was slow; she'd been swallowed by a blackness weakened only by the feeble attempt of a flashlight whose bulb had grown faint with years probably greater than those of her guide. Every few steps she would shake it, the battery would rattle within like old bones, and the light would brighten, but its rally had little oomph and before she could properly study a bit of dust-free wall, it would fade again. She took a picture, blinding herself with the flash, and decided to tuck her camera away until she saw something truly unique.

After running her finger through the detritus on the floor, she stared at it, thousands of years of silt and powdered sand. On her fingertip remained the remnants of sloughed off ages. Then, she reached out and ran her fingers along an untouched section of wall, breaking off a crust of dirt that dropped to the floor with a poof. The hovering dust shimmered, targeting her eyes and nose. She could taste those ages on the air, dry and almost tangy. Lost, like old memories.

Hieroglyphs paraded across the wall: animal shapes and wavy lines, straight lines and simple characters lined up in mathematical precision. She'd studied a few of the symbols in one of her travel books, but their meaning proved less than Greek to her. At least she knew a few of those letters from the sororities at EWU and math class assignments. Summations, standard divinations and theorems. She was far more familiar with the math, always harboring a heavy disdain for the popularity contest that the sisterhood sustained. Joining the hieroglyphs were images of magnificent beasts and gods, the rulers of the land, and representations of the common duties of everyday life. She knew all that writing told tales and morals, and explained the proper ways of living and dying. The depth of this culture—a fairytale itself—astounded her.

The designs and decoration within this mastaba were nothing like those of the tombs in the Valley, but Jeannette felt a kinship with the modest depiction of life. She jiggled her flashlight again and studied a scene of people lined up facing one direction. Were they dancing? Lining up for free rations of grain? Their true actions as mysterious to Jeannette as those of the sorority girls back in college.

A stone caught her foot and she aimed her flashlight at it. She wondered if the rundown state of the Old Kingdom tomb was typical, earned by time, or if it had been robbed by raiders, either modern or ancient. The corridor soon branched off and at the intersection in an alcove, a piece of pottery rested. It was intact, and she brushed the side of her hand against the surface, displacing the sleeve of dust. In the weak light she could see a long-necked animal next to an ibis and some squiggles in reds, blacks and whites. With instant solemnity, she knew shouldn't be down here. It wasn't right for her, a mere tourist, to tramp around in such a pristine archeological site. She'd probably screw something up, maybe break something irreplaceable, and she didn't welcome such guilt.

She called out to the boy. No answer. She called again. "Hey, kid?"

Her words slumped through the hollow of the tomb.

Footprints led to the left down some steps, and she followed them at a careful pace, keeping her arms tight against her chest to avoid touching another thing.

"Hey? Where are you?"

Dread tickled the back of her neck. What if he'd tripped and snapped his neck? What if he'd broken a five-thousand-year-old vase?

"We should leave," she yelled, but her cry went flat, consumed by the passages and stone.

Another few steps and a darkness, almost tangible with its density, claimed its territory upon the floor mere shuffles away, sucking dry the glimmer from her flashlight. Two handles of a wooden ladder, almost modern and free of dust, peeked over the edge of the hole in the tomb floor the size of the tractor inner tubes she'd used to float on at the lake in her childhood summers. Aiming her flashlight, she tried to illuminate the pit down the shaft, but the light only exposed a few rungs of the ladder.

"Hello?" she called down into the shaft. "You down there?" Her voice limped to the bottom of the shaft, weakened by the sinister and creepy vibes that materialized with her worry.

Straining her ears, all she could hear was that ticking hum of silence, the noise left behind when all other sound sat back for a noontime siesta.

She squinted down into the hole. She didn't want to go down there. She really, really didn't. Entombed bodies rested down there. But the kid had probably climbed down; she would have explored this shaft when she'd been young and stupid.

"Hey. Kid?" She tried to add steel to her voice, mimic the tone of someone who no longer considered the scratching on the windowsill hilarious. Instead she noted a tinny edge to it, the sound of someone just this side of flipping out and escaping to the safety under the open sky.

She squared her shoulders. She was not going to freak out. Sure, she knew that it was highly likely a mummy rotted away at the bottom of that shaft, but what if her guide had fallen in? It wasn't even a remote possibility that she would leave him down there. She wasn't the kind of weak horror movie stereotype to flee at the first sign of creepiness and abandon others to some grisly end. She was not a helpless cliché; those kinds of people were despicable.

With a little struggle she stuffed the flashlight into her pants pocket; the skewed path of the light flushed the shadows from the ceiling's corner. Then she grabbed the handles of the ladder and placed her right foot on it. The rung held. With a little bounce she tested the steadiness of the ladder. It would hold.

Gingerly, she descended. Her gaze adhered to each rung as it rose before her nose like the baskets of an amusement park ride; her hands, pale, almost glowing, clutched onto the worn wood as sweat began coating her palms.

One foot, one hand. Descending. Into the domain of a mummy. Where she might find the body of her guide. His body swarmed by a legion of scarab beetles.

If she focused, really listened, she could almost hear the metallic clack of millions of beetles crawling over each other, their exoskeletons clinking in concert as if in celebration of such a tender meal. She knew that sound; pre-trip she'd watched any movie about Egypt she could dredge up, even the scary ones.

As she strained to hear any indication of movement below her, Jeannette's foot hit cockeyed on the next rung, skidding off. Scrambling for the rung, her hands, damp with anxiety, slipped from the smoothed surface of the ladder: her palm dangled, her fingers gone inch by inch, and then the tips lost their purchase. She knew then, in that moment she *knew*, the beetles would have another offering on which to tame their hunger.

For a brief moment she felt weightless, then reality once again asserted itself through the rigidity of the floor. As she hit the ground her jaw snapped shut and her body tumbled. Reaching out to brace herself as she rolled, pain sparked a map across her body: her butt, her leg, her wrist and arm. In an instant her world turned sharp and piercing. Her flashlight dug into her hip, then disappeared, and with her eyes squeezed shut she wondered if it would still work. When she smacked her head against a stone, she didn't worry about it anymore.

Chapter 2

GROANING, JEANNETTE FOUGHT TO PRY HER EYELIDS APART. It proved a Herculean effort. First one, then the other fluttered open, and each only a slim crack. Nothing. With the booming bass in the back of her skull, she'd expected that the simple act of seeing would spark some additional pain—sharp, dull . . . something. But there was nothing, no seeing at all. The room had dematerialized in the complete absence of light. She could be floating along the edge of the universe for all she knew, except for the scent of dry stones and dust, and the firm support of the floor beneath her side. A circus pachyderm balanced on her head, using it in its act as a replacement for its brightly-colored ball. With questing fingers she explored her scalp; sharp bolts of pain danced across her synaptic nerves straight to her eyeballs, and suddenly there was that light she'd sought, only brilliantly white and piercing.

A few seconds slipped by and she opened her eyes again; the pain had mellowed to an ache. With newly inherited timidity she reached back to feel the wound a second time; her fingers came away tacky. From her years of forced first aid videos and classes through Starvine Laboratory's safety training, she knew she should apply a cold press. The dry voice of the video narrator came to her mind. "Do not apply ice directly to the skin. Hold the cold press on the affected area for half an hour." The bump rivaled a goose egg, but bled little. After a quick survey, she discovered pain in her right wrist. At least her legs felt mostly fine, except for her hip. She could praise God, or Allah, or whoever watched over this place, that she hadn't fallen into a fissure of magma, or a pit of deadly vipers. But such beings did not exist in her world.

At least it didn't seem that there were any beetles.

She held her breath and listened. No metallic chittering. She giggled, then snapped her mouth shut, not liking the way it sounded.

It was claustrophobic, this utter blackness, but she'd never been one to give sway to panic. She breathed in deep, long and lung filling. Inhaled again. Again. The air tasted earthy, dull with stagnation.

With her heart still running races around the track, she got to her knees and began brushing along the ground, scouring the floor for the ladder, the flashlight, the kid, anything. As nimble as dead fish, the fingers of her useless left hand crawled along the cool stone of the floor as she cradled her right close to her middle. She'd never been one of those ambidextrous prodigies who could throw a ball, much less write, with her off-hand.

Nothing. Blind and lost and alone.

She squeezed her eyes shut and considered what she did have. She rolled back onto her tailbone, a twinge of pain reminding her of her misfortune, and pulled off her daypack. High tech nylon scored by the tight weave of miniscule strands of material. Water resistant, abrasive resistant, it was an outdoor gear masterpiece. The salesman at the Spokane store on Monroe Street had told her it offered everything she required for a daypack. She'd told him she had plans to vacation in Egypt and he pretended to be sufficiently impressed. She knew he was pretending, but she'd still preened under the attention. She liked that other people saw her as adventurous.

Gabby had acted unimpressed.

"About time you went out and did something adventurous," Jeannette's friend had said. About time, indeed.

The airport-friendly combination lock barred the entrance to the pack's main compartment. Her emotional yardstick slid another few inches into the dangerous realm of annoyed.

The main compartment contained her money belt with most of her cash, passport and credit card, as well as a lapis lazuli ankh pendant with a little bug design she'd purchased that morning in the El-Balyana stalls. But right now, most importantly, a small first aid kit remained locked away until she could develop night vision or spontaneously hit the right code on the lock.

"Damn," she said aloud, jumping as her voice filled the dark chamber.

Rising to her feet, she turned in place, eyes spread open to capture any stray spark or sneaky ray of sunlight. Nothing.

Blinded without the sharp aim of a mud-slinger.

Remembering the rabbit hole she'd fallen through, she tilted her head back, searching the ceiling for the shaft's mouth. Her eyes roamed everywhere, eager, wanting, desperate for something. A way out. Carefully, she pushed one foot forward along the stone. The bottom of her boot scraped against the floor. Stretching forward with her good arm, she took another step, and another, inching her way along until her knee collided with something sturdy. She mentally added it to her inventory of hurts. The object reached about waist high with a slightly rounded top. A shelf? Tired, she propped her hip up against it and dropped her backpack onto the shelf. She was trapped here, in the dark. Alone. Thoughts of being buried alive and the ravenous scarab beetles eating at her flesh flashed through her head in 3-second shorts. She sniffed, swallowed.

"Jeannette. You are a scientist. You enjoy scary movies. Do not freak out now." She tilted her head back and called into the nothing around her. "Hey, anyone here?" Silence. The teenager must have ditched her, and wasn't that the pinnacle to a splendid day. Abandoned. Again. Just her life.

Jeannette shook her head. Walking down that pathway lead to nowhere good. She needed to start thinking logically. She scooted her butt up to rest on the shelf.

Her intended seat shifted to the side, the grinding of stone rebounding amid the chamber. She sprang to her feet, turning to look, an automatic response of the sighted. But there was nothing to see down here.

Or, was there?

A faint glow illuminated the darkness to her right. A square section of light, like the rising sun at five a.m., highlighted an opening. She could just make out the top landing of a set of rising stairs as the light dimmed slightly, then flared up like a newly caught candle. A torch braced in a sconce lit aflame, then another, this one down a step, closer to her, followed by another, and Jeannette began to feel like she'd fallen into some Hollywood adventure film as the entire room became visible by the wavering brilliance of equally spaced out torches.

That lit themselves.

Fine wisps of smoke curled to the ceiling. Jeannette stared at the torches, mouth popped open by untended muscles. The shifting light drew shadows over the intricately decorated walls. She clamped her eyes shut and counted to ten, taking a deep breath as each number came and passed. She opened them again. The torches still blazed, stairs that she swore did not exist when she had explored the floor above still led up, and the decorated walls surrounding her were like nothing she'd seen before.

The reds and ochres that spread across the richly painted chamber became crisp once they'd emerged from the gloom, as if painted there the previous day; the dust she'd experienced on the level above was as absent as her young guide. Patterns of ankhs and pharaoh heads and squiggly lines covered the stairway wall as the steps climbed into the unknown. Pictures of squatting caricatures of Egyptian men with multi-colored hair crowded near the floor. Centered along another wall were images depicting the tale of a man facing Ra. She knew it was Ra because a disc of the sun rested on his head. Women with long, black hair dressed in white spread seed upon the ground; others harvested grain. There were paintings of green trees and brown trees bearing fruit. In the curved arch of the ceiling a phoenix spread its wings, the feathers fluttering with the hypnotic flicker of the torches. Osiris, Bast and a wig-less woman near a glowing arch. An image of a heart weighed against the feather of Ma'at, another of hunting waterfowl, the next of war chariots, stages of life and the afterworld pledged in layers of milk and lye. All faces in profile, all eyes staring at her.

She tore her eyes away, then realized two things. The ladder and flashlight were missing, which certainly caused her alarm, but worse, something that caused her to question the number in her deck of cards, the hole she'd fallen through no longer pierced the ceiling.

Materializing stairs, torches coming to life . . .

She stared at the ceiling again. Still, no hole.

The serpent of unease wrapping around her insides turned into a dragon. Dropping her gaze from the walls she reached for her bag. That was when she saw it.

Against the wall opposite the stairway lurked a large sarcophagus, the lid resting askew.

Involuntarily leaning away, she scanned the sarcophagus. That must have been what she'd sat on. It seemed impossible that she could have budged the lid with the simple act of sitting. The weight of the stone slab would have taken many men to move. The slabs were chiseled from solid stone, weren't they? She scolded herself for her lack of research on the practicalities of ancient Egyptian life and death. On previous tours, the guides had filled in the knowledge gaps from her pre-trip readings. But for this expedition, she had only one errant boy guide who'd probably unearthed something priceless and was preparing it for hawking, forgetting about the poor American woman lost in a maze of antiquity and delirium.

From the side of the sarcophagus spied a pair of painted eyes, wide and intent. Everything down here watched her.

Maybe the lid wasn't stone, but a hollow, plaster counterfeit. A mimic of history for gullible tourists. That explained her ability to move it. A laugh built up inside her throat, but it never came to life. What about the ladder, and the hole in the ceiling? She turned around in place, watching the eyes watching her.

She felt deserted.

Where had her damned guide gone?

Maybe he was a vindictive little punk who wanted to pull one over on the easy vacationers. He'd moved the ladder, and the hole's absence had to be some optical illusion perpetrated by mirrors and the uneven lighting.

Or possibly, though more far-fetched, some old mold, like those people in Salem had ingested in the early days of America, flourished down here. It could also be that the fruit drink from the café on the corner where the kid had solicited her had been on the fermented side. With enough time for thought, she knew she could devise a plausible explanation.

To her right rose the stairs, and to her left, near the sarcophagus, another passage led deeper into the complex. Maybe the kid had been injured. Honestly, it was against her nature to think badly about him. He'd doubtless gotten lost, and now wandered the ancient paths as any child his age would, guided by youthful good luck.

She stood on tiptoes, plucked a torch from its holder, and wished she'd packed her four-leaf clover. She needed some of that luck, and twenty-four wasn't so young anymore.

The torchlight caught an image of the Eye of Ra, omniscient and red, and a shiver crossed her skin. With a glance back at the stairs—a little voice in her head urging her to 'just get the hell out'—she faced the tunnel again. She'd leave once she assured the kid wasn't lost down here, injured and scared.

She grabbed her pack and slung it over her shoulder, careful of her injuries, and crept past the sarcophagus, certain the opening loomed wider than before. Not looking in for fear of catching a peek at something dead and rotten, she stepped into the darkened hallway, calling out. "Hello?" Her voice hung flat in the narrow hall, the acoustics wanting. It surprised her to find a network of passages and rooms. Each dry, empty antechamber sucked the fluid from her mouth and mocked her with hostile silence. As she wandered from one small chamber to the next, she expected to find piles of offerings, maybe gold or jewels, or even pottery, but the rooms housed only one blocky sarcophagus. Otherwise empty, they had been left incomplete—or emptied under ill-intentioned methods.

"Kid." Her calls had turned into a mantra, lacking the passion of initial panic and had morphed simply into a word that slipped from her lips each time she entered a new room. "Kid?" Her guide played an amazing impersonation of somebody who was just not there.

When she hit the end of the passages, having explored each alcove with no sign of life, she began retracing her steps to that first room she'd tumbled into. The kid must have been on the upper level after all, and had not fallen down the threshold into crazy land like she had. Just her luck.

Exhausted, dragging her feet across the stones, she almost tripped on the flat surface. She just wanted to return to her hotel and sleep. The dreaded knowledge of the long trip back in the bike's sidecar—assuming she could even return that way—and the fact that she was running out of water, sapped away her optimism. Trips were designed to be fun, a bit of adventure, a bit of pampering. She was ready for the spa treatment now. The tour planners had touted it as part of the package deal. She'd never had a spa treatment: no foot rubs, no facials. The knowledge that a hot bath and massage waited for her spurred her forward, though all she really wanted to do was close her eyes and open them again to her hotel room, the soft bed and bowl of fruit, the funky scent of the detergent that tickled her nose to the edge of a sneeze.

Damn it. This wasn't what she wanted.

Frustrated, she stomped across the floor, her hard-soled hiking boots clomping as her mind soldiered through her options to make it back to El-Balyana, let alone Luxor. With her thoughts leap-frogging from walking miles, to hijacking a camel, to the cost in dog lives of a taxi trip to her hotel, she didn't see the figure standing near the opened sarcophagus as she rounded the corner.

When she did, she froze.

Within the eon caught between one blink and the next, she absorbed details of the monster from a bad B movie: short, about her height, wrapped in linen gauze. Arms bound to its sides, it twisted and writhed, struggling to free itself from the linen embrace.

Then it moaned, a noise tapped straight from its slim chest, desperate and hungry, and Jeannette couldn't contain her own scream.

She spun away, another cry breaking free. With energy mined from welling panic, she hobbled from the room, pain flowering through her hip. The stairs, the only possible way out, were still lit by the flickering torches. Hopping the steps two at a time, her pack jangled with each lunge. Her breath erupted in sharp staccato. Mindlessly, through tunnels new and unfamiliar, she ran until she saw an exit. Warped moonlight streamed in through solid supports, and she could hear the evidence of people outside, lots of people, walking and talking, calling out. She burst through to the outside, remembering it should be day and desert and desolate, but all at once it was none of those things.

The moon bloomed fat as it hung low on the horizon above the rounded edge of the foothills. The glow reflected on the river, which curved at least half a mile closer to where she'd emerged than it had before she'd entered the tomb.

"Watch it," someone said behind her and she turned.

Something was definitely rank in the state of Denmark.

A man, towering above her, dressed in a white, Egyptian style kilt and nothing over his chest, scanned her with puny eyes peering from the head of a jackal. A fly settled on the tip of his pointed ear; he flicked it away as he walked on. She stumbled backward, retreating into the tomb, caught by the world beyond, poised on the borderlands of sanity.

A fair number of short, dark-skinned people with black hair, dressed in anything from the white linen illustrated in all the paintings to scraps of dirty cloth, passed before her like fall leaves floating on a river determined for the sea. Mixed within their ranks were men and women of night black skin, others paler with large beards, and Asians. All of these were normal by any other standards, because walking among them were animal-headed people. Mini-gods, she'd immediately reflected. A cat head and cow head, and jackal and some bird heads, all mingled with the humans on the ancient street. Her mind having gone blank in overload, all Jeannette could do was watch and breathe and think "this isn't real."

Reaching back, she touched the sticky bump adorning her head. That must be it. She must have concussed herself and now she was either in a coma or hallucinating. A very simple explanation.

Or that LSD mold she'd remembered reading about had infested the tomb, and she'd inadvertently taken in a whiff. It wasn't witchcraft her mind had been blighted with, but Egyptian mythology, which in some Jungian paradigm had to fit. She was sick and concussed, and now trapped in some headspace that grabbed at the details squirming through her brain, and this was the make-believe existence it had created for her.

She nodded shallowly with false assurance, her breath coming in unsteady sips. It was near impossible to ignore the stuttering of her heart.

A short man sporting the head of a crocodile stalked up to her and snapped at the air before her face. She pulled away, making herself small. His shoulders hunched under his bulk and he walked with a long spear that rose over his head. "You aren't of the family. Get out of that tomb, flat-face. I'll tell the Overseer you're cursing the dead if you don't get now." He bared his teeth and she flinched, then nodded, raising her hands in some I'm-doing-no-harm gesture that did little to impress the guard, and she stepped beyond the tomb mouth, away from him, impeding the folks traveling the mortuary hill.

"Are you lost?" She flinched at the question, and then turned to see a man. A human. Her relief made her so giddy she nearly smiled.

"Yes." She nodded. "Where is . . . ?" She glanced around. "Where am I?"

He looked at her with open curiosity. He wore a simple length of cloth wrapped around his waist with minimal adornment. "Ah, a foreigner. Are you here for the *Bakhu* festival? To receive an oracle?" He studied her for a moment; she swallowed and offered a weak nod. "The festival is held at Montu's temple." He pointed toward the river. Beyond the line of buildings of the ancient city, a bonfire blazed in miniature at the center of a large complex. She nodded again, as if suggesting he'd given her all the answer she needed.

"Yes, thank you." She did a half bow and the man shook his head as he descended the hill, muttering about missionaries and outsiders.

The cogs within her brain screeched to a halt. Had he just spoken English? And that crocodile man, too? Her brow furrowed; it wasn't English, she was sure of it.

She glanced around, in awe at the buildings, the full moon, the animal-headed mini-gods walking amidst the people of Egypt. Ancient Egypt, for that was exactly where she stood now, and how in the world had her mind created something so detailed, fully supplied with even the defunct language of the people of the river?

"Maybe my water was tainted," she said to herself, "because this isn't at all what I expected."

"Nor I."

Turning, she saw the mummy three steps behind her. Its wrapped arms and legs, now free, were loosely bound at the elbows and hands; its body's aged linens sagged at its waist; flashes of dark, shriveled skin were visible through the slipping gauze on its face. Eyes, withered and loose within their sockets, bore down on her.

21

Chapter 3

WARMTH SEEPED INTO THE KITTEN'S BONES as she nestled deeper into the heap of her brothers and sisters, all seventeen from her birthing batch. This bordered on the pinnacle of comfort, perhaps even peaked it, to be swallowed by contented purrs and lulled into a half-doze where time and impending duty meant nothing. Simply one of the litter, she hoped she would always remain so.

A foot jabbed at her shoulder. With a hiss and spat, she let her sibling know that he could put his ungainly leg elsewhere. She settled back into place, eyes in a half-sated squint.

Then a commanding *chirrup* pulled the kittens from their pile, the nap officially called to an end, and she tottered to an unoccupied patch of the stone floor and arched her long back in a morning stretch. Her claws extended as her paws reached across the cold stone; her tail waved in slow arches through the air. A fly buzzed overhead, drawn to the fine tuft of fur crowning the tip of her ear. She flicked it away with disinterest.

An elderly lady who had long ago perfected the transformation into the human-bodied form, the sacred attitude of the Lady Bast, entered the chamber. "Children, time for your morning exercises," the matron said, her voice a lovely melody of serenity. Though they all *awwed* in protest, the kittens followed her command, knowing not to push her patience. Napping was much more fun, but the matron's word was a law unto itself and her sharp, orange eyes cataloged those who lagged, those who showed greater eagerness.

As one unit, the litter followed the matron. Through eyes framed by silvering fur, she'd seen more inundations than the kittens could count, learning wisdom and spells as all of the children of the Lady did. As the kittens would, for they were all *mi-nether*, reflections of the Goddess. They padded behind the matron, leaving the sleeping chamber with tails erect like a salute, each kitten trying to match the exact pace and positioning of his or her neighbor so as not to stand out. They were a mass of identical black, marching with identical sway and step.

The matron led them through the familiar golden hallways arching high over their heads, into a small inner garden open to the sky above. A limestone-lined pool shimmered in the center, filled with waters from the *Iteru*, the sacred river that brought with it all life. Reaching up from the water, the speckled peak of an obelisk ascended at least three heads taller than the woman. Lush palms lined the garden, perhaps the favorite place for the children of Bast to roll and play, tussling with their brothers and sisters. Early morning light, thin and pink, illuminated the rounded tops of the stone walls. The kitten lifted her gaze to the cloudless sky; it was far too early. But today commemorated an important transition: it was their first viewing of the Goddess Sopdet in the month of Thoth of the time of the flooding. Today began their first shifting lesson, and so she sat amongst the others, waiting politely for the matron to speak.

"Children. To reach adolescence, to leave kittenhood behind, you must master the art of changing your form from that which it is, to that which is holy and of the Lady." She smiled at them; her fangs, worn with age, had dulled to a pale yoke color. "It is in your blood, and I'm certain each one of you will reach perfection before the new moon rises." As she purred reassuringly at them, the kittens secretly exchanged glances with each other, silently sharing fears and concerns.

Then the matron clapped her hands once, and they all jumped to attention, small bundles of energy frantic to please. "Now, line up. Yes. Face me." The kittens, each a black smear against the vibrant green grass, aligned themselves in a neat grid pattern and waited expectantly. "Good." She purred again. "Now, close your eyes." The young female did as guided. Around her were the noises of her sibling counterparts, shuffling, buzzing with expectancy. The beat of her heart thumped inside her ears, and she wondered if her heart hadn't somehow moved from her chest into her head and if this was the first step to the change. "Take a deep breath," the matron said, "and imagine yourself in the two-footed form. Then, let the mind's vision become reality. Be two-footed."

With a great inhalation, the kitten did imagine, just as the matron had instructed. *Be the wind, be the laughter, be the joy, be two-footed.* A nursery chant taught before they could even speak ran through her mind over and over, its repetition a salve to her nerves. Then, something within her shifted. The thudding of her heart bounced like a wooden ball across the sanctuary's hard floor, her hearing all but swallowed by Apep, and suddenly she lost her balance, toppling to the lawn with such lack of grace that she knocked over her neighbor to her right.

She gasped. "I'm so sorry." She'd never been so clumsy. Springing away with contrition, she jumped to her feet and reached out. Hands. She had hands, and immediately she fell to the spongy ground again.

"Well, done," the matron told her, her approving smile turning her

23

usual dour face into one much younger.

The kitten looked down the length of her legs—long human legs—and lifted her hands up before her face. Smooth-skinned, beige fingers. Her thin body naked, hairless, and so tall. She glanced around at the others, hoping she wasn't the only one to get the transformation on the first try. She didn't want to be better than anyone else. She didn't want to be different.

Three of her siblings had also managed the change and wore identical looks of concern.

* * *

Hours later, the nursery overflowed with yearlings once again. It felt, to the female, like a reprieve. Exhausted relief coursed through her little body: she hadn't been taken away. By the end of the lesson only four of them had failed to reach the goal of their metamorphosis. Those four had not advanced to adolescence like her and those of her litter who *could* change. They were different, even more than she who had been one of the first.

Only the careful set of her features, betraying no pride or concern, kept her part of the litter. Even to show one tiny bit of self-confidence stemming from her quick transformation could ostracize her; she'd heard of such things happening.

There were stories passed around the litters. All of the young ones listened eagerly, promised by a brother or sister from an older birthing batch that these stories were as real as the whiskers on their mother's muzzle. Tales of those who stood out, those who learned quickly, grew faster or slower. Those who didn't *fit*. They disappeared. Gone away from the warmth and safety of the mass of siblings. The ideas of *different* and *away* and *alone* scared the hiss and spit out of her.

They were not individuals, but one of many. She liked it that way; it meant she would never be lonely.

That afternoon she'd morphed from one form to the other, changing shapes with the natural ease of a tadpole into a frog. Back in the sleeping chamber, the slowest of the litter practiced again and again, tutored by the others to achieve their own change so they wouldn't be left behind. While explaining the feeling of the change to a sister, the adolescent's mind wandered to her next lesson, to assume the lion form of her cousins of Sekhmet. After perfecting these changes of shape she would then learn the magic of Lady Bast and the skills of a midwife and guardian. She and her siblings were highly prized, the girl kittens going into midwifery while the males entered into the guardian guild to protect the recently deceased with their cousins of Anubis. It was what all the children of Lady Bast had done for eons.

Night settled on the litter, and she snuggled close to those of her birthing batch, a pile of kittens linked together by tails and fur and the blood pumping through their veins, at peace with the knowledge that things were as they were supposed to be.

"Sanura. Sanura, rise up."

Warmth seeped through her flesh and she didn't want to move, but someone called out to her and the voice sparked feelings of contentment and safety. Something in her *ba* arched up to reach it.

"Sanura." That voice. *"Focus your mind on me, my dear one."*

Slowly, like a gentling whirlwind, her thoughts settled and she opened her eyes. The sleeping chamber, its brightly muraled walls depicting the charges of the children of Bast, enclosed her where she slept buried within a ball of familiar family.

"Sanura." That word again, that name. It floated about her like a hot summer's breeze, blowing through the hollow center within her chest, leaving a bit of itself behind. *"Attend to me, Sanura."*

"Sanura?" she asked, her voice somehow transparent, residing mainly in her head. "Is that my name?" She'd never had a name before.

"You are my Sanura," said the voice.

Seeking the source of the words, Sanura looked around, eyes blinking under the new weight of the name, and there, under the arched entryway, stood a human-bodied woman wearing the headdress of authority and a shimmering torque around her neck. She recognized the golden eyes of the Goddess without any hesitation; it was Mother. The Lady Bast who called to her with mind and voice and presence. With her next thought, Sanura slid from the grip of her body and float-walked over her siblings to drift before the noble Lady. The Goddess' *ba* pulsed like the tide of the great delta and Sanura was as helpless as the river reeds wrapped up in that power.

"Mother!" she cried.

Sanura caught something in the Goddess' expression. Behind the joy and love rested the taint of worry, or perhaps concern. Something like expectation. The adolescent couldn't clearly define it, but acknowledging it erected the hairs on her body in an unpleasant way.

25

THREE GREAT LIES

But then the Lady chuckled and Sanura no longer felt afraid. Above all else, her mother loved her. With that truth cradled in her heart, she leapt into her mother's arms, buried her questing nose into the soft fuzz along the Goddess' neck and inhaled deeply. For months she'd wished for this, to be with her mother again, to return to this complete sense of belonging and rightness.

"*Your* ba *is so young.*" The Lady inhaled a deep breath—eyes closed in joy—then she opened them again and Sanura caught a delicate hint of sadness. "*So sweet, my lovely child.*"

With soft fingers, Lady Bast stroked Sanura's body from crown of head to the base of her tail. The soporific sensation soothed the young female, and soon she felt herself relax, her *ba* settle into the protection offered.

"*Sanura*—" she stroked again, "—*I have a task for you.*"

Sanura's breath weakened. She glanced at the rest of her littermates, all sleeping in a jumble of limbs, her own body amongst them, motionless. Then she returned her gaze to that of the Lady.

"Y—yes?" she asked. She would do anything for Mother, this divine Goddess who had given her life, who guarded the lives of so many.

Lady Bast leaned down, her golden eyes soft at the corners, and breathed into Sanura's face. With her warm breath traveled a ray of calm. Sometimes the simplest gesture could convey a river of reassurance. Or maybe it was just the sweet scent of her mother.

The Lady ran a finger along the bridge of Sanura's nose, and the young feline smiled, too tense to laugh. "*There are two wanderers where the* Iteru *flows. They are lost and afraid.*" With this simple statement, Sanura's world shifted. They were lost. And afraid.

With a quick dart of her eyes Sanura looked beyond Lady Bast's shoulder out toward the world beyond the nursery, the protective walls of the temple. "They are alone?" she asked, her voice quavering and small. The Lady nodded, her ears erect. "Out there?"

"*Yes. Out there.*" Lady Bast's voice was warm, but heavy in a way Sanura had never heard before. "*I need you to do something for me. Only you can do this.*" Her mother purred and the girl nuzzled closer, her paws kneading, seeking comfort. "*Will you do this for me?*" she asked, her voice as gentle as the caresses her tongue had performed the day her litter bubbled up from Nu, born of thought and intention more so than any earthly performance.

Sanura swallowed, her throat suddenly dry, ignoring the sudden weight pressing into her from all around. "Of course . . ." With a pounding chest and her tongue cleaved to the roof of her mouth, Sanura's body twinged from tail to ear. "But I don't know how to find them. I do not know how I can help."

She stared at the uraeus upon the Goddess' head, the rising cobra a symbol of her power, her authority. She couldn't meet her mother's eyes, but instead stared at the ruby glint of the serpent's folded wings. "Why me?" she wanted to ask, needing to know exactly how she had stood out from the others when she had tried so hard to be just like everyone else. Why wasn't another of them picked? Like one of her brothers who would grow up to be a guardian? Why not another of those who'd changed first, or who hadn't changed at all? But she didn't ask, the unknown truth breeding far more fear that the lack of knowing. Of knowing her deficiency.

"*I will guide you.*" Lady Bast licked Sanura across her nose. "*I will guide you and watch over you the entire way. Even if you feel that you are alone, know that my love is with you always, and I watch you, always . . .*"

Her mother had told her where she needed to go. Her mother had told what she needed to do. And it was all *out there.*

"*You must leave today,*" the Goddess said, and Sanura did as she asked, even if it was the scariest thing she'd done in all her life.

Chapter 4

THREE HEARTBEATS LATER, the proximity of the walking, talking mummy unnerved Jeannette into action again.

By weaving herself between the strangest mix of people imagined by the collective subconscious of the universe—or her own concussed daydreams—Jeannette danced to skirt her tail. Soon enough, the mummy's lurching shuffle left him swallowed within the oddity ball. Even those fabled stories of 1920s freak shows couldn't compare to the men, women and beasts surrounding her. Certainly a wolfman covered head to foot in hair, or a geek who ate bugs and nails would be balanced on the odd end of the teeter, but a woman with the head of a lion just passed by, followed by a pack of jackals yipping about the state of the temple they were pledged to guard—and Jeannette could understand every yip and bark. Their unnaturally colored fur glistened, black as night, and she wondered if she'd just incurred twice the bad luck of a similarly colored cat's passing.

The types of people weren't the only odd flavor to this place. The light stretched thinner and colors looked sharper, like a badly tuned television. Flavored with the dust from the marching procession, the air had an unpleasant tartness to it. Two buildings down, a merchant carried a stick with seven shriveled heads dangling from it on gossamer lines. With sharp nods and hand gestures, he haggled with a goat-type creature topped with the head of a man whose flurry of hair could have been tended to by house mice. Everything was a strange fusion of facts straight from her pre-trip texts and things that she'd never even thought to dream up. Many of the women, black hair braided or worn straight, eyes darkened with kohl, wore white smocks held up by a strap knotted over one shoulder. Most of the men wore long, white kilts, the fabric crossing in the front, that she'd learned were *shendyt* from a display in the Cairo museum. Some even ran around naked, and Jeannette gawked worse than a virgin at a strip club.

But those defined normality. Nudity definitely belonged in the catalog of normal.

Jeannette glanced over her shoulder. The mummy, a single specimen of his kind, stumbled along about twenty yards behind her having its own issues with the crowd. It turned its head to follow the path of a jackal-headed man, and then submissively dropped its gaze when the jackal glanced its way. Nobody else gave her stalker a second notice; apparently the risen dead were as notable as sparrows on a power line.

The sun was lowering behind her in the west—at least she assumed the sun in dreams still set in the west—casting everything in long shadows touched by gold as she dodged between the people. She wondered where the day had gone; it had been afternoon when she'd entered the tomb a million years—and a couple million orderly brain waves—ago. Rough, mud-brick buildings lined the wide street, free of litter, free of cars and the last physical traces of dead dogs. The buildings had been built on a grid, regularly spaced with five paces between each one, and she realized she'd wandered into a subdivision. Maybe they called it Desert Oaks or River's Edge, some name akin to the landscape pre-development.

Perhaps this dream didn't stray much from reality after all. Leave it to her overtaxed brain to supply her delusion with urban sprawl. As she watched a woman lugging a child on her hip, a theory snapped into place. Jeannette wondered if all of these characters were everyday tourists and businessmen, and her sick mind dressed them up in animal faces and white dresses in the form of three-dimensional paper dolls. That they were all normal, and she had somehow stepped sideways, her perception skewed as if staring into one of those funhouse mirrors from the wrong angle, giving them this appearance of the past, of myth. She knew that all the crazy had to be explainable, just something beyond her brand of education. She went hard science, not that fluffy, soft drivel that involved subjection and feelings.

Maybe she'd slipped through some portal into another dimension entirely. She laughed at that. That was too fanciful even for her.

Near the foot of the hill, people clogged the street. Guarding her right arm with her torso, Jeannette tried to avoid touching anyone while still attempting to blend in. Which was a joke in her khakis and beige button-down blouse, black backpack tightly bound to her shoulders. While she had brown hair, it was practically pale compared to most of the people here, whose hair shimmered as black as the jackals' backs.

The scent of baked bread curled around Jeannette's head, and her stomach rumbled. Her collection of protein bars were for desperate times, when she was starving and not merely hungry, and right now the bread smelled too good. After another block, Jeannette came upon a small shop, a display table stacked high with bundles of oval bread that were dead ringers for mid-sized portobello mushrooms. Searching behind her to make sure the mummy wasn't anywhere near, she stopped and stared at the piles. Still radiating warmth, the yeasty scent reminded her that she hadn't eaten since before her adventure with her mislaid guide.

She hoped he was dealing properly with her concussed body.

She stared down at her feet and swallowed. A sense of drowning washed through her. Nothing to be done about her body now, that existed in the realm of Untouchable at the moment.

"You want bread?" a gruff man asked, pulling her back to the surface. He was shorter than Jeannette, with a bit of a belly, dressed in one of those white kilts, although this one hadn't been white for some time. Spotted and rotting, his misaligned teeth could have been planted in his gums by an elderly man with palsy. A brown cat sat at his feet.

Perhaps, while existing in this delusion, she should pretend to be a part of it, treat it like a vacation. Eat the local food. See the sights. She'd read about coma victims in one of her magazines and how nobody knew exactly what went on in the brains. When she woke up again she hoped that, assuming a coma was her predicament, she could describe everything that she'd experienced to the doctors. Though she guessed that probably wouldn't be the case. Nobody ever told stories from beyond that veil.

"How much is it?" She hazarded a guess that Egyptian pounds or American dollars were not legal tender.

"One kit," he said.

Good guess. She nibbled on a fingernail, wondering what to do, then pulled her finger from her mouth to study the dust caught in the dry creases of her skin. She beat her hand against her pants.

A thin man with a shaved head lit a lamp positioned to the left of the stall, then moved onto the next one down the street. The baker squinted at her. "Pilgrim? You from the sea?"

Jeannette blinked.

"Are you here for the Sacred Bull Festival of Montu?" he asked.

Montu, the place at the edge of town with the huge bonfire. "Ah, yes."

The man nodded, then unwrapped a bundle of five pieces of flat bread and handed her one with a stiff nod.

Hesitating, she took it. "Thank you," she said, shocked at his generosity. Then, because 'thanks' might not reflect her gratitude, she bowed to the man. He waved her off.

The bread tasted sweet and contained grit throughout, but it adequately filled the hole in her belly. She knew, from her research, during the grinding of the grain sand inevitably mingled with the flour and hundreds of mummy dental autopsies showcased the abrasive effects of such a mineral-laced meal. Ripping off another bite, she shuttled the knowledge away and joined the current of people again: dream bread couldn't grind down dream teeth. Though it could apparently appease dream hunger.

Three little girls ran by her, a white ibis flapping through the crowd to keep up. So many were trekking to that Montu temple place that the traffic moved as freely as that in the tourist markets back in Cairo. From her vantage, halfway down the slope from the tombs, she could see the crowd around the bonfire. Maybe somebody there could tell her more about what level of Dante's hell she'd landed in. At least it was something to do.

She needed something to do.

"Do not simply abandon me to the desert." The words induced a crop of goose bumps to sprout across her skin and the finer hairs to parade down her neck.

Jeannette turned toward the voice, dry, like mice rummaging within autumn leaves. Behind her stood the mummy from the tomb. Still. Unmoving.

She took an automatic step away. Was he bent on attacking her, escorting her to her grave at the point of a cursed finger? "Why are you following me?" she asked, her own voice high and sharp, hovering between panic and annoyance.

The mummy limped toward her, arms held out, fingers twitching. "You disturbed my repose. I now wander." He scanned the busy road. "You must help me, woman. Hathor can no longer guard my rest."

Woman?

Her emotional teeter dipped toward irate.

"Don't call me that." She retreated another step. "Just leave me alone, demon." She spat at him, imitating the local Egyptians from her realm of normality to ward off the unwanted.

He flinched; she assumed it was a he by the timbre of his voice and the fact that he called her 'woman.' The mummy's linen dressings had yellowed with age, loosened in their weave around his limbs. The leathery glimpses of his flesh she unwillingly caught triggered something primal within her. Turning her body away from the horror movie reject, she dashed through the crowd, enticing cries of irritation from everyone whose foot she stepped on or ribs she elbowed. That thing was dead,

31

dead and stalking her. A woman with a black, furry face snapped at her. She decided to abandon the crowded thoroughfare and sneak between the neatly lined up houses.

Which was a mistake. She swore she could hear the leathery creak of mummy skin and the slap of dehydrated feet against the stone-paved road as she darted between the single story buildings.

"You cannot leave me." The voice was close and wavering. "My judgment in the West is unfinished and I do not know this place. Someone must be repelling my way." Yes, definitely a man. And not someone old, she thought. Someone unsure.

"Me either. I'm no help," she called, not even looking over her shoulder as she pressed past two young women carrying baskets on their heads. The scent of bog water followed them as they headed toward the main road.

"You awoke me, woman. Stop your flight." She skipped over a reclining house cat and then she heard, "Please."

Jeannette stopped and slowly turned around. The emotion coloring that single word sounded so human that she couldn't deny his plea. The mummy lumbered toward her, quick for a guy who'd been dead for thousands of years and didn't seem to have good motor skills. Through slips of his gauze his shriveled flesh taunted her, and she quickly looked away, only to feel her eyes drawn to him again. He was mesmerizing, like a roadside accident.

"You're disgusting," she said matter-of-factly. "Completely nasty. Why aren't you dead, like mummies are supposed to be?" And why wasn't he trying to eat her flesh? Was that his plan? Lure her into a sense of responsibility for him, a sense of compassion, and then whammy! Or was that zombies?

The mummy, his thin, crinkled lips failing to produce an adequately human expression, pondered the question as if she'd really wanted an answer. She huffed, a sound between a groan and a whine, ready to turn and continue her march to the bonfire, when he said, "I am dead, but this does not appear to be *Yaaru*." His eyes roamed over the gathered buildings. "I do not remember weighing against Ma'at's scales. Nor my *ba*'s flight by day. I remember . . . nothing." His voice trailed off, then he tried to glare at her, their gazes level. It wasn't all that effective; his jaundiced eyes were sunken in their sockets. "Obviously this is not the Afterworld—" Jeannette opened her mouth to inform him he was trapped in her delusional coma dream, but he talked right over her, "—

32

though it is filled with the Gods, and I believe the reason that I have not moved on properly is because my tomb has been disturbed. The spells have been broken." He covered his chest with a hand. "My heart scarab, too, is missing."

He said this with such intensity, an unexpected pulse of concern jolted through Jeannette. Then her gaze dropped to the center of his chest. "Really, I don't want to hear about your missing organs." And she really had no power to help him, anyway; this was all fiction, completely brewed up by her brain. She turned to leave.

He grabbed her arm and whirled her around. The nearness of the mummy's face, his soul sucking mouth, hollow gaze, set her heart knocking in her chest; fear that he would chomp a juicy hunk out of her neck overdosed her system with adrenaline. "Where is my scarab, woman?" He squeezed her arm with unexpected strength. "My heart scarab is missing and without it my heart—" The hand over his chest clutched into a fist. "My *ba* does not return to me. You were there when I woke." His yellowed, raisin eyes squinted at her. So close, she could count his lashes if she had the desire. "It must have been you."

"Listen," she tried to reason. "You're dead. You shouldn't even be up and walking, let alone missing your organs or scarabs." She forced her voice steady. This close she could smell an odd spiciness about him, nothing rotten at all, no scent of decay. "Now, just skip on back to your tomb, slide into your coffin and go back to being dead!" Her voice rose with every word, ending in an embarrassingly loud tone that drew the attention of the people on the less crowded side street.

Still, none of them came to help her.

The mummy leaned in even closer and whispered harshly, "I cannot return to my tomb, you dolt. Do you know nothing? The sarcophagus is opened; the spells have been broken. My *ba* wanders, lost. It might already be consumed by the Devourer of Souls." The fingers gripping Jeannette's arm quivered.

She knew she'd read something about this *ba* thing in one of her travel books, but since it wasn't history, she hadn't actually studied it. "What do you mean?"

He leaned away from her and his mouth dropped open. His tongue reminded her of a strip of beef jerky and she wondered if it had that smoked flavor. A startled giggle bubbled off her lips. With a violent shake of her head, she shed that icky image.

"It means," he said, his dried eyelids grinding against his eyes, "that I

33

cease to exist. Completely. Here and there. No Afterworld. No rebirth." He reached out and smacked her across the back of her head like a harsh taskmaster would a misbehaving student; she dropped to her knees, the blinding sparks of pain subsuming all other sensation.

"Oh, camel spit, are you hurting?" For a moment there, he sounded human.

Tears welled up in her eyes as Jeannette cradled her head lump under her cupped hand, assuring no other bumbling fools would smack into it. "Yes," she said through gritted teeth. "My head. Now if you would back off and stop hitting me—" She should have packed her pepper spray, even if it had been number two on the list of restricted items from the tour planners.

The mummy took a step away. The dancing sparks in her vision dimmed and she could see his toes through the gauze. One toenail hung on by a thin strip of skin.

In a half crouch, she walked over to a building and sat against the mud wall. Ignoring her unwanted stalker, she pulled her pack into her lap, dusted off the layer of dirt it had gathered, and muddled her way through her combination, eyes still dewy with pain tears. The lock only had three digits—her birth month and day.

Jeannette opened the lock and unzipped the main compartment of her backpack. She fished around with her left hand, pulling out things willy-nilly and piling them around her. A light jacket, her Nalgene bottle with five swallows left, a compass on a key chain, box of matches swiped from the hotel lounge, a creased photo of a guy with dark hair and darker eyes, a packet of gum, a tour book and finally she withdrew her first aid kit.

Unzipping that she removed the ointment and some sterilizing pads. Also within the kit were stomach remedies and painkillers. She popped two painkillers before nearly finishing off her water.

"Great Atum who made the sky, what items of mystery do you have here?" said the creepy dead man. "Are you a vizier? A priestess?"

Jeannette took an alcohol wipe and ripped the foil package, then proceeded to dab her bump with it. It no longer bled, but still it sprang to life at any glancing touch. "Of course not. Everyone has this stuff." In reality, her unbidden thoughts supplied. Then she applied ointment to her finger and dabbed it to the wound. Who knew what infectious germs infested this prehistoric place? Then she chuckled; coma dreams were probably pretty sterile. Still, her years at the lab had pounded an antibacterial addiction into her as solid as tooth brushing and her morning coffee.

When Jeannette finished, she zipped closed her first aid kit and stuffed the things she had taken out back into the backpack. Then, directed by impulse, she snapped a picture of him with her camera. Most likely a worthless shot, but it lightened her spirits to see him blinking against the flash.

"What—?"

"Nothing. Don't worry 'bout it." She replaced the camera. The mummy loomed over her. "Mummy-boy, stop staring at me." Nothing unnerved her like a stare.

"Do not call me Mummy-boy," he said in an arrogant tone, sounding quite insulted. "I am called Abayomi. I am the third son to the Chief Grain Measurer and a scribe for the granary. I deserve your respect." He glowered at her. She ignored him. "Do not ignore me."

She lightly tapped the bump on her head. Other than wrapping her head in gauze, there wasn't much else she could do. And no way would she play dress-up like Mummy-boy in Halloween Land. "Oh, grow up," Jeannette said. "How old are—were you anyway? You're acting like a spoiled brat." Then under her breath, "Smacking people like a five-year-old."

He propped his hands on his hips. "I have seen the inundation twenty-one times," and then, "I am not spoiled." He looked away from her. "I did not mean to harm you."

"You're twenty-one?" Jeannette laughed, pulling her hair into a loose ponytail. "Pretty short for an adult man." He stood up straighter as she rose to her feet. "You're no taller than me," she said.

"Well," Abayomi sized her up, "you are rather large for a woman."

She put her pack on, and when she heard his diagnosis, ruffled in indignation. "I am not large for a woman. I'm petite." He'd probably fall over in shock if he ever came upon one of the university's basketball players. "It's not my fault you people are all runts."

"And you look sickly with such pale skin," he concluded, and damn if he didn't sound amused. She didn't know what to be more shocked at: the fact that she was speaking with a dead man or that the dead man was teasing her. "Are you weak of constitution as well as large of bone?"

Haughty little twerp, she thought. At that, she turned her back on him, her ponytail swishing in her dismissal. He reached out, landing his hand on hers, and the dry brush of his decayed wrappings sent her skin

35

into quivers. She jerked away.

"Don't touch me." She spoke without any intention, her words having a mind of their own. "You're filthy and dead, and I'm sure I'll catch something fatal if I stay around you much longer."

Jeannette stomped down the hill, toward the party cooking up at this temple of a cow on the border between city and river land, munching on the rest of her sweet bread. Behind her, the sound of the mummy's stumbles followed.

Chapter 5

A MENAGERIE OF PEOPLE gathered around the stone temple. Though the most populous were normal humans, a large number of mini-gods filled out the crowd. From crocodiles, to falcons, to bulls and cats, all straight out of the Egyptian mythology Jeannette had learned for her college humanities credit and later reviewed in preparation for this trip. A smattering of human-headed animals highlighted the gathering, and a small sphinx caught her eye, though she didn't think that a sphinx should have a rattling tail. Baboons and large cats, with brightly colored birds flying about, all assembled around a giant bonfire blazing next to a sitting priestess and her huge bull.

"That bull is purple," Jeannette said, amazed that a strangely-colored bull still had the power to shock her. The giant bull stood serenely on the temple landing like a tamed lamb.

"It is the famous *Bakhu* bull, sacred to Montu."

Without so much as a twitch in surprise, she glanced to her right; just behind her stood the mummy. With a droop to her shoulders she turned back to study the bull; twice as tall as the sitting woman, it chewed its cud, mimicking a king-sized dairy cow from a cheese commercial.

"You understand," Abayomi said, his voice a soft echo of awe, "the bull delivers oracles. People from all over Kemet make pilgrimage to this temple to ask *Bakhu* for answers. Perhaps he can bring me Re's light and tell me why I am not in *Yaaru*. And . . ." Abayomi brightened as he set his withered eyes upon her, ". . . he has the powers of Isis and can heal wounds. Maybe he will heal you." Though his facial expressions were a mystery behind his wrappings, Jeannette could hear the mummy's smile in the tone of his voice.

She returned his gaze skeptically. Gaily colored bulls that could heal injuries and answer life's questions? "Right," she drawled. She wasn't the type to be taken in by chocolate-coated cotton, but perhaps if she mingled, fit in with these crazy people, then she could find some answers, or simply entertain herself until she woke up. "After you, Mummy-boy."

Abayomi closed on her, his feet dragging across the ground. "Abayomi, you insolent woman! I have informed you of my name."

She retreated a step, maintaining her distance, a challenge in the sardine-can packed crowd. "Don't call me woman, that's rude. I have a name too." Abayomi continued to lean toward her; she edged her back into someone's elbow. "It's Jeannette."

Dense air bloated the space between them until Abayomi pulled himself upright and tilted his head. "If it is so, Jeannette—" he said the word slowly as if tasting its texture, "—follow me, perhaps if the Gods allow it, we will be granted audience by *Bakhu*." He brushed past her and forged his way through the crowd. "I have never received an oracle before."

As his gauze-wrapped back slowly wove its way forward, Jeannette found herself anchored to the spot. This dead man—the only animated mummy she'd seen amidst this cast of freaks—that had badgered her for the last hour, pestered her, creeped her out, now gallantly led the way into this unknown world. She swallowed, waffling between slinking off like a guilty dog and following him into the heart of this zoo to find answers.

She'd never been a coward. Chin lifted high, she charged after him toward the oracle. Her banged up head pulsed with each step.

A mingling scent of perfumes, unwashed bodies, rich incense and cow manure wafted on the breeze as she inched through the mass of people packed around the bonfire as if it were Homecoming night. Encroaching on each other like bacteria colonies vying for real estate on a thin, glass slide, she couldn't move without bumping into someone. Under her boot she almost squished a monkey that kindly told her to watch her step.

"Sorry," she said to the small, black face, and then someone jostled her unceremoniously into Abayomi's back.

He twisted around. Even in the light of the flames his eyes still held a darkness unmarred by the fire's shimmer. "Are you intending to push me into the red-heat of the fire?" The wrappings covering his face shifted as he spoke.

"N-no." The intensity of his eyes caught her, before so lifeless and now somehow even more dreadful. Her fingers furled into a fist. "I wouldn't murder you, even though you *are* already dead."

For a moment they were trapped in one of those stare-downs that always made Jeannette self-conscious, and then he laughed, a dry chuckle. She wondered, what would happen if he got wet? Would he re-hydrate?

"If we wait here, we will be given our turn," he said. She blinked, yanked from the hypnotizing shift of gauze to where he pointed. The body of the long line they'd just queued in coiled around the left hemisphere of the bonfire to the mouth of the temple. At the head of the line, next to the mighty bull, the priestess perched on a four-legged stool.

When the beast turned its head, Jeannette could see that a single horn nearly reached as far back as its meaty hip and she doubted she could completely encompass the horn's base with the combined range of both of her hands. The horns' bulk contrasted oddly with the golden disc mounted between them.

"So, that's a magic cow?" Jeannette said, impressed by his sheer size, unlike the rest of the crowd that took an oversized cow in as much stride as a talking mummy.

"The *Bakhu* bull is the magical, blessed oracle of Montu that can understand Ma'at in ways those focused on worldly issues cannot." The linen around Abayomi's eyes creased as he studied her. "You surely do not know a thing, do you?"

With a scowl she lifted her nose. "I know about more things than these . . ." she nodded to the men, women and animals waiting in line— the monkey glared up at her and hopped to the left—then let her scrutiny settle on Abayomi, ". . . people. I have a biology degree from Eastern University," she shook her head, realizing he'd probably not understand a word she said, "—a school. Though, I think most of the things I'm seeing here have tossed everything I know out on its ear." Her voice trailed off like a weak echo.

Abayomi bent forward to look into Jeannette's face. Though she found it difficult to read the mummy due to his lack of visible features, she could still tell a great many things from his body language. Right now, she knew he was interested, and that proved more than a little unnerving. "Where is this school you speak of? On the delta? I studied writing from a local master."

"No, you prehistoric man, it's on a different continent." She sighed and pressed her good hand against her forehead.

"Is it an impossibility for you to engage in normal conversation while we wait? Why must you harbor such an ungracious attitude, woman?"

"Don't call me woman, mummy," she growled. His body stiffened, began to turn away, and her story fell unbidden from her lips. "Fine, what do you want to know? I'm not from around here. I'm twenty-four and wanted to be a nurse until I decided I couldn't deal with whiny, suffering people, so now I work in a lab. I have a cat named Archibald. My mother is dead. I've no siblings—" his jaw dropped open, and she quickly looked away from that ruined tongue, "—and I've never been married." There, that should really shock him. At least she hadn't had a divorce already like Gabby had. At least she wasn't an unwed mother at seventeen like her own had been.

"You have seen twenty-four inundations and you are unmarried? You are not a priestess?" In the distance the cow bellowed, and Jeannette glanced along the line of pilgrims to see the beast walk a few feet, then stop to sniff the ground.

"No, I said I work in a lab. Biology, germs, microscopes?" All mysteries to this ancient world. "Nothing you would understand," she said under her breath.

The cow stretched its neck out to the next man in line; its nostrils flared as the animal took in great huffs of air. The man dropped to his knees in some overdone symptom of veneration. "Priestess?" She huffed in hollow amusement. "Honestly, I don't really even think I believe in God."

"Which God?" Abayomi asked curiously.

Jeannette hmmed thoughtfully. That was not a conversation she cared to fence about. "So, tell me about yourself."

"I was married, but then my wife was bitten by a serpent."

She tore her eyes away from the bull and looked up at the mummy. "Did she die?"

"Yes. Isis did not kill the poison within her." He spoke so matter-of-factly that it seemed unreal that this thing, this monumental thing, had happened to him.

"I—I'm sorry." They stepped forward as the line progressed. The smell of wood smoke hung heavy in the air, battling the more heavily rooted scent of marsh. "How long were you married?"

"Two inundations." He didn't meet her eyes and she wondered just how blasé he truly was in his heart.

Perhaps it was best to move away from such treacherous ground. "What is this inundation you keep talking about? We call it years, the cycle of seasons, the rotation of the earth around the sun." She lifted her arms in some grand gesture that included the solar system and beyond.

"The Sun God Re watches over us all." He closed his eyes and raised his hands before his chest. The blackened tips of his fingers poked through his wrappings. Then: "Inundations, the annual flooding of the great river *Iteru* that brings the fertile, black soil. May it provide for us as Pharaoh protects us."

She snorted, biting back full-fledged laughter.

He dropped his hands. "What is your amusement from now?" he asked with a grumble.

"Oh yeah, sure. It will provide for you until the future Kemet folk dam it all up and then bye-bye *Iteru*." She knew all about the history of the Nile and the Aswan Dam. Oh, this poor, poor ignorant fool and his long lost culture.

His glare burned into her. "You speak riddles and presume I am a fool. I know that this is not the Kemet in which I lived, and I know this is not the land from which you came. Perhaps what you think you know is silly drivel in this world, as in mine."

She abruptly stopped laughing; what if what he had just said was true?

"I have to find out what's going on. How I can wake up, get back to normality . . ." She shook her head, her long bangs dancing in the movement. It suddenly felt so hopeless.

The mummy placed the palm of his hand on the top of her head and she shivered, even as she appreciated the thought behind the gesture. "Do not worry. The Ennead will look after you, traveler, as they will look after me. It appears that we have both lost our way."

And hadn't they.

Jeannette pulled away and they settled into silence as she listened to the conversations bubbling around her. The locals discussed the forecast of the harvest, how much wheat and barley they would bring in, the amount the pharaoh and temples would take. It sounded like a terrible life, nothing but work and the abundance from your endless labor bound for someone else's table. What kind of justice was that? She knew that these people loved their gods, but which ones listened to the complaints, the endless prayers for prosperity and fertility. To beg to have your wife of two years saved from a snake bite. When your back broke under the yoke of unlucky breeding, even prayers couldn't undo thousands of years of tradition. She'd never heard any answers to her own prayers, back when she was hopeful and naïve; did the gods here show greater interest? Had Abayomi ever heard the voice of the Ennead in anything but fever dreams? She hoped she wouldn't be wedged in this mind trap much longer. It left a bitter taste in her mouth.

Finally, they were next.

"I shall go first." Abayomi stepped forward, and Jeannette rolled her eyes. So much for chivalry in ancient Egypt.

41

THREE GREAT LIES

The priestess of *Bakhu* sat, back straight, on a stool golden in color with fine carvings spanning the distance between the legs. She wore a flimsy veil over her face that reached the tip of her nose, doing nothing to hide her smooth features. A linen dress of white, bound at the waist by a braided belt, pooled on the ground. The woman listened as Abayomi quietly asked his question. He bowed his head low and dropped a golden object into a plain bowl placed near the woman's sandaled feet. Jeannette had no idea where he'd had the object stowed under his wrappings, and she really didn't want to imagine its hiding hole. The bowl overflowed with offerings, and Jeannette realized that she had nothing to give.

She slipped off her pack and quietly unzipped the compartment to hunt for something that might appease the priestess and the bull. What would a bull want anyway? Certainly not her first aid kit, nor chewing gum. She was all out of cow treats.

A pointed object jabbed her finger. She fished it out. The gold pen presented to her for two years of dedication to Starvine Laboratories. Well, not real gold, not like a few of the shimmering items that the cow sniffed and drooled over, but it was a ballpoint. Maybe they would think it a useful tool and still give her her prophecy. She gripped it in her hand and hoped.

The stars splattered the sky and though she had grown up in rural eastern Washington, she had never seen the sky so clear, so brilliant. The moon had long ago given up its sky reign, and she wondered at the hour as a yawn struggled to contort her face. Man, she was tired. It hit her hard, like the terrible news of a close relative in the hospital, or the man you loved saying his final good-bye. One minute it was all excitement, the next, exhaustion infiltrated her bones.

"Jeannette." The sound of her name pulled her out of her reverie. "It is now your turn. Ask about your injury." He touched his hand to the back of his head.

While spacing out, she'd completely missed Abayomi's prophecy. Annoyed, she stepped forward to face the priestess, bowed like Abayomi had, and placed the pen in the bowl, tucked between a tiny bronze statue of a man and a woven strip of linen. The priestess said nothing, but she hadn't for Abayomi's gift either, so Jeannette figured she was okay.

The woman simply sat, and the silence between them became stifling. "Go forth," Abayomi whispered to her over her shoulder. She sneered at him. She was getting to that.

"Hello. Umm, I was told you could heal me?"

42

The Priestess nodded once, a slow motion movement, and the bull lifted its great head and sniffed Jeannette. The shoulder of the beast surpassed Jeannette's own by a few inches. It might have been intimidating, but an endless line of people had just stood next to it without any worry, and she wasn't about to show fear in the face of the unknown. Warm air puffed up the downy hairs along Jeannette's arm as the purple bull breathed on her. Then the woman said, "Your affliction merits no concern."

Jeannette's brow knit in annoyance. "Well, okay. Fine." She'd already guessed she wouldn't die from her injuries, but the veiled woman didn't have to be rude. "Also, could you tell me how to get back to reality," she said in teeth-grinding tones she usually reserved only for her boss during his bouts of unreasonable requests. Abayomi groaned disappointedly at her. Quickly, she added, "Back . . . uh, back home?"

The priestess reached up and touched the bull's horn; her head rolled back. A gentle palsy set upon her body as, apparently, the answer to Jeannette's question was being zapped through the woman's body from the bull's sacred horn. The bull chewed its cud.

"The reed-grass is now silent, the birds have stilled," the priestess said, her voice flat and lifeless. "At the dawn, they come forth and sing the sacred greeting. The road to home is no easy path. Follow the fledgling into the beautiful west. Beware those dwelling with a false heart, their *ba* drifts in truculent waters."

Jeannette waited.

The priestess said nothing more.

"But—" Jeannette began, but Abayomi grabbed her sore arm and dragged her off.

"Hey, let me go." A throbbing ache scorched her shoulder. Stupid, useless bull. "She didn't answer my question." Jeannette stared at the woman and her bull over her shoulder as Abayomi dragged her away.

"That was her answer. You act like you have never heard the answer of an oracle before." Though she couldn't see his face, she was certain he'd just rolled his eyes at her.

"Well, I haven't." He let her go and stopped to look at her. Jeannette held her arm close to her chest, providing a protective shield with the uninjured one. "Most people I talk to deal with facts and science and truth, none of this woodgy-woodgy crap that needs a secret decoder ring to decipher it all."

Abayomi shrugged, the resin along the edges of the linen strips

43

flaked from the constant abrasion, sounding like the slide of snake belly on stone. "I do not know about your secret ring, but she receives the prophecy from the bull, a conduit of the gods, and relays it to you. And if you consider her words, it bears the weight of importance. Begin again at a new day, or a new life." He lifted one shoulder and let it drop with casual disinterest. "Find this fledgling and avoid those of false hearts."

She ran her good hand along her arm, mulling over this random prophecy. Now, away from the heat of the fire and the crowds, she wondered what season it was. The night held her in a warm bundle, as the prophecy held onto her mind. It was as bad as that fortune cookie she'd gotten from China Palace last Christmas. "You will be visited by three great lies." At the time it had been hilarious and she kept the thin strip of paper in her wallet. Honestly, lies were a dime a dozen.

They began walking again, away from the town, and the scent of the river subsumed all other odors with a thick mucky odor. "You're not the fledgling are you? Like some fledgling mummy?" That would be her luck. "Roughly wrapped and crusty, moaning and lurching around seeking brains?"

Though only hollow hints of his tanned eyes and the edges of his lips were visible in the dilute light, she could just guess at his expression, and it made her laugh.

"What do you laugh at now?" he asked, sounding tired. "You certainly are a jovial type. Jester in the court of the pharaoh, that was your role, I am certain."

"Me?" That brought even more laughter. "That's a good one. I think I was voted most likely to be a mortician my senior year."

"Mortician?"

"Yeah, someone who prepares dead people."

"Oh, an embalmer." He nodded. "Then, you enjoy treating the dead?"

She laughed harder. "God, no."

In the lonely, vacant streets, more open and sparse than in the city proper, Jeannette paused to look around. The late hour must have chased everyone into their homes and she and the mummy were the only ones around. That thought sobered her, alone with a mummy in the dark. "I don't suppose there would be a motel around and that they'd accept Egyptian pounds?"

"There are guest houses for pilgrim commoners, but I am lacking payment." He stared at her, unblinking, his arms hanging like dead weight

44

at his sides. Whenever he moved it was jerky and stiff in the style of claymation, but when he remained still, it gave her the someone-crawling-over-your-grave shivers.

"What about that gold you dropped into the pot back there?" This man could frustrate a Tibetan monk.

"That is for the Gods. You do not mix the gold for the Gods, placed among my treasures during burial, with that used in everyday commerce." He sneered, his tooth, brown and loose in its socket, wiggled.

They hadn't walked long before they emerged from the edge of thinning town. She looked up one side of the roughly cobbled road and down the other. Few buildings lined the road; everything slipped to rural within a one-hundred yard stretch. Maybe she could convince the locals that her money was 'from the gods' and they would take it in exchange for dinner and a bed, maybe a hot bath. She was certain that in the morning when she opened her eyes, she would be smothered in the soft embrace of her queen-sized bed and dosed in that spicy scent from the laundry detergent that had annoyed her only the previous day. That in the morning it would swarm around her head in a pleasing reminder of what the world should be.

"Come with me." The mummy went to grab for her arm, but she pulled it out of his reach. He was way too touchy-feely.

"Would you quit grabbing at me, damn it. My arm is hurt."

The mummy grunted. "I apologize. But why must you be so disagreeable, woman?"

"Quit calling me woman, dead man. Jeannette, remember. And I can find lodgings." She stared long and hard down the dark road lit only by the streak of stars in the sky, toward the river buildings sparsely dotting the landscape. "It can't be that difficult."

"If that is your impression." He huffed, a kind of strangled groan mutated by his inability to fill his lungs properly thanks to thousands of years of desiccation at the hands of natron and the desert air.

No shops or hotels lined the riverfront like those from daylight and sanity; instead, the area reeked of muck and decay. Rough, moist earth tripped up her feet after she'd left the well-defined street for the immediately rural farmlands near the flood boundaries. In a history book she'd read about the time of King Arthur, she learned how travelers would knock on the doors of farmers living along the road and ask to sleep in their barn. Seeking a farmer with a barn, she didn't quite find what she was expecting.

THREE GREAT LIES

"Where do you people keep all your tools? Your livestock?"

"I am no farmer. And I would suspect they would not keep them where the crocodiles and snakes might travel." He surveyed their dim surroundings. A few small, square houses, both single and two-storied, were dispersed across the fields. Some had scaffolding of some sort on the roofs—the ancient version of sun shelters used at every one of Gabby's dog shows scheduled on hot, summer days.

Abayomi watched as Jeannette began banging on doors, asking for an inn or to pay for a room. It was more discomforting than her haggling attempts back in the real Egypt. The homes of plaster covered brick had tiny windows highly placed so she couldn't peer inside, and at the late hour few people opened their doors no matter how incessantly she banged. Those that did shooed her away.

"I have money!" she said, her tone beseeching in a way that was vaguely embarrassing, but nothing swayed them to offer her boarding.

"This sucks." She chewed on her thumb nail as she surveyed her options. Exhausted and aching, it seemed a lifetime ago when she'd risen early to tour El-Balyana, then that kid had practically hijacked her on that long, baking bike ride to the middle of nowhere where she'd whacked her head. Shoulders slumped, she left the farmers' lands and continued toward the void ahead of her that marked the Nile River. Secretly, in her inner gut, she hoped that the closing of her eyes, the momentary re-boot sleep would offer, would be the catalyst that forced everything to right itself. Bump her out of this weird PCP dream.

Squat buildings of the same mud-brick construction, topped with roofs alive with large palm fronds, poked up along the flood zone. Knocking on the door of one reaped, yet again, no answer. Scrutinizing her surroundings—reedy and generally deplorable—and assuring her isolation, she tried the door.

She hoped that trespassing didn't warrant the punishment of beheading.

"What are you doing?" Abayomi whispered at her.

"Finding us somewhere to stay for the night." The door opened easily.

Chapter 6

A SOFT, WHISKERED NOSE nuzzled her face, and with a sleep-addled brain Jeannette reached out to stroke her cat Archy. Archy pulled away from her hand, and she sought him, running her palm across the sheets. But her bed was rough, and as she touched Archy again, she wondered who'd shaved her Persian cat. A yawn contorted her face. She hadn't slept well and her neck ached. Finally, as her backpack crinkled against her cheek, she realized she lay on the cold ground, and its vampiric hunger had sucked out her cherished warmth.

Ancient Egypt. She couldn't still be there.

Archy nuzzled her again.

Opening her eyes, she could just make out the pointy face of a brown, foot-long rat.

A scream wrenched itself from her lungs and she slapped a hand over her mouth, but she moved too late to snare it from escape. The rat scuttled away beyond the jars without so much as a good morning, and she jumped to her feet, afraid someone might have heard her, might grab her for invading private property and cut off something: her hands, her head, maybe all her hair.

"Mum—Abayomi, get up. We need to get out of here," Jeannette said, her voice heavy and old in the darkness.

She stuffed her jacket into her pack, shot her arms through the straps and tip-toed to the door. Abayomi was leaning against the wall in exactly the same position he'd propped himself into last night, his eyes open, but unseeing. "Are you awake?" Pressing her ear to the shoddily constructed door, she listened hard for guards or someone shouting about intruders, but all remained quiet. She cracked open the door and peeked out. Within the strengthening traces of pink in the direction of the river, she couldn't see anyone nearby.

Impatient, she glowered at Abayomi. "What is wrong with you?"

He blinked at her, shaking his head. With apparent effort, he pushed himself to standing and examined his hands—palms facing himself, finger tips browned. Rotating them repeatedly, front to back and back to front, he seemed in awe that such things existed. Hands, what a concept.

"Abayomi?" Jeannette said. Still, no sound arose from outside, but she wanted to leave before the single rat brought back a plague and

47

whoever owned the small warehouse came to inspect his inventory.

"Mighty Amun, why am I still lost in this place?" he said in a voice so low Jeannette knew it wasn't for her ears.

Her own despair a leaden stone in her chest, she couldn't agree more, but refrained from mumbling her own pathetic prayer. She had no Amun to call to—not that prayers and wishes held true power. She wouldn't make deals with nonexistent gods. "We need to go."

Slowly, her grip tight on the handle, she opened the door wider, and then, with a churning belly, she stared down at her own hand. It no longer ached.

Jeannette shook her fingers and flexed. She would not be mesmerized by her own appendages.

The slip of world peeking through the gap at the door invited air loaded with the earthy scent of the Nile, lacking the acrid exhaust from vehicles. She wrinkled her nose, the inside dry and crusty, and inhaled. Around her spread out the same world as last night. The same flat land, the same river. The same damned smell of decomposing plant life on the air. Though the sun had yet to rise, the morning blossomed under a cool, gray sky. The sky of *ancient* Egypt.

She hadn't returned home.

At the river, a few people bent over woven fishing nets, heaving them this way and that with the full force of their weight; they ignored her and Abayomi and she was grateful for the peaceful silence. A pack of cats infested the area like needy children, nudging the men, batting at the nets. One of the strays slunk away with a fish tail in its mouth. The entire area near the river felt anticipatory, the birds only warming up for their morning chorus, and in that calm, just for a second, she no longer felt like she was sinking.

But she *was* sunk. Fixed. Somehow lodged here like a fallen log in a rapids, trapped and beaten and helpless.

She hated feeling helpless. Too many years she'd been helpless and she wasn't about to roll over and lie there and take whatever the universe dealt her without a fight.

Cautiously, she slipped through the doorway into the sparsely developed farmland, the border of the city a defined edge along the rise of the land, beyond the reach of the voracious floods of the Nile. Abayomi remained confined in the door frame, making himself a target for all eyes to converge on in his graying linen. "Come on," she urged, gesturing for him to follow as she headed back toward the crowded settlement of the Egyptian subdivision.

Something deeply internal, more than an instinct, set her being abuzz. Unlike Abayomi, she wasn't willing to stop and ponder the horror of the morning, the deceit of her working hand. The night's sleep had not returned her home, hadn't whisked her back to the world of reason and science and truth. A place where animals didn't hold conversations she could understand or where mummies didn't lurch along by her side. Her brain still clung onto this fabricated world of magic and mythology. Still in a coma, or drugged, or . . . or lost. She just didn't know.

"What the hell am I going to do?" she wondered. Abayomi, a few paces behind Jeannette, gave her no hints.

Maybe she had to retrace her steps, go back to Abayomi's tomb where this entire detour had begun. Find that hole and climb back up through it. Bent forward, eyes taking stock of the rise and fall of each foot against the dirt track that gave way to paving stones, she returned to the city. Her passage took her from the farmland to the city proper, through one small alley to another, guided like a gerbil through plastic habitat tubes. A number of people within the town busied themselves in the pre-dawn, mainly those Jeannette would classify as servants, carrying things back and forth as diligent as ants toiling for the hill, dumping baskets of waste into pits alongside the street. Their rough sandals struck the brick-cobbled street in an offbeat performance.

The scent of livestock tainted the air, and she stopped to audit her surroundings, realizing she was completely lost. Her stomach gurgled, and Abayomi remained shrouded in his gloom, trailing her like a miserable mime. That didn't bother Jeannette; she had her own worries to contend with. She brushed the back of her head with her palm. No pain. Holding her hand up, she studied it. Completely fine. Had the purple bull actually healed her? The sky had brightened and she blinked against the rising sun, her eyes burning. She took a slow, deep breath. Then another. She would not freak out. She would *not* freak out.

The tomb had been built on a hill; she remembered the long hike down to the Montu oracle that could *not* be the cause of her healed head. Grabbing a protein bar from her pack to munch on, she turned in place a few times to get her bearings. A side street began a slow assent, so she followed it as it slunk between a procession of blunt buildings. She only had to get to that mastaba, and everything would be alright.

"Where is it you lead us?" Abayomi said, a sad accent to his raspy voice.

49

THREE GREAT LIES

"To the beginning. To your tomb."

The roads of this portion of town had been laid out with random abandon, but eventually she found a main thoroughfare populated by early shoppers, their heads topped by colorful baskets and jars, and eyes brimming with duty. A party of naked boys drove five complaining goats down the center of the street. The musky scent of the animals overlapped a rich aroma of fresh bread, grilled fish and some unknown spice, but could not overpower the mouthwatering might it had. Jeannette's stomach growled. She was thirsty, and grimy, and had to pee.

In a large, open square a group of well-dressed men and women, and a few animal-headed types gathered. A loud voice carried like a command over the crowd.

"Now, this next slave is quite the prize. Just arrived from her birthing batch, too young for full initiation into the arts of midwifery, this one is a clean slate, perfect for cultivation in any field of service. The ideal maidservant for the mistress of the house, or even for the mister," a man said. "Fresh, and pliable, she can be trained in any occupation. Look at her proper stance as a servant, she already understands her place. Let's start the bidding at three deben."

Jeannette halted mid-step, her knee bent, ready to propel her up the hill. She couldn't believe her ears. Couldn't even fathom. The man's words reverberated through her mind, making it hard to breathe. Abayomi halted next to her. They looked at one another for a long moment as the bidding commenced; he blinked his atrophied eyes, a slow, grating motion. Yanking her gaze from his, she faced the loud auctioneer.

Nearing six feet tall, the man's stomach hung over the precipice of his kilt rivaling that of the Buddha. Black hair hung to his shoulders, exposing his ears and a thin, white scar bisecting his left cheek. Bands of silver encircled his throat. Next to him cowered a young girl, naked and downcast. She was maybe eleven or twelve—her body hairless, no hint of breasts—though Jeannette's skill at aging tweens was comparable to her prizefighting prowess. The girls' skin was dark like all the native people, but she was one of those fantastical types, with the head of a cat furred all in black. With a pronounced muzzle and overlarge ears, hollow gaze snared by something near her feet, she looked even more lost than Jeannette in this alien world.

"Seven shrouds of linen for the girl," said a man, his long white robes almost see-through they were so filmy.

"Abayomi, do you see that? That perv is going to do terrible things to that girl." She reached out for him, her fingers ghosting across the stiff material of his wrappings before she remembered just what he was and pulled away.

The mummy scoffed. "I think the fate of a slave would not rate so high compared to your own dilemma."

A stupor of disbelief stalled her brain, but then her contempt for Abayomi's lack of compassion shocked her back to action. Jeannette, adrift in a land of drugs or possible head trauma, had no knowledge on how to right her capsized life. But this girl—degraded to a Blue Light Special, her life worth the equivalent of a few sheets of cloth—perhaps Jeannette could do something for her. "I'm not going to leave someone that innocent," she thrust her finger toward the girl being manhandled by the fat auctioneer, "to be defiled by that pervert." She gestured more sedately at the finely dressed man.

The bidding progressed, and still Abayomi wouldn't budge from the edge of the market that dealt in misery and human souls. "It is not my place to interfere," he said.

"I will take her for two bronze jugs and a sheet of linen. My final offer, Master Slaver," came another bid from the crowd.

Making her decision, Jeannette stepped forward and raised her arm.

* * *

The Master Slaver couldn't be more pleased with the new addition to his pens. When he'd awoken early that morning, the eye of Sopdet still rising from the Netherworld, the girl had been waiting at the market gates, huddled like a beaten kitten. She handled easily; she understood her true value. That was evident in her posture and her ceaseless refusal to meet his gaze. Though he had questioned the girl, asked her why she wasn't back with her brood of *mi-nether*, all she would reveal, with ears held back, soft hands gripped together tight enough to cause her knuckles to whiten, was that she'd been cast out. The little whelp had begged him to "place me with some nice people" and he'd promised her—oh, he'd surely promised her—that he would put her in the finest of homes.

Damned domesticated cat.

But then sometimes these windfalls, these pampered princesses, won his highest fare, and he wasn't dim enough to turn away this gift from the Gods. "Praise be to you, Oh Re," he said with chest out and head held high. He would fulfill the *mi-nether's* request and place her well, into the hands of a merchant, or an officer of the army, offering up fine linen and debens, jars of beer, and silver. He was in the business for profit after all—this was not an orphanage—and the pharaoh's power lay in the straight spears of his army and the flow of coins from palm to palm.

The Master Slaver dominated the brick platform, the slave pens, the entire slave market in fact, his intimidating presence flooding every stone like the great *Iteru* during inundation, drawing fearful gazes from passersby, as well as resentment from those who longed for his power. He didn't mind that petulant look from those lesser; such jealousy fueled drive and a driven citizen was often an asset to the pharaoh.

"If it pleases the Gods, she is certainly worth three deben. Young, completely willing and eager for any task." He gripped the adolescent's chin and forced her head to the side; she flinched and he bared his teeth in a grin. Perhaps he was too rough, perhaps she couldn't abide the touch of a man, either way, he liked a little fear in them. It kept them docile.

"Three deben, not a kit less. Who wishes for a perfect servant to please your every wish?"

The sun had already breached the horizon and its persistent heat had begun to build in the market commons. Today, no breeze stirred from the river, a sign the day would best be endured in his garden, with his lovely wife and daughters to dote upon him. Furthermore, it would be prudent to complete his business early for the benefit of his merchandise, before the slaves resembled melted wax husks and turned nobody's eye.

The early crowd mulled around the platform, watching as he presented them with the slave, tempted them with ingratiating words and the promise of an inexpensive sale. A stout woman watched a flock of songbirds flitter through the square; the girl offered no temptation there. His guards stood nearby, silent sentinels at the platform's border and the along the edges of the square. Each of the prospective buyers assessed the naked *mi-nether*, their obvious appreciation of her evident by their greedy grins, appraising eyes and fleeting glances at each other. Like hungry crocodile amongst the cattle, the scent of their desire intoxicated him. "A willing girl for all duties." He turned her around, letting them feast on every inch of her. She cowered into herself, and he licked his lips.

One hand lifted from the crowd. "Seven shrouds of linen for the girl." The Master Slaver studied the man, his fine attire, the high cheekbones, obviously hailed from noble ancestry. The merchant lifted his chin and remained passive, donning a veil of imitation indifference. The twitch in his jaw, the crinkle around his kholed eyes, the Master Slaver could read all of these; this man wanted the daughter of Bast.

"The Gods thank you for your offer. But certainly," he said, stepping behind the girl, pulling her shoulders back to force her into an upright stance, "this young daughter of Bast, beautiful black fur, free of lice, mange and other diseases, is worth double that price, Master Merchant." He scanned the crowd, making eye contact with each of the buyers showing any glint of interest.

"Gracious lady," he said to an old matriarch. Dressed in white muslin, the shoulder straps embellished with the gossamer likenesses of the wings of Isis, he judged her as upper class, though no noble woman. The pleated skirt was bleached, undyed to anything finer. "This girl would do splendid in your household. A rarer find will not be found this season. Such a hard worker and easy to train. Fastidious as all of Bast's daughters are." He nodded once at the woman, communicating the wisdom of the purchase.

At his side the girl cringed; he tightened his fingers around the delicate bones of her shoulder, her skin clammy against his own smooth fingers. She mewed softly, but did not oppose him. Certainly, he wondered what heinous action had caused her dismissal, but without such black marks publicly disclosed her worth amounted to barrels of dates and beer and the favor of Renenet, and he wasn't about to ask unnecessary questions to earn unwanted answers. His wife, may Isis shine always upon her, was a voracious woman, and Akana and Mesi, his most lovely daughters, had a perpetual need for *things*, clothing, perfumes, wigs, as regular as the rising sun. He had little time to squander concerning himself with the girl's past deeds.

A rotund man, almost as tall as the Master Slaver himself, raised his palm high into the air, the heavy flesh under his arm swaying with the action. The fresh rays of the sun reflected off the man's shiny, bald head. "I will take her for two bronze jugs and a sheet of linen. My final offer, Master Slaver." He held tightly to a *was* scepter, the sharp eyes of the Seth animal peering from the curved handle, and wore the skin of a young leopard marking him as a lesser priest. Seth and Bast did not have the friendliest of associations. But this was business; the Master Slaver couldn't be bothered with such rivalries, he was here to make money, provide for his family and dedicate his votive offerings to the Gods, not place lost kittens into the best homes.

Casually, with a warm smile for the priest, he acknowledged the bid, most favorable for him and the pharaoh. He could not hope for a better price; the buyers within the crowd all watched the priest from the edges of their gazes. "Sol—"

"Wait!" The entire market assembly turned toward a pale, foreign woman dressed in odd, fitted cloth around each leg and linen shirt. Her hair, uncovered by a wig, matched the color of aged papyrus, and her skin, lighter even than the Canaanite next to be sold, reminded him of the emmer wheat that lined the *Iteru* during shemu. Most certainly a barbarian from across the sea, she hopped up and down, and waved her arms high above her head, performing some absurd display—perhaps a tribute to her foreign Gods—drawing undue attention to herself.

Then she proceeded to bid against Seth's priest. "I'll pay three bronze jugs for her!"

Well, apparently a rich barbarian.

He waited three breaths, measuring the priest's sullen glare, and saw no further competition there. "Sold! To the foreigner for three bronze jugs. May the Gods smile upon your gracious coffers. Attend to your due—" he gestured toward his assistant who sat on a low stool, his lap smothered by a long parchment, who dealt in the collection of payment, "—and you can receive your goods."

The woman nodded, her misshapen eyes round, astounded, like she'd bid due to a momentary spirit possession and now wasn't exactly sure how to proceed. With little grace she elbowed her way through the crowd toward the barter scribe as the next slave mounted the platform, the strike of his bare feet against the floor battering out his reluctance, and the demure daughter of Bast slunk away to her unknown future.

The Master Slaver shook his head. What did it matter if this foreigner stole the prize from a priest, as long as he got his fees, and the pharaoh and Gods were not insulted? His jurisdiction in this business was over. He flourished his hands and gestured toward the Canaanite prisoner. "Now, this stout man is perfect for work in the fields . . ."

Chapter 7

WHY IN THE WORLD had Jeannette gotten involved? Had bid on a *slave?* One minute she was arguing with the walking, talking case of the need for bleach, and the next . . . she was caught totally unawares. Her hand lifted, raised high and waved at the fat slaver; words sprang from her mouth. Her stomach roiled as she participated in the slave auction, worse than when she'd scarfed an entire cheesecake as a kid. However, she needed to do something, didn't she? She simply needed the courage to intervene, and it had infused her, as all-encompassing as that crippling sadness that overwhelmed her whenever she watched a nature program where cute animals died. Now she found herself digging through her money belt, intending to pass off modern Egyptian pounds as money the cashier should willingly receive. The cat-headed girl stood submissively behind Jeannette, naked, gaze locked on her bare feet, and Jeannette felt completely evil for having just *bought* her.

Not that she planned to make the girl wash clothes or scrub any floors or grind emmer wheat into sandy flour between two stones. Jeannette was going to clothe her, and set her free.

"Will this do?" Her hands shook as she pulled out the cash. Maybe, if she talked fast enough, the cashier would take the money. "This is worth a great amount in the lands I come from." She added a smile for good effect.

"What is this paper? It is more fine than papyrus." The man rubbed the Egyptian fifty-pound note between his fingers. "Very nice, but this is not payment." He shrugged with a shake of his head, his black eyes narrowing as he returned the money. "It is not silver or copper. Silver or linen or the bronze jugs you offered, that is all." He sat up stiffly and crossed his arms, tiny beads of sweat ghosting his close-cropped hair and temples catching Jeannette's frantically wandering gaze.

She glanced behind her, hoping Abayomi had a few more hidden gems secreted within his gray wrappings, but he was nowhere to be found. She huffed and ground her teeth. Her only support was a pre-teen slave with the head of a cat and the spine of a jellyfish. Sizing up two guards stationed between the cashier and the platform to the left, her anxiety threatened to burn clean through her. The quickest escape route lay behind the money man to his right, away from the guards, beyond the open commons down a skinny alley. Other than the unwanted money, her passport, and an assortment of day-trip essentials, the only possible thing of value to these people might be the lapis lazuli ankh pendant she'd bought at the flea market. Praying its worth amounted to three bronze jugs, she dangled the pendant from its silver chain, hoping that not having the money didn't land her in a holding cell to be presented on the slaver's block the next morning.

"How about this, will this cover her?" She shook the blue ankh, symbol of eternal life.

The cashier examined what she had in her hand, and then sprang away, his little stool toppling over. Grabbing an amulet at his neck, he held it out toward her in a gesture of shielding.

"Where did you get such a thing?" he asked, then louder he cried out, pointing with his free hand, stepping farther and farther away, "Tomb robber! Desecrator of the sacred!"

"What?" Jeannette said. The crowd arched their necks, heads turned, eyes narrowed. Her fingers constricted around the necklace ornament, the six points of the design digging into her palm. "No! I didn't rob any tomb; I got it at the market."

"Get back, you crocodile. Curses brought down upon you and your children! Your ancestors to Apep." The cashier's long finger, stained with ink, marked her for his comprehensive curse. The guards squared their shoulders; one took a step toward her, spear gripped tight in his fist. "May vengeance find your sleeping cot. Sekhmet! The defiler is here. Sekhmet, feast on her heart!"

"Wait!" Jeannette reached out to calm the man, then gave up her plea as the phrase 'tomb robber' whispered throughout the crowd, more virulent than a venereal disease on Greek Row. She had to disappear, quickly. Her eyes landed on the alley beyond the screaming man, beyond the reach of the guards and crowds and angrily spat curses.

"Listen, that's all I have." Jeannette grabbed the hand of the girl, pliantly waiting behind her, and slipped the pendant into her pants pocket. "If you don't want it, then fine. I'll come back with three bronze jugs, or whatever it is you want, to pay for her later, but we're going now." Nobody blocked the way to the alley, if only for seconds more, and Jeannette tugged on the cat-headed girl's arm as they barged through the thinning crowd to the opening.

"Stop, you cannot take her! You did not pay for her. Thief!" His cries of 'thief' and 'defiler' chased them with the persistence of angry hounds to the thin opening of the alley. And behind the words chased the guards.

The girl barely kept up, and it felt like dragging along a petulant five-year old in need of a long nap. Jeannette shot a glance over her shoulder, looked into the girl's peculiar cat eyes and commanded, "Run." Those almond eyes widened, and suddenly wings seemed to have sprouted from her feet she ran so fast. She chased after Jeannette as they sprinted down the alley, the sound of the lumbering pursuit trapped in the commons, the slim mouth of the alley holding them at bay.

"Woman. Stop now! By order of the Master Slaver, stop."

Another glance and the receding face of an angry guard swallowed her vision, fueling her panicked steps.

A 'T' in the alley demanded a quick decision, and she slipped to the right, back toward the main thoroughfare, her grip cemented to the girl's wrist.

"Where are we going?" the girl asked, her voice vibrating with a rubbed quality, like a cricket song or a purr through her shallow huffing.

"No idea," Jeannette said between breaths, wondering at her next course of action when a hand reached out from beyond a wooden door frame and pulled her in, yanking the girl in after her.

The door slammed, and in the dim light of the room she could make out Abayomi, his posture as stiff as the limestone statues that lined the temple entrances. At the sight of him, an off feeling washed over her, something unfamiliar in an unfamiliar land, and she named that unexpected feeling with rising horror: relief.

Pressing her butt against the wooden plank door, hands on her thighs, she panted, trying to absorb the awkward emotion, to eat up the quiet debt she owed. Her ponytail end brushed against her ear. Refusing to face him, to even look up, she took the time to gather her thoughts.

"She went this way," came the cry from the direction of the market, muffled by the thick brick walls.

The double cadence of two approaching men brought with it dampness to her pits and the accompanying stench of fear-sweat. Abandoning the door, Jeannette went to the naked, freaky girl, blocking her with Jeannette's own body from potential x-ray vision and bloodhound noses.

The grinding of a not-too-distant door roughly yanked on, the door banging open, the barking orders of the guards had Jeannette threshing out a plan. She pushed her way past clay containers to a high window on the opposite side of the building.

"Come here," she said in an urgent hiss, waving at the girl. In an instant, the cat-headed girl hopped over and put her foot in the cup of Jeannette's hands as she hoisted the girl up to the window. "Crawl out. Hide at the Montu temple. We'll find you."

Another door banged open. A dog barked. The girl's bare butt, followed by her feet, slipped through the small window. Now, only Jeannette and the slow, lumbering mummy were left.

Apparently that wasn't what the mummy had been expecting as he watched the window, open mouthed.

Jeannette scanned the building: clay jugs and wide mouthed vessels, woven sheets, burlap-styled bags fat with unknown goods. "You, come." She didn't have time for elaborate explanations. Abayomi shuffled to her and she pushed him into a crouch between two large jars, throwing a stiff sheet over him. "They're not even looking for you, so stay hidden. Montu temple. Got it?"

She sprinted to the door, threw it open and charged right into the chest of a guard. The man, a tiny bit taller than herself, had the wide eyes of the suddenly shocked. Jeannette rebounded from the man's hard chest, twisting her body for a turn. But the man guarded the slave auction, probably experienced in grabbing people rebounding from his body parts, and with a snap of his wrist, snatched the back of Jeannette's shirt.

Jeannette continued her twist, praying for the strength of modern invention and the glory of polyester. Her shirt held firm. In Jeannette's peripheral vision another guard approached in slow motion strides, spear point leveled as if to skewer her for the annual company picnic.

She raised the heel of her hiking boot and slammed it onto her guard's foot. The action canted her body; she cartwheeled one arm and yanked her shirt from his hand with the other. His furious cry of pain pierced the distant noises of people.

She spun around and bounced off the rough side of a building, spring-boarding off it for all she was worth, and sprinted toward the sounds of the crowd, praying for a path back to the main street and population.

Chapter 8

FOOTSTEPS JOUNCED TOWARD HER from a side street and Jeannette froze. Taking a breather, she'd been gazing at the sky above. Not a cloud in sight. Not a bird. Not a magic flying carpet ready to whisk her to safety. Scanning to the left, then the right, she readied herself to bolt, but then recognized the sliding gait immediately. She snapped her head around the corner. The mummy headed her direction.

"You! How did you find me?" She searched for guards, but none chased after the dead man. She popped up to her feet, the threatening cloud of lead having drifted away.

The mummy shrugged. "The Gods guided my way. Follow me." With nothing more, he turned and—hobbling along as fast as his atrophied muscles allowed—led her back toward the main street.

"The guards are there," she whispered loud enough to make the whisper a lost cause.

"We are not returning to the market."

As they neared the busy cross-street—closer to the temple of Montu and the river than the slaver market up the hill—he bee-lined for the temple. His head swiveled this way and that as he searched for something. Jeannette followed cautiously, she too searching, eyes peeled for guards and danger, hoping to find a cat-headed girl waiting in peace. A woman with a pot on her head glared when Jeannette bumped into her. "Watch yourself," the woman said, her scowl the vicious mirror of a wicked headmistress.

At the back of the temple, near a gathering of women surrounding a well, they found the girl. She saw them and slunk in their direction, radiating for all to see an air of guilt.

"You're safe," Jeannette said, delighted and more than a little shocked.

"We should get out of sight," Abayomi suggested. Jeannette agreed, grabbing the girl's arm, relieved to feel those clammy fingers wrap around her own. Jeannette turned from the chatting women, who watched the three with casual glances, and slipped down a sparsely populated street.

The mummy followed, this time Jeannette did not even attempt to lose his tail, and after poking her head into three buildings—all three filled with furniture and the scents of life—the fourth proved vacant. She wished she'd been this bold last night, then she wouldn't have had to sleep with rats. They climbed down into the building's cellar, the air cool and earthy. Little light reached them from cracks in the mortar above, so Jeannette snuck back out and nabbed a lamp from another house, the owners gone, probably busy with a normal life. Lighting the woolen wick with one of her matches—nearly a full box—she set it near the stairs and collapsed in utter fatigue. Letting out a sigh, she whispered, "How did you know? Back there? That I would go that way?" Her left boot strings dangled, undone, and the little plastic sheath on the end of a lace had frayed somewhere in the last two days. Maybe it hadn't been days; maybe time had grown fat and lazy, and stole more than its due. She re-tied her laces.

The mummy glanced at the cat-headed girl, then tore his eyes away to face Jeannette. "It was obvious the alley proved the best route to escape if your tongue delivered you into some complete disaster." He paused. Still tugging at her laces, she shook her head, the veil of her hair shielding her uncertainty. He acted like he knew her so well. "The number of people at the road would have slowed the initiation of any escape, and the slave corral would not have been a place you would have wanted to approach." Lifting her head, she blinked at him through her bangs. The spent flesh of his lips turned up into a brief smile. "And if you did go down the alley, the left turn would bear you to a small garden. You had to go right or be trapped." He huffed a roughshod laugh. "I did my own scouting."

Obviously, his earlier stint of reticence had ended. Maybe, he'd come to terms with his own personal dilemma, instigating Jeannette to foster a new brand of resentment.

"And then," she asked, "after I'd run?"

"As I said, the Gods guided my path."

Like she believed that.

Then he gave the cat-headed girl the most attentive appraisal. Jeannette waited for him to drop to his knees and begin genuflecting against the floor, kissing her feet or something equally besotted. Jeannette studied her too, trying to envision what set Abayomi into a spasm of awe. Defenseless nakedness. She needed some clothes.

"You . . . Are you a sending of Bast?" he asked, his voice curious, hopeful, and a little reverent. "Can you offer me your aid? I must get to the Hall of Two Truths. I must find my heart scarab."

Jeannette closed her eyes, reopening them onto this girl she'd saved from slavery. Rescued from sordid, sexual debauchery at the calloused hands of a fat ploughman. No way a god, however far-fetched the entire concept was, would allow such misuse.

"Abayomi. She's not a god. Get over it, would you?" Jeannette cringed at her own words. "I mean, you're probably scaring her."

The girl glanced from Jeannette to Abayomi, her eyes bright and wild. She shook her head. "I am not—" Her words crumbled on her tongue and she blinked her gaze back to Jeannette: opened, closed, opened. Methodical. "He is not scaring me," she amended, her voice vibrating deep in her chest.

Like all the animal-headed people running around she had the mundane body of a human, but her head, black and furry, had the shape of a Siamese cat's. Two pointed ears perched on the top and a crop of whiskers sprouted from a muzzle that housed a line of sharp teeth. The orange slits of her eyes revealed nothing, and Jeannette realized she couldn't glean a thing from that feline face, harder to read than even Abayomi's dead flesh. The line of fur faded along her shoulders and back into perfectly smooth skin.

"Bast is my mother. I am a daughter of Bast." The girl glanced away, her shoulders stiff, her ears pulled back the slightest amount. "She calls me Sanura."

"Did they hurt you? Are you okay, Sanura?" Jeanette asked. Women's laughter reached the cellar from above. Jeannette felt cagey.

"I am fine," said Sanura in that same purring voice that sounded so alien, like computer-generated vocals the digitally skilled plastered over the Internet in songs and voice-overs. "What is it that—I am yours now. Is there anything you need?" She performed an awkward half bow, diligently averting her gaze.

"No! Really, you're not my slave. I'm freeing you." Jeannette threw her hands in the air as if tossing a pile of handbills, each one coated with the ineffable right of freedom. "You're no slave."

The girl blinked. Open, close, open. "Then, I thank you." She bowed again.

Abayomi snapped his mouth closed and turned away from them, facing the blank surface of the cellar wall. He opened his mouth to speak, then hesitated. Jeannette guessed that his next words would antagonize the burgeoning nest of bees that her nerves had become.

"We are now in an unfortunate dilemma." He took a step toward the stairs. "The guards are searching for us and this place of refuge is not adequate." Then, with a shuffle of dirty feet, he turned to face them once more. His gauzed face remained a mask, though the slow rumble of his voice led Jeannette to think the poor man was pushing his long dead brain into overexertion. His face angled toward hers, though his eyes looked afflicted by a wandering disease—one of them aimed slightly upward, the other off to the left as if afraid to be pinned down. "And, you have stolen," he turned away, "what others deem is a slave."

Already primed, her hackles ruffled. "Did you hear the things he was saying about her? He was going to sell her as some harem girl or prostitute or something!"

In jagged jerks, he nodded. "Yes."

A heavy load pulled her heart to her stomach. "You're okay with that?" she asked, her voice small and rushed.

Again, he twisted his body to avoid meeting her accusing eyes. In that one gesture, the pedestal he'd managed to climb upon crumbled to a pile of rubble. He opened his mouth to continue speaking, but before he could dig his grave any deeper Jeannette interrupted. She knew his answer.

"We need to go. We can't stay here forever." How broad was the slave market men's reach? "They'll find us soon enough."

"As you say," Abayomi said hollowly. "We stay here until the fall of night, then to the docks."

Abayomi puffed out a long breath, looking at neither Jeannette nor their ward, but at the flicker of the lamp flame as it burned steadily in the still air. The activity on the street above, only one story up, was muted. She hated the silence.

A grumble bubbled from her stomach, breaking it.

"Fine." Jeannette forced the words between clenched teeth. "So I screwed up. They wouldn't take my money. However," she fluttered her hand in a blurred gestured toward her best guess of the market's direction, "I'm not about to send the girl back to the slaver merchants." She barricaded her face behind her palms, peeking through the gaps of her fingers. "I've really screwed up, haven't I?"

Abayomi studied her, and shook his head. "You have drawn notice of those you are best to be hidden from. Even if you found the money—" Abayomi opened his eyes and cast them upon the girl, knees clutched to her chest, "—I'm not sure they would allow you freedom, since you did make a fool of the Master Slaver and tried to use gold from a tomb to purchase her." He threw his gaze at her, aimed it like an accusing finger. "You do not steal from tombs, do you?"

"No! And it wasn't gold," she tried to explain, but her protesting stomach interrupted again.

"I realize you are a foreign woman, but what were you thinking? There are three people in every city you do not cross. The head priest of the dominant temple, the local nomarch appointed by the pharaoh, and the master slaver. Didn't you even think?"

No, she couldn't say that she had.

"I saw a girl whose liberties were being stripped." She slapped her hands against her thighs, a childish action, but she felt so impotent she needed to lash out at something. "Where I'm from there is no slavery and everyone, pharaoh or farmer, has the same rights."

Both the girl and the mummy went silent; a kindergartner would have been less flummoxed from interpreting differential equations. Then shadows of scorn hardened the girl's unsophisticated purity. "But," said the girl, "the farmer has no education, little responsibility other than to tend the fields. They do not have the same power, or the same worth."

"I can't believe you're okay with your lack of rights, of—" Jeannette took in a deep breath, "—of enslaving children."

Abayomi glared at her. "I am not one who questions the laws of the pharaoh, nor can you." Tilting his head, he studied them, his heavy contemplation landing first on Jeannette, then the poor girl huddled near her. "It is how things happen. Pharaoh and," he lifted his shoulders, shaking his head the slightest amount, "the Gods condone it. Who am I to argue and say it is wrong? I am only a scribe. You say that in your land everyone has the same rights, but such a thing is impossible, improbable even. The pharaoh's word is law. And the Gods'." From one end of the cellar to the other, he paced; a line of his linens had begun to unravel and trailed along the ground behind him. "We all serve the Gods, Jeannette, even you. Even her." He nodded at the girl, who stared at him with the wide eyes of dashing innocence. "And if the Gods—her mother even—deemed that she should be sent into slavery, then that is what is to happen." He stopped his desperate migration, and focused all his intensity onto the dirt floor, his voice ratcheting with each flurry of words. "If the Gods deemed that my wife would die after only two inundations together, then so be it! If the Gods deem I die of disease and get stuck in some in-between place with a foolish, insolent woman, and that I lose my heart and cannot have it weighed so I can go on to the Fields of *Yaaru*, then it must be so." As he forced out his injustices, the heat of his anger faded into quiet resignation. He glanced about the ground, his manner scattered, and finally sat.

His utter faith in the order of things, his acceptance of life's hardships, stirred something within her that brought about an intense feeling of indigestion. She'd long ago given up on a single God, she doubted that a mass of them, furry faced or not, could do much better. How people put their faith into something as intangible as divinity, she couldn't comprehend.

"But what if your gods are wrong, your pharaoh is wrong?"

His head snapped up, the swift action of a spring uncoiled, and if he'd had any fluid in his body, she knew he'd be spitting he spoke so vehemently. "Watch what you say. I can save you from slaver guards, but I cannot save you from the Gods' anger."

"You don't get it!" she snarled back. "I don't believe in your gods' anger. It does not affect me. I *do not* believe in your gods."

A gasp from her left, tiny, yet heavy with the weight of astonishment, tore Jeannette's attention away from the fury wrapped in linens to the girl she'd just rescued. Sanura's mouth had fallen open and her ears spoke epics with their tense angle.

"My mother, she loves and protects me. My sisters and brothers teach me how to live properly, teach me about my place in the world. If Mother asks me to do something, anything, I will do it, even if all I want to do is be a part of the litter. It is my duty and it is my pride and pleasure." Then, the girl closed her vivid eyes, her voice soft, almost inaudible, even in their underground hideout. "I didn't ask to be picked. I didn't ask for it."

The mummy began rewinding a loose strip of linen around his thumb. Jeannette, speechless, awkwardly patted the girl. Pulling the water bottle from her pack, Jeannette offered it to Sanura, who leaned forward and sniffed the side.

"It's water." Jeannette shook the bottle with a slosh. "You want any?"

The girl nodded, took the bottle, running her fingers along the hard, plastic surface, then drank from the wide mouth. Solemnly, she returned the bottle to Jeannette, and then she asked, "How can you not believe in the Gods?"

It hadn't been an instantaneous process, but she was certain it started years ago, when Jeannette had been as young and naïve as this young woman beside her. She'd been visiting her aunt in a tiny fly-spot of a town along the Canadian border. Her father's sister, who'd modeled an even more messed up worldview than her dad ever had, dragged Jeannette to church Sunday after Sunday, broiling away in polyester dresses of soft, Easter hues within the run down house of God. The steepled church housed one of those sin-obsessed denominations that worried more about other people's business than keeping their own church house in order. Or maybe it had just been that particular preacher; that old man, colossal behind his podium, railing against this evil and that, had accomplished nothing more than making Jeannette feel like a belly-crawling creature of sludge.

That was God's man. At the time she believed in him, trusted him. She'd go home and read the Bible, short passage by short passage because the language had been as alien as Shakespeare, taking notes like her school teachers had taught her.

One morning, trying to please and impress, she'd approached the preacher and began to ask him the questions that tormented her day and night. "Sir, why was Cain afraid of all those people out there when God cast him out? Where did all those people come from?" He gripped her shoulder, firm for such an old geezer, and led Jeannette to her aunt, telling his parishioner that, "you have a lot of teaching to do on this one."

Thus marked a month of Hell before Jeannette could escape home, begging her mother to forgive her for all of the terrible, wicked things she did, for the evil thing she was. Cried against her mother's chest for God to love her.

Her mom never again sent her to visit that aunt.

The young mini-god stared up into Jeannette's face, waiting.

"I just don't."

"But why not? When you can see them everywhere?"

With a sneer Jeannette could feel twist apart her face, she glared at the little puppet, echoing the doctrine she'd probably heard all her life. Were they all brainwashed and blind? "I don't see any gods anywhere. On the streets are people like you—" the girl flinched under the force of Jeannette's vitriol, "—with animal-heads and talking dogs and freaky things straight from myth, but are they powerful gods? Do they answer *my* prayers? Do they talk to *me* about life and death and the meaning of all this crap?" She shook her head, her hair flying wildly. "Never. I don't put stock in purely imaginary things."

Sanura's eyes drowned in matte black and again she snarled at Jeannette. The girl's protective streak stretched as long as the Nile itself.

THREE GREAT LIES

"My mother is the Goddess Bast. She answers my prayers. She talks to me! You are hollow and empty and I feel sorry for the loneliness you must feel." The two women eyed each other, and the girl deflated, sinking into herself, as lost and alone as Jeannette felt, even with a goddess by her side.

But she'd certainly hit her mark.

Abayomi remained quiet, still on his side of the cellar, a mouse hiding from squabbling hawks. He'd tied his finger gauze up in a scruffy knot. Jeannette couldn't help but notice how he'd agilely avoided their conversation. He must have had sisters.

They waited through the back-end hours of the day in silence, the only noise shared between them Jeannette's and Sanura's rumbling stomachs. When darkness set, Abayomi pushed himself to standing. "We leave now. We must still be quiet, even at night the guards should be about."

"Brilliant observation," Jeannette muttered as the three snuck out of the abandoned building, capers in the night. "Miss Marple's got nothing on you."

He rolled his eyes; the whites seemed whiter now, perhaps the copious amount of eye rolling collected moisture from the air and lubricated the organs, washing away the stain of death. "You hide behind your riddles again. Stop arguing and let us leave before they catch us."

"The men are after me." Sanura glanced down the empty, dark streets. "If they have me, they might let you go."

"That is not the case," Abayomi said. "Jeannette has already made her enemies in this city; it is best if we all leave for now."

Jeannette glanced at the mummy. "You don't have to run, too." Why he wanted to help her was a mystery; she was perfectly fine taking care of herself.

He shifted one shoulder, a robotic action, and stared her hard in the eyes. "No matter my actions, I am bound within this world of mystery until I find my heart scarab."

She wasn't sure if he was accusing her, or making up an excuse to keep them all together. Again, she found herself frustrated by her inability to interpret her companion's features or actions.

The girl considered some knowledge only she knew and nodded at him. "Then, I will help you find it."

Abayomi's posture relaxed and he dipped his head at Sanura. How in the world had Jeannette ended up in this quest to save the maiden's life and the squire's soul? But as long as she ended up back home, she might as well help these people while on her own search for reality. "I'm in. I'll help you, too," she said to Abayomi, then to Sanura, "Don't worry, we won't let them have you." Jeannette twirled the girl around by the shoulders, facing Sanura down the alley. "Let's go."

* * *

In the low light of the moon and fishermen's fires, Jeannette could see a number of vessels moored along three jutting piers, rocking gently in the shallow waves, shadowed beasts in the night. Three men squatted on the grassy riverbank, gutting the evening's catch. The fires shone against the river's still surface while a gaggle of mewling cats and a few dogs begged for scraps.

A sizable barge heaped with what looked like grain consumed the north side of the widest dock. Other flat, open rafts with nothing on them rested on the opposite side, while a line of five small reed canoes that looked ready to sink at a sneeze were tied up on the south dock. Fastened to the end of the central dock were two planked ships, a pole protruding vertically from the center of each craft.

Finally, something was going their way. Jeannette hadn't expected so many possibilities. "We should take one of those." She jerked her chin at the planked boats.

"It is night, the sailors will be sleeping. Plus, we have no payment for boat fare," said Abayomi. There he went again, raining on her parade. He hadn't even considered she might have meant to steal them.

The girl made a noise half a meow, half a whine. "They're coming. Fast."

Activity emerged from the city's main road. In a sharp cadence, a man mounted on a horse seeped from the darkness, then another.

Abayomi gawked. "What is that thing? A demon?"

Jeannette glanced between Abayomi and the horse. "What? The horse?" Of all the things to sweep his feet out from under him, she wouldn't have bet on a simple horse. "It's just an animal, uh, from the north."

For a few more breaths he stared at the animal, then shook his head. "Here." Abayomi grabbed the two women's arms, trotting down the south pier with them in tow. For once, Jeannette didn't try to pull away, worried more that he led them toward the least water-worthy looking boat than the possible infection of some contagion of the flesh—drowning being the more immediate calamity. An old man's form became distinct in the faint light as they crossed the dock; his sunken face watched them impassively from the north dock, chewing on a reed. Abayomi pushed them into a small reed boat, meagerly sized to fit two adults. He grabbed a tarp of rough weave before he climbed into the boat after them, packing Sanura between the two.

"Why are we in *this* boat?" Jeannette asked under her breath, her skin crawling every time the mummy brushed up against her. Abayomi fiddled with the rope, untying the small watercraft, and pushed against the dock. "Can't we just swim?" Water soaked her clothing and she propped her backpack on her chest hoping to save her electronics. Luckily, her cheap watch claimed to be water-resistant, but her camera had no such advantages. Abayomi wrestled with the fish-scented tarp until it covered them, submerging them into a blindness that triggered her baser instinct to freeze.

"Many snakes and crocodiles. The hippo, too, is deadly. It would not be safe." His voice came from so close, it brought up unwanted images of his lips brushing against her hair.

Jeannette hoped the current would sweep them away from this danger. But counting on her luck, a worse calamity would befall them oarless on the Nile. She squeezed her eyes shut, not dwelling on ill fate.

As the horses trotted closer, Jeannette held her breath. Since Abayomi didn't need to breathe—though he certainly sighed enough— and Sanura was as quiet as a cat, Jeannette could only hear the beat of her own heart slaloming in her chest, surely giving them all away.

"Stop fidgeting," Abayomi whispered, and Jeannette tried even harder to be still. Cool water soaked the back of her shirt, oozing up her neck. She had no sense of gliding down the river, of being caught in the current of freedom. They felt anchored.

"Did you see a daughter of Bast and a woman come by, old man?"

The words settled down upon them with the heavy weight of inevitability and Jeannette shivered. She could feel the heat of Sanura pressed against her side. This girl was as motionless as a rock.

Then from Jeannette's side of their boat, she heard, "Hey. You want me slip you out of here?"

68

Chapter 9

THOUGH THEY HUDDLED IN SILENCE, Jeannette's mental clock ticked away a marching band percussion, loud enough to rally the away team stands. Fear sweat dripped down the sides of her temples where her hair grew thinner, pulled tight by her ponytail.

"You want me help?"

As close as she could approximate, the voice, an odd guttural grumble, spoke from the level of the water's surface. Abayomi shook his head at her.

"Who are you?" she whispered.

Abayomi puffed out a gust of disappointed air; from too close by far, she heard the guards questioning the ancient prune of a man near the barge.

Heaped together in a little leaky boat constructed of river reeds, guards hunting them down like death row escapees, with a disembodied voice oozing up from the river surrounding her, Jeannette wondered if this was her end. This make-believe world was winding down, because the long sickness of her body—filed away in some anonymous foreign hospital—had finally rendered her brain to cottage cheese.

"Me is you help."

That made no sense.

"Help you, you give me cat."

Sanura, her body pressed against Jeannette's, stiffened. Heat radiated off her. Jeannette heard a soft hiss, like a slow leak from a balloon.

The guards stomped around along the docks causing an unnecessary racket. The guy in the water probably wasn't a guard. Another slaver?

"Why?" she whispered. Abayomi shushed for her silence again.

After a brief pause, the voice came once more, blending with the soft lap of water against the reeds. "Give me cat. I push you to river."

The deep voices of angry men grew louder. Perhaps they'd reached her dock. "The woman is a slave thief. An urn of beans for you if you tell us where she is."

"I saw them." The voice was wheezy, brittle, like Jeannette's faith in mankind.

She hated being caught in this quagmire of bad options. She didn't imagine that getting nabbed by the guards was a livable option, but giving this man Sanura? Maybe the mini-god was just a drug-figment, but right now, pressed tight to Jeannette's side, she felt solid and real. Plus, she'd just saved the girl from an equal fate, and Jeannette didn't appreciate wasted work.

She hated to do it, but Jeannette didn't see another option. Little bits of detritus fell from the tarp, ticking against the firm material of the backpack she clutched to her chest. "Fine." She held her voice low and steady as she spoke through the thick reeds of the canoe. "Get us safely out of here and *cat* shall be yours." She stressed the word "cat," pointing out the man's bad grammar, finding some stable ground in the mockery.

Another hiss, and Sanura pulled away. Jeannette's head swirled and she longed for fresh air. The girl beside her trembled.

"What are you thinking?" Abayomi whispered. His anger heaved over her like a storm cloud brimming with lightning and thunder. "You cannot hand over Sanura. Plus, you have no idea who you are talking to."

She leaned toward Abayomi, pressing down on the silent girl, and spoke so quietly her words were barely a breath. "And neither does he."

With only shallow dips and sways of the boat, the sound of sloshing water offered the only real assurance that they were moving. A gentle splash of water toward the foot of the canoe, as of someone rowing to press them along, gave her the only notion of their mysterious liberator.

Men's shouts, the stomping of feet against the wooden pier—farther away by the moment—the deep rumble of the man chuckling in the water, the cool flood through her clothing, and the cold shouldering her companions gave her were Jeannette's only sensations within the cocoon of reeds. She hated relying on this unknown person. She wanted to throw aside the tarp to see what was going on in the world around her: to assure herself of the dream's existence; to prove to her racing heart it had a reason to race.

She wanted to tell them it would be okay. She wanted to make promises.

With neither of her fellow fugitives deigning to speak to her, Jeannette began to pass in and out of a half-drowse until pinpricks of light began to steal through the tarp's weave. Her back ached; a knot on steroids had been pumping iron under her right shoulder blade, and being dry had become a lost memory turned sweeter by age.

"That boat! It's moving," someone called.

Signs of people active in the early morning roused her from her stupor.

"Look there! Jawbones is pushing a boat."

"Where you going Jawbones?"

Sometimes the man in the water would reply: "Just down river," or "Move away," or he would make that throaty chuckle that spurred within Jeannette a growing feeling of cornered prey.

"What cargo you selling, Mr. Riverman?"

"Foodstuffs," came his sharp reply. Jeannette's nerves were churned to butter.

The heat and used-up air filled her lungs with lead and she couldn't help but squirm.

Finally, the gentle rocking of the boat ceased and the sound of reeds on reeds scraped past her head. The boat hit something, and Jeannette gripped her pack tight against her chest as the angle changed and the boat slid up a shallow slope.

"Out now. Me cat."

Jeannette threw off the canvass, swallowing down scents of fermented mud and fish guts. The sun floated over the horizon. Scanning the water by her canoe, she didn't see a man at all, or another boat.

"Hello?" she called out softly, ignoring Abayomi's shushing noises and Sanura's turned-away face. Pulling out one leg, then the other, she stumbled from the boat, gripping the spongy reeds as her boots sunk inches into the shore's muck. Shadoufs bordered the edge of the bank, irrigation ditches at their bases taking water to the thirsty land away from the waterlogged marsh. Tugging with each step, thankful for the secure fit of her new boots, she slugged her way toward firmer ground and looked around.

At the foot of the boat, scant portions of him visible above the surface of the water, skulked a crocodile longer than her boss' luxury SUV. He was big and green and terribly toothy. Jeannette stepped away, impaled by the intelligence in his tiny, nugget eyes. She secretly wondered if mud in those eyes would really accomplish anything and wanted to be far away from this monster.

"Here, tasty little kitty," said the crocodile, Mr. Jawbones himself.

The Riverman had landed them just downriver of a wharf where the natives squatted along the river's edge, gutting their catch from the early portion of the day.

"Hand over cat." The Riverman lifted first his front claw, then the opposite rear claw as he crawled his way toward Jeannette, impressing

71

upon her the sheer size of the mythic crocodile. She took another step back. "You no break promise."

Sanura slunk over the lip of the opposite side of the canoe and Abayomi shuffled to put himself between the Riverman and the girl. Jeannette could imagine the wheels grinding in his deteriorated brain as he tried to spin up some strategy to get them out of there, measuring how quick they would need to run. Though, this time, he'd had no time to scout out an escape route.

Jeannette faced the crocodile, squaring her hips, and gripped the straps of her pack. "Yes, I promised you a cat, but not Sanura." She turned from the mouth of teeth, and trotted over to the fishermen, sighing her relief at finding what she'd hoped. Her limited experience with such places proved: where people gutted the fish, strays swarmed. Three cats huddled over a pile of offal, and she grabbed the closest one—brown with a short tail—by the scruff of its neck. It hissed and spat, clawing at her arm as she brought it down to the river.

"Here. A cat. Our deal is over." She squeezed her eyes shut as she tossed the frantic stray to the crocodile and the Riverman seized it out of the air in one gulp. Somehow, it hit her harder than the dramatized nature programs when the wild dogs took down the baby impala. With burning eyes, Jeannette sliced her hands through the air; now they wouldn't have to run from yet another lynchman.

No!" Sanura screamed, tripping forward to her knees, hand reaching out, fingers straining for the empty space between woman and beast. Mud coated her legs and hands, marring her perfect nudity. Moving toward the girl, the mud sucked onto Jeannette's boot, delivering her to her own mud coating as she tumbled to the ground. Sanura's accusing eyes flickered between the crocodile and Jeannette. "How could you sacrifice a little brother?" Sanura clenched her fists and punched the mud, teeth bared and shoulders hunched. Jeannette pushed herself to her feet, scraping the mud plaster from the bottom of her shoe.

"Mother Bast, why have you sent me to these people?" Sanura leapt to her feet, skirted around the prow of the boat with Abayomi scrambling after her, and charged at the crocodile.

"Son of Sobek, I am a daughter of Bast. You have done a grave thing this day." Unfurling her body, she stood up straight and thrust her finger at the crocodile on the ground. "I curse you with the hatred of the men of the *Iteru*. I curse you with the power of Bast. Until the stars fade from the sky, until the great River leaves dry its banks, they will hunt you down until you are no more."

The Riverman tossed his head, open mouth revealing the jagged arsenal within. His ridged tail slapped against the water's surface and without any other warning he lunged from the water, his entire bulk propelled by a strength designed to take down a ton of buffalo on the hoof.

Teeth flashed. The Riverman's head snapped to the side, the jaws poised for a death-grip. Jeannette, actions on autopilot, threw her clump of mud in a sideways toss that splat against the snout of the giant carnivore, nowhere near its eyes.

Already opening the act with desperation, Abayomi had a hand on Sanura's shoulder, pulling her backwards, away from the bone daggers seeking her blood.

A nerve-sizzling crack echoed down the river as the jaws slammed shut. A flock of gray sparrows took flight, chirping in alarm. Jeannette's chest heaved, brain laboring to assess the death count of the scene.

The crocodile slid back into the water, no body of a young mini-god dripping from his jaws.

"You word no good. I tell all others not trust you," he said. Then he swiveled his great head toward Sanura, pressed into the soft riverbank, Abayomi crouching over her like a guard dog.

"I crocodile. I eat you." No malice colored his voice, only a kind of grandfatherly amusement for a granddaughter who'd cried with the realization that her dinner of steak had been yesterday's pet cow. "The stone of nature shown in the tooth. Silly." He turned and slunk back into the water, Jeannette's mud grenade disintegrating in the current. A tail flick heralded his withdrawal.

Sanura's body rocked with unbidden sobs; her ears drooped, eyes, cold and full of pain, pressed on Jeannette.

Jeannette stood silent.

"I cannot believe you," Abayomi said to her, teeth clenched, gaze on the girl.

Spite bubbled up within Jeannette, as corrosive as battery acid. "Would you shut up? I just saved our lives." She glared from the man to the girl, body all over cold. Crazy, and backwards, and brainwashed. "You know what?" She threw her hands in the air and then tugged tight the shoulder straps of her backpack. "I'm sick of your disbelief. Go disbelieve in something else." They were all fools. None of them were dead, or enslaved. Yes, one cat did get killed, but the crocodile didn't get any of them. By the great moral scales in her head, their lives mattered more than one cat. She turned from the boat and the broken girl, from the river and the accusing mummy, and trudged up the slope of the bank to ascend a small crest.

"Where are you going?" Abayomi demanded. His shock and worry and pent up frustration almost fetched her back, but the dual look of contempt they'd had in their eyes, Sanura's smoldering silence, pushed her on.

"You don't need me, and I certainly don't need you." She laughed, an acerbic mockery of amusement. "Good luck."

"Jeannette!"

She kept walking. Bone white teeth flashed inside her mind.

"Jeannette. Get back here! You are a fool to separate from us."

She did not turn back.

"This girl is your responsibility," he shouted. "Foolish, selfish woman. Be gone with you then!"

She didn't want to look at them. Them or their disapproval.

* * *

She topped the hill and pulled up short by the view before her. A grand city stretched along the fertile run of the river, rising up a fruitless hill that crawled away from the flood zone.

Hand still shaking, she forced herself forward, not looking back for Abayomi and Sanura. She kept moving, refusing to acknowledge his taunts, his calls for her to stop. She couldn't deal with them right now; her frustration egged her on. The cat's yarl echoed in her mind. She didn't need them and their judgment, and they certainly didn't need her or her willingness to act. They'd proven that. They'd be fine without her, probably safer, too.

She flicked mud from her knees.

Waterways scarred the tanned landscape cradling the city. A shrine of antiquity. Jeannette bet more than a bucketload of Egyptologists would sell a kidney to be right where she stood at this moment. Mixed within tall square buildings was a sea of mud brick huts surrounding a central zone of ancient Egyptian cosmopolitanism. Everywhere were statues: men, women, ram headed lions and endless gods. She could smell the stockyard on the river side of the city and could just see buffalo and elephants and other beasts that should never have been comfortable in the desert, not to mention the donkeys. So many donkeys. And people. Normal people, the dark skinned, short Egyptians in white linen, and enough of the animal-headed ones to cause goose bumps to sprout at the utter improbability of it.

The streets were paved in square blocks so level she didn't stumble once as she jogged into the city, her heavy boots leaving a trail of mud nuggets. Her pack rattled against her back, and she kept her eyes open for anyone like her. Someone else who might have plunged into this land of crazy and knew exactly how to return. Someone with petroleum fibers and pale coloring and a height few of the locals could claim. Someone from her world.

Criers calling for the worship of Amun filled the air, praying for his shadow to fall upon them. Surely, this must be the center of it all. All travelers must pass through such a city. It was inevitable—she had to find an answer here, a way to return to where she belonged more practical than the oracle's words.

Everyone seemed busy, some laden with wrapped packages, or bundles of sticks, or pulling recalcitrant donkeys burdened with clay pots. So many, they were like an invading army, charging up the market to buy and sell with violent force, and she lost herself within them.

She refused to look behind. They really were better off without her.

"Mighty Amun, watch over us, and this, your city." A man, spread flat along the pathway reached out for the feet of passersby. "Mighty Amun, watch over this city of a thousand gates." She stomped by, ignoring his insanity.

She also tried to ignore the pit that settled in her stomach as she continued on. Losing herself in the city, she was a stranger in an even stranger land. She crossed many streets greater than the main thoroughfare of the last city she'd been in. Here, there were even more bizarre people, odd skin tones, even odder dress. A bubble of hope warred with her churning stomach. Maybe, just maybe, she could find someone to help her here.

Her stomach growled, reminding her that food would be a really good idea too.

Though the people all spoke in a language she could understand— some had thicker accents or spoke in broken phrases, like the Riverman had—she still couldn't read the hieroglyphs or more common writing. She had no idea what a bird and feather and then a curvy stick might mean.

THREE GREAT LIES

Her money belt contained fancy paper and the ankh, and she'd already caused a scene with that. Maybe her mp3 player would dazzle someone into giving her food, or, knowing her luck, they would think the noises came from a demon and call in the priests for an exorcism. Somehow she had to earn, or maybe steal, some deben or kits—or whatever they used—so she could eat, so she could survive long enough to get home. Survival first, she told herself. She bet Gabby never had to earn money on any of her trips. Gabby'd never leave the safety of bank machines.

The market of the city could compare to nothing in modern Egypt. It was the Mall of America of street fairs. Stalls and huts crammed the borders of the roads even as the shoppers crammed the streets with a higher density than even downtown Spokane during the world's largest road race. There were fishmongers—she steered clear of those and their bevy of cats—and copper smelters and shoe weavers and even brewers.

"Master Craftsman, a deben ring for these jars."

"The rug is average. I offer one ration of grain."

"Beer, one mug for one kit. Beer."

The muddled calls of the bartering energized her. All around her were people going about their lives, nothing out of the ordinary. Just the worries of buying food for dinner, clothing, and furniture. It all seemed so simple.

A pile of woven sandals caught her attention. Her own boots still squished, though her pants and shirt had dried in the growing heat. A baker had a pile of flat loaves organized on a sheet woven of light brown material. They looked delicious and smelled like heaven itself. With a smile and a bow, she asked the man the cost for the bread.

"A kit."

"Well, what exactly is a kit?" She had to get information, and asking seemed easier than pretending she knew anything about this place.

"A ten portion of a deben." He squinted at her and took a step closer to his merchandise.

"Ah, thank you," she said, teeth gripped tight together. "Very helpful. But, what is a deben?"

The man's weak mouth turned sullen. "Leave this place. I don't need no beggars." He shooed her with the back of his hand, the cordage of muscles in his arms more of a deterrent than his actual words. Jeannette spun away and immediately bumped into someone.

"I'm sorry." This sucked.

76

"Oh, it is of no worry," said a friendly voice.

A friendly voice. Jeannette glanced up at a tall woman, her eyes so dusky, the brown melted seamlessly into the pupils. Skin of flawless ebony, she obviously came from the south. A Nubian. The woman, older than Jeannette by a few years, pulled the tip of her long, white robe up to her shoulder, covering the edges of her broad collar. Mostly white. Jeannette noticed a brown smudge on the robe where she'd collided with the woman, and cringed. The woman's hair was braided with bronze beads woven into the ends. An easy smile revealed white, crooked teeth.

"You are new here?" she asked.

Jeannette simply nodded, unsure what to say to someone who was talking to her, not yelling at her, not accusing her.

"I was once new here as well. I understand how hard it can be to find your place here. Perhaps I can help you if you tell me what it is you need."

Jeannette opened her mouth; it was dry and slimy, which reminded her she had no water. With a swallow, she tried again. "I'm trying to get some food and water, maybe some money. I really . . . I don't belong here. I need to return to where I've come from."

"Follow me," the woman said with a slight dip to her head, and she turned and walked down the market street, the lightweight material of her robe flowing behind her like gauzy wings. She led Jeannette to an open plaza with a wide well in the center. Many women and children were gathered around a raised, bricked lip surrounding the well, chatting, pulling on a shadouf to remove the water. As Jeannette drew closer, she could see a kind of bench carved into the inside of the well for people to step down and fill their jars. She wondered how safe the water was, just sitting here, fairly open to waste and the elements. There had to be dirt in it and, though she didn't want to think about it, sewage. At least she had iodine tablets.

The woman stepped under the sparse shade of a nearby building and gestured for Jeannette to go use the well. Jeannette approached the woman with the shadouf, smiling. She was certain her teeth would crack from all the effort.

The woman raised her eyebrows.

Jeannette twirled her arm at her, a 'carry on' gesture. "Just observing."

"What, you judging how I fetch the water?" She delivered Jeannette a distrusting sneer, a prisoner of her xenophobia.

Jeannette shook her head. "No, just learning."

"Don't know how to get the water?" Her sneer relaxed into a snide smirk. "It's easy. Just dip the bucket in and pull it out." The woman stepped onto the bench and pulled down on the long rope dangling from the end of a pole that was balanced on a small support structure. The bucket tied onto the end of the longer section of pole dipped into water and filled. The woman then relaxed her hold on the rope, and the heavy counterweight on the other end of the pole did all the work in lifting the water. Jeannette nodded; it was simple, but effective. She thanked the woman, who laughed but stepped away, and tried her hand at pulling out her own bucket of water. It *was* easy. She filled her water bottle, drawing the attention of the other women, and stepped away. Jeannette felt all eyes on her as she searched for her iodine tablets in her pack and dropped a portion of one white tablet in the bottle, shaking it up. Though still thirsty, she dropped the bottle into her bag, giving the iodine time to do its chemical magic. Still agitated from the face-off by the river, she felt a little ease relax the tension gripping her body. She'd figured something out. Survival wasn't an impossibility.

"There is water; now we shall find you a method of employment."

Jeannette practically jumped out of her skin to find the friendly woman at her elbow. "Yeah, thanks." Jeannette grinned, nothing so teeth shattering as the forced smiles she'd been giving the other locals.

"I am Tabiry." The woman inclined her head, her thick collar tinkled. It must have been metal, like a mantle of thin bronze. Jeannette noticed that the woman hardly even had a glisten of sweat to her brow, while Jeannette always had a trickle of it dripping down her temple, sneaking down her spine.

"My name's Jeannette Walker. Ah, Jeannette will do." She'd need no last names here.

"May Amun be pleased for this meeting, Jeannette."

"Ah . . . Okay. Yeah, may he be pleased." Jeannette rolled her eyes at herself as Tabiry turned and guided her down other market streets—a maze worse than the market in El-Balyana—and finally stopped at a small crossroads.

"That is the Master Brewer of this the market precinct. Address him as Master Brewer and I shall tell him of your knowledge of beer."

Jeannette raised her eyebrows at her new friend. "I know nothing of brewing." What was Tabiry suggesting she do, lie to the man? Her learning curve would make her useless for at least a day.

78

"But," the woman said, her eyes strangely bright, "you know nothing of anything. Beer is easy. And amongst those of Kemet, it is expected that a woman perform the brewing. You would be doing him a service."

Jeannette wondered why a woman had to brew, hoped this wasn't some weird marriage custom, but didn't feel like arguing. Exhausted from the day's events, she just wanted something to go her way. She felt it her due. Approaching the brewer, an old man with a face lined as deeply as the hills harboring the city, she smiled her most congenial smile. Her cheeks ached. He looked at the women, not bothering to turn away from a large, pottery jar—reminiscent of an Erlenmeyer flask—that he was stirring with an oversized wooden spoon.

"Master Brewer." Tabiry harbored the air of politeness, but her tone gave Jeannette the sense that she thought herself of higher station. Jeannette wondered just who this lady was. "I would like you to consider this woman to aid you in the toil of making beer."

He snorted, swallowed, smacked his lips, and then said, "What does she know of the brewing of beer?" After a cursory examination of her dress, he barely paid a glance to Jeannette, favoring the Nubian and his big flask. The scent of fermented grain, nothing so bitter as strong ale, hovered around them in a dank cloud.

"It is made from the grain of this land." Jeannette feigned confidence with an energy she knew wouldn't last. "Fermented for the proper period of time to produce the liquor of pure inebriant that you, fine Master Brewer, brew here." God, she sounded so lame. She'd taken a wine tasting class the winter after she'd moved to Spokane to try to meet new people. She kicked herself for not taking the beer class instead, but it seemed too plebeian at the time. "I am merely offering my services to do the menial tasks to release you from the burden of them." She had the urge to bow, but checked herself and only dipped her head. "I am certain I can aid you in making a drink that is fit for the gods." She studied the man's reaction through her bangs.

He didn't even look up. "No, girl. I do not need you."

"Girl?" She pressed her fists to her thighs in exasperation. "I'm older than I look. Back in my home I have a job of great importance," she kept her voice steady and almost pleasant, "and you would be a camel's ass to pass me by," she finished at a volume she hoped only she could hear.

His thick eyebrows crawled up his high forehead, expanding the wrinkles into crevasses; his frown deepened. Jeannette couldn't force herself to look at Tabiry, sure she'd disappointed the woman.

With a sigh, Jeannette released her fervor, her shoulders slumped, and she faced down the busy street, beyond to where the river lay, and the fish gutters did their dirty work, and the leaky boat she'd come in on bobbed against the shore. She couldn't help but wonder about those fools she'd left behind.

It had always been a shortcoming of hers. She just didn't know how to act in new situations without plenty of observation time first. "Well, Master Brewer. Can you tell me what it is I am lacking so I can alleviate your worries?"

"You are not of Kemet. You do not know the fine art of brewing. What more do you ask of me?" He grunted at his flask.

"I know I could easily brew this beer, and do it better than anyone . . . Other than you, Master Brewer." She didn't stop her bow this time. Her limbs felt heavy; she needed a nap. The trip across the river had not been restful, but she didn't want to leave without something. "Do you think anyone around here might have need of me? I work hard and fast. I pick up tasks quickly. I'm able to do any duty." And if he didn't know someone, maybe her new friend did.

"Little girl," he said. *Little girl?* She couldn't believe it. What a rude idiot. She pursed her lips, but kept her mouth shut. "You release the donkey lead with too little effort."

Jeannette shot him a look. He was staring at Tabiry, who gave him a single nod. Then he chuckled and tossed Jeannette a long, wooden ladle. Reaching out with science-geek adroitness, she hit the ladle with one palm and fumbled to catch it with the other. "Stir this until I return." He wiped his hands on a stained apron as Jeannette shook her stinging hand. Grabbing a basket, he wandered off down the market, his shoulders rolled forward in a painful-looking hunch. Stall keepers sent out greetings as he passed by.

Jeannette glanced at Tabiry. "What just happened?"

The woman turned to Jeannette and flashed her brilliant teeth with undiluted friendliness. "You have found a job."

"With your help." Jeannette blinked and looked away. She didn't mean to sound petulant. "Thank you, Tabiry."

The ladle's handle had been smoothed down from wear and the bowl at the end was stained brown. "Stirring. I guess I can figure that out. But I think I need to wash first." Jeannette held up her hands, dismayed by the brown shadow of mud over them. A vessel of water with another ladle squatted along the wall of the building. Jeannette scooped out some water and rinsed off her hands as best as she could without a bar of soap. Then she stepped over to the clay flask—the moist, pungent air tickling her nose—slipped the ladle in, and began to stir.

With a nod, Tabiry bade Jeannette farewell, and said that she would see her soon. "One must help a fellow newcomer," she said and floated away like a dream. Other people walked by, stopping to stare at her with curiosity and amusement, but moved on from the sight of a foreign woman stirring a pot.

Chapter 10

A MONTH OF SMELLY TOIL—and a crash course in brewing and obedience—had passed under cloudless skies, and each night a pittance gilded her palm. Jeannette thanked the Master Brewer; though the coins were worth a spit-on-a-fire, at least he didn't pay her in beer. The few coppers and the use of a sleeping pallet stashed in the back of the small shop, tucked in amongst stacks of dried barley and finished bread loaves, seemed like masked-bandit robbery for the hours she'd given. It certainly marked the do-you-want-fries-with-that? point of her career.

Four hours of stirring pots, flaking the bread that fermented into the beer, pouring, drudgery in the morning, the afternoon meal and siesta, and then four more hours back to stirring, flaking, pouring, and drudgery in the late afternoon. Her nights, thankfully, contained none of these tasks.

During each morning's flurry of activity—before the curtain of heat closed down the day—she watched the animal-headed people pass by and counted the variety. Heads of cows, others of cats, jackals, alligators, and vultures. A man with a ram's head and long horns. A vulture with a snake head flying low above the crowd. And on and on the procession went.

One thing she noticed, none were adolescents.

Mi-nether, she'd heard them called. Perhaps, like Sanura, they too were all children of their respective gods. Performing their jobs, honing their training, doing exactly the things expected of them from the first day to the last. And wasn't that a unique concept. Children of gods, trying to do what was expected of them. If she were a child of Bast or Zeus or Odin, she'd certainly not allow herself to be chained down by lame rules and let weaker people walk all over *her*. Sell *her* on the slave block.

A lion-headed woman strode by, each step full of purpose. The crowd parted, clearing her path. Jeannette ripped a hunk off a loaf of bread and chewed it thoughtfully. So many gods. How could these people keep them all straight? You could never please them all. The ancient Egyptians certainly landed themselves on the center step of a Penrose staircase coming up with that cosmology.

But then, if she thought about it, weren't there many Christian gods? Each god somehow brought to life by each church and their own distinct expectations of the divine? God the Father, the Son and the Holy Ghost.

The Jealous God. The Forgiving God. And the Son: Jesus the Redeemer, Jesus the Judge and that sweet Lamb, the one who snuggled up with sheep and died for all our sins. New Testament, Old. The Koran. Mother Mary and all the Saints. People really did choose their own gods, and as she watched the procession of *mi-nether* she realized you had better pick well.

Not one mummy lumbered by. Or anyone like her, modern and light skinned.

Only when Tabiry came to visit and they toured the vast city together did she set aside her loneliness.

She swallowed her last mouthful of bread and drank down the beer dregs from the bottom of her mug, which, to Jeannette's taste buds' eternal boredom, also tasted like bread. It wasn't terrible, fairly weak as beer went, but she really missed cold, filtered water. And ice. And ice cream. Coffee. And anything with a familiar flavor. She swore her teeth would grind away from the sand baked into the loaves, and judging by the locals' ghastly dental status, she didn't think that a far-fetched fear.

The Master Brewer tapped the side of the mixing flask with his ladle.

"I'll attend the jug until the sun hits the Camel's Back. Then I'll need you to flake the bread and mind it until nightfall."

Jeannette jumped to her feet and nodded at him, having dropped her vacuous bowing habit when she realized such actions only turned her into a dancing bear. "Yes, Master." She glanced at the western hill cradling the edge of the city and measured the height of the sun from its smooth hump. The sun hovered about four fingers above the Camel's Back. She'd learned by comparing the drop of the sun with her watch that when it hovered near the horizon a finger measured about a fifteen minute chunk of time. Plenty of time to continue her explorations. "I'll be back later."

Tabiry had told Jeannette this city was one of the great capitals: Thebes, the center of religion and commerce, and the second seat of the Pharaoh. Though the landscape and layout of the city diverged from what she remembered about Luxor during her tour of the real Egypt, bits of it were familiar enough. With one foot on the east bank and the other on the west, it had crawled up from the Nile to the rise of the Theban Cliffs, the crowning rim of which was the Camel's Back. The distant hills corralling the city were celebrated for a protruding point beyond the hump of the Camel, which the locals called the Peak. To Jeannette, who had been born and bred in Washington State, it looked more like an ambitious foothill.

She had explored only a small portion of the city, and as she wandered, and ingratiated herself to the local merchants and craftsmen, she always sought out other people like herself, displaced and out of time. Had her eyes open for something familiar.

One month, and nothing.

A full cycle of the moon, lying down and hoping, wishing and praying—she prayed for a while; oh, how God found his way inside—that tomorrow morning would be the day, the day when she opened her eyes and saw the familiar. Maybe it would be the pristine white of a hospital room. Maybe her bed back in Luxor—she wouldn't be that far away now. She'd even take waking up bloody and bruised in the mausoleum of the partially unearthed mastaba. That kid, whose name had never reached her ears, shaking her awake. "Miss, Miss," he would say. "We must go now, Miss. Another forty pounds if you wish to stay."

But lately, each morning as she opened her eyes, the homespun sounds of an active city had been predictable. Expected.

Part of her felt like she was giving in. *Knew* she was giving in. Forgetting. Accepting. If she was, nothing would ever be the same—she didn't believe in the *mi-nether*, the mummies, or any gods. Didn't want to believe.

But wanting didn't seem to rule this roost.

She wondered how Abayomi and Sanura were faring, and hoped they were safe. Though she'd known them only scant hours, something about those two ceaselessly tugged at Jeannette's mind. Those two had also been blown off course, if by varying degrees. Did they find places to stay? Food to eat? Did they avoid the crocodile's domain like she did? They'd stolen into her thoughts more and more, those two strangers she'd fled with on her first day here.

But she wasn't completely alone, she reminded herself. One woman would certainly care if she fell into the Nile and washed out to the sea. She changed course and trekked through the crush of stalls and shoppers to the collection of smithies near the river where Tabiry was sure to be found, working under her own Master.

Rounding a corner, she bumped straight into a man with the head of a long-beaked bird. Jeannette gasped. Though she watched and categorized the animal-headed people, she'd made a concerted effort to avoid interacting with them, let alone touch them. How did she deal with mini-gods? They weren't like *people*. If her brief interaction with Sanura was anything to go by, they were marionettes with invisible threads, heard whispers from god-like parents, and were touched by the cruelest mental malaise: a sense of purpose.

Dressed in cloth dyed the blue of the early morning sky, the *mi-nether* blinked his eyes of the same shade and clacked his long bill at her. He had a thick, black wig that hung past his broad shoulders, bronzed from the sun.

"You are not from this land," said the man. He tilted his head to the side, blinking his curiosity. His voice tinkled, an unnaturally high sound that should have come from a cartoon fairy. A long tongue darted out through his curved beak. Again his eyes slid closed, a mechanical twitch that made him look less real than an animatronic puppet from Disney World.

She hesitated, then forged on. She wouldn't get anywhere if she panicked and stuffed her head between her knees. "No. I'm lost here, and I want to go home."

The son of Thoth stood perhaps a foot taller than she. Disproportionately small, his head looked ready to slip apart from his shoulders, supported only by the mass of his wig.

"You must speak to the Sky Watcher at the Temple of Amun." A trilling chirp followed his words and he clicked his beak in lazy punctuation.

"The Sky Watcher?" Sounded like some more mystic woodgy-woodgy to Jeannette, but pissing off another mini-god probably wasn't going to get her invited to any of their parties. "Who is he? An astrologer?" Her lucky numbers probably wouldn't be much help.

Another snap of his beak and then the ibis-headed man said, "*She* is in the Temple Precinct, opposite bank of the necropolis." He flashed his blue eyes at her again. "Near the waters of the *Iteru*." He lifted his long arm and pointed north, across the Nile to the eastern side.

The opposite bank. Since her arrival to Thebes, Jeannette hadn't gone back to the docks. Too many memories. The sharp scent of rot from the reed canoe. The chilled water seeping up her neck. The anger in the mummy's voice. The betrayal in the girl's eyes. The crocodile. The thought of it made her spine itch.

"I already asked some woman with a purple cow, and she didn't give me an understandable way to get back." The mini-god remained silent, head tilted, eyes blinking. The silence grew viscous. "Is the Sky Watcher another oracle?" Did she honestly care? Jeannette realized she did, though she longed for an honest to goodness straight answer. However, information, even if random and indecipherable, was better than wasting away stirring fermenting pots.

"She will answer your question with truth," said the mini-god. Then he swung his head around into a hairpin turn. His body followed, and he walked away. Just abandoned her with ripe questions on her tongue and not even a 'good day to you.'

More mysteries. Something in her chest expanded and burned, and she recognized it as worry or curiosity, and just a little bit of dread.

Part 2: The Sky Watcher

One Man Can Not a Temple Build

Chapter 11

GRINDING HER SHOULDER INTO THE DOOR, Sanura pushed it, and then pushed again as the wood scraped against the rough, hard ground. During a tremendous inundation, long before she'd even been born, the flooding drowned the soil and footsteps must have churned it into a wasteland. No hand had moved to level the mud, and it had dried into a substance as hard as the stones of her mother's temple walls. Now, due to the angle of the shack, no breeze filtered through to cool the interior, giving it the qualities of a brick oven during the height of each day.

Sanura yawned and inspected the river nearby. It was mid-dawn, and a mist hung over the surface of the *Iteru*, arresting all sound in its pervasive reach. Time held its breath. Memories of mornings in the nursery rolled through her head, like the wooden toys she used to play with. Bouncing steadily forward, the impressions were always a leap or two ahead. It seemed that with the right thought she could pin them down, touch them, bind them for study, but then a bird squawked and the silent magic was shattered.

The mornings were the best times to search the city for Jeannette, harboring activity throughout the town, protecting it with the remnants of the cool night air. She missed her leisurely naps.

The terrible hut was about three hundred of her paces upriver from the docks, which they passed each day to enter the seat of the ruler of two lands. At the docks, people already gathered. There the women would come down and sell beer and grain, linen and jars. Men would haggle, offer fruits and pots and more grain. It was interesting and it was loud, and it was more than a little bit scary. Abayomi, a worldly scribe in his own time, had even balked at the unknown, such as wall-sized looms and knives of shiny, silver metal.

"I am beginning to think this a poor plan." Abayomi followed her out of the shack they'd been abiding in like common rats.

Sanura studied her companion. His shadow self, his *ka*, had been poisoned by doubt and worry, and Sanura didn't have the skills to heal him. She'd barely even learned the change; the healing arts were certainly beyond her ken. As he began the trek into the city, she watched him. It wasn't the first time she took note of the droop to his shoulders, his unraveling linens. If something wasn't done soon, Sanura feared he would lose himself and his existence would end. Unfortunately, as that parasitic fear niggled in her gut, she knew it blossomed from no taught lore, its meaning elusive and vague.

So many things she just did not know.

"Mother," she mentally cried out. "Mother, please. Why don't you answer me?"

Closing her eyes, she summoned the image of Bast. The pure black of her fur, those sharp eyes and the love reflected there. Her mother. Her God. Taking in remembered words, the brush of her mother's thoughts and touch, Sanura steadied herself.

Though her heart still ached.

She wished—but no, she shouldn't make empty wishes. Things were done, things were decided upon, and Sanura could do nothing else but face forward and make the best decisions possible with the limited amount of knowledge she had.

Trotting, quite adept on her feet by now, though her hands and knees told the tale of her experience, Sanura caught up to Abayomi. Her tube dress danced around her knees, scratching her skin. The size was not quite suited to her frame and the straps constantly slipped off her shoulders. He waited for her, always waiting for her. Looking up into his masked face, she smiled.

"What do you mean 'a poor plan'?" she asked.

He reached out and she took his hand. Together they continued towards the great city. The noise, missing from their riverside hut, adopted an intensity outclassing even the deafening cries of an ibis flock taking flight. Sanura realized she didn't care for cities.

"That woman ran off," he halted and stared off into the still gray western sky, "That proves she did not want to be with us."

"She is here."

Abayomi looked down at Sanura.

"And she needs us."

A groan hissed from the mummy, flavored with disbelief. "Jeannette needs a solid switching, that is what that woman needs. Needs some respect and appreciation beat into her."

Sanura growled, but only half-heartedly. Abayomi certainly had a point, and she still bristled when her memories took up the little brother who'd been sacrificed. Still, the teeth of time nipped at her heels and a blossom of alarm unfurled within her a little more each day. Her mother had given her a task, and she would not fail.

Three Great Lies

"We have not been there yet." Abayomi gestured down the *Iteru* where a brown haze tainted the mist.

Abayomi had told her that he knew Jeannette hid in this city, somewhere. The Gods spoke to him, though he considered himself only a hollow man. "I am sure we visit the temple precinct and she hides in the market," he'd explained. "We visit the farm huts and she is at the jar makers. We search the district of gardens and manors, and she is drinking beer with the priests of Bast."

He squeezed her hand fiercely, but Sanura didn't mind.

They turned to the right, walking along the border of flooded farmland on well-traveled paths. Her bare feet squelched in the saturated soil. The river swelled, reaching closer to the city here than it did near the higher land their hut squatted on. It curved gently to the northeast, the banks lined with riotous growth, a shrine to the determination of life. She sniffed the air, her senses bombarded with fragrances never experienced, a trove of knowledge in each whiff. A language totally foreign.

They crossed into the city and she spied some guards at the entrance of a manor house; she clung to Abayomi's padded palm and edged closer to his side. One guard, a short man with a tanned kilt, had a monkey perched on his shoulder. Sanura lost herself and smiled at the creature.

"Abayomi." She tugged twice on his arm. "Look at that. Right there, on that man's shoulder."

Abayomi glanced over at the guards, then snapped his face forward and sped up their pace. "It is simply a monkey, Sanura," he said, dragging out the 'a' at the end of her name. He said her name in so many different ways. Sometimes quick and sharp, other times, quietly, softly, especially when he wanted to show her something new. But lately, more and more her name adopted a weight, as if just saying it took unwelcome effort. At those names, she couldn't meet his eyes.

Once they moved beyond the guards, he pulled her to the street's edge and dropped to a crouch, drawing her towards him. "Sanura, you cannot draw attention to yourself, especially from the guards. They might know who you are. Remember, there is not a person out there like us. No mummies, no young of the Gods. We must be like beggars, like shadows, below their notice. You do understand this, do you not?"

She nodded. Yes, they had to keep to the shadows because of their uniqueness. Yes, she understood this, but she didn't always remember its importance. To her, the important thing was to find Jeannette; her mother trusted her to help the woman. She had to help the two lost souls. This secret she kept tightly bound beyond her tongue.

His tan flesh shifted behind the gauze, slips of it visible through the loosened wrappings. She didn't want to meet his gaze, see his disappointment. "I'm sorry," she said. He was the adult; she shouldn't be bothering him with her own task. She swallowed past the nastiness in her throat. "But, the monkey—"

He nodded. "I know. There are many different and new things. Come on, let us get some food for you and then visit the artisan's precinct. I am sure what we see there will delight you." His tone had lifted, and Sanura sighed, looking up to his face, to the smile that reflected in his eyes.

Together, they entered a section of town that held the taste of a fresh kill on the air. The smell settled on the roof of her mouth, towards the back, and she tried to lick it away with her tongue.

"What is wrong?" asked Abayomi.

She mewed, ears pulled back. "The air tastes funny."

"Oh, does it?" He took in a great gulp of air, then nodded. "It is curious. The melting of metals. Copper is melted at the quarries to shape it for weapons; it seems unwise to have it done here, within the city."

They came upon four men surrounding a small, brick dome that radiated heat. One of them repeatedly stepped upon a sack of hard leather attached to the base of the dome. Smudged with soot, they glistened with sweat and grunted in their work.

"It looks like a terrible job," she murmured. One man's gnarled hand was a finger short, another had old, twisted scar tissue slicing up his arm.

"It is very hard work. Come, let us move away."

As they left the smelters hovering over their little dome, a slick, black cat slipped from behind the smelter's hut. It sat, curled its tail around its body, then began to lick its paw. A pain pierced Sanura's chest as she watched the animal wash itself. She tightened her free hand, relaxed it, tightened it again. Such an alien appendage.

The cat rose and trotted across the street, passing by a gathering of three flat-faced people and then disappeared in an alley. Sanura wanted to call out after it, to hold it close to her chest, to feel its fur. Wanted to have it lick her nose. She *wanted*. Her eyes began to itch.

A harsh voice lured her attention away from the budding ache in her chest, and she blinked roughly to see a lovely woman, skin the bistre of the fertile river deposits. The woman stood tall, nodding and rebuking

91

two other Nubian men, both covered in the filth of smelting. In contrast, the woman glowed with cleanliness, wrapped in white fabric knotted at the side, and decorated with necklaces of fine golden beads. The men wore nothing of note, simple loincloths and braided sandals. She must be their master, Sanura thought. The woman's hair hung in braided ropes, long and well-tended, not the typical wigs of the women of Kemet. Sanura continued to watch the group as Abayomi led her by the hand. Leaving the small section of town carved away for this filthy business, she kept her hand over her nose. The woman appeared unaffected by the heavy, metallic odor, for all her elegance and grace.

The woman lifted her hands and shook them at the men. Their shoulders hunched and Sanura recognized that stance instantly. They had done something wrong and were being scolded. Their grief was written not only in their body language, but a kind of intuition bubbled within her. She felt it from them, like a heat on the air.

And from the woman, beautiful in form in all ways, something within was rotten.

Too soon Abayomi led her from the haze cloud and into the artisan's quarter, where beautiful pots, jars and statues came to life under skilled hands, each adorned to be fit for the Gods. Sanura followed like a sleep walker. She'd never felt that before, that sense of *knowing*, of understanding a thing so totally it was as if the knowledge were born within her very *ka*. She knew it wasn't a typical skill from the Matron's lessons. Nothing normal her brothers and sisters would ever be taught.

Abayomi halted near a local well and a pile of rubbish. "Here, some goose wings left out for the cats."

She clamped her lips closed in an effort to steel her nerves. Would he notice her unnaturalness? Would he abandon her because of her freakishness? But the mummy smiled, picking up a gnawed bone, and again his pink lips mesmerized her.

"Are you well, Sanura? Has your *ka* been stilled by Apep?" he said. The way her name slipped from his lips was soft, the ending of it lifting with concern.

She shook her head, a rapid wag to her chin, ears erect in their resolve. "I am well." She took the bone he held out patiently.

He paused a moment, not saying anything. Then he relaxed his shoulders. "Well, if you do require anything, you must tell me. I am no oracle. I cannot read the winds." He laughed, the sound low and comforting, like a purr from the depth of his chest. Then he sobered and said, "We will find her. Do not worry."

She nodded again, taking refuge in the knowledge that he hadn't forgotten. That Jeannette still walked in his thoughts, like she haunted Sanura's.

"Hey, you there."

Abayomi and Sanura stiffened and as one turned towards the voice. A broad woman with great birthing hips approached with sure strides; her tunic, frayed at the edges, was plain and unadorned.

"I've a job for swineherds like yourselves. If you're not too good for it."

Abayomi growled. "I am no swineherd, woman."

She gestured at the pile of waterfowl parts. "You're eating garbage; you're beggars then?"

Abayomi scowled, and Sanura remembered what he'd said earlier that day: Pretend to be beggars, be hidden from the eyes of the guards. Perhaps they were not as invisible as he had hoped.

"Come with me. I've a job for the likes of you." She looked Abayomi up and down, then surveyed Sanura in the same haughty fashion with wrinkled nose and chest puffed out like a breeding pigeon. "I can give you quarters and a pittance of grain and beer, as well as all the fish guts you want," she said to Sanura.

Something mewed to her side and Sanura looked to see the black cat. Sitting upright, staring right at her. The cat tilted its head, then stood and brushed up against Abayomi's legs, discharging his anger with the brush if its fur.

Sanura fisted her hands to stop their shaking. "We'll," she began, but her voice cracked. With a swallow, she continued, "We'll do it."

* * *

When Jeannette had been young and optimistic about her place in the world, she'd often gallop horse-back across the local vacant fields. The horse, a half broke appaloosa, would toss his hind end in a half-hearted buck. It was her neighbor's horse, and they were so poor there wasn't even a saddle, just the bridle and the tight grip of thighs on his barrel chest. Her friend, Brenda Somethingorother, rode next to her on a white mare stiff with arthritis but well trained in her day.

Riding like that, across endless, open land, friend by her side, Jeannette didn't think she'd ever felt so confident, so comfortable. They raced through grasses that swept the horses' knees, letting the pair have their bit so the wind stole her breath away. She'd never felt so alive. It was a singular memory, one of such emotional iron that it struck her, even today, as something never reattainable.

Gabby, her best friend, had stuffed Jeannette in a box labeled 'backwards' and 'small town'. Judged and found lacking. If it wasn't Jeannette's taste in music—alternative over hip-hop—it was her clothing choices, her TV shows, the things she didn't have, the places she hadn't been to. Gabby traveled everywhere, had even toured Rome twice. Her dogs won trophies. She'd been married, though the marriage expired in a messy divorce. Jeannette figured adult friendships tended to develop into something unbalanced; it was simply the way things were once the unguarded affection of children had been pitched aside.

But now, she had Tabiry. This woman, beautiful and classy, came out of nowhere and befriended Jeannette. A total stranger who had apparently nothing to gain. On her free days, Tabiry escorted her throughout Thebes, delightfully absent of any snide amusement whenever Jeannette lost her words.

Hammers clanged steadily from the nearby smithies as Jeannette waited for Tabiry to emerge from the rear of small gilder's shop. The heavy scent of metal and fire kept her company. For her entire adult life she'd wanted this, this kind of equal friendship, this joy of just spending time with someone. Too lucky to be real. Part of her held back, waiting for the loss of interest, the cold shoulder once Tabiry found something new and fascinating to entertain her. But so far, that hadn't happened. And Jeannette had nobody else.

She pulled her rubber band off her wrist and flash braided her hair; the wind hadn't been playing fair for a few days now.

The door opened. Proud as a goddess, Tabiry strode toward Jeannette with chin high and shoulders squared. She greeted Jeannette with a ready smile and Jeannette had to remind herself to smile in return, she was so disarming. "Good afternoon to you," her friend greeted while handing Jeannette a round fruit—kissing cousins to a papaya—and a handful of dates.

"And to you." Jeannette took a bite of date. Sometimes, when things went Jeannette's way—and in a kind of a twisted fashion things were going her way—she would brace herself for the worst. Not because she felt the world conspired against her, but because, somewhere, she'd learned that maybe, just maybe, she wasn't good enough for the sweet life.

But here she was, with a good friend, becoming accustomed to a wholly exotic place. Surely, if Gabby saw her now, her old friend would be more than a little impressed.

It was amazing how good you felt once you weren't scared and alone.

"What are your plans today?" Jeannette asked, chewing around the pit of her date. On wealthier days they would dip the dates in honey. Swimming in sin, they were so sweet.

The sky above was a washed out thing, and a dusty wind deposited an hourglass of grain in Jeannette's nose, ears and eyes. She should have worn her shades. Not a day to spend outside, but she was loath to cancel her time with her friend.

"My Master has taken a day to visit the shrine of Ptah." She shifted her shoulders in a shrug, then tilted her head at Jeannette. "You had mentioned getting some beads to go with your *kalasiris*."

With almost reverent strokes, Jeannette brushed her fingertips along the soft, flax-derived linen covering her hips. With nearly painful care, the dress practically glowed as white as a nurses' uniform. Though only a low quality frock, it had cost her a month's salary, that and the simple sandals. The sand her boots collected could have supplied its own glass factory, plus the scent of them could turn a dog's nose.

It amazed her, that one article of clothing, so basic to every citizen, cost so much. No wonder so many people remained naked. How could anyone ever scale the pecking order when a month's blisters gained her one dress? Hell, with her monthly salary back at the lab, a new wardrobe wasn't an inconceivable goal. Not a fancy one, but still.

"Will your master be needing you again today?" Tabiry asked, taking a tiny bite out of her own date.

"Yeah. I have the height of the day to rest," Jeannette said. They all had the afternoons off. A lifetime of split shifts. A gust sandblasted her face; she dropped her eyes shut. "Maybe we should do something inside today."

"If you say. I must bid farewell to some friends, though; I will be leaving the city for the workers compound soon."

Jeannette cracked her eyes open, pressing the fluttering skirt of her dress to her thighs. Wisps of her hair beat her cheeks, slicing her nose with pixy knife edges. "You're leaving then? You got the position?" A burning sensation nested in Jeannette's throat.

Tabiry smiled, nodding. "Yes, I am to work for the tombs. It is a great honor, may the Hidden One always bless me so." She bowed her

95

head briefly. "It will be hard work, but I am always of service to great Amun." Again she bowed and Jeannette wanted to curse this god, this hidden deity who would take away her only friend.

"If it is possible, I would love for you to visit me." Tabiry gripped her hands before her, a curiously unsure gesture. "When you deliver the beer for your master, if the time allows for it."

Jeannette couldn't hold her grin in. "I'll be there. Don't worry," she said carelessly, "it won't be a problem."

Tabiry smiled, *glowed* with happiness.

"We'll always be friends, Jeannette. Now, let us escape from this wind, shall we?"

Chapter 12

"YOU SEE, WE TAKE THE GRAIN and let it ferment directly, none of this bread business." Jeannette inhaled the moist air as she poured the finished beer into smaller jugs for trade and sale. At the back of the room, a large, square container nearly overflowed with the loaves she'd soon have to shred with her fingers. "It's a lot more bitter, though. Maybe it's the hops."

"Hops?" asked the Master Brewer. Elbow deep, he scrubbed at a trade jug with a dash of water and some sand. His stirring arm, bulky from constant use, choked the mouth of the container.

"It's the flower of a plant. Like a cone of the cedar, only less woody."

Following a night parked on the roof to beat the heat, Jeannette had finally convinced him that cleanliness was next to godliness. Describing the tiny demons that swarmed over old food and excrement, bringing rot and disease, he finally seized on the idea, though it had taken the aid of many jugs of weak beer. Even with the disinfecting properties of alcohol, she worried about nasty, host hopping bacteria. She only wished the physicians would listen.

"We use that in lots of beer. I don't know where the plant comes from, though." The scent of toasted grain caused her mouth to water. She loved this part of the process, making the malt. She'd explained that yeast could be added directly to the grain mixture for the fermentation. "Flaking the bread takes too much time," she'd said. But he'd told her that 'Discovery fills the time, but Osiris fills the mind.' Whatever that meant. All she gathered from that was that Egyptians weren't keen on new ideas and they had a sick obsession with their gods.

The afternoon had been productive; adequately clean vessels lined the wall.

Tabiry had been gone for three days.

She could no longer deny that this place, as crazy as it all was, was *real*. And that acknowledgment—dragged from her by lonely nights tucked between bales of barley—plunged her into a fever to return. This wasn't her native land.

The Montu oracle had told Jeannette to follow the fledgling. Sanura? Certainly young and clueless like a newly hatched chick. Barely swallowing the truth of it, Jeannette marveled at how the woman had known Jeannette would meet Sanura, find her on the slave block. Now she wondered about the warning of the false heart. Abayomi? He was the one seeking his *ba*, perhaps it was wandering. It was mystical, the oracle's power, like folks who pick up the phone before it rings, or those who refused to ride the train the day it derailed. Intuition? Or maybe magic.

Like people with heads of animals? Like landing in ancient Egypt? The walking dead?

* * *

Waking instantly, heart frantic, Jeannette scrambled to a sitting position and stared blankly into the darkness. An image of an ibis had snuck into her dream, dropping muted feathers from a starry sky. The night still held dominion, and the sepulcher silence swallowed her gasps. She was forgetting something. Something important. It wasn't Tabiry, because thoughts of her didn't drive her into this utter panic. Maybe Abayomi, her dead companion who hadn't been such a bad sort, or Sanura, the fledgling she'd sprung from a life of slavery. They seemed to be bound up in so many fragments of her day, cropping up in her thoughts like some grand unification principle. Her worry for them a familiar companion.

But they weren't the trigger, either.

Her mind flashed through the last day, then the last week, jumping from highlight to highlight, demanding a spark of recognition.

What had she been dreaming of?

Then it came to her. The ibis crossing her dream. The son of Thoth and his message about the Sky Watcher. *She will answer your questions with truth.*

She lay back down, cradling her head against the fabric bag stuffed with woven rushes. Another oracle. She hoped the woman didn't have the head of an ass, or her tail turned colors based on the amount of cream she'd had in her morning coffee, or she spoke in Klingon. Jeannette needed answers, and the ibis-headed man had said the Sky Watcher would give Jeannette the truth.

Truth—in a world of fairy tales, Jeannette craved the truth.

* * *

98

Her morning chores completed to her satisfaction, Jeannette told her master, "I'm going to the Temple district." He said nothing with his mouth, but the dance of his bushy brows expressed it all. "Curious. Be careful." She wondered what exactly she should be careful of.

"Is it troublesome to cross the river?" She hadn't gone anywhere near the river since her ride with the Riverman and her departure from Abayomi and Sanura. She'd treated it like a cordoned off hazard sector: Do not enter, angst zone ahead. There wasn't any personal protection gear for that.

"You will need to offer payment," the old man said. "Here." He dug around in a junk pile accumulating in the corner of the shop, and ferreted out some belt-width strips of leather. He also handed her a small, sealed trade jug of beer. "This should get you over and back."

Grinning like a teenager just offered the Corvette keys, she thanked her master amply. She stuffed the trade items in her pack, catching the zipper on some frayed fabric.

"I owe you. I will never forget this. Thank you, Master. Thank you so much." And to top it off, because old habits are harder to ditch than comp-sci majors with liquid courage, she bowed a few times, too.

He cleared his throat, taking a step away from her. "It's nothing. Do not accustom yourself to it." He handed her a freshly poured mug and lifted his own. "For your *ka*." He gulped down the brew, and she took a swallow of hers. "Now, get out of here." And he shooed her with both hands.

With hyperactive eyes, she sought out the river's opposite bank from the southern port. At some point the waters had receded, though the river still reached wider than the Columbia as it sliced the center of Washington, dammed up and converted to a series of lakes frequented by fishermen and ski-boats. The river stretched to her left and her right—huge river barges breaking up the sun-bright surface—and apart from the curve near Thebes, it was a straight shot to the ocean.

A woman and man walked by, hips nearly touching in the intimate way of longtime lovers. A reed basket piled with linen filled each of their arms, but that didn't negate love's magnetic pull. Jeannette had taken a trip to the Puget Sound once with the man she'd thought she'd be with forever: Ricky. They hopped on a ferry and visited one of the tiny islands protected by the wide embrace of the Sound. The entire trip they leaned against the deck railing at the front of the ferry, the day cool enough to require a jacket. Three whales had surfaced near the ferry and Ricky had leaned close to her, their bodies touching all down their sides creating a tight seam. He'd kissed her then. She still remembered that moment: the touch of his lips to hers; the cool breeze carrying its salty scent. The feeling in her heart, like her body couldn't contain that kind of emotion. Their lips lingered. Nothing passionate, but something full of *more* than passion.

The couple passed behind a clump of papyrus and with them passed her memory. She'd had somebody once, but that was long ago. Here on the drying marshes, amidst the piles of fish guts and, farther down, women washing clothes, she almost looked for her lost friends. An old habit, like jumping at every white dog after your Bichon Frisé had been missing for six months.

In the harbor seven docks pierced the river. The four most northern, double the width of the remaining three, were covered in litter from the morning trade, and reed and wooden crafts lined the three smaller ones. A few men lingered around the boats—one of them plucked at a dark goose carcass—talking, drinking beer, and chewing on reeds. Distant associates of the hay and grain farmers back in her neck of the woods. They surely gossiped about their catch, or the rise of the river. "Did you see the perch I caught?" "What do you think of the inundation this year, think we'll good a good crop?" Probably. Tied to the land. Such reliance could only cultivate common concerns.

Avoiding a man with a grim set to his frown, she stepped forward to haggle.

"I am to cross the great *Iteru*, and I want to hire your magnificent boat." She dipped her chin in a sharp nod and did a game show hostess arm sweep at the boats. "Which of you is willing to ferry me?"

The men studied her curiously, mumbled amongst themselves, and one shrugged a single shoulder in a manner that said, "I guess, if no one else will take this job, I'm bound by some God-derived duty to take this woman all the way across the river at the height of the day when I'd much rather sit here and chew the fat with my buddies, drink some beer and maybe watch a boxing match."

However, instead of all that he said, "We aren't crossing now. Come back later."

"But, I need to go now." Jeannette couldn't put this off any longer. "I will pay."

The man shrugged, unswayed by either her needs or her payment. "Then, go talk to Nekhebu; he will take your job."

Another of the men laughed, a condescending, superior kind of burping sound, and scratched at his thinning hair. "Nekhebu will certainly take you."

"Why? Why would he take me and you won't?" She probably shouldn't ask, asking always led to too much information and a knowledge of things she didn't want to know about, but she couldn't kill that curiosity.

"Nekhebu's brother was taken to the magistrate for tomb robbing. He now has his brother's family to care for, all of those children, but none of his wealth." The sailor gulped from the jug he held loosely in one hand, his shoulders hunched over with labor and years. Maybe thirty-five of them. "He needs all jobs."

"The trial is today," said the frowner. "He will finally know when his brother is to die."

"Die?" Jeannette interrupted without intending to. They all looked at her. "Well . . . Yes. Of course the thief will die."

"Death is better," said the man who'd told her to go to Nekhebu. "The man has been beaten daily." He shook his head, steeling his features into a bleak façade of approval. "He's paid affront to the pharaoh. To the Gods."

The frowning man looked away, his frown pulling his mouth into a bow. "Death is a gift."

"Ma'at will see her due," said another, no longer burping up his amusement. "She can never be fooled, let alone by fools." The men all agreed, nodding heartily with their friend. A bloodthirsty attitude—a tried and true brotherhood.

"Those who do not live with Ma'at all die." The man shifted his shoulders, straightening his back. "It is the curse of a heavy heart." Gravid glances shot between the men, and then they pointedly said no more.

"Alright," Jeannette drawled. "Where can I find this Nekhebu guy?"

Following a pointed finger, away from the main port, she saw a small cove corralling a few rafts and canoes. Some swarthy folk lounged in their boats, fishing with rod and line. "There, where the fishers are. He will be there. He will be the one with the black sash." The men gestured with limp tosses of their hands, away from them and toward the small fishing armada, as if warding away the evil that hounded the man for his brother's deeds.

Jeannette nodded her thanks and left the men with their gossip and beer. Once she arrived at the small fishing cove, having pressed her way through papyrus thickets shading the sky above, the man with the black sash stood out like a neon sign. A kind of dark aura emanated from him, evident by his hunch, the haunted look in his eyes, the noticeable no man's zone that moved as he moved, scattering all other folk as he continued with his business.

Raising her arm, she called out to him. "Hello there."

Huddled in his little boat, a defeated refugee of a due process-less system, he glanced up, then searched around himself.

"Nekhebu, I would like to hire you." Now she had everyone's attention, boatmen and shore men alike. Even the man with a fish bending his rod chose to gawk instead of pulling in his catch. Nekhebu continued to look over his shoulder, possibly searching for an Egyptian with his same name, floating behind him in the water, wearing a sun hat and drinking a Mai Tai. That, surely, must be the man this woman wanted.

"Would you—" she waved him to the shore, "—just come over here. Yes you, in the black sash." She began digging her sandal toe into the green algae layer covering the mud. A young girl, nose a snot factory, sat close by on a reed mat and had forsaken playing with her stick and reed doll to stare open-mouthed at Jeannette. It was as bad as asking a high school boy on a date, right in front of his pack of buddies that he never went without like a fashion accessory. Not that she'd ever done that, but she could imagine.

Finally, he began rowing toward her. Shooting her suspicious glances the entire time, it took him an eternity to finally beach the reed canoe on the mud flat. Though she wore local clothing, she was still a pale ghost to these people, a foreigner from across the sea. Skeptically, she studied the canoe. The sight of it drug her across the harsh landscape of her torrid reaction to Abayomi and Sanura's anger, their distrust. Her abandonment. A whiff of vegetable rot fought the overpowering odor of fish. She didn't like it; she would get soaked and that smell would be defeated by nothing but bleach. Unfortunately, it was her only option.

"I need to cross the river to the other side and back. Will you take me there?" He stared slack-jawed at her; a desperate, haunted look had roosted in his eyes. "I will pay you. Are you listening to me?" Maybe he'd been struck dumb. Cursed by the god of remorse. Probably, he was just overworked. Fish camouflaged the bottom of the boat and she wondered where she would even sit.

"You need to cross the *Iteru*? At this time of day?" Nekhebu shielded his eyes as he looked into the sky, a washed out blue, beautiful yet so overused as to instill in her a blasé attitude.

"Yes, please. You take me across the river and bring me back, and I will give you this fabulous leather and some of my own special beer." She smiled, nodding at the man, reminding herself of the nameless boy back in El-Balyana, now a distant, ancestral memory, nothing that had actually happened to her.

Nekhebu took up the long lengths of leather and proceeded to finger the grain, stretch it, bite it, sniff it and then even lick it. Jeannette watched in awe, unsure exactly why he was doing the things he was doing, unsure if he was serious. With her mouth shut, she waited for his diagnosis.

"Both strips of leather?"

Jeannette nodded. "One now, and one when I'm returned."

The little girl coughed, then rubbed at her snotty nose with the back of her arm. Dirt outlined a snail trail from the girl's nose to her upper lip. Homeliness like that had to be some birth defect. Or maybe she'd been dropped on her face as an infant. It was entirely possible. Jeannette shuffled away a step, still focused on the fisherman.

"Fine, I will take you then. Two leather pieces and your beer. Is it good beer, woman?"

Woman? Jeannette sighed. "Yes, of course it is good beer." Then she became somber, her annoyance kept at bay by her need for the ferrying. "By the grace of Tenenit, she works through my hands. Under her will, I shape the beer. She watches as I pour it into pots. Tenenit works through my hands." Jeannette dipped her chin in obeisance. Nekhebu looked suitably impressed, nodding at her in a way that suggested he supported her in her prayer.

They did that here. She invoked the names of their gods and the people's piety rose in garish delight like peacock feathers. It was a nifty trick she'd learned; speak the name of the divine and await their religious compulsion.

"Quisa, come get this fish."

Jeannette was surprised when the little urchin jumped to her feet, snot and all, and began unloading the fish from the small boat, unceremoniously dumping them into the mud. One, a silver fish with large scales, flipped and flopped, not quite willing to give up its last gasp. In no time the two Egyptians had the boat emptied, then Nekhebu paused stoically by his boat, a frown of displeasure on his lips, waiting for her.

The man had an impressive way of looking worried, displeased, and contrite all at once. He needed to decide on one emotion and live with it. He'd probably be happier that way.

Since she'd been living subsistence level on bread, grains, unknown fish flesh and beer, Jeannette had lost a few pounds and it was a tribute to that new lightness of foot that she stumbled fairly gracefully into the canoe. Nekhebu grumbled about her near flip of the boat, but did them all a service by keeping it under his breath so Jeannette could pretend she didn't hear. Squatting in one end, backpack in her lap, she exercised her stillness as the fisherman rowed them easterly under the eager winds.

It took longer than she'd expected. The little boat had to watch for other river traffic and avoid the large barques lined with rowers. As they traveled the river, the day turned calm, the wind finally taking a Valium and giving her hair a holiday. Split ends frizzed her ponytail into a cat tail. Everyone here shaved their heads and wore wigs, and though she could acknowledge the wisdom in that, Jeannette didn't want to. Her hair was brown, *light* compared to the wigs of the Egyptians and natural hair of everyone else. It made her different, in a good way, in a way that made her feel edgy and even a little bit exotic.

She'd always been just a plain Jane.

By the time they reached the far bank near the temples, something captured her attention without any chance of its release. Now that she'd been residing in the land of gigantic stonework, she tended to measure grandness on a different scale. Here, at the east bank temple precinct, she had to develop yet another measuring stick. Jeannette leaned her head back, letting her eyes crawl along the surface of a statue. A colossus with no equal. For I am Ozymandias, king of kings.

No doubt.

"You'll still be here when I return?" she asked Nekhebu, eyes still on the statue as she climbed out of the boat. The fisherman sat with arms crossed across his chest adopting the manner of a petulant child, apparently unimpressed by the impressive. "I'll pay you the rest when I get back."

The colossus stood alone on paving stones of pink granite, the single representative of its species, overseeing the entire harbor, the river, maybe even to the edges of Kemet itself. How such a monster had torn itself away from dust and stone, she had no idea. It was an engineering marvel, even more so than the pyramids she'd witnessed in the real world, humbled by age and a modern mindset.

"Yes, I had already agreed." He looked up at her, his dark eyes full of too much . . . hurt, anger, frustration—an entire dictionary of pain—that Jeannette didn't want to look at them anymore.

During the river crossing, she'd asked about his brother, a stupendously stupid move. He'd gotten angry, called her a woman of loose tongue, swore his brother had nothing to do with the thieves. "My brother lived straight and true. Thoth's judgment shall see the truth in the lies."

She didn't blame him. Now he had nephews and nieces to feed, and the system taxed almost two-thirds of a fisherman's catch. It wasn't a fair system, for certain, but Jeannette had only tried to be thoughtful. Obviously, another miscalculation. She could poison a well with her social blunders. Though making friends was a challenge, it seemed an easy enough task to piss off the average individual with the simple act of speaking.

Slipping away from the shore, she trespassed deeper and deeper into the precinct. Finely dressed men, hairless and white sandaled, strolled the streets with heads held high, the road defeated by their sure strides, none of the frantic scurrying and hunched shoulders of the working class. The scent of perfume followed each like a lazy swarm of bees, banishing the typical stench of sweat and labor

Each new precinct, from the merchant zone she resided in, to the priests' and scribes' homes she walked among now, all the way to the extravagant temples, was like another step up the socioeconomic food chain. The poverty to riches spread just begged for a social revolution, but she was no ancient Che. Such business was *not* her business. The Thoth man had told her she'd find her truth here, and perhaps the truth would solve her own problems. Keep your sights to your own household: a good motto to live by.

A woman in long, white robes with a golden sash walked in Jeannette's direction. She carried a lidded jar of gold and ivory, covered in images of men and animal-headed gods. "Excuse me," Jeannette said. The woman stopped, lifted a questioning eyebrow. "I'm looking for the Temple of Amun."

"You are a pilgrim?" she asked. Her voice carried steadily.

"Yes, I am not from here and I wish to beg Amun for his light."

The woman nodded in understanding. "You see that building with twin obelisks. Beyond that is a courtyard. Walk through there and you will arrive at the Temple. Remember your offering."

Jeannette nodded and turned to face the way the woman had directed. "Thank you," she began, but her breath changed gears from speaking to gasping.

The shadow of this place, packaged in ruins and tied up with the limitations of imagination, was abolished by its undeniable existence. A blazing sun in a flat land. Even artists' renditions, those who prided themselves with realism as well as the free thinkers that waved about a whimsical license like a flag of honor, couldn't capture the power, the majesty, of what lay before her. To see the Temple intact, gilded, painted in the vibrant ochers and greens, golds and brilliant whites, negated all imaginings that any person from the modern world could dream up.

A set of shallow, broad steps rose toward the courtyard entrance, bordered by enormous stone pylons etched with the chronicle of wars fought and won, glory earned and righteousness prevailed. The tapered towers dwarfed everything but the sky-piercing obelisks, leaving Jeannette feeling small and insignificant—not an unrealized emotion in this land of extremes. No giant herself, barely breaching five feet tall, the seated colossi rose four, maybe five times her height. They stared into the desert, eternally watching for some invasion, or maybe they merely waited for the time when they could rise and tend to their own business, so lifelike they were. In the distance, along the edge of a large pond, a flock of geese honked and nibbled at the grasses sprouting along the marshy edge. An older boy sat near the birds, watching Jeannette, unmoved by the surrounding splendor.

Facing the stairs, she climbed with the conscious pace of someone entering hallowed ground. Something in the air, an atmosphere of power, squeezed her heart, her lungs, her brain even. A statue of a sphinx guarded each step, only it didn't have the head of a human, but that of a ram; strong, heavy horns curved tight around its head. The details of the horn ridges, the fur nestled within the depths of the ear, the powerful haunches, all jumped out under the sharp light. The ages had not had the chance to erode the faces to extinction, to reduce the artwork to vague outlines and decapitated lumps of stone. Each of these beasts was poised to leap forth.

She marched forward soundlessly, an endless climb to heaven. Two obelisks delimitated either side of the stairway. They cut through the washed out, cloudless blue, the base of each easily twice her height. Along their beige sides were chiseled intricate hieroglyphs. Craning her neck, she saw each had a pyramid topper pointing to the heavens. She rubbed her shoulders and inhaled long, deep breaths. She stood in the center of a grand complex, the passage of years, millennia probably, marked by different styles of construction. Unadorned walls of smaller bricks gave way to larger blocks crawling with more hieroglyphs, cartouches, and carvings of the pharaoh and gods. All of it in perfect condition.

And still, it went on.

Before her stretched the courtyard, guarded by giant osiride—statue-columns—each the image of a god, legs swaddled, wearing a double plumed crown. Arms crossed his chest in the pose of a resting mummy.

In pictures the osiride were beautiful, a testament to an ancient culture's artistic inclination and skill. In reality, though they still held that beauty, it now turned dark and foreboding, the eyes of judgment digging into her very heart, to see her flaws and fears and failings. To measure her worth and find her inadequate.

She hoped they didn't find her unworthy, and come to life to cut and lay her open.

She passed through the colonnade, a solitary breath of life in the deserted courtyard, her chin propped high with defiance and will. The long passage of osiride became covered by a roof of stone—a wonder that the columns could support such a weight. The roof shunted away the light, dropping her into deep shadow. So quiet, just her and a cast of stoic statues cut from the bones of the earth. Oil lamps and censers lit the way, filling the air with incense that hung motionless in the stagnant air.

The path became a hallway, void of any breeze with a ceiling low enough to put a Morlock at ease. By the time she reached a long bench stationed the edge of an inner garden, the thick air had set her head to floating. An open archway on the left led deeper into the great unknown, her own location one of the lesser variety. At the moment, Jeannette didn't care. She plopped down on the bench, its legs ending in great paws, hoping to clear her head. Dizzy, panting slightly, she wondered if the incense was narcotic, because the tips of her fingers and toes began to lose the tangible sensation of existence.

Hunched over, a sea level native gulping air in the Andes, she cradled her head in her hands, keeping her head low to forestall passing out. She slowed her breathing, one deep inhalation after another. The drugged air swam around her like tiny mites, silent and insidious.

Breathe in. Exhale. Breathe in.

THREE GREAT LIES

When she lifted her head, the spin of the universe had faded into a gentle tilt and her stomach no longer danced the mambo. Surrounding her in a crescent-moon arc, a cadre of brown monkeys, quiet and sedate, sat. About fifty in number, with faces from the deep brown of the *Iteru* mud to a reddish-pink, they blithely munched fruit. A large, red-faced monkey, her fur a golden brown, lowered the green fruit and looked straight at Jeannette.

Chapter 13

"HELLO," JEANNETTE MANAGED with a brain crammed with cotton balls. Then, because it seemed polite to show interest, "What kind of monkeys are you?"

The moderately-sized monkeys, who had been peeling the inner meat from the fruit rind, also stopped chewing to watch her. The central monkey drew back her lips revealing wicked canines. "We are royal monkeys. We are baboons." Her voice was pleasant and soothing, almost motherly.

Though the numbness hadn't subsided, Jeannette no longer felt in danger of going slack and cracking her head on the stone floor. She'd already had one bad blow to the head, and here, in this back hallway of the Temple of Amun, no magic cow waited to sniff her healthy.

She giggled. "I'm sorry; I didn't know."

"That is fine. Why are you here?" the big monkey asked. Each of the baboons modeled fluffed out manes, their tails curled around their rumps, but the talking monkey dominated the others with her size and the intelligent glint to her black eyes. The pungent smoke lazily swirled around the watchful congregation. Movie directors would cry for this kind of effect. The fumes made Jeannette want to lie down and close her eyes. Just for a moment. Ride the lazy curl of incense to a land of peace and apathy. She lowered herself down onto the bench facing the baboons, heaving one leg up, and then the other. With a bump she barely felt, her foot hit the wall behind her. Her pack cushioned her head, the water bottle relegated to the topmost edge. Somewhere inside awaited two small jugs of beer, one for her offering to the Sky Watcher and another for Nekhebu, along with his extra strip of leather. Somewhere. Inside.

"I'm here to meet with the Sky Watcher. Probably some drugged woman and her sacred dung beetle," Jeannette said through the clouded haze. A bubble of laughter popped in her mouth, and then, as the smoke muddled her sight and she had to scrunch her eyes closed, her laughter slipped into a tired sigh. For a handful of seconds, Jeannette was sure the baboon had smiled, but she'd probably just flashed her deadly teeth: the length of Jeannette's fingers and stained a pale brown. Weren't baboons herbivores? Fruit munchers? Under another fierce yawn, she hoped they didn't want to eat her.

Three Great Lies

"What do you wish to know from the Sky Watcher?" All the baboons were now facing her, sitting on their rounded rear ends, neglecting their meals in obvious fascination with Jeannette. Musky drafts of incense brought about a triple sneeze. After she rubbed her nose, Jeannette giggled again. Just a little, because the hysteric urge vanished in the next breath.

She forced herself upright, a potato in a slouch. Anxiety flittered along her nerves like restless butterflies. "The truth." The monkeys stared. "It's just that I'm not—" She pressed her fingers into her forehead, her thumbs supporting her cheekbones. "I'm fairly certain that this place isn't real, you see? Isn't logical." While Jeannette's eyes roamed over the statues, the paintings and carvings of the temple walls, she considered the entirety of this Egypt with its talking monkeys and animal-headed men and women. All in her head. "I used to think I was in a coma . . . or drugged, and this place was all a dream. Now," she gently shook her head, "I've no guess at what's happened. I'm trapped in this place . . ." she lowered her voice to a whisper, "lost." The matron monkey tilted her head. "I'm just floating with the ground nowhere in sight." Jeannette's eyes burned; she buried her face in her hands. "I need to find my way back to my world. I want to go home." Exhaustion swept through her body.

Her eyelashes trembled, and she squeezed her lids shut. She wouldn't give in to that. No point in crying over every roadblock in her life. Sinking back to her side, she let the lethargy sweep over her, even though experience had proven that taking a snooze wouldn't whisk her back to reality. She'd tried that trick already. A month of rising with Re had passed and that dream had long ago lost its power.

"You wish to return to where you came from?" the large baboon asked. A smaller baboon sitting behind her hooted.

The seamless, stone bench cooled Jeannette's clammy hand. She rubbed her palm over the surface back and forth, back and forth. "Yeah." That had been the goal all along. "But this world won't seem to let me go."

"Where you came from, is that your home?" The primates looked at her, their intensity unbearable, but it had to be borne.

Jeannette nodded, and slipping her eyes closed, listened to the soft hoots. "And the Sky Watcher is supposed to be able to tell me how to get home," Jeannette said. Hit with a yawn, her jaw popped under the fierceness of it. "Maybe I am drugged up, or in a coma. Hell, maybe I time traveled." Somehow teleported here because of a bad transporter accident from a future she didn't remember living in. "I know I hit my head."

"Do you still think the truth can be found in such explanations?"

Safeguarded from the haze of unreality behind the void of her eyelids, she considered that question. The earthy smoke lingered thickly all around her, filling her lungs, fogging her senses. "No. I don't spend my days feeling drugged or crazy. Actually, I feel just like me."

"The Sky Watcher only trades in the truth, but it is your duty to not turn your face away."

She peeked at the baboon through slit lids; the world shimmered like a heat mirage as the smoke swirled in the calm of the hallway. In her ears she could hear the beat of her heart, slow, steady, a marching pace for her brain. Her watery eyes met with the beady ones of the large baboon. "What do you mean?"

The baboon sat motionless, then pulled her lips back into that fierce grimace. As she spoke, the words rebounded off the walls, each one targeting Jeannette without error. "Awaiting within the Twelve Gates the serpents poise to strike. Strength will not open the passage. Gold will not open the passage. The Hall lies silent, broken only by the lamenting from the Honorable House and the sorrow from the wandering *ba*."

Jeannette furrowed her forehead, feeling the collision of the skin, the drop of her eyebrows. "Wandering *ba*," she parroted, thinking back on the mummy's own search. "Abayomi. He's not very nice."

"Be that truth or not, a man's ruin lies in wandering."

"But he's dead, why doesn't he stay dead?"

"It is his soul he seeks, his soul that cannot find its return path. The weight of his experiences must be measured against the feather of Ma'at. Then, and only then, can he step upon the Fields. He will be forever trapped in the balance, stuck, unless he can find his true heart."

A shiver scurried up her spine and danced along her neck and arms like fleeing mice. The baboon had just described Jeannette's own predicament. The matron did not look away, gripping Jeannette in an unwavering gaze.

"I think he thinks I stole it," Jeannette said, her voice a distant sound, wafting along with the incense trail. The boundary between her skin and the stone below her had dissolved. She was sinking. "He doesn't like me." Her words sank with her.

The big baboon hooted; a second and a third joined her. "By your actions toward him, you are not a very easy person to like."

A raw hole expanded in Jeannette's chest. She pried her eyes open wide and pushed herself to sitting, feeling the slow detachment of her skin from the stone, her pack, the fabric of her dress. "Tabiry likes me." But Jeannette stopped the excuse before it turned into a whine. She took in a deep breath, ending with a cough. The air held little oxygen. "What do I do?"

"Sometimes kindness can ease the distance toward mending past misdeeds."

Jeannette opened her mouth to tell the talking beast—who had only just met her and already threw about judgment like red cards—that she *was* a kind person, but the baboon lifted her long-fingered hand and Jeannette found she could not speak.

"Do not argue with me. I will answer your questions, but I will not argue useless quarrels."

Jeannette swallowed away the block in her throat, momentarily tempted to slouch into a pout, but instead said, "Then this Honorable House, is that Sanura, the daughter of Bast?" The ground solidified under her feet; her skin had pimpled in the cool air of the inner temple. The baboon remained still. "What do I have to do for her?"

"The reflection of the heart is blackened by worry and the blinding disease of fear. To find the truth one must count the grains of the sand, or harder still, one must face the reflection with eyes wide," the baboon said.

Jeannette sat upright. "What does that even mean?" The baboon didn't elaborate, her nose at the end of her long muzzle twitching. Jeannette's fuzzy brain rolled it around. "Sounds like self-delusion or something." Jeannette scowled when the damned monkey refused to elaborate. "I'm no shrink, curing that can take a lifetime!"

"Choice words coax the wandering kid back to the river." The cadre burst into a chorus of hoots and shrieks, the sound expanding within the small garden and hall to bursting, pressing against Jeannette's eardrums, filling her head and her thoughts and—

They stopped. The silence broken only by a buzz in her ears.

Jeannette's heart sank. She wasn't a compassionate person, she didn't do *choice* words.

"And once he's got his heart scarab and she's past puberty, then how will both these things get me home?" Home, apparently, would be a distant goal she'd reach when her teeth were all ground to dust and her hair had fallen out at its own leisure; she clasped her hands together in her lap to stop from warping them into fists. Part of her wanted to take to her feet, dash away from this place and the grim reality of the baboon's words. Wanted to tear down the walls of the temple and dry up the waters of the great river and just escape and be free and not have to worry about returning to where she came from, or Abayomi's soul, or Sanura's elusive sense of self. Why she listened to a talking baboon anyway, she didn't know.

The other part of her, the analytical mind, told that overly large selfish part to shut the hell up.

"This temple did not crawl from the soil of its own will. It takes an army. It takes sacrifice. Isis spoke the spells and gathered up her dismembered Beloved; she did not succeed alone."

Jeannette sighed. "I get you."

"They are the key. Only together can you name your enemy and open the Gate."

"But, where is the Gate?" Or did the baboon mean metaphorically, that once these quests—duties, chores, assignments—were finished, that *poof*, she would pop back home?

"Return to your first morning."

"What? I have to go back in time?" Like when she came here, to ancient Egypt? She was mostly joking when she mentioned it.

The baboon bared her teeth and then closed her eyes. "Return to where you were born again."

Jeannette didn't figure the baboon meant where she'd re-found a God she'd never once chosen as her own.

It must be Abayomi's tomb—her passage into this world. In an icky kind of way, it could vaguely represent a birth canal.

Before her fall through a tomb shaft, before she even set foot in Egypt, she had been required to attend weekly meetings for work to discuss *very important things*: upcoming deadlines, new clients, the latest technique in identifying airborne pathogens. She and Gabby would sit in the back, texting each other about far more important things, like which movie they would catch that weekend, or if the bookstore was having a sale. Then her boss would bark at her, "Jeannette. I've got a new project for you. Top priority," and her ears perked up like one of Gabby's dogs when you sweet-talked it with a peanut butter biscuit. She liked new things; she liked a plan, a schedule, to follow a series of methods to reach her final outcome. Now, plan in hand, she'd expected to feel excited with this new purpose. Instead, that previous hibernation returned to smack her down with the full force of a Greyhound bus charging down the interstate. But she had *something to do*. Admittedly, a vague something. Incense smoke flushed through her mouth and nose; her vision drowned at the edges. In a slow, methodical process, she reclined back down on the bench, pressing her back into the temple wall. Jeannette found herself in a cloud, supporting her gently, soothing away the anxiety and fear she'd been living with for the past month.

The cooling balm of hope.

"Thank you," she mumbled to the baboon and her entourage, "for talking to me. I still have to find to the Sky Watcher. I'll see what she . . ."

Her words trailed off, but before she lost awareness, she heard, "May Amun, Lord of All That Is, guide your steps."

* * *

"Excuse me." Someone rocked her shoulder. A rope of pain hobbled her back. "Miss, you must wake."

Rising, she reflexively twisted her neck, drawing her ear to her shoulder and evoking a series of pops. She glared at the pack intended as her pillow, now resting on the stone-lined floor. A young man stood over her, his eyes pools of cinnamon with the merest up-curve on his lips. Seeing him, she felt lonely.

"I'm up." She rubbed at her eyes. "I'm up. Thank you." Note to self, don't sleep on stone benches. A dull throbbing heated up her hip, warning of future pain.

"You should not be here," he said, though nothing in his easy posture hinted at any real reprimand. "Do you need help? Something from the Temple of Amun?" The young man, his chest shielded by a silver aegis, raised his eyebrows. His bald head shimmered in the low light.

"I came to speak to the Sky Watcher." A blanket of wool, or maybe the entire sheep, had wrapped itself around the inside of her skull.

"She is in trance now," he said mildly, "communing with the Lord Amun, the Hidden Father of the Sky. You will have to come back at another time."

Just her luck. Fever vision tendrils clung to her thoughts as tenacious as London fog. She pressed her wrist to her forehead; she didn't feel overheated. Probably, she'd inhaled something mind-altering,

114

and odds were high she'd been stoned on psychotropics masquerading as holy incense. She laughed bitterly. She'd never even smoked pot in college. It was one of those moments she wished she had a save point to her life.

"When should I come back?" she asked and stood from the bench, that torture chamber for her spine. Along the corridor, the statues of Amun-Re stood sentry, their crowns tall and beards long. Their painted eyes seemed to have centered on her, like the wandering eyes of the Mona Lisa.

Goosebumps waltzed up her arms.

"You can try again in two days."

"Two days?" That seemed an awful long time to commune with a god. Didn't the priestess have to pee?

The young priest studied her. "Are you okay, Miss? You look unwell."

"I'm fine, thanks," Jeannette said. The priest nodded, that placid smile resting on his lips. Too calm, maybe he'd snorted too much holy incense, too. "Okay, two days." After digging around in her pack, she pulled out a jug of beer and handed it to him; he stared at it, eyebrows bunched in question. She strolled away under the barrage of the statues' gazes, taking in huge gulps of untainted air. This time as she walked among the massive stature of the temple, the double colonnade, the tales of gods and pharaohs painted greater than life-size along the huge blocks of stone, she let her brain relax. Soft memories of her dream oozed in between thoughts of "I wonder whose cartouches those are?" and "I wonder why that obelisk isn't pointy at the top." Memories of baboons and Abayomi and Sanura, and a sense of guilt, all jostled with her admiration. With complete faith in her homing pigeon feet, she found herself at the temple's exit, quietly passing the company of guardian rams.

Out here, beyond the headquarters of the Egyptian god, the sun flirted with the western horizon and the shadows stretched long and thin. Though only hours had passed, it felt like she'd conquered a week of overtime. On the bottommost step of the stairway, Jeannette eased herself down with the care of a pregnant woman. A different boy herded the gaggle of geese, bouncing a switch at them whenever one would stray from the flock. A breeze toyed with the heads of the tall grasses along the pond, dipping them in sinusoidal waves. The open area, with its green grass munched short, reminded her of Riverfront Park in Spokane, though the temple grounds still resembled a wild place, half tamed by a gentle hand—a place where feral dreams and hidden fears ran unmolested and the important things, the heavier thoughts kept buried deep inside, could rise and take form.

A small, gray goose honked and split from the group, its gait, though an off-kilter waddle, was quick. The boy cried out a sharp, wordless command, hit the ground with the stick, and the goose abandoned its getaway, edging back into the watchful domain of the gooseherd, strutting like it had meant to return at its first wayward step. Riverfront Park had always been covered in Canada geese, as well as ducks and gulls that crapped on everything. Even during Gabby's wedding there had been the hazard of slipping on goose droppings.

Easy as sliding into a heated pool, Jeannette found herself slipping in that hazy space between memory and resignation, remembering Gabby. Her friend's wedding day, late in September, had risen cold, but the afternoon blossomed into a perfect fall day. The forecast had threatened rain, and Gabby had annoyed Jeannette for the entire week preceding the event with her whining and worry. It never rained here, in Egypt. A year's forecast of sunny days. Everyone in the lab had treated Gabby like a carrier of that season's flu, but Jeannette had to put up with it. Unwelcome side effects of friendship.

Gabby's cousins had hoisted up the wedding arch, and their friends from Professor Fry's cellular biology class had decorated all of the chairs with little silk flowers in pinks and blues. Who would pick pink and blue for wedding colors? Jeannette told Gabby those were baby shower colors. Gabby didn't listen. Gabby never really listened.

Gabby's dogs had been there, groomed to silky perfection and decorated with blue and pink bows that nearly strangled the poor things. They panted the entire day. Gabby's sister and best friend from high school were her maids of honor. Jeannette helped during the wedding, forced to take over the set-up once Gabby left to dress for the big event. Nobody else had stepped forward. Her friend hadn't complained about any of Jeannette's spur-of-the-moment decisions, so she guessed she'd done alright.

And then there was the groom. Jeannette had never seen a man so handsome in a tuxedo. Sure, all men looked good in tuxedos, but he wore it like it had been made for him, and Jeannette knew for a fact that it had been rented off the rack.

Each time he passed by her, pacing a path in the grass like the foxes at the county zoo, Jeannette couldn't help but admire the fit of the jacket, the line of the trousers. He'd caught her looking once and their eyes met. He looked away. Jeannette felt amused and angry and a little bit hurt. The hurt, though, had mainly gone away by the wedding. Mainly.

Watching Gabby walk down that aisle, Jeannette remembered thinking how beautiful she was. She'd always been a pretty woman, far prettier than Jeannette. And now, years later, after the divorce, after the bitter tear stains Gabby left on Jeannette's shirt front, after the doling out of his and hers, she couldn't help but feel angry still. Angry about the Trick. Angry that Gabby swooped in and took away Ricky, the one man Jeannette had ever loved, stole him away with her coy smiles, her wit, her outgoing friendliness.

Obviously, Gabby hadn't learned that one important lesson: A man snatched away from another woman easily strays. On the day the divorce became final, vindication visited Jeannette, overdue prize winnings. Though, as she wasn't a complete dragon, she made an effort to keep her expression supportive and good-natured. Through it all, she stood by her friend who had never once considered how much she'd hurt Jeannette. Through it all, everything Jeannette had eaten tasted of sour spite. And through it all, she'd been angry. Angry at Gabby. At Ricky. At herself. Angry that she'd ever loved him. Ever trusted him.

Two geese began a squabble over a piece of orange fruit near the muddy edge of the pond, filling the once quiet air with raucous fury. Their wings beat at each other and the boy ran to them crying out.

"I know how you feel," she muttered. "It sucks when someone takes what is yours."

She stood abruptly, ready to get home, get back to brewing. She didn't want to remember that she'd been a fool. That she'd fallen for the Trick so many other women had.

She shook her head, dissipating the cobwebs. That entire trip down Screw-up Lane was as helpful to her right now as a thirty percent off coupon for an oil change.

Then another memory clouded her mind. Thoughts of baboons and tombs and a bench not-quite-there. The information that Sanura and Abayomi played an important part in her escape from this place. And that she *could* return home. That was what the baboon had said, wasn't it? They were the key, and Abayomi's tomb the Gate?

On her return to the docks, Jeannette took the river walk, withdrawing from the oppressive melancholy the columns and elaborate paintings brought on. She didn't want to be surrounded by beauty. The

117

breeze off the river cooled her skin as she sauntered along, kicking at clumps of grasses, hands gripped around the backpack's shoulder straps. Earlier that day the fishermen had left their fish waste on the bank—now off-gassing putrescence—and the piles were infested with stray cats. The cats spied her as she approached and scattered, each darting through the bushes like its tail burned with fire.

News traveled far.

Nekhebu sat in the papyrus reeds, weaving a small figure out of the flexible fiber of the plant. She stood by him quietly, watching as he crafted the doll, probably for the snotty girl he'd inherited. He finished the doll before he glanced at her.

"Did you get what you needed?" he asked, turning the green doll over to inspect it from all angles.

She looked into the dimmed-down sky. A cloud hovered on the edge of the horizon south of the Camel's Back. Perhaps she'd have solid answers in two days, when she could gain audience with the Sky Watcher. "I'm not really sure what that is, Nekhebu."

He looked at her, his eyes rich with surprise.

"I'll have to return anyway. The Sky Watcher was communing with the gods, or something." She rubbed at her temple. "Would you just take me back to the western shore, please?"

Nekhebu nodded, tucked the little doll away amongst the reeds of the papyrus canoe. Jeannette was sure he'd lose it, its camouflage perfect. He began to row, muscles straining against the current. She would have helped, but the canoe lacked another oar, so she sat back and watched the world pass her by.

When Nekhebu finally reached the shore, Jeannette hadn't even realized the passage of time. In this sluggish reverie, she paid Nekhebu his additional strap of leather and the beer, and handed him one of her few deben.

"For the kids," she said.

The copper coin rested on his open palm; he made no move to take the money. "Just take it," she said, already regretting her momentary softhearted lapse. It was just that she knew what it was like to be falsely accused.

The coin disappeared and Nekhebu cleared his throat, a kind of embarrassed noise meant to disturb the uncomfortable silence. "I'm sorry the oracle wasn't there to meet with you."

She offered a tired laugh. "Yeah, me too. I had the funkiest—" she shook her head. "Listen, do you know anything about the Sky Watcher at the Amun Temple?"

"Everyone knows of the oracle, but few have a chance to actually meet with her. She's very choosy with who she grants audience to." His fingers dug through the side of the canoe and pulled out the doll he'd crafted while waiting at the Temple.

"What about baboons?"

He tilted his head down and eyed her through his lashes. "Well, the Sky Watcher is a baboon," he said uncertainly. "The Temple has a group of them, or so I've been told."

But Jeannette wasn't listening anymore.

Chapter 14

RELAXING BACK INTO THE CUSHIONS, the Master Slaver rubbed his belly. The morning meal had consisted of a rich assortment of figs and dates, filtered barley beer, and some bread with sweet honey. His mind jumped forward to the evening meal promised him, and though he no longer felt the pangs of hunger, his stomach almost purred in anticipation. Not only would he dine on bread, beer and the fruits of the *Iteru*, but Adi would roast some of the fish her husband had hooked yesterday. Adi and Tabu were hardworking and meek slaves; Re had blessed him the day they were presented to his home.

It was a failing of some, men and women of an afflicted *ba*, that they didn't accept their role as serenely as his slaves accepted theirs.

His jaw ached; he forcefully stopped grinding his teeth. His home was not to be poisoned by the heat of his other matters. He raised his mug and Adi filled it with the fruity wine he'd earned from an auspicious trade with a man from the pharaoh's court. Not only had he earned wine for his family, but an ox and plenty of silver. Such good fortune allowed his wife and beautiful daughters to bring in the seamstress for new dresses; he also prescribed a new *shendyt* for himself. He would save it for special meetings with Lord Re's priests, or perhaps even a meeting with the pharaoh, though the Master Slaver would never be so presumptuous as to assume such goodwill.

But, it was good to be prepared.

Akana entered the room, the pleated skirts of her strapless sheath dress swished around her calves, the golden-ochre of the dress setting off the copper bangles that rang as she swung her arms in carefree delight.

"Hello, my daughter," he greeted her. Akana and Mesi, his contribution to the flourishing population of Kemet, were his pride. He had had a son, but the boy had succumbed to an affliction after only two inundations during *peret*, and now his body lay in the west. They had given him the name of Akhom. The fiery breath of Sekhmet could not cure his son. Isis, the Queen of the Earth, did not know the affliction's True Name; their magic had no power to kill the poison. The moon rested in the underworld the night the priests covered his son's fevered body in herbal mud and chanted prayers until the first call of the benu bird. The Master Slaver had exchanged his coffers for the divine votive offerings he'd heaped upon the altar, and still, his boy was no more. When Akhom's struggle ended, they wrote his name down within the pages of the book in the House of Life, and the Master Slaver walked within the red lands for his mourning.

In spite of the loss, the Master Slaver knew his luck ruled strong that two of his children had grown to adulthood.

"Hello, Father." Akana smiled at him, showing off her strong teeth. Recently she'd finished washing; he could still smell the heavily perfumed oils she'd dressed her body with. "Mesi and I are going to the well."

He almost suggested she let Adi fetch the water, but knew his daughters had reached that age where they had eyes for husbands. Inevitability compelled their desire for their own households. His wife, Merit, kept their household tight and oversaw the farm with a precision he admired with all his heart. She had already begun matchmaking for their daughters, though the Master Slaver knew Akana was as headstrong as her mother and would turn away the pharaoh's son himself if Merit had set up such a union.

His girls were getting older, and the evenings filled with "Daddy, another story," sitting on the roof during *akhet*, were long put to rest. I beg of you, Oh excellent spirit of Re, Lord of Mercy, he began in silent prayer, guard my children with your ever vigilant eye.

"When you return, we should play some twenty squares."

"Father," his daughter said, voice quiet and deferential, though he could see the strength of her mother in her lifted chin. "I think that Mesi and I might walk by the river near the Palace, if we may." Akana dropped her gaze, her thick lashes shielding her eyes so he couldn't see into their darkness. This day had come far too soon. He cleared his throat and grunted his assent.

Her head popped up, all obeisance vanishing as she bounced to him and planted a quick kiss upon his bald crown. "Thank you, Father. I'll be back as Re's solar barque hits its zenith."

He chuckled; she always spoke more piously when she got her own way. "Be back before that. Your mother will need help with the trade bundles." His daughter's shoulders slumped. "Do not skirt your duty, Akana. You must learn from your mother."

"But I've spent years learning from Mother." Akana slammed her lips closed in a frustrated frown. "Yes, Father. You are right. We shall return before too long."

"Oh, Akana." He drew her name out with a sigh. "You may walk

121

along the river, I'm not forbidding that of you, but you cannot spend your time daydreaming there." His daughter brushed her fingers along the edges of each bracelet, letting them fill the air with a soft tinkle, pointedly not looking him in the eyes. "Your time will come soon. Do not worry. Re watches over you. Isis has blessed you with wit and beauty. Do not rush things."

Akana glanced at him again through those thick lashes, and let a warm smile transform her face from sullen to utterly beautiful. The Master Slaver mentally cataloged the boys who'd already been asserting their interest in his oldest daughter. Next to each name in the long list, he devised brutal executions if they ever made her cry. Driven onto a spike while still taking breath might be too good for them.

"Father, shouldn't you be leaving?"

He brushed crumbs from his thick belly and nodded. First light had already passed and he must attend to the slave pens before Re's power reached full bloom. And today, he had a special meeting.

"Yes, my daughter." He rose from his cushions, rolling to his side to push himself up standing. "I am to my duty. You have a fruitful day." He smiled down at her and she grinned in return, flashing him her teeth. He ran his tongue over his own worn ones. He huffed; he didn't relish getting old, of having Adi boil down his food into a mash.

Leaving the house, he first entered his garden. A light breeze twisted through the acacia and tamarisk trees, causing the songbirds to join in with mild chirps. He found his wife in their small, personal temple. Musky incense filled the air, only to be swirled by the wind along with dislodged leaves that floated down to the pond, joining a collection of other such castoffs. A goose honked and lifted from the water in a flurry of wings. The morning dawned perfect in his garden; he wished he could sit here with his wife and enjoy the day. Just enjoy a quiet day.

"Merit, I am off."

His wife, her thick, black wig in perfect form, lips red and eyes heavy with dark outlines, looked over her shoulder at him. She offered a sharp nod. "May you please the Gods and Pharaoh with your diligence, my husband."

"And you, my wife," he finished formally.

She returned to facing the marble image of Taweret, whose heavy breasts held the nourishment for all of Kemet.

The Master Slaver left his home to attend the slave pens, nodding and waving at neighbors, sometimes praising those respectable enough to warrant such honor. A pleasant stroll on a typical day. This morning, though, he modified his path and proceeded through neighborhoods he infrequently attended. He aimed downriver, around the gardens of the Montu Temple, and turned west along the precinct layout where the houses sat tighter together and the streets began their rise up to the mortuary hill.

He crossed a heavily trafficked roadway filled with merchants, scribes, priests and slaves going about their important business for the pharaoh, and then back into the tightly woven pattern of the city, an orderly grid, unlike the sprawling chaos of the older cities like Thebes. Standing before a bread maker, he didn't wait long before an older man wearing a short, white *shendyt*—its ends neatly tucked away under his belt—and wielding a gilt staff approached him.

"Master Slaver, may your sweat and industry bring glory to Pharaoh," said the older man.

"Master Scribe." He offered a nod. "And I praise your sharp reeds and sharp mind. How is the accounting going?" This master worked for the nomarch and collected taxes from the citizens, a worthy position in Pharaoh's court. The Master Slaver took the time to enjoy juice and beer with the Master Scribe on occasion, and learned his children's names.

Because only a bread maker drew customers to the junction of the two alleys, it held few passersby. Which is why the two men had chosen this spot to meet when the need arose. A small dog raced down the street, barking, filling the blossoming morning with unnecessary noise.

"Well, sir," the Master Scribe said. "I have something more for you." He held out a tightly rolled scroll, wound together with a long, woven string.

The Master Slaver took the scroll and nodded. "I will look this over."

With a nod the Master Scribe turned towards the main street. "I'll send the boy by again if I have more information."

The Master Slaver watched his friend walk away, then looked down at the scroll in his hand. He clenched his jaw. They would not get away with this.

With a set frown, he no longer greeted those he might know. He continued up the alley, deep in thought. A pestilence had taken root in his city, perhaps it spread even farther afield than he knew. An increased guardianship upon the tombs was in order. His jaw clenched again. Nobody would undermine the divine order. Not as long as Re saw through his eyes.

He turned left towards the Slave Market. He would need to set up more scouts, more guards. The idea that a citizen of Kemet would perform such sacrilege . . . A throbbing settled into his temple that could fell a camel. Reaching up to rub at his head, he noticed a *mi-nether* youth coming down a side street. Her head was turned, looking behind her, and she had on a simple dress. With cautious intention, she moved low and hunched over, bringing to mind illicit intentions. Her head turned, gaze shifting about, constantly on the search. And when she looked at the Master Slaver, her orange eyes caught his, and her cat ears dropped to hug the back of her head.

The Master Slaver stopped, halted by the gut-yanking feeling this young *mi-nether* solicited. Children of the animal-headed ones rarely came to the city, and never unescorted. This one, a daughter of Bast, must surely be that lost slave from so many days ago.

And as she turned from him and sprinted away, he sucked in a great breath of air and charged down the road.

* * *

Gasping, Sanura pumped her arms and legs to keep up with her rabbit-racing heart.

He'd seen her. She knew it, as sure as she knew her mother had wanted her across the Great River to this place that had almost destroyed her. Across the alley, down the street, up onto roofs, she scanned for a place to hide, a place where she could be small, unnoticeable. It had to be away from people, for she was a daughter of Bast and would stand out in any crowd.

Abayomi had taught her that.

How naive could she have been? Abayomi had warned her not to cross the river. But that dream she'd had . . . He didn't understand dreams like she did. It was possible he didn't even dream at all.

She worried about him, unable to pass through Duat, gain his judgment from Anubis and Ma'at. Its unnaturalness made the fur behind her ears itch.

That morning Sanura had woken up early, before the first light, before the call to duties. She'd left Abayomi standing in his half-slumber, not fully aware, but not asleep either. He stood perched in that in-between state, motionless like the statues lining the temple walkways, images coaxed from marble and granite with no beating heart. No *ba*.

She shivered in the cool shadow of a mud wall, body wracked with panting. Two women walked by, arms wrapped around clay pots, chatting with words that couldn't penetrate the buzzing in her ears. Sanura pushed her back into the building, trying to disappear, to meld with the hard mud. She must hide. The man had seen her, the slaver who'd handled her like chattel, who'd hurt her chin, her pride. Her feelings. Never before had she experienced such brutality, and never before had she experienced such excitement as when Jeannette and Abayomi had stolen her away.

Abayomi breathed harsh words, curses, damnation about Jeannette. Though he released such vile things, his true voice held a kind of sorrow without any true animosity. Jeannette had hurt them both in her race to abandon them and the consequences of her impetuous choices.

Sanura inched her nose around the corner, sniffed, then peeked an eye. The alley was blank. Quiet. Her ear flicked, the hairs on the back of her neck lifted one by one.

Springing into the air, she twisted around. A massive hand swiped at her, missing by a whisker's breadth.

Behind her, an evil demon from her past.

"You gave yourself to *me*," the Master Slaver said. His eyes narrowed to slits of menace, his teeth bared in a snarl.

"No!" she cried out, a sharp mewl, and ran through the pattern of blocks, through back alleys and people's gardens. She ran. Blindly, she ran.

"Get back here, slave!"

Sanura didn't spare a glimpse for the man. She ran, ran for her life.

"Guards, catch that girl. There!"

A boy, smaller than even Sanura, skipped out into the road before her. Their bodies collided; one of her sandals sailed through the air and landed beyond her reach. "I'm sorry," she tossed away in a rush of breath, then rebounded to her feet, one foot punching the paved street as she pledged herself to her freedom, head forward, bloody knee slicing through air.

The overfed but agile slaver chased her, calling for aid from family guards. She didn't look back, but the voices and beat of feet against paving stones put them at four. The mortuary hill rose just before her. Sprinting up that hill, her lungs and legs wailed at the pace and her heart telegraphed her exhaustion to the rest of her body. A waste pile filled an alcove not far down the right branch of a side street and with exhausted relief, she tossed herself into it, wriggling deeper into the refuse, clenching her eyes and mouth shut against the rotting muck.

Buried at the heart of the garbage pile, she couldn't breathe; even with a calloused hand cupped over her muzzle, she battled for each inhalation. Tears budded at the corners of her eyes, fighting against the acrid air. Quiet and still, she waited. Voices, muffled but audible, cried out and two people raced past her hideout. Her chest spasmed.

Silence.

Lingering, she counted to twenty in the hush. A coughing reflex triggered a gag. Then another. Lungs screaming for air, she pushed her head through the pile, vegetable scraps and animal waste clinging to the fine hair over her head and face.

Dragging in huge lungfuls of air, the odor penetrated to the back of her nose and she could taste it on her tongue. She sneezed once, twice, before she could sweep her gaze over the streets and buildings and trash. Nobody lay in wait; only a single black cat sat nearby, blinking its orange eyes in feline disinterest. She climbed from the heap. Trash painted her in greens and browns, a splatter of yellow and some red. Grime clung to her dress, long ago having given up any semblance of being white. At least laundering it upon her return would be no hardship. A bit of pomegranate shell clung to her unshod foot; she dislodged it with a shake. Quick scrapes of her hands down her arms and body, over her head and ears, brushed away most of the garbage. Throughout her attempt at cleanliness she watched the cat.

That cat licked a paw, and then drew the paw over its head. The action pulled a pang of loss from Sanura's own past, missing her carefree days as a kitten with her birthing batch. After Sanura finished brushing away the larger chunks, the cat stood and trotted away. Sanura followed. It headed up an alley that mounted the hill to the tombs.

In her sleep last night, the sweet scent of her mother captured Sanura's senses. Her mother had walked ever forward, revealing only her straight back to Sanura. Her desire to reach up and hold the Lady Bast's hand burned her, but she only followed behind, watching the shift of her mother's shoulders, the swing of her long arms. Sanura struggled for a breath. She missed her mother, her sisters, her brothers.

Though the world where the *Iteru* flowed was harsher than anything her innocence could have allowed her to imagine, Sanura persevered. Her mother had asked a task of her, had sent her to walk among the people, and Sanura would rather face a river full of the sons of Sobek than disappoint her.

Now, following a little black cat, she found herself standing before the entrance of a mastaba secured by twin columns, a heavy stone slab spanning across the lotus blossom crowns.

She smiled. "Thank you, Little Brother," she said to the cat, who blinked once and then hopped away. Closing her eyes, she silently thanked her mother, too. Sanura knew she never walked alone. A warm breeze ruffled the tufts on the ends of her ears. Never alone.

She snuck into Abayomi's tomb, unsure of what clue her mother wanted her to discover. Torches illuminated the tomb, and she wondered if Abayomi's family tended his house of rest. Processions of cattle and entertainers marched down the walls. These would attend him in the afterlife. The Gods waited for him. Osiris escorted by Isis and Nephthys, the great eye watching all who entered. It showed the balancing of his heart, Anubis kneeling at the scales. And then, Sanura saw it.

Saw exactly what her mother had sent her to find.

Chapter 15

THE MORNING AFTER JEANNETTE'S EXPEDITION to see the Sky Watcher, a raw throat and a pummeling ax to her temporal lobe were her divine blessings. The entire prospect of facing the world was too much. She wanted a sick day and ibuprofen. The Master Brewer hummed some dull tune that seeped through the thick walls. Rolling over and stuffing her head in the straw wasn't going to drown out the noise any better than the insulating mud. Something about the droning plucked at her nerves, only deepening her agitation with each inhalation and *hmm hmm hmm* that followed.

With effort she attempted to pull on her khakis—which stood at attention under their own power—and realized every market hut in the precinct would ban her if she browsed their goods in those. With a sigh, she skinned them from her leg like a dried hide, moving slowly to cushion the pounding in her temples, and put on her *kalasiris*. It was probably the incense, the narcotic smoke she'd inhaled for hours to give her hallucinations of prophetic monkeys.

But what the baboon had said.

It wasn't something to toss aside. False dreams or real visions. Here, in her personal unreality, did the difference really matter? Here, in that same unreality, was it so unbelievable that a *baboon* would speak words of wisdom.

A bug crawled over the side of a jar; Jeannette watched it with half a brain cell. Assigning a separate brain cell to the concept of scrubbing her clothing only caused it to jump into the morass of the cowering collective. Her country for a washing machine, or servants. Unfortunately, she had no country, and servants didn't get servants of their own.

"Amun's light upon you," the old man greeted as she passed through the brewing room. She grunted in reply. To that he began humming again.

Eyes at half squint she stared at the master. The sadistic jerk chuckled—maliciously, if the sparkle to his recessed eyes and twitching lips were anything to gauge his mood by. She attempted to smooth down her hair.

"Good sleep?" He wiped his hands against his stained kilt and took up a large ladle. The morning light swept over the room from the high windows. She blinked, once, twice, then exhaled a gust of exhaustion. She wished he wouldn't speak, but it sure beat the droning hum.

"I need to wash my clothes. And myself." Apathy sucked away all nuance to her words. Just getting by proved difficult here, and today she didn't even have the energy to feel indignant about it. Another day of robotic hard work, because life didn't get lived in ancient Kemet without a lot of hard work.

He squinted one eye at a brown stain on the front of her dress. "Yes, but first I need you to take these jars to the foreman of the guards at the vizier's tomb."

"The workers compound?" Tabiry would be there. They'd met up before. Tabiry had asked Jeannette to pass on a written message to her gilding master in Thebes, and Jeannette had gladly done so. A little bit of spirit wriggled inside of her as her mind touched upon the image of her friend, though the foreman was a pompous jerk whose fat hung off him like jelly rolls. Like that pedophile slaver. And there always existed the possibility that Abayomi and Sanura might be hiding out there. If she was going to chase prophecy, it was as good a place to start as any. She sniffed herself. The stink wasn't that bad.

"Go fetch Mered's donkey. And be back by sundown. The hippopotami come out at sundown."

"There aren't any hippopotami in the hills." He might as well have warned her of desert leeches. "They live in the river."

"Ah! So you aren't petrified of sense."

His attention returned to straining the beer, so she stuck her tongue out at his back. But honestly, her annoyance lasted only as long as a leech in the desert would. He strained the beer through layers of cloth and sand by her suggestion, and now everyone wanted to wet their whistle on the Master Brewer's famed 'thin' beer.

The bass of her headache eased into a background buzz after rehydrating her brain with a quart of water. The morning breeze sighed across the floodplain as she gathered the donkey from Mered, a farmer upriver who grew wheat and cultivated a patch of giant garlic that exploded with flavor.

"Come on, Ass." She swatted the donkey on the rear with the flat of her hand. Flailing her hand through the air couldn't dull the sting. The donkey flicked an ear. "We don't have all day." She smacked him again and Ass brayed, taking his first resistive steps. Her dress strained against her knees as she lugged the donkey back to the brewery, his ears bouncing with each stiff step. She mentally mapped out the rest of her day. Go to the compound, drop off Raia's beer, look for Tabiry and the wayward constituents to the oracle's equations, then maybe hit the river, wash clothes, wash body, work until evening. It was a break from the everyday, but a party and hors d'oeuvres it wasn't. Walking through fields of tall grasses, she grabbed handfuls of leaves, tiny serrated swords that stained her fingers green. A tickle to Ass' nose with the grass secured his obedience. His prehensile lips reached out to gather up the offering.

"I'm back," she called out to her master, the donkey in a half trot-walk alongside her.

"Good. You should have been gone to the village already." His frown might have been disapproving, if it didn't twitch at the corners.

"I am sorry, Master. I am but a slow, stupid foreigner who cannot work with such a dismal beast." She held out a handful of grass; Ass lipped it from her palm and munched.

The Master Brewer grunted. "Let's load him."

Together, Jeannette and the Master Brewer strapped two large jars, sealed with wax, to the donkey's back. Balancing one on either side of him, a sturdy leather harness, padded by a thick blanket, kept the jars in place. Ass shifted his body weight onto one side and relaxed a hind leg by tipping the hoof on its front edge. Jeannette tossed some of the straps over the donkey's back, and her master tied them with an elaborate series of knots and bows. It had to be more sophisticated than a ship's rigging because the old man took such care with each connection. His beer: far more valuable than the cost of one ship and crew. Jeannette contentedly let him do the majority of the work.

"Here's your pass."

Jeannette took the pottery chit, smooth to the touch of her thumb, and tucked it carefully into a pouch on the donkey's tack. This, she couldn't lose. One merchant, one pass. She didn't even know if you could reapply for this bit of plastered clay stamped with the nomarch's mark. The halter lead in one hand, she strained to get the donkey moving again. He balked at first, propping himself up against her tug with his sturdy forelegs. Then, like a stiff nut giving way under copious amounts of WD-40, the donkey abandoned his defiance and followed along at a sedate pace.

Her master laughed. Jeannette mocked laughed back. "Yeah, so, so funny."

She left the city on the tail end of the merchant peddlers' morning exodus, traveling on straight, bricked streets heading northwest until the paving gave way to dusty roads and thirsty desert stretching to the edge of civilization. The washed out sky sprawled endlessly above, an impermeable lid on the grainy atmosphere. The tombs of Thebes were not monster pyramids made popular by their inconceivable grandeur, but were burrowed into the desert hills, hidden from opportunistic thieves. The discreet graves rested along the side of the Theban Cliffs, tucked within a system of ravines. Secret. Hidden. Safe. The way to the workers village wasn't secret, though. Everyone knew the way.

Within the compound, the workers and artisans labored under sequestered oppression tighter than any high profile murder case. Not because their art might be influenced—all the art everywhere looked formulaic and traditional—but because of that perpetual problem of wealth: someone always wanted it. A confined and overseen group had less opportunity to sell off ill-gained wares. Remove the opportunity and keep honest men honest. Still, a more comfortable prison couldn't be found.

Though grave robbing received the ultimate punishment: death, even the death of your family, the temptation was undeniable for many. Set out the good china, Faust is coming to dinner. Needless to say, Jeannette secured the ankh necklace from the flea market out of sight, stashed away in her money belt that never roamed from her backpack.

The town of the tomb workers crouched in a secluded valley under the eclipsing presence of the Theban Cliffs. As Jeannette hiked up the hill at the speed of irritating donkey, eyes always on the ground, her breath came in ragged gulps. The donkey brayed every time she switched his rear with a supple stick to maintain his sluggish momentum. The two sounds created some seriously unmelodious noise. Scorpions and snakes, and the ever elusive desert leech, posed serious threats, so she didn't mind the slow, watchful pace. But nothing deadly came out to eat her that late morning. In fact, the highway was lifeless other than the procession up the hill. No green crops thrived along the road; only the bones of the earth sprouted from the soil: limestone and dust.

The smooth advancement of the uphill trek abruptly hit a brick wall when the donkey refused to take another step, and the last of her bribery grass had disappeared behind eager lips twenty paces down the hill.

"Ass, you will move." She spoke each word clearly, to assure the donkey understood her. He seemed to have bonded his feet to the bedrock, so even as she hoisted the rope over her shoulder and bullied forward, she couldn't nudge the imbedded weight of the donkey.

Someone laughed at her. Jeannette straightened up.

A boy in his teens ascended the hill below her, his own donkey doing what it was supposed to be doing: walking. He wore a typical short kilt, his calloused feet bare and dusty.

"Stupid woman, can't move a donkey."

Jeannette blinked, then furrowed her brow at the obnoxious kid. "What did you say?"

"Only stupid women don't know how to handle the donkey. Why don't you take up the saddle!" He laughed again, an eagerly mean noise. Ass craned out his head toward the other donkey that whickered at him.

"At least I've got shoes," she called after the brat. Jeannette wished she'd tripped the hoodlum as he'd passed. Unfortunately, he, and his donkey, cruised up the damned hill and Jeannette was stuck in park with a defiant beast whose sole purpose was to make her look like an idiot.

"Ass, why must you be . . . so well named?"

Other donkey handlers passed her, some offering help, some laughing like the shoeless loser had.

"Smack him good and hard," one older woman suggested. Jeannette's hand already throbbed.

Another told her to make loud sounds or rattle something to get him going. Open to anything, she guzzled the water from her plastic bottle and stuffed in a handful of road-side stones. A muddy brine of pebbles swirled against the plastic, creating the perfect percussive noise.

Ass' ears pulled back. She lifted the water bottle and shook it hard. The stones beat against the curved wall of hard plastic. Ass stretched his neck out and brayed, taking his first steps toward an energetic lope up the hill.

"You have got to be kidding me." She let Ass half drag her up the remainder of the hill, rattling her bottle every time his steps lost their pep. Still, the trip exhausted her. The sun hung angry in the sky, whipping her sweat glands into a frenzy of over activity, and a rock had slipped in between her sandal and foot, rubbing a spot raw. But worse, she had no water.

As she queued up in line behind other couriers of produce, shoes, cloth and leather, bread, and beer, she tried to force her breathing through her nose. Even the donkey huffed. A jackal trotted along the line of people, sniffing at their feet, the donkey's hooves and anything it could get its nose close to.

The line moved. Another jackal trotted by, ears alert and tongue lolling in the hot day. Finally, Jeannette had her turn.

"Pass," said a familiar Nubian guard in a deep, droning voice. His head bald offered up the perfect surface for an eternal sunburn, though he had none. She handed him the chip of pottery. The pole-ax at his side sparkled with the same exuberance as the man's sweaty head. "Any drink to share with us, Brewer?"

She smiled at the gate guard. "I'm sorry, but this beer is meant for Raia, the Head of the Guard, a man of honor who protects the vizier's tombs. I am duty bound to deliver the beer to him only." She patted a jar.

He nodded her in and said, "Next time bring me some." Next time, she would.

The construction site toiled with the driven activity of an ant hill under siege. There were men who designed and laid out all of the afterlife scenes smothering the tomb walls. There were those who coaxed statues from formless blocks of stone and others who inlaid the sarcophagus with gold and jewels. A large quarry rested near the village and bunk houses lined the streets. The place reeked of wealth and it amazed her that in a land so rich she earned the equivalent of less than a dollar a day.

To Jeannette's estimation the workers outnumbered the guards about four to one. The armed men lined the streets like sculptures of flesh in an array of browns, spears in hand. Most of the men were fairly fit, and she'd been there long enough to become acclimated to their differences and acknowledge just how attractive some of them were even with their terrible teeth. She'd always had a thing for dark and swarthy.

Ricky had had the nicest brown eyes.

Keenly, the gaze of the guards hounded her as she followed the roads to the Head of the Guard's building. She kept her actions obvious and her hands where they could always be seen, not that she was anywhere near something valuable. And what would she do with any ill-gotten gains, stuff them away inside a beer jar? She'd be searched on the way out. Still, she figured there was no point getting skewered on account of a misunderstanding.

A small hut surrounded by a milling group of guards marked the end of her journey. The hut barely breached the innards of the village; she'd have to go deeper to refill her bottle and find Tabiry. She already missed her at-easy-reach water.

"Is the foreman within?" she asked one guard, less scowly than the others, less ready to chop her hands off or impale her on a pike.

The guard nodded and shifted his spear from his right to his left hand. He opened the door and yelled into the building. "Boss, got some beer for you." With a jerk of his head, he invited her inside. "Go in. I'll watch the donkey."

Jeannette pressed her lips together to smother a grin. "Yeah, thanks. Just don't drink the beer." She brushed past him and stood in the open doorway of the cool building.

Raia, obese and handsy, had about forty years on him, though age could be an unknowable measurement with skin subjected to the elements day in and day out. "Your wheat beer, sir," she said with a subservient tone, making her want to vomit on her toes.

The man oozed sleaze. The last time she'd delivered the beer Jeannette had to practically leap over the low table to escape his questing fingers. No way was she going that far inside this time. He came out without any argument, smiling at her as he inspected the jars. Who knew, maybe he was aiming for dashing, or friendly, but really his temperament resembled that of a spoiled rich boy from the Heights and he had all the appeal of a bad case of food poisoning. He called out to some of his men and she gave half an eye to them wrestling the jars from the leather straps, afraid to pull the main force of her attention away from the location of his paws.

"Won't you stay and enjoy a drink with me?" he asked, his hand already drifting her direction.

Jeannette stepped close to the side of her donkey. "Oh no, I'm afraid I must decline. I'm very busy."

His body rumbled in a deep laugh, popping out another chin in the process. "Oh, I insist."

Jeannette went rigid. He hadn't insisted last time. Glancing from one guard's face to the other, she found no support in the amused or slippery eyes. Her master had told her to never refuse a direct order from anyone of higher rank. A foreigner, such as herself, usually weighed in as the squatter at the base of the totem pole. Plus, he wasn't simply higher rank, he was *foreman*.

"Come in, Brewer."

Plastering a rigid smile on her face, she dug her knuckles into the donkey's flank, where stomach met hind leg. Ass brayed, launching himself up the street. "Oh, so sorry, but—" she turned towards the fleeing animal, "— I must catch my donkey." Running as if trying to lose her shadow, she silently thanked the donkey for being such a cantankerous bastard.

Oddly, even the lack of air in her lungs relaxed her a little. Anything was better than that man's presence. Except maybe being swarmed by insects. Or contracting a flesh eating disease. Through a maze of streets the donkey loped, his rattling hee-haws warning the pedestrians to clear the way. A teenage girl leapt for the donkey, but missed the lead by inches. Many yelled about her unruly livestock and apologies drained from her lips as she chased after him. "Ass!" she cried out, but the donkey was on a rampage. Dipping to the right, he zipped through a passage between buildings taking her deeper into the village. Utterly unfamiliar, the place held a certain malevolence that only being trapped and uncertain footing could bestow.

His tail swished around a corner.

She didn't relish the idea of getting accused of something she hadn't done or going places she shouldn't be. The main road—behind her? toward the hillside? lost in the labyrinth—tugged at her sense of well-being. The road out of this town. The road back to Thebes where she belonged.

When she finally found her runaway donkey, he'd half inserted himself into a small lean-to near a hut that could have fit in her old apartment's kitchen, chowing down on dried grasses laid out in a trough for a pair of black and white goats who didn't seem to mind sharing. One of them looked up at Jeannette, its jaw rolling in a sideways chew. Her chest heaved, pumping air into her lungs. She walked up to her beast and patted his rear, calmly so he didn't freak and bolt again.

"That's a good boy. Stupid donkey. You weren't supposed to sprint to the other side of the compound." Sweat stinging her eyes, she began securing the straps and padding that thankfully hadn't tripped him and broken his leg. "Now come on, let's get out of here before we're accused of cursing the dead."

Above all else, she had that distinct feeling of being in the wrong place at the wrong time. One didn't wander the workers compound of their own volition. Her feet itched and her fingers felt numb with the weight of it. She had wanted to see her friend, find the mummy and daughter of Bast, but right now that had dimmed to a faded promise on the dry slab of her tongue.

Someday, somehow, something would be easy.

The musky scent of goat saturated the lean-to with an undertone of clean grass. With arms the weight of truck tires, she grabbed for the donkey's lead and pulled his head towards her, moving to pet his soft nose.

A noise.

She ducked behind Ass' bulky frame, fearing the guards and their questions. What business do you have here? Under whose orders? Open your pack, your non-existent pockets. Strip down, we know you're hiding something. Back to Raia you go, he'll sort it out. Instead Jeannette caught sight of two men, weaponless with the squared off beards of men from the north, not guards. About ten yards away from her and her donkey-blind they stopped, one facing up the road, the other facing down. One of the men rubbed at a wicked scar slicing across his shoulder, a kind of absent-minded action people did when their mind was focused on other things. The shorter man glanced around—an SS Agent ferreting out a hidden assassin.

The scarred man leaned close to the other. "I've five more jars to pack and we're ready. You have anything to add?"

Jeannette bowed her head in relief. They were just merchants, like herself.

The lookout nodded, then licked his lips. "I do." He scanned the street continuously.

Merchants who were also worried about the guards because they too got lost?

Something about their shifty actions and stiff posture convinced Jeannette it wasn't quite the picture she wanted to paint. She held her breath and watched from behind Ass, who tilted his hoof and took another mouthful of grass. "Give me another day. Then we get them out of the city."

The scarred man nodded. "Tomorrow then. No later. Not all guards can be swayed from Re's light." He turned his back and slipped around a hut; the other disappeared the opposite direction. The street sat empty, Jeannette's memory the only proof of their existence. Ass shook his head. She swallowed hard, the unease of understanding drying out her already parched throat.

She slowly rose to her feet and looked around. Nobody appeared to be about. She could hear nothing but the munching animals and her pulse thrumming in her ears. "Let's get out of here," she whispered into the donkey's upright ear. She took his lead in shaking hands.

Scanning each passage as she made her way back to the main road, her progress was nothing to boast about. Luckily Ass must have had his fill of disobedience and didn't struggle as she led him out of the sparse shanty town. Finally emerging from the subdivision of huts, a guard practically fell upon her.

"You. I don't know you. What were you doing back there?" He aimed his spear at her and she lifted her hands up high above her head, stick 'em up style.

"Nu-Nothing! I was delivering beer. My donkey ran off and I had to chase him." The rough weave of the donkey's rope bit into her palm and fingers.

With casual, haughty authority, the guard lowered the spearhead, pressing the iron into her breastbone. In a flash flood of dizzying fear, her morning headache rushed back through her skull, clouding her vision. The metal scorched her skin and a low groan rumbled in her ears. This was it. Her end. He would press that sharp iron through her bone, tearing it up into tiny spears of its own, and the bone and weapon combined would pierce her heart, ending it all. Ending it.

The corners of his lips crept up, the arrogant amusement of a man with just enough power to make him want more.

"I didn't do anything." Her voice hitched.

The faint imprint of his smile took on the mantle of a full smirk. He began to search her, his hands skating over every plane of her body. From one grab-man to the next, at least he loosened the spear point from her chest to get his thrills.

His hand slid down her hip.

"But . . . but two men were talking." Fingers brushed her inner thigh. Oh God. "About taking jars out of the city. And—"

The guard stepped away; his spearhead swept back toward her. The motion had to be sharp, but to Jeannette it seemed submerged in molasses, a funeral march to her own wake. She clamped her mouth shut; fear stink poured from her skin. "Were they now?" he asked.

She nodded, not trusting her voice, and he lowered the business end of his spear to the side. "Can you describe the men?"

Attention on the spearhead, she did, and he nodded as he listened.

"I see. Sounds like tomb thieves."

Wiping her knuckle across her eye, Jeannette nodded, wishing her headache would go away, that she had some water and he'd just release her so this entire day could be written off as bad and she could start all over tomorrow.

He stared at her, and something in his expression, maybe that twist to his lips, the narrowing of his eyes—she didn't quite know—warned her. Her blood went cold; his spearhead arced through the air, right for her.

She dropped to the ground, thankful for gravity and adrenaline and every force in the universe that currently sat in her corner. The spear sliced through the air and penetrated the earth as she rolled underneath the donkey. The guard yanked it back, ready for another thrust, but she'd already taken to her feet. Running. Sprinting for the safety of *away*. Ass, without any coaxing, kept pace.

Behind her, the hammer of feet snapped at her heels. No time to look, she envisioned a phalanx of guards hot on her trail, spears lifted, hefted, sailing through the air to fell her right there in the streets, like a thief, like a common dog.

Which, she was not. She would not end up a mutt-pancake.

Brain on super-compute, she scanned the street, took a left, a right. She recognized a house, two story with a green door and broken loom leaning against the wall. Ass ran with her, tracking her every turn. The guard's footfalls slowly fell away. Erupting onto the main street, Jeannette tumbled to her knee. Popping to her feet again, she charged by men and women. Other guards and merchants with donkeys.

"What's that?" an old woman scolded as Jeannette nearly flattened her out.

She was *not* a common dog.

Ass galloped ahead, giving her that extra burst all the way to the edge of the village. Out of my way! she thought, no time for breath, and nearly wept when the inspection line solidified into view, long and unhurried.

Delivery men and women, merchants and artisans, fed the exit line that separated Jeannette from liberation. Pressed to the end of the line she lifted her chin, sucking down gulps of air while still scanning her surroundings. Dried saliva glazed her mouth, collecting in the cracks of her lips.

It was all such a joke. For a moment, maybe just an instant, she'd understood this place. Now the law hunted her down, reducing her to a street dog, lost and alone and desperate to survive. Visions of forgotten bodies lining the streets back in El-Balyana harried her every time she blinked. Nobody cared about those dogs, and nobody cared about her. Perhaps this represented a type of karma: become that which you had the audacity to mock. It tasted rancid on her tongue.

Exhausted. Panting. Running. She was always running. It seemed an unending race to get away. And she never seemed to end up anywhere.

She nodded to a familiar border guard, smiled, made friendly by desperation. Ass stretched his long neck, sniffing at another donkey, providing a shield between her and any flying, first-class tickets to the underworld. From the edge of the busy throughway her pursuer stood tall, spear at his side like a flag of nobility, and watched her. Their eyes locked; her body went cold, glacial as the Spokane waters in the dead of winter. That same amusement caught the edges of his lips, the arrogance shadowed by bitter anger. He pointed one long finger at her. "I'm coming for you," the gesture said. "I'm coming for you and next time I will have you and nobody will stop me from cutting you open and eating your heart."

Jeannette turned away, crowding the man in front of her, trying to swallow down her panic and desperation and fear. She smiled and nodded at unheard questions. Her headache pounded away.

Chapter 16

A BROWBEAT HUSBAND, late for his anniversary dinner, couldn't slink in with any more finesse than Jeannette did that afternoon. Dull inside and out, she left the silver kits and pottery pass on a low table and sought out the dark safety of her room, filed away in the back of the brewery enclosed within the heady scent of grain.

What was she going to do?

"Jeannette, were you going to the river this evening?" the Master Brewer asked from the other side of her door.

Her breath hitched, a shuddering inhalation, so she covered her mouth with her hand to smother it. She couldn't tell her master, couldn't confess her brainless actions. How she'd almost been skewered on a crooked guard's spear. How he'd touched her, made her nearly pee herself. How she'd babbled about the thieves, hoping to distract him from his baser desires. Biting her palm to staunch another desperate noise, she discharged a sharp pain, an earned punishment for not remembering a most basic lesson: this world was not on her side.

She couldn't tell her master about the guards; he didn't need to be involved. His safety leapt fathoms into the not-so-doomed zone if he didn't know anything about it.

"Girl. Are you listening?"

"Yes, Master. I'll go in a moment."

"Don't let Re's light dim too much before you go. It is dangerous at the cusp of darkness."

She grabbed her pack and re-stuffed it, brutally thrusting in her pants, her shirt, the payment for the soap. The backpack had aged: no longer black, and worn around the edges by the abrasive wind. She remembered buying it back in Spokane, and her leather boots, which she never wore anymore. That salesman had nodded with interest at her upcoming trip. A million miles away and a million years ago.

She inhaled, trying to cool her stoking panic. The guard was positioned in the artisans' village. Surely, his duty trapped him within like all the others assigned to the segregated population.

Think, Jeannette. She squeezed her eyes shut.

And if he hadn't chased after her, screaming for the other guards to catch her, he obviously didn't want to bring attention to Jeannette or himself. Sure, it was her word against his, and while everyone would trust the lies from his lips over God's honest truth from her own, he must not want any scrutiny landing on him, his whereabouts, or his actions.

By degrees, from loosening muscles, to calming breath, Jeannette relaxed. She scrubbed her face against the rough linen of her sheath dress, avoiding the unidentifiable stain. It needed washing, too. The state of her person and clothing was embarrassing. Back in her own time and place she would have never interacted with someone as filthy as her, like those sign holding beggars that sprouted from every major intersection. With one final breath, she left her room to face the brewer.

When she entered the brewery, he stood there, hands on hips as if he'd been waiting all afternoon in that exact stance. "Stay with the men and women. And mind the crocodile." Maybe his eyes lingered on her face a little too long, maybe not.

"I will." She hated the crocodile, silent death in waiting. "I'll filter the beer when I get back." She waved to the master and trudged off to the river.

In the almost quiet of the early evening, she could feel her temples pulse with each step. She should drink some water. After rinsing out her make-shift donkey rattle and filtering the water through a slightly less filthy corner of her dress, she waited the requisite iodine time and took a swig. Her iodine tablets were nearly gone; she'd taken to splitting them into even tinier pieces, reducing their efficiency. If a gut bug would end her, so it must be. It would soon be a decision out of her hands. Trust her luck and it would be the spear, swifter and less depressing.

"Damn it." She blinked quickly. She did not want to die, by bacteria or execution.

Maybe today she should give herself a break and just pay the laundry men to do the chore for her, but she couldn't stomach throwing away her wages on something she could easily do herself. On the horizon, the evening sky stretched clear on to forever and the air's heat index dropped from insufferable to something tolerable, just like every other evening.

First chore, though, was to trade for this land's shoddy version of soap: a mix of salt, ash and goat fat. She wondered about lye, or bubbles, or anything that might actually clean. Couldn't you make soap out of olive oil or milk? She had no idea how to get good glycerin from animal fat. Another distillation process, no doubt. With all of these half-formed inventions in her head, she only proved a danger to herself. By some twisted miracle, she'd probably devise a bomb. The ability to learn about old fashioned and ancient skills had never landed in her lap, and knowing how to test for dioxins in the soil with thousands of dollars of lab equipment wasn't even remotely useful here.

Halfheartedly, she traded for the soap.

A nearby guard watched her. Jeannette smiled at him, nodding like an idiot. She earned a scowl in return.

"Don't forget the oils," the soap seller said. Though her age was indiscernible—everyone appeared old before their time—the sandy bread had defeated her teeth with its ferocious tenacity. "Though, you're not a maiden even by the will of Isis." The woman cackled. Jeannette took a step back. "You still might find a man if you rub scented oils into your body. And kohl your eyes. Be pleasing, and one will find you desirable. Your beer is excellent." The woman nodded. "Everyone talks about it, foreigner."

Jeannette stared at the woman, startled.

Ignoring the idea that Jeannette needed to please a man, she asked, "What do they say about my beer?"

The woman cackled again. "They say, since the pale foreign woman came to be with the Master Brewer in the market precinct his beer slides down one's throat without the drinking straw. It fills the belly and rivals wine for the flavor."

Though knowing that the woman's words were well aimed flattery, Jeannette still had to rein in her gaudy grin of pride and vanity. The hard working men and women of a drink deficient world had noticed that she'd filtered the beer and added various fruits for flavoring. Of course anything adlib would turn a few heads. It had been a hard-earned experiment from weeks ago; convincing her master to change his methods could only have been pulled off by a sixteen-teen mule team and her nagging, yet gilded, tongue.

She wanted to rush back and tell her master, but he'd just glower at her boast. Still, she would hold her pride close to her heart.

Jeannette nodded at the old woman. "I'll take some of the wax."

The woman barked in laughter, and handed over a small pyramid of wax that fit in Jeannette's palm. She paid the woman. Sweet perfumes wafted from the wax: too sweet, too perfumy. Jeannette strolled away, gaze skipping from one person to the next—had that woman tried her beer and enjoyed it?—and scoping out each guard—did he know of what went on in the village on the hill? Was he in cahoots with the thieves?

One guard, slouching against a plastered shop wall, grinned at her as she passed, displaying half a smile of stained nubbin teeth; she stood tall and nodded at him without meeting his eyes.

Amidst the citizens rushing to perpetual duty, an adult daughter of Bast passed on the opposite side of the street from Jeannette, dipped her chin, and faded into the city. The sparse encounter triggered Jeannette's dream-meeting with the Sky Watcher. She had to find her old companions. Another line-item to worry about. Anxiety rolled over in her gut like a waking dog. She doubted that they would want anything to do with her after that whole fiasco on the river bank with Mr. Jawbones and the stray cat. Neither had even asked how Jeannette had felt about it. She snorted. Wasn't that typical? She'd felt awful; she hadn't wanted to kill the cat, but it was the single viable action that had come to mind at the time.

She glanced back over her shoulder—no daughter of Bast stood by, watching Jeannette trudge toward the river.

To be completely honest, Jeannette hadn't given them the opportunity to ask how she'd felt either.

She hiked over the small hill and followed behind a couple men as they descended towards the river. Now, at the same river's edge, she was on the lookout for Jawbones. Children, under the watchful eyes of parents, splashed in the water between bouts of beating clothing with sticks. Their giggles tinkled through the air, like the happy sing-song of fairies. The landscape swarmed with cats. A fish gutting operation had taken root down river from the washing nook, and the wild Egyptian cats feasted on the leftovers.

Passing three women elbows deep in the river, Jeannette found a vacant spot on the river—not too hard this late in the day—and dumped some of the fat and salt concoction onto her travel pants. Squatting in ankle deep water she began scrubbing away in the cool refreshing waters of the *Iteru*. At least she only had a few items; the man next to her had an entire basket full of sundry undyed linen items. The area had a rocky beach, possibly imported from the south so people had a solid surface to squat on. The stones were worn smooth from use, but a few had jagged edges that dug between the tendons of her feet, forcing her to shift and shuffle until the blunt daggers quit harassing her footing. Under the mindless labor, bubbles of memory took her back to her lab. The mixing of chemicals, the beakers, the meticulous notes. The gloriously clean working environment. Honestly, the job had been tedious, and not really all that important in the grand scheme of things, but at least it wasn't hand scrubbing clothes with cold water and worthless soap. She wished that she could grab the ear of all children and implant within them the need—the imperative—to find a career that gave them meaning, a job to feel good about and look forward to every morning at 6 am when the alarm clock screamed them to wakefulness. But with a glance around her, at the naked, grubby boys playing in the river to the equally bare girls walking by with water jugs on her heads, she knew that she could never give these children such advice. They were trapped, stuck within a world that solidified a system where choice wasn't even an inkling. They were all born to a job, born to a position, and they would follow it through until the Pharaoh changed their destiny or the *Iteru* swallowed up their souls. This wasn't a world of dreams and hopes; it was a world of living with the roll of the dice.

And here she whined about not having had a fulfilling job. Not *loving* her job. Sometimes, she forgot this place she'd woken up in. Sometimes—she angrily twisted a gray sock—she didn't have a clue. She had to stop dreaming of a dead past and focus on the here and now.

Casting a casual glance at the fish gutters, something stole her attention that upended her world yet again. The sock caught in the current, and she had to snatch it up from the river's cradle, splashing her mostly dry dress into a sodden mess. On the riverbank closer to the docks, knife in one hand, dead fish in the other, squatted a mummified man.

No other mummies had crossed her path during the months she'd been in this ancient land.

She draped the sock next to her dripping pants on a thatch of stiff grasses to dehydrate in the moisture hungry air. The mummy sat on the pebbled beach, a metal knife ready to puncture another fish, a large mound of gutted bodies speckled with flies were heaped by his side while a smaller pile of discarded bits grew behind him. A flurry of cats darted in and away to steal whatever they could, scattering at any provocation.

It had to be him. The dead man who haunted her destiny. Jeannette's mouth twisted, sour with the taste of regret and practiced apologies.

Pulling on her pack, she walked up to the man, her skirt flipping in the warm breeze scooping off the river. He stopped his fish massacre and looked up at her. Her heart beat heavy and rusty. Something about his surprised eyes captured her attention—dark, full and moist. His lips glistened in the lowering sun.

"I've been looking for you." She breathed through her mouth, tongue pressed to the roof of it. If she'd not adapted to the scent of the river and all its bounty, she'd surly be tossing her cookies at the concoction swarming the man.

Abayomi nodded, focused on scraping large scales off the fish with his bronze knife. "We have been here." His voice cracked. He swallowed. "Waiting." Fish scales painted his front, his feet, the ground before him in shimmery rainbows. "I see you have not been driven onto the stake yet."

"I'm made of sturdier stock." Jeannette looked around. "Is the girl around somewhere?" Jeannette didn't see the young daughter of Bast among the workers.

Abayomi lowered the red fish onto the crusty linens of his lap, and Jeannette found herself grimacing in disgust. She thought *she'd* been filthy. "That's kind of . . ." she began, gesturing at his hands, his lap, his blackened feet. He looked himself over. "Maybe you need to be rewrapped."

Head bowed, he shook it in denial. "I cannot," he said. "My wrappings hold within me the breath of Osiris. Within them are spells of preservation. The Lord of the Sacred Land himself promises me renewal. I cannot willingly abandon that." His voice dropped softly. Perhaps he was sad, about his wrappings, being mobile or something else entirely, she wasn't sure.

He'd changed in the time since she'd last traveled with him.

"Well, we should dip you in the river and wash off some of that gunk." He looked so bad that she felt oddly conspicuous being seen with him. Though, she knew she was no dilettante with the brown smudge down her own front.

"Sanura is working at the laundry, scrubbing in the dark all day. They make her wash the undergarments of women in menstruation." He did not meet Jeannette's eyes. "They call her the Forsaken. That Bast is not watching Her daughter." His voice had gone rough, hard.

Something splashed in the river nearby. The wind lifted Jeannette's hair, spiraling long strands of her ponytail to brush against her cheeks and nose.

"Do you blame me?" she asked.

Abayomi looked back up at her. Yes, there were whites around that deepest brown and blackest pupil. "Why would I? Why do you think you have anything to do with it?" Then, he shook his head. "Jeannette, you are like a tomb. Do you know that even though the burials of the mighty are all hidden away, their entrances camouflaged by crafty stonework, that someone will someday find a way within and take away the treasures of the afterlife? It will not happen tomorrow, or next year, but in time, the protection of stone and earth will crumble away. You think you are so fortified, you think you alone hold within your arms the fate of life and death, but eventually, you too will crumble." He spoke this proclamation like a judicial sentencing. "And when you do, you will know that you do not stand alone."

Her eyes narrowed. "I don't think I'm all that."

Abayomi settled his gaze forward, towards the ships upon the river. "I have seen it. In glimpses." His voice deepened in intensity with unnamable emotions.

She had nothing to say to that.

The tacit hush stretched uncomfortably thin. Jeannette shrugged. "So, when are you done here?"

He dropped the fish with a splat onto the pile of its dead comrades. He held his hands away from his body. "Now."

"Don't you want to gather your day's wage?" she asked, shocked. Time and money were not so disposable.

"It does not matter. Sanura is happy with fish scraps, I do not have hunger, and we have been passing our nights in the fish shanty with the other workers."

"Why even bother working then?"

"It is the duty of every citizen to contribute to Pharaoh's domain."

No jest lurked in Abayomi's open answer, and he seemed startled at Jeannette's shock-widened gaze. "Why work if you don't have to? The pharaoh doesn't know you from any other dead man in his empire."

"What else would we do? We looked for you, which amounted to little success. So wait for you, and we work." He looked away, back rounded in a bow.

"You looked for me?" She pulled her shoulders back, leaning over the sitting man. "I've been looking for you, too. What do you mean you've been waiting?"

"We have been waiting. Waiting for you to find us when it was your time to find us."

She shifted her gaze down the river. Pink traces flickered across the water heralding the ending of the day, though the opposite bank still sat in full light. A steady buzz of insects droned underneath the everyday sounds of the river: people talking, the water slipping along the bank, the plunk of fish bodies slapping against each other after men and women scooped out their innards.

"Fine. I'm here now. I found you. But we should finish," she said. "I'll help. We need that pay." She opened the small compartment of her pack and found her own knife. The blade needed sharpening.

"*We?*" A little curiosity wrapped itself around the utter annoyance of the word. It was good to hear a little bit of his old self.

With a length of the leather cord used to strap the beer to Ass' back, she cinched up the skirt of her dress, inelegantly baring her legs to avoid a fish-blood abstract design on the white canvas of the linen. She was tempted to go naked, many women did, but she couldn't see herself stripping in front of a man she knew. A pink-scaled fish looked at her, black eyes the same dead or alive. Not like Abayomi. His eyes no longer looked the same.

"Yes, we." She squatted next to him and snatched up the fish. Slime caused her grip to slip. "Listen, I'm sorry that I left you at the docks," Jeannette whispered to the dead fish in her hand, unsure whether she'd spoken loud enough to make herself heard. She didn't look at Abayomi as she apologized. She didn't want to see his look of triumphant 'ah ha!' Instead she jammed the short blade into the belly of the river fish.

"I regret letting you go." His voice was an echo of hers and she wondered what filtered through his mind as he reached down for the dropped carcass and continued his work. She sawed along the center line of the fish's underside. The knife caught on the thick flesh and she twisted the blade to tear it away.

She forced a laugh, a flamethrower intent on burning away that awkward tension. "I got a job, too. A brewer's apprentice. And I met this woman." As she struggled to keep a grip on the fish, she told Abayomi about her life. She breezed through her meeting with Tabiry and finding her place at the brewery, but when she hit on her hazy description of meeting with the Sky Watcher, Abayomi stopped her.

"So, you, a commoner and foreigner, went into the inner chambers of Amun's temple?"

"I guess. What's the big deal?"

He chuckled. "Ignorant swineherd, only the priests can enter into the inner sanctuary."

"They didn't kick me out." She smiled at him with a flash of teeth. "And I did get a conference with the monkeys."

He blinked at her and she could see the deep brown of his eyes, dark like the soil of Kemet. Darker than that bastard Ricky's had been. "Monkeys?" he asked.

She grinned at him, teasing him with reticence. The stare down lasted longer than she anticipated, and her desire to tell him about the prophecy outweighed any pleasure she would get from holding out on him.

"Yep. I met with the Sky Watcher." She marched through her hazy memories of her time in the temple. "At least I think it was her," she said mostly to herself.

"The Sky Watcher?" he repeated. Perhaps he hadn't changed so much; he still had limited conversational skills.

"Yes." She nodded. "Amun's oracle. And she told me that I needed you guys. Well, that's not the only reason I came looking for you," she said in a rush. And she knew that was true. As she sat there, chatting with the once annoying dead man, she felt oddly content. "But, I need to help you find your heart scarab and help Sanura to find herself, or something. Face her reflection." Then, "I didn't steal it, you know," tumbled out of her mouth. "Your heart."

"If you say so."

She squinted at him. "I do." The pile of dead fish hadn't grown much over their conversation, but enough beady eyes watched her that she felt a little judged. "Then we go back to your tomb and the magical gate will open and I'll get to go home."

He squinted at her. "Magical gate?"

Jeannette shrugged. "I guess." The fish felt heavy and cold in her hand. "I think that's what the big baboon said." At the moment, the bright, hopeful future she had envisioned gathered a bit of tarnish. She cursed and dropped her head back to face the endless sky. "I'm sure of it. She talked about these gates and how strength couldn't just open the gate, or gold. And then she talked about the key. That you guys are the key. We need to . . ." she thought a moment, "we need to name our enemy at the gate. I'm sure that's what she said." Or maybe it was the drug memories she was certain of.

She wanted to move on, suddenly unsure of anything.

"Then I stumbled on two men talking about taking things out of the workers village. That they were hiding from the guards. I think they were taking things from the vizier's tomb, the one being constructed in the valley on the cliffs." She turned towards him. "So, guess it won't be years before those tombs get plundered."

Abayomi dropped his fish, almost jumping to his feet. Maybe he planned to run off and save the gold and jewels and art from its illegitimate future right then and there. "What did you do?" She'd never heard such life in his voice before. Well, unless he was yelling at her.

She chuckled, the flavor of chuckle that didn't really express amusement, tapping the side of her knife against the fish. "I ran away."

"You ran away?" His mouth dropped open and she quickly shifted her gaze. "That is it? You just . . . ran away?"

"Yeah." Not very heroic. "I mean, there was this guard and he chased me. All through town." Her voice cracked at the memory. "He tried to stab me."

"How did you get away from him?" Abayomi asked, gentle concern overshadowed by the Matterhorn of incredulity.

"I told you, I ran. And once I got in the line to leave the town, he didn't follow anymore."

"You must be watched over by Isis herself. First," Abayomi shook his knife at her, "if the guard attempted to kill you after you told him of your suspicions, he was certainly in the employ of the thieves. He should have killed you with the knowledge you had. You could turn them in, destroy their entire scheme. Surely you have the eyes of the Gods on you," he muttered, then more loudly, "Second, you cannot return to the workers village. He will be waiting for you."

"But, what if my master tells me to?"

"Then, you will be killed." Abayomi said it so pragmatically, her alarm was kept at manageable levels. "The messes you get into."

"Not everything I do is a mess," she argued for the sake of argument. He made her sound like a walking, talking catastrophe.

He rolled his head towards her—such a natural movement she almost forgot the man was dead—and said, "The slave market."

"You didn't have to follow! And the girl was being sold into slavery."

"What is wrong with slavery?"

What a bastard! With all her might, she hauled back and threw the fish at him. It smacked him in the center of his chest and he stared down at the smear, mouth open in amazement.

"You just threw a fish at me," he said.

Her passion faded, and in a small, malnourished voice she said, "Yes."

Then he laughed. A sound so loud, the people all around stopped their work. Fish gutters, children, a few fisherman nearby all looked at him, but he didn't cease. He laughed and smiled and his eyes blazed with some inner energy that took her breath away.

"You are one of the oddest people around, Jeannette." He remembered her name; didn't call her woman or swineherd. He'd said *Jeannette*.

"I'm odd? You're the walking dead."

"Yes, I know. But that says nothing about my nature. You, however, are odd through and through. The plant reveals what is in the seed," he said sagely.

She studied him, then snorted, taking it for the compliment that it must have been.

When he finally caught his breath, he bowed to the other fish scalers who slowly returned to their labors, a few making shooing motions at him.

"Sanura will be back just before sundown, after the laundry closes for the night." Abayomi studied his fish. "We will do what we can here, earn our grain, and then decide, with Re's light shining upon us, what to do next."

Jeannette nodded, unable to staunch her smile. Together, they passed the time with guts and fish scales and few words. And with only seven nicks during the entire process. A minor miracle.

By the time the sun's reflection wiggled closely below it on the river's rumpled surface, Jeannette had long ago given up the impossible goal of cleanliness. Apparently God didn't gut fish. Fish slime, blood and bits of white flesh covered the front of her dress. She looked like an assault victim on the streets of Atlantis, nearly as bad as Abayomi.

Then it finally sank in. After he'd been laughing, laughing *hard*, Abayomi had had to catch his breath. Jeannette had seen it. The gentle filling of his torso, and equally subtle deflation. She would swear by all she held as truth that Abayomi would, every so often, breathe.

Something hooked his attention and he looked up, looked beyond Jeannette to the space behind her, to something that had to have been magical or mystical or just so damned amazing because he burst into a delighted smile. Even through the dark bandages and dried skin, it transformed his face. Happy. As happy has anything she'd ever seen.

Jeannette glanced over her shoulder, then took to her feet. Fish scales and other unidentifiable parts rained onto the river's shore. The cat-headed girl walked towards them.

Chapter 17

SANURA'S SHOULDERS SAGGED. Her dress, though torn in several places, was clean, and mismatched sandals adorned her small, tanned feet. Jeannette noted these things with a clinical attentiveness—they were facts, measurable data of the physical world. But the true metal of the girl was measured in the set of her eyes, the carriage of her ears. These expressions on her feline face revealed that she was not beaten. Even if she had almost been forced into slavery and now worked a pariah's job. Even though she wandered a land as strange to her as it was to Jeannette. They were all alone here. Lost lambs.

Those eyes shifted to Jeannette, narrowed, and the ears, so jaunty before, drew back.

Jeannette's gaze dropped to the weave of her shoe, a knot where the knitter fumbled the reeds catching her eye. "Is it too late to apologize?" she asked.

A charged pause pervaded the space between them, then Sanura said, "It's never too late." That odd musical trill was a forgotten surprise.

"I'm sorry." I'm sorry I killed that cat. I'm sorry I left you.

Sanura's ears relaxed, pointed upwards once again, and the corners of her eyes softened. The girl stepped forward, and dipped her chin.

"It's all right," Sanura said. "You are forgiven."

For a breath, then two, they stood there, eyes joined.

Jeannette filled her lungs. "Thank you." She glanced away, suddenly awkward under the burden of forgiveness and sisterly love. "Let's get your pay, gather our things and get clean." She slapped her hands against the stiffening sludge crusted on her dress and glanced at Abayomi's linen wrappings. Iridescent fish scales shimmered over the length of them, giving him a mystical, merman look. "We're disgusting." A fly buzzed around her face; she swatted it with an impatient flick of her wrist.

Looking himself up and down, Abayomi shrugged, reflecting the guise of indifference with body language because a bandage-wrapped face told few stories. "There is little that can be done about my linens."

With a tentative lift of her eyebrows, Jeannette asked Sanura, "Do you think we can launder him at the place you are employed?"

Sanura smiled, not generally a reassuring effect with all those teeth. "Yes, I think we can dip him . . . and you. Personally, you smell lovely, but

151

I can understand your clothing might become hard to move in." She giggled. The sound struck Jeannette as young and refreshing. The girl deserved so many more chances to be this carefree.

During her conversation with Abayomi, the sun's light had melted away to a soft, purple glow and the air had cooled. The city settled into quiet inactivity, a complete one-eighty to the thrum of the morning and early evening. A tender wind sighed down the river valley and the twilight insects took up their chorus amid the random squawks, squeaks and barks of the river's other nightlife.

With a basket of fish guts under one arm, Abayomi stood, his wrappings crinkling in at the elbows and knees. Jeannette gathered her clothing that had dried under the ravenous rule of the sun, and through the pitch-like darkness of the streets, followed Sanura to the laundry, only a couple hundred yards away near the river. It made Jeannette laugh, a bitter, dry kind of chuckle, to realize just how close they'd been this entire time. The heavy scent of fat, ash and salt, an almost stomach-grumble inducing scent to those who never ate their fill, did little to smother their own personal *Eau de Parfum* of fish guts, sweat and river water. Mall saleswomen spritzing them with a cloud of perfumed mist would do nothing to subdue their very special aroma.

Outside the laundry, ropes stretched along the length of the long, skinny building, where, in the arid heat of the day, the linen cloth would dry in record time. The inside reminded her of the brewery. Large clay pots rested over fading coals or dead fires and charcoal littered the floor. A respectable affair, it probably employed over thirty people.

"Strip down, Jeannette, and we can get you clean first," Sanura said.

Jeannette paused and pointed at Abayomi. "I'm not getting naked in front of him." Her arms crossed her chest.

Curiously, they both stared at her. "Why not Abayomi?" Sanura asked. Jeannette shook her head with an added elaborate eye roll for effect.

True, women pranced around topless and both of the sexes could be seen completely nude, but modesty was a habit not easily forgotten. Though, if she wanted to be honest with herself—the apparent theme of the day—the idea of a clean body couldn't be denied, and she did have the clothing she'd just washed in the river. A good scrubbing with some of the handmade soap and clean clothes could turn her entire situation on its end—tail to top. And right now, that wasn't such a bad thing.

Jeannette scanned the menagerie of clay vessels. "Is there any warm water left, and are there any large bowls or tubs I could use?"

With help from Sanura, Jeannette stoked up a fire and manufactured a modest bathing area formed from mixed-sized jars and slightly damp fabric. If only she'd had access to a giant refrigerator box, then it would be a child's dream fort come to life. Abayomi shied away from the open flames under the heating jars and waited near the door. Shielded from everyone's eyes, Jeannette stripped down and tossed her dress around the fat belly of a jug to Sanura. Squatting on a three-legged stool, she methodically scrubbed her skin raw with handfuls of sand and soap, then rinsed off with a splash of warm water from a wide-mouthed jug. She even washed her hair, and wasn't that a nice feeling?

She made an incredible mess, but couldn't find it in herself to work up an ounce of remorse. Too many other things had used up her last reserve of "I'm so sorry."

With extra attention to the cuts on her hand, probably infiltrated with who knows how many different breeds of bacteria, she took an alcohol wipe from her first aid kit—an endangered species by now—to break up that rowdy convention by wiping down every cut and scrape she had. The worst injury from her fish dissecting stint, a slice across the fleshy heel of her hand, earned a latex bandage—again, another of the few remainders of its kind.

Once clean and dressed in her khaki pants and button-down cotton shirt—encasing her torso and smothering—she emerged from her soggy corner, skipping over a puddle, and returned to Sanura and Abayomi. Light from the torches scattered against open jugs of water hoisted over heating fires. The two sat quietly, Abayomi on a stool and Sanura leaning against his leg, his hand on her head. Jeannette pulled up short. They looked content, like family.

Eyelids half-closed, Sanura looked her direction.

In a low voice, Jeannette asked, "Sanura, where's my dress?"

Sanura popped up to her feet before Jeannette could protest and led her to a covered pot with a steady fire burning underneath. Steam escaped the laundry pot, rising from under the lip of the lid, and peeking inside, Jeannette saw her dress floating on the surface. "You didn't have to do that for me!"

"It was no problem; you were busy." The girl flicked an ear at Jeannette.

Jeannette pursed her mouth tight, deeply touched at the automatic kindness. She nodded stiffly, then smiled at the cat-headed girl. "Thank you."

Jeannette's fingers snagged at knots as she finger-combed her hair, still dripping and soaking rosettes on her blouse where it rested as she studied the filthy mummy. And now, like that one onerous deed left after a long day of chores, only the replacement of his bandages remained.

"Do you think he'll be normal?" she whispered to Sanura.

"Isn't he already?"

Jeannette didn't know what to say to that.

Abayomi, the onerous deed, had moved to the doorway, inching away from the two women. His wrappings, stained with travel and fish bits, sagged at elbows, knees and other active joints. They looked fragile, like the next gust of wind might swirl them away and carry them into the west without the man inside.

"We have to re-wrap him," she said to Sanura. "He won't last much longer if he remains in those ruined things." She planted her fists on her hips and studied him. "Sanura, he seems to think if we unwrap him, it will stop him from being mobile . . . undead and all." Abayomi seemed to grow smaller under her scrutiny. He looked to the right, then to the left. "What do you think?"

Sanura blinked; her large pupils flashed green in the firelight.

Abayomi shifted his weight from side to side as if ready to bolt. "I will be fine . . ." He glanced towards the door.

"Perhaps if we re-wrap him in sections. A foot, a calf, all the way to his head—

"I'll cease to be!"

"No," Sanura said. "Jeannette has magic." The words rolled off her tongue.

"Magic?" Abayomi and Jeannette stared at Sanura. "Wait! What? I do?"

"She does?" Abayomi sounded equally dumbfounded.

Didn't Sanura have the magic, being a goddess' child and all?

Sanura squinted at Jeannette. "Yes, I can see it in her eyes. Especially when she is near you."

The crackle of the fire filled the empty air. Abayomi and Jeannette sized each other up, measuring with experience and a hurricane of gut feelings just how much trust existed between them. She stepped closer to him.

"I cannot say that I am eager for you to unwrap me." Panic flavored his words, twisted them high and drawn out. His hand pressed against the wall behind him.

"You are already unraveling." Jeannette pointed out a visible patch of dark skin on his forearm. She didn't want to see her newly reunited friend, however frustrating he could be when he put his mind to it, attacked by a pack of feral dogs thinking he smelled like a doggie treat.

"But . . ." He grabbed at a hanging strip of elbow cloth, almost black in the low light, and tucked it up along his arm.

Jeannette reached out and touched his bicep. The feel of his arm, the emaciated flesh beneath the cloth, didn't creep her out like it used to. But, it was still icky. "It's okay. According to all the horror movies I've seen, a mummy isn't killed by unwrapping it." She didn't want to tell him that she'd only seen a few mummy movies and unwrapping hadn't been a plot hook at all.

"This, ah, horror movie is a lesson in embalming?"

Jeannette almost nodded yes, but then shook her head. "No." She sighed softly. "It's entertainment. Like a play."

Abayomi leaned away, head shifting in miniscule shakes of denial.

"Just one portion at a time," Sanura said, joining in on the 'rewrap Abayomi now' rally.

While Jeannette continued to sweet talk the dead guy, Sanura ripped long strips of linen cloth she'd scavenged from a pile of remnants stored in the corner. The widths of the cloth strips were non-uniform, but when Jeannette tugged at one's length, it held as readily as any modern weave.

"Okay, Abayomi," Jeannette said. "Just sit over on that bench and we'll get to work." His eyes were horror-wide, drawn to the fresh strips of bandages gripped in her fists. "Don't worry. I will be very careful. I'll say all the prayers over your new wrappings as I go."

"You—You will?"

Jeannette nodded.

"You are not a woman of Anubis. How do you know the spells?" His voice, reduced to something small and needy, pained her.

She ignored the liquid guilt that filled her inch by inch, every nook and cranny of her being. "I've read parts of the Book of the Dead. The . . . uh . . . Coffin Texts." Very small parts quoted under some interesting pictures of scrolls and wall decorations she found on the Internet. "I will cast all the spells; they'll just be in my own form." She assured him with a nod. It wasn't a complete lie. Anyway, it couldn't be simple mumbo jumbo that kept him alive, kept her here, and let Sanura even exist. One wrong word on her part wouldn't cut the strings that made him—an Old Kingdom mummy—talk and walk and be a general pain in the butt. Something bigger played a role here—she didn't really want to dwell on what—and she had to trust the daughter of a god's intuition on this. She patted his shoulder, pushing him towards the bench, trying for helpful and feeling stiff and uncomfortable like her sun-dried pants.

He said nothing more and shuffled where she directed. He moved like an old man. Well, he was a few thousand years old, depending on the point of origin. As he sat, she took a deep breath and bounced a little on her toes. Now or never.

Jeannette squatted next to his ragged feet, dangling her hands between her legs; her knees popped in the crackling hush. Sanura hefted a wide-mouthed bowl over to them and, sitting cross-legged on the ground next to Jeannette, offered a long strip of linen. White and clean, it measured longer than Jeannette's arm-span. Taking her time to sit as well, Jeannette finally reached out for Abayomi's left foot. As she drew close to the grimy limb, she hesitated, waiting for his okay. He jerked his head in an approximate nod.

Filth from walking barefoot across the mostly dirt roads of Kemet had provided the bottoms a sturdy sole. She placed his foot in the bowl of her lap and removed the wrapping, one circumference at a time. One loop. Then another. Slowly, so as not to startle him. The accumulated crust flaked off in her lap. Though she attempted to suppress it, a shiver of disgust wriggled down her spine. Mentally, she began to recite the biological classification of a tsetse fly.

She didn't want to look at the foot, the skin. It was dead. She held dead flesh in her hands. But then the toes wiggled and she couldn't help the bark of strained laughter. Dark brown and of the consistency of a fifty-year-old sun worshiper's, his skin had a pinched look, almost baggy now that the linens no longer pressed it together. Swallowing down her automatic ick response, Jeannette poked him with a finger. He watched her. Maybe he glared; it was a challenge to tell. Though still leathery, the flesh wasn't as stiff as she imagined a mummified corpse's should be. A far cry from his hide when he'd first lurched after her back at the fires of the Montu Temple.

She ran her fingers under the arch of his foot; he jerked and squirmed, trying to pull his leg away.

"Ha! That tickles."

With a gush of breath, she said, "I know."

Hand over her mouth, Sanura tried to smother her giggle. Another measure of tension lifted with her mirth, freeing something tightly coiled within Jeannette.

The girl handed Jeannette the short pot of steaming water; an earthy odor curled up from the bowl. Plant detritus floated on the surface, and as Jeannette swirled a cloth into the water, she tried to catch as few leaf bits as possible. With the wet cloth in hand she began to wash Abayomi's foot. Cradling his heel in her lap, she brushed the cloth firmly along the sole. His toenails were whole and generally clean if thick, and the skin began to soften under her massage. She scrubbed the ancient skin up to his ankle, sloughing away layers as well as years. Underneath, his flesh was pure.

Jeannette couldn't imagine . . . didn't see how . . .

With her thumb, she caressed his fresh skin, naturally beige but untouched as a newborn's. She looked over at Sanura, expecting some explanation. *Did I do this? Am I seriously magical?*

Sanura only smiled, a non-verbal response that said "I will spill no secrets" and handed Jeannette a strip of cloth. Numb, Jeannette began to wrap the limb with fresh bandages, firmly, but not so tight as to reduce his range of movement.

In a low voice, barely a breath, she prayed over the new wrappings. It'd been years since she'd said anything positive to any kind of a god— except for Asphaltia, the Goddess of good traffic and parking spots—and the words came as easily from her mouth as teeth.

"Please God, Anubis, Lady Bast—" her gaze zipped to Sanura, but she kept going "—bless these linens to keep Abayomi. To protect him in his search for his heart scarab and his *ba*. To help him find his place in Heaven, or whatever Afterlife he belongs in," she finished in a rush.

Her fingers tingled as the linens dragged against her skin.

Slowly and with great care, she unraveled the gauze along both legs up to his groin, washed the thin limbs, and then rewrapped him in clean cloth, chanting her low droning prayer. It wasn't so long ago the simple concept of touching his skin gave her the willies to the extent that the idea of being eaten alive by crabs did, but in less time than it took to finish his second leg, she'd grown used to the feel and appearance. When she finished his legs he stood from the bench, eyes half-closed. She wondered if he lost himself in some meditative head-space, a kind of protective shield from the trauma.

"Umm, do you want . . ." she gestured foolishly toward his crotch,

157

not wanting to presume, not really wanting to continue. "How about your arms next."

He tilted his head at her, but raised one arm in a long stretch before him. The horror movie directors would have hired him on the spot.

"Just don't moan at me." She began to unravel his hand. With the flat of her thumb, she pushed against his skin like she would a boiled yam. It curled up just the same.

"Why would I moan at you, Jeannette?" Abayomi sounded tense, so she ignored his question and continued her mumbled prayers of mummification.

"Please, Anubis, let Abayomi into the promised land. Osiris, guide his way."

She conquered his arms quickly, though she lingered at his hands, gently rinsing the length of each finger. Finally, she stood back and examined his swaddled chest, slim and undefined. With the sensitive tips of her fingers, she ferreted out the end of a long band of linen ingeniously tucked away above his hip. "God, bless this man." The stiff linen crackled as she stripped it from his body, looping his abdomen three times. The next strip started where the last ended and as she unwound this one little objects tumbled out from his death bandages: a turquoise, wide-legged A; a man shape with a loop for a head; a brown eye of Re; and more. Bits of gold, too. She collected each with care and added them to a growing pile, wondering at each one's meaning. What power it was supposed to hold. Tucked under his chin was an oblong shape of blue-green porcelain. All of it, beautiful. Probably priceless. His body, on the other hand, told another story. Pale candle light danced over the breadth of Abayomi's chest and shoulders, illuminating the wrinkled texture of his skin and the white embalming scars. His nipples jutted out from his sunken, hairless chest, and his stomach curved inward. Anorexic.

But dead men didn't starve.

Jeannette dipped the washing cloth into the bowl of water. The water was again hot and clear, the herbs more fragrant than before. When Sanura had prepared the new bowl of washing tea, Jeannette wasn't quite sure. She wasn't sure of a lot of things right now, such as why her hands had that tingle she sometimes got when she stood next to a power station; or why running the cloth down the dead flesh didn't drop her straight into the land of Heebie Jeebie; or how his skin had changed as completely as any caterpillar from a cocoon; or how Sanura fit in fixing up a new cleansing bowl in the space between one breath and the next. Maybe the mini-god could stop the pace of time. After all, time was one of those tricky things you could never be sure of.

The tips of her fingers had pruned up. She splayed her fingers wide, lifting her hands before her. They shook when she held them stiff.

Sanura held up a length of cloth and Jeannette took it. After the washing, Abayomi's flesh no longer resembled day-old worm carcasses dried out on the pavement. Other than his unnatural thinness, he looked—normal.

Jeannette held the next wrapping up to get its measure. With an apologetic shake to her head, she handed it back to Sanura and after quiet deliberation on Sanura's part, the girl grabbed another strip and gave that one to Jeannette. Jeannette offered her a smile. Due to the length of the wrapping, she gave Abayomi's stomach and lower chest an entire layer. Then she laid on the next, and by the third layer, she began to tuck the items back into the places she'd found them. She wished she'd drawn a map, like she did when taking apart complicated equipment with bowls full of nuts and bolts. Never ceasing her divine mumblings, she slipped the painted lozenge into the place below his chin and then all that remained were his head and groin. She wasn't sure which one was worse.

Abayomi's eyelids hid his eyes. For most of the ordeal he'd gone into a strange trance, taking slow, deep breaths and letting Jeannette maneuver his body like a pliant, life-sized doll. None of them spoke much, and only Jeannette's uneven chanting broke the silence. Her throat had grown as raw as her hands, and her voice droned on like a rough, flat stream. A small smile touched the edges of Abayomi's lips visible through the gaps of the linen. For a few seconds she stared at that smile. She didn't want to look at his face. It would be uncovered. Defenseless.

The groin would have to be next.

"Okay, spread your legs a bit. Please," she added, her voice as steady as she could make it.

Eyes still in a nap pose, he stood and, with an audible click in her throat, Jeannette swallowed and began unwrapping Abayomi's crotch, cursing herself at each rotation around his hips for her mad suggestion to replace his bandages. Letting her mind drift to happier places, she chanted her nonsense prayers. When the linens lay in a coil around his feet, she couldn't help but look. Jeannette's skin grew hot around her ears. As expected, everything had shriveled under the abuse of natron. Or maybe he was always like that. She chanced a glance at his face. Eyes still closed. Washcloth in hand, she bathed his flesh, the cloth sloughing away the outer layer of death. Disallowing her brain any more curious side trips, focusing on her prayers, the awkward job of washing and wrapping his groin soon ended, the flesh now renewed.

"How you do feel?" she asked.

He opened his eyes and smiled, an almost lazy expression, like Archy would make after waking up from a sunbeam nap. "You have gentle hands."

Her eyes slipped off his face like hot butter off a roasted ear of corn; her palms had gone clammy. "Just one bit left."

She sat him down and began to unwrap his head.

The river of linen around his head had been some of the cleanest on his body. Standing behind Abayomi with the final end pinched between her thumb and forefinger, Jeannette's heart twisted into a tornado of emotions. Halting the procedure, she shook out her hands, trying to bring normality back into her raw and sensitive fingers. Sanura had shredded another extra-long strip of fabric and placidly waited for Jeannette to take it. With a little tug, the aged wrapping had gone loose around his throat, then around his face and finally it slipped off his head all together into a rag-doll pile on the floor.

"God," she said, "in all forms, for there are many we broken humans have created, please keep Abayomi safe."

With the same magnetic power of a road side accident, she found herself staring at the back of his head. Mostly bald, thin wisps of black hair stood between his scalp and the ceiling. A glance at Sanura—hoping to see in her reaction just how bad his face appeared—gave her no hints; the *mi-nether* remained quiet like a God-loving church girl at sermon. Right next to her thigh rested a fresh bowl of herbed water. Jeannette blinked, wondering once again when time had skipped.

Jeannette valued honesty, and rarely took detours down the highway of self-betrayal. Since she'd found the man by the river, she'd not once thought of Abayomi as a monster. Well, maybe a walking mythology with a definite hydration problem, but not a living horror. These weeks, living in a land not quite his own, had changed him. Had *healed* him. How could she consider him a monster when he laughed and did thoughtful things? How could a man be a monster when he helped young cat-headed girls feel safe?

Bending over at the waist, she dipped the edge of her washing linen in the steaming water. Though the room was warm, another shiver shimmied over her body. Most of the fires had died to hot charcoal shifting between red and black in a dance that seemed to match the pacing of Jeannette's prayers. She set the cloth onto his scalp and began rubbing in circles, constraining herself to gentle, slow movements. As she ran the warm cloth over his skin she swore the stupid man purred.

"You like that?" she asked, not sure if she was accusing him.

He nodded, but said nothing.

Then, bracing herself with a huge breath, she side-stepped around the bench and faced him.

Pinched, loose skin sagged from his chin and sharp Egyptian bone-structure. But unlike the dried up dead men she'd seen on her tours, Abayomi had thin lips and eyelids that were now open. In fact, his eyes looked *normal*. She'd been noticing them the entire afternoon. Where before they had been dehydrated brown nuggets, now they resembled a dollop of chocolate surrounded by a sea of cream. Beautiful.

He smiled at her, a dimple cracked in his left cheek. "Not so pretty, am I?'

Jeannette's ears burned. "Oh . . . well, ah . . . You're a mummy, so it's to be expected."

Something sad whispered within his eyes, but it was fleeting and in its place landed a roll of weary exasperation. Jeannette cursed herself for being a complete and total cow.

"Yes, I suppose so," he said.

"It's not that bad," she muttered, knowing she couldn't take away the hurt.

He turned to Sanura, and she blinked one of those contented cat blinks and said, "I see your life as the surge of the annual inundation: powerful and ready to overflow its banks. Your body is full of magic and is beautiful."

Jeannette squeezed her hands together, popping her knuckles. She knew *exactly* what Sanura meant, but it had eluded explanation until the daughter of Bast gave it form with words. Intangible life swelled inside him.

With quickness and a wandering gaze, she washed his face, around his ears, and dabbed at his closed eyes. She never once looked at his entire scrubbed face. Seeing his fresh flesh was too much for her, gut wrenching, like listening to Gabby babble about her happiness and impending engagement. To Ricky. She wasn't quite sure why, but Jeannette just couldn't face Abayomi. Maybe it was a fear that he might be ugly. Or attractive. Maybe it was guilt because she'd been such a dragon. Under the power of her monotone prayers she replaced the last of his wrappings. Doing most if it from behind his back.

"Keep him safe, God. Keep him whole. Allow him his heavenly rewards. Let him be happy. Let him be free. Let him find his peace."

She stepped away, leaned against the laundry's mud wall, completely drained.

Clean, and smelling so much better, he stood up tall and seemed to expand with a breath, fill the entire room. What once was brown with age and travel now glowed white and fresh.

"How do you feel?" she asked.

Perhaps, in this realm of magic and dreams, death was not the last bow and life had far more substance than mere shadow.

"Wonderful. I feel wonderful." He turned towards her and smiled. Caught in her chest, her breath stopped. She nodded at him, trapped by those eyes, warm and accepting and encompassing things she couldn't understand.

Sanura gathered up Abayomi's filthy wrappings and began feeding them to one of the laundry fires.

Jeannette joined her and tossed in a few strips. "Burning the evidence?"

"Burning what is no longer needed." The flames ate the dry linens, sending up sparks and black smoke.

Jeannette wished all unnecessary things could be dealt with in such a convenient way. Take all those hang-ups, take the uncertainty, take the worry and let it all burn.

That night they slept in the back of the Master Brewer's shop, Sanura curled up between her and the mummy. In brief windows she'd seen him, wearing nothing but his natron flesh, and then even that had been removed. How could she look him in the eyes and pretend nothing had changed? Tomorrow, they would go to Abayomi's tomb and find that gate and she'd be out of there. Undoubtedly she'd never see them again. The thought seemed to trip over itself as Jeannette listened to Sanura breathe.

Chapter 18

JEANNETTE WOKE TO THE DRY HUM OF HER MASTER, and for once it didn't drive her to the mouth of dementia. Squeezing her eyes shut she hoped that his general mellow nature would deflect any freak out he might have at her overnight guests. She rose, attempting to slip away without notice, but Sanura mewed and curled closer to her side. The awkward situation confounded her. She'd never been trapped like this before; she had no sisters to contend with. Legs crossed, Abayomi sat leaning against the wall, his dark eyes on her. He must have slipped apart from them sometime during the night, not even disturbing her.

She looked from Abayomi down to Sanura, tilting her head with her eyebrows bunched in a what-do-I-do-about-this? gesture. He shrugged.

They remained in her room—more storage than anything marked by her personal tastes—Jeannette trapped under a small arm wondering what to tell her master, when he tapped at her thin door. "It is time for you to introduce your friends, Jeannette. Beer waits for no man."

Jeannette huffed. "Yes, Master." She unwrapped Sanura from her body.

A sliver of Sanura's bright eyes peeked at Jeannette. "Is it time to rise?"

Jeannette nodded and Sanura stretched her small body long, the entire process ending with a high 'nrow' that could only be interpreted as pleasure.

Soon, they surrounded a low table, each kneeling on the floor. Jeannette adjusted her cushion and stared into the mug of beer. Back where she came from, she never really drank beer. She'd always been more of a wine person, the bitterness of beer offering little attraction. Taking in a mouthful, she swallowed it down. Here, beer was akin to life.

Jeannette first shared a look with Abayomi, his linens white and eyes glistening, then with Sanura, whose twitching ears showed all the signs of feline interest. Though her facial features were a mystery, Jeannette had learned that those ears told all. Jeannette half-smiled to the Master Brewer, not really sure where to start or how much to actually tell him.

Introductions. She'd start with introductions.

"Master, this is Sanura." Jeannette gestured at the cat-headed girl, then turned to Abayomi. "And this is Abayomi." Then she faced her master. "This is the Master Brewer, who has been kind enough to take me in and share with me the vaulted skill of brewing." She smiled at him, and he offered a half-nod to each in turn.

The Master Brewer gulped down some beer and finished with a hearty smacking of his lips. "Names are not all that define a man," he said, his voice gruff.

Jeannette sighed. "Sanura is a daughter of Bast." *In case you hadn't noticed the cat-head on her shoulders*, she completed to herself. "She was training to be a midwife," Jeannette said uncertainly, and Sanura blinked, twitching a whisker. "And Abayomi is an embalmed, dead man walking." She paused, then remembered. "He used to be a scribe."

Abayomi closed his eyes and shook his head, but didn't interrupt.

The Master Brewer studied each of them, and Jeannette dropped from sitting on her knees to her butt. This wasn't going to be quick. "A scribe and a *mi-nether*, you certainly collect odd friends."

Jeannette began to smile, then noticed the look on his face. Mirthless. Her smile died of abandonment.

"So it seems," she said, waiting for him to reveal whatever it was he was probing for. It felt like one of those moments made eternal by teenage coming of age films where the father grilled the girl about what she'd been up to the night before. Drugs, sex and knocking over the local convenience store all plausible misdeeds.

"I see you managed to wash yourself and the crocodile did not eat you." His tone suggested such a thing would have bothered him little.

"I did some washing." She kept her voice steady and met his eyes. Her friends remained astutely silent.

"It seems there is someone else you haven't introduced me to, yet."

Jeannette dropped her facade of patience. "What are you talking about?" He'd always seemed a little senile. Or maybe she'd contracted a ghost only he could see. An Egyptian haunting, just her luck. The bad sci-fi horror movie plots kept adding up.

"What else might you have tripped on? Jeannette, you walk with your forehead leading you down dark paths and your eyes plastered to the ground." Then her master shook his head. "Re, high in the sky, light this one's way," he said in benediction. Abayomi grunted, and bobbed his head as if amused. Now, Jeannette was really confused.

"Why are you praying for me, old man?" She didn't mean the 'old man,' well, really, she did, but she hadn't meant to say it out loud. He didn't appear to take offense.

"Because, Jeannette, apparently somebody needs to since you don't do it for yourself. A guard has been watching the brewery since the prior evening and he remains there now. Walking the street, but he never strays far. I know I did nothing to earn such esteemed acquaintance."

Her heart took notice of what he said before her brain did. "What do you mean?"

"Just what I said, would you listen? You gather troubles like a goat gathers grass seeds. A guard has been waiting for you. He makes the entire street nervous."

"How do you know he's waiting for me? Maybe there's been a crime and he's waiting for the culprit. Maybe he's just here to protect the citizens. Maybe—"

"Jeannette," he said sharply.

She shut up. Letting her fingers trace her shinbone, guilt turned her bile rancid. She knew she should have just left, but she wanted to say good-bye and she wanted a good night's sleep and she just wanted to not worry about anything for one damned moment.

Honesty stepped forward and whacked her with a clue stick. She'd found comfort in her small life here in Kemet and she didn't want to throw it to the wolves. Too much time had been wasted sitting around, pouting, stuffing her head under the entire dunes of the Sahara. She was more than a little ashamed.

She tugged on her ponytail. It'd grown long enough to chew the end of if she wanted to.

"Jeannette!"

"What? Fine. So, there's a guard." Did she tell him, or would it be better if she didn't? Then, he wouldn't know anything and he wouldn't be in trouble. Stupid, stupid, stupid Jeannette. She shouldn't have come back.

Sanura petted the length of Jeannette's arm until Jeannette stood. The girl looked up at her with those huge, vibrant eyes. Jeannette looked away. With her face hot and chest heavy, she cowered her way to the front of the shop and peeked out to the street. There he stood in his short *shendyt*, spear by his side, right at a juncture between the road and the alley to the well. He didn't look familiar; certainly not the man who'd chased her back in the workers complex. People gave him a wide berth as they passed on the street, eyeing him as if he would strike viper fast.

She returned and said, "I shouldn't tell you why he might be here, but he probably is here because of me." She took a deep breath.

"Master." He held himself motionless, eyes swallowed up by his wrinkled face. "I am leaving." Nothing so much as a twitch. She snorted quietly. Maybe he'd be glad to see her go, but she'd hoped for some kind of reaction . . . sadness maybe? A little nod of understanding. "Not solely because of the guard. I have to do what the oracle said, and help Abayomi and Sanura."

"Good," the Master Brewer said. "About time you dealt with that."

Jeannette frowned. She inspected his face for even a scrap of evidence that he cared. Nothing but lines of age.

"Oh girl, what is that sad face for? The Gods call and you must answer. Stop acting like you're marching off to your own death."

She blinked and exhaled through her nose. Sanura was watching her. Jeannette looked elsewhere, at a red pot that she had no expectations from.

"We will leave immediately. I don't want the guard to get you in trouble."

The Master Brewer barked, a horrid mix of laughter and a snort, and his stoic expression sloughed away. "Jeannette, if you return, you have a place here. I always wondered why you left the oracle's words locked away in your heart's well. Nothing good ever came from ignoring the Gods' words. You must go. Stop with this mourning when you haven't lost a thing."

Sure, nothing. She'd never had a thing in her life to lose, and Kemet held no great promises. "Fine. Good health to you."

Her master looked at her, his squint and frown holding silent words. She wondered what he wanted to say. "Re will watch over you. Have faith in the Gods."

Abayomi dipped his chin, and Sanura nodded, eyes wide.

"You must forgive me if I'm too worldly to put much faith in the gods," she said. "But, thank you nonetheless."

"Even if it's all you have?"

She laughed, scratching at the back of her head. He must know she had more than invisible specters of judgment and pride to rely on. "But Master, you just said it." She grinned. "I have you, and I have Abayomi and Sanura. I will do what I can with the help from those who have already proven their worth." She'd never meant anything to anybody. It was new, this sense of belonging. Sanura reached out and pressed her palm against Jeannette's leg. Her gentle touch brought a calm stability to Jeannette's inner turmoil. She would do what she could for her friends.

He nodded, one sharp motion, and the loose skin under his chin waddled at the force of it. "Good."

Jeannette gathered her pack and the wages she'd earned and with a few good-byes—and blessings from those who put value in prayer—the three left the brewery by the alley door. In silence, Abayomi and Sanura followed Jeannette's lead through the city, streets she'd grown familiar with during her stay in Thebes. People acknowledged her, others hawked produce, enticing them to look at a pile of the freshest cucumbers to be found in the great city. Children climbed sycamore trees near a well. One of them hooted, scratching himself like a monkey. Children's games remained the same through the ages, and apparently through unique universes. Maybe it was simply the imagination that remained consistent.

Before them, beyond the city's boundary, the river cut the world in two, a fluid knife of force and age, beautiful yet brimming with dangers. Tall grasses lined the edge of the marshland—a few putting on seed heads—golden in the light of the rising sun. Their sharp-edged blades brushed together in the soft wind, creating a gentle, rattling tune. Jeannette stopped and looked out at the world spread before her. Abayomi stepped up to her right side, his presence a solid force. Sanura slipped up along her left.

"So, the Sky Watcher oracle told you that we need to find my *ba* and Sanura's reflection? Her, what would you call it, her inner spirit?"

Jeannette watched the distant fishermen throw lines out from their little boats, each 'plunk' creating ripples in the current. "Pretty much."

"Well, I am eager to be reunited with my scarab so I can move on to the Afterworld. Though, I am uncertain who stole it, if it was not you." Abayomi stared at her from the corner of his eye, touching a place at the center of his chest. She readied herself to argue her defense, but he cut off her tirade before she could even present her first scrap of evidence. "And I know that it was not."

"Okay, so what exactly is this scarab thingy? It's not some cockroach that lives under your skin or anything." Enough disgust scorched her words he sighed at her. During his cleaning, she'd found nothing crawling within his flesh, only the pristine layer hiding underneath the old. At his sigh, she struggled to keep her expression neutral but she couldn't quite stop one bubble of the giggle she struggled with. The look he gave her could have soured beer.

"Don't give me that look. I don't know what you're talking about. What is it, exactly, that you're missing? Explain it to me, as if I were a

167

foreigner from a different place and time." She smiled sweetly at him. Sanura coughed, the noise surprisingly close to a chortle if Jeannette was any judge.

With all seriousness, he placed his hand upon his chest; his long fingers fluttered against his wrappings. "This heart, I received it from my mother, it has resided within me since my birth to take my measure as a man. When I go to the underworld, I will be judged by the gathering of Gods. The scarab will restore life to my heart once I have been judged." The conviction in his voice was disturbing. "I await the benu bird to lead me to the underworld. I am still waiting, wondering why it has not yet come. My heart scarab, a carving from the stone of Horus, the deep blue of the evening sky during Shemu, could fit within my cupped palm, and was missing when I awoke. Now my heart might speak out against me if I am to be judged without it, though I strove to live a good life during my living years."

Sparked by his words, she remembered seeing display after display of different little beetle carvings in the museums, fat little guys with things carved into the back or underside. "So, we just find this carving, and that's it? You'll be happy? Complete?"

He squinted, looking off into the distance. "I am unsure. Maybe once the scarab is returned, the benu bird will come. All I know is that I am snared. I am certain that this country is not the Perfect Land. At least, it is not the reward I was taught awaited me."

"I think there are many things we are raised to believe in that are not true." Sanura's eyes were bright, almost glowing in the morning light. Jeannette couldn't believe Sanura would say such a thing. She'd always seemed to have complete confidence that everything would end up full of sweetness and light like all the blindly faithful did. Jeannette wanted to ask, but the daughter of Bast simply looked at her, then turned her head away.

A desire to reach out, gentle whatever pain the girl kept hidden within her almost overtook Jeannette, but she didn't have the casual confidence in such gestures that Sanura did.

As they walked up the river away from the main docks to a place of gathered fisherman, Jeannette considered Sanura's words. Birds filled the air with a cacophony of chitters, taking wing as the three passed a particular thatch of grasses, then landing in the exact same place once they had passed it.

"I think that is just the way life is. Our parents tell us to live well, do as God demands," Jeannette added with a shrug, "to play fair and share. As we get older and try to live within those restrictions, we find those lessons get us nowhere as adults."

Abayomi laughed harshly and stopped in his tracks. He turned to the river and she followed his gaze to the fishermen. "Play fair and share? Your parents were very cruel to tell you such things, Jeannette. Life is not fair. The only thing we can do is live a good life by the Gods and they will allow us into *Yaaru*. It is what we all strive for. A spot in the Fields to live eternally."

Sanura nodded slowly, as if heavy thought gummed up the flex of her cervical vertebrae.

Jeannette opened her mouth, ready to enlighten them about the true existence of gods, but shut it with a snap. They each believed so strongly, she didn't want to waste her breath.

And perhaps she didn't want to break that hope they both held. Sometimes, she wished she had that same staunch fidelity to some code or belief. Those kinds of people always seemed happier than she ever was.

Then, in the distance, a shout hit them from behind, launched from the city they'd just abandoned. They spun around in unison; punching through the city's edge, the guard stationed in the midway of the merchants' zone was running toward them, one arm holding the length of his spear to his side as his legs pumped in fury.

Abayomi grabbed each of the women's hands and leapt down the hill toward the docks. Jeannette twisted her wrist, reversing her grip so she held his hand and tugged him towards a reed canoe on the far end of the gathered fishermen. He surrendered to her pull and let her lead as panic and fervent wishes alternately raced throughout her body.

A man wearing a black sash and short kilt stood by the canoe, watching them. Jeannette couldn't believe her luck.

"Nekhebu! Please, take us down the river. Please," Jeannette pleaded, sending sharp glances over her shoulder.

Nekhebu did nothing. Gripping a fishing pole in one hand, his eyebrows bunched together and one side of his mouth tilted up. He didn't throw aside his pole, or jump into action like her frantic tone suggested he must. He'd seemed a little slow before, now she wanted to whack him across the head for this shortcoming.

"I cannot fit all of you in my boat." His eyes surveyed the odd assemblage. "Why are you in such a rush? I just returned with my morning catch." A flood of fish swamped one end of the little boat.

169

Three Great Lies

"Please, Nekhebu. I did nothing wrong, but a guard, he is after me." She swallowed, glanced over her shoulder again, but the guard hadn't appeared over the little rise yet. She turned back to the fisherman. Damn, there was no way he would help. If he was smart, he would turn them away. "And," she swallowed, "right now, I have little to pay you with, but you can have it all. Nothing compared to what your help is worth. But, you will be saving my life and I will be eternally grateful."

The other fishermen within earshot stopped their tasks.

"Guard?" Nekhebu suddenly became twitchy, scanning the riverside up along the slope toward the city. "I shouldn't get involved," he said with an urgent shake to his head.

Jeannette grabbed his arms. He looked down at where their bodies connected as if uncertain he should allow such an intimacy with a stranger. A cry from the direction of the city caused her fingers to tighten. Behind her Abayomi said her name slow and low, scolding, or warning, she wasn't sure.

"Nekhebu," she said dropping her volume. The audience they'd gathered leaned towards them. "I know the guards are involved in tomb robbing. I know it. They know I know it. They will kill me if they catch me." Then, a flash of intuition punched her in the gut. "They are probably the ones who framed your brother."

Nekhebu stared at her, dumb and lost, and then comprehension lit his eyes, twisting his weathered face into a mass of resentment. He snatched his arms away.

"I will believe you, foreigner. I will trust you, by Hapi's promise of the inundation, I will. But, you will never again ask such a thing of me. Never. Now, get in."

Jeannette scampered into the little boat, unsuccessfully kicking fish out of the way; Sanura sat on her lap, and Abayomi climbed in behind her. Fish tainted water soaked her pants. The boat was so cramped, she had to lean into Abayomi, her backpack pressed against his chest. Her body had grown stiff with tension while the guard called out, his voice growing with each passing second. Abayomi wrapped his arms around her and Sanura. In her ear he whispered, "Relax, Jeannette, we are in the Gods' hands now.

But she couldn't relax. Even as they pushed out into the river, ensnared by the unbridled current, even as the distance between her and the guard expanded, her fingers dug into the reed boat's side. Then she leaned over one side, sending the boat to rocking, splashing her hands through the water, paddling with her ineffectual makeshift oars. Nekhebu would get in trouble. Her master would get in trouble. The guards would be relentless. Why had she even come back? Selfish, selfish, selfish. She wanted to bang her head against a rock, then maybe she'd get a clue. She'd been blind and selfish, working harder to avoid acknowledging her situation than at any other task she'd chosen to undertake.

"You cannot flee us!" came the faded words. "You're actions prove your guilt. You will be punished for your crimes against Pharaoh!"

Jeannette didn't turn and look for the guard, to face his false accusations. Exhausted, she hunkered down against Abayomi, his surprisingly strong arms combined with the warmth from Sanura sapping some of the anxiety from her like a slow drip from a tree. She realized she had treated this entire interlude as an extended tour to a wondrous land, even with its hardships. Not as a displaced expatriate, not as a stranger in a dangerous world. Not with open eyes.

The guard eventually stopped yelling, but she still didn't look back. Instead, she closed her eyes against the brightness of the sun and wished she'd filled up her water bottle before they'd set off. The flow of the river carried them away, removing her from immediate danger. But she'd got someone else involved again. She owed Nekhebu. Though she'd tried to be a conscientious person, she had still put someone else at risk. She didn't want to look at her companions or the flat, busy river surrounding her. She envisioned Spokane with pine forests, automobiles and cloudy skies. The memory of rain and snow and coffee stands bringing with it its own melancholy.

As the journey along the river stretched into hours as measured by the steady march of the sun, she half listened to the other three talking about Abayomi's magical scarab and where it could possibly be. Nekhebu talked about tomb thieves and where they might stash their goods. That seemed like the simple part of this crusade. The scarab was an object, something to hold, something capable of being found. Solving Sanura's portion of this quest comprised a completely different cluster of problems.

Finally, her exhaustion, and the rocking and the quiet murmurs, lulled her into a fitful doze filled with evil men hurtling spears and the heads of baboons at her, and the only way home was through death.

171

Chapter 19

HOURS PASSED GLIDING ON THE GLITTERING SURFACE OF THE *ITERU*. Jeannette's jaw popped on a demanding yawn. Something slipped underneath her back; a heap of fish did not provide a comfortable seat. This mighty river, the longest in the world, cut through the desert with gentle curves, its banks lined with temples and shrines to beloved gods. Crocodiles also held their revered place. Nekhebu expertly sailed far away from their promise of death.

For a time, a flock of small geese escorted them downriver, honking to themselves until they paddled to the bank and watched as the little boat floated away. Jeannette missed them once they'd parted; around her, everything held its breath, the splash of the oar and murmur of the water against the boat's prow the only sound.

Having passed the time in a meditative half sleep, Nekhebu's harsh, "We have arrived," cut short her mental vacation. He climbed from the boat and pulled it through clumps of papyrus onto the bank. Their passing disturbed a black cloud of gnats. Jeannette held her breath and set her eyes at a squint.

Once again, she smelled like fish. And she'd just been clean. Sanura laughed, and mumbled something about the rich scent and rumbling stomachs. Jeannette tried not to feel totally defeated.

Abayomi and Nekhebu stood on the bank, discussing something apparently important if all the hand waving was anything to judge by. Nekhebu shook his head. The dark skinned man and white mummy contrasted against each other, framed within the backdrop of the smooth, muddy shore. No docks lined this part of the bank, in fact Nekhebu had mired the little canoe away from any settlement.

No guards held them at spear point, either.

Above them, the sun had scorched all color from the sky. Though she had a good tan, the skin of her face felt tight, and she knew she'd probably be as pink as a baboon's butt by tomorrow. She licked her lips.

With Sanura by her side, they approached the men.

". . . guards. Yes, they were involved. I'm sure of it. They accused my brother of taking pottery and gilded statues. He lived the life of a fisherman; he had no want for such luxuries. They killed him for their own treachery!" Spittle coated Nekhebu's bottom lip.

172

"What?" Jeannette had to have heard wrong. It had seemed such a distant possibility. "He's dead?"

Nekhebu sprang on her, his typically dull face twisted with rage. "He is dead. They sliced his head from his body! My brother. My brother is no more." With a force of its own, Jeannette fell away from the power of his anger, his pain. "His children have nothing. No home but my own small hovel. And those—" he thrust his finger toward Thebes, "—cursed men did this to us. Tore our family to shreds."

The fury of a madman swirled in the whites of his eyes. It came back to her, all at once, that if the thieves had enough power, she too would have her head sliced from her body, adding to a basket of like heads, all thinking 'Where did I go wrong?' in that last split second of consciousness before the electrical signals realized the pathway had been severed.

Though she knew it was more than a little silly to hang the fate of her life on action dramas, it was an incontrovertible fact that any innocent hero had but two choices: run and save her butt, or face her accusers. The first option meant she'd have to hide from the tomb robbers and the guards, because she couldn't distinguish one from the other. Anyone in authority could be in on it. Trust no one. Well, except for Abayomi and Sanura. Or, she could confront them. Find a way to publicly prove her innocence and get the dirt on those rat bastards. Yeah, right. Fat chance there. Thankfully, she only needed enough time to complete her oracle requirements: Abayomi's heart scarab and Sanura's soul searching.

Damn.

She spared a thought to Gabby and what she would do in Jeannette's situation. Then she dismissed any effort needed to unravel that what-if scenario. Gabby would have never gotten in this situation; the woman led a charmed life. If Jeannette's friend wanted it, it was hers—lickity split—until she no longer wanted it anymore. No, Gabby would have smiled at the guard and he'd have offered her wine or grapes or a ride home on his pet dragon. That's what would have happened to Gabby. Jeannette, well, she didn't have such luck.

"Nekhebu, I'm so sorry that they killed your brother. I hope from my heart that Anubis watches over him, that Ma'at finds the truth." Jeannette felt a pit of fire burn in her belly. None of this was fair.

Nekhebu clenched and unclenched his fists, darting his gaze from left and right. He needed a better job to support his double-sized family. He needed justice. "I'm going back," he said. Jeannette faced him and bowed deeply.

"Nekhebu, I must thank you from the bottom of my heart. You saved me in a moment when I had no other options. I owe you much." She began rummaging in her backpack, searching for the little package bound with pliable leaves. Having learned her lesson, she didn't offer the ankh necklace. "Right now I've little to give you, but this—" She held out the small bundle. "Please, take it." Nekhebu took it, and unwrapped the little pyramid of wax she'd bought only yesterday. "Your wife might enjoy it. And," she charged on after finding what she was scrounging for, holding out her hand, "take this. I promise you more." She dropped her few copper debens and a silver kit into his open palm. "If I can, and I am not gone from this place, I will pay you more for this great thing you did for me and my friends. I am forever in your debt." She bowed at the waist, words useless in her deep regard for the poor fisherman.

"Those are evil men you run from, Jeannette." Nekhebu's previous dimness had gone. "If you survive, I will welcome your gifts."

With little else to say, he returned to his boat and began the toil of his upriver journey.

By the time they began walking to the city of Montu's Temple, the sun had embarked on its solar pathway to the opposite horizon. Sanura led them through tall, wiry grasses that stung Jeannette's arms until they reached bared farmland and hiked to the developed edge of the city on a path lined with chasms for ruts. Placing her feet with delicate care, Sanura picked her way along the churned soil of the central mound. Not so graceful, Abayomi and Jeannette each took a side rut and followed in her wake.

The city, stirring after the heat of the day had dipped, was no different than what she remembered of her first night in this mythical world, though it had somehow diminished. Had grown smaller, or duller, or less fantastic in her absence. Maybe the masses of people no longer alarmed her. Or the strange dress. The dry taste to the air. She was a little surprised the slaver wasn't there to greet her, or the artifact thieves, or maybe even somebody else she'd unwittingly pissed off along the way. Each one would be eager to scold her, threaten her, try to kill her. Danger skulked behind every corner, where before there had been a world full of fresh new experiences, endless possibilities—even if she hadn't treated them that way. Now that optimism was dashed by the hard knowledge that this world would never run by the same, expected rules of her fair and orderly one.

What would she do if the guard found her this far down the river? She didn't want to die a headless death. Or any death at all. This wasn't a good place for her life to meet its end.

Hands lifted in a half-reach nearly touching the others, she kept close to her friends, following behind with vigilance, scanning the crowd for the myriad threats that hid amidst the everyday people of this ancient place. Though no monsters popped into existence right at her feet, ready to chase her down, pin her to the ground with the copper head of a short spear, she didn't discount their existence, hidden in waiting like ninja.

Instead people carried baskets; naked children giggled, sprinting together in a mob, trapped in some vital contest beyond the ken of adults; men in robes or long *shendyt*, carried rolled scrolls, noses up in the air. A man passed, tugging on a reluctant donkey, and Jeannette couldn't help shouting, "Bribery of grass always worked for me."

The man nodded at her, and waved in thanks.

The place, known to her simply for its mortuary hill and magical cow, seemed so organized now, so tidy compared to the sprawl of Thebes.

"Let us go to my tomb first and see what we can discover." Abayomi was already steering the three towards the hill of ancient tombs. With his back straight, his gait consumed the ground.

Sanura trotted up to him and slipped her hand into his, then grabbed Jeannette's. Jeannette squeezed her hand, and Sanura squeezed back. Together they trudged up the hill, leaving the merchants and homes and temples behind, slipping between the people, blending in with the impetus of someone with a price on her head. A few black jackals patrolled the streets, sniffing at ankles and then trotting on.

A pair of women, arms laden with fruit and vegetables, entered a tomb downhill from Abayomi's. As ancient and defenseless as these tombs were, people still paid homage to their beloved dead, feeding their *ka*. Keeping the spirits alive.

Finally, the twin columns guarding the open mouth of Abayomi's Old Kingdom styled tomb posed before them. The mummy stood as stoically as the Colossi. A flash of memory hit Jeannette: the supports leaning at cockeyed angles, the signs of millennium of sand nibbles wearing away the carvings' details. The layers of dust, the fine paintings. The eye that watched her within the sarcophagus chamber. Her first meeting with Abayomi as he hunted her down like a persistent nightmare.

"Is this a family mastaba?" Sanura asked, pulling Jeannette back to the present.

Abayomi nodded. "Yes, my family were scribes for the Temple for generations."

"What did you do as a scribe?" Jeannette asked. Maybe he took notes, like a secretary for the local rotary club.

Abayomi puffed his meager chest out with pride. "I am trained in all forms of writing and arithmetic. I was in charge of recording the cattle brought in to the Temple, and who had owned them."

"Really? That's it?" She wondered if he'd be at all impressed if he understood the amount of schooling she'd gathered up like playing cards. *I've got one BS in Biology, a handful of minors, and I'll raise you complete literacy.* She almost told him—maybe he'd be impressed—but he turned sharply on her.

"There were many cattle brought in. I also traveled to the farms to assess the landowners' value in cattle before each inundation."

She nodded quickly, widening her eyes to show just how much he dazzled her. "Oh, of course." She didn't want to anger him right now, didn't want him to leave her. She just wanted them all to get along. "It would be a lot of work."

His gaze lingered on her. As if accepting her reaction as honest-to-goodness awe, he nodded. Then he turned and faced the opening to his eternal place of rest.

Subtly, a junky's spasm invaded his hands proving his calm false as he placed a foot down with utmost care to mount the steps leading to the entrance. A few passing people, *mi-nether* and human, watched them with craning necks; Jeannette acknowledged them with a nod as she and Sanura followed their friend. Abayomi crossed the threshold between the two large columns, muttering something about Ammut and hoping his heart was not already eaten. Amun's name fluttered from those same desperate lips, as well as an array of other gods whose natures she knew little about.

He was drowning, she could see that—drowning in a possible future of eternity in limbo. His faith made real his damnation through a lifetime of supplication and the sacred words of texts. That very truth flowed in and out of him like his renewed breath. Right now, she saw a condemned man hoping and praying for his own salvation. Hoping and praying that he would find what he desperately sought.

He was as lost as she was.

Meeting Sanura's eyes, Jeannette tilted her head towards Abayomi. Sanura blinked her slow blink, then offered Jeannette a slight nod. In unison they moved, and two strides later they stood behind him. Though her memories were fuzzy and tainted with the panic of the moment, Jeannette didn't remember seeing much in the tomb when she'd first fallen down the tomb shaft. Her impression had been of something unfinished, and as they stepped into the flickering firelight of the mastaba, the place still bore the feel of emptiness through careless abandonment.

Those same inexplicably lit torches lined the stairway, casting everything in dancing shadow and light, and Jeannette boosted up Sanura—a tiny wisp of a thing—to jiggle one loose from its sconce. The girl's eyes reflected green. They moved silently through the tomb like visiting ghosts, their presence a passing sigh across the walls and floors that would withstand the ages. Surrounding them marched the sanguine scenes of the mundane lives of ancient Egyptians, happy in their duty, joyful in their lives. Finally they descended into the burial chamber. Abayomi stretched his legs in long strides, abandoning his half-lumber, and approached his large sarcophagus. Bending at the waist, he searched the inside, the sound of his hands sliding along the walls and corners mixed with curses of failure.

"Here." Jeannette handed over the torch. He snatched it from her and pushed it down into the sarcophagus, casting the tricky light into every corner of the square container, revealing nothing more than the wooden coffin within. The flames licked at the edges of his wrappings and Jeannette tensed, ready to push him to the floor and roll him around like the educators in elementary school had taught her if he flared up like a Roman candle.

"I don't see anything. Even my canopic jars are missing." A small shelf above the sarcophagus stood empty. He slumped against the colorful brick wall and propped his head up against it with a bump. He groaned, low and mournful, a sound edged with a sob of desperation. Jeannette had never quite appreciated Abayomi's personal horror until right then. That sound laid it all out for her, plain and bare and open for all to see.

"Well, what do we do now?" she asked.

"It must be tomb robbers, even here down the river." His words snapped like frozen rose petals that fell to the ground and shattered on the stones. "Even with the curse of the Gods upon them, they still took from my tomb!"

Jeannette hoped Sanura would have an answer. She was *mi-nether* after all, the daughter of a goddess. Jeannette acknowledged that she'd already accepted mummies and oracles, tomb robbers and animal-headed people. If these unreal aspects of this *otherworld* barely caused her pause, accepting Sanura's divine blood should be an easy step. If the preserved dead walked, why couldn't gods as well? Science proved none of it. But apparently, here in this lost land, science didn't reign. Jeannette just had to toss away her obstinacy. Not an easy task, but one she wouldn't let defeat her.

Somewhere along her journey she didn't think this place a lie anymore.

But Sanura said nothing, simply watched Abayomi, her hands grasped in front of her, her chin dipped, almost resting against her chest as in silent prayer.

"Oh come on," Jeannette found herself saying before she could kill her forced optimism. Abayomi looked so beaten, she had to try something. "We'll find your scarab; it can't be that hard. We just need to find out where these thieves keep their loot. And then you'll have it back and . . ." Jeannette waved her hand through the air, ". . . you can do whatever it is you do when you have it. You can go to your Afterworld, meet your final rewards." She smiled at him, nodding.

His posture didn't change. He'd always been the positive one; it was a new and distasteful challenge to deal with this sullen Abayomi. She wanted to do something, though all she could offer was a four course meal of empty promises.

"Well, we need somewhere to stay tonight, a warm, clean place. I'll find one. Maybe another brewer will put us up."

She turned and headed for the lit stairway.

"Wait!"

Jeannette stopped; Sanura stared up from the corner she'd bee-lined for once they'd walked into the sarcophagus chamber.

"Did you want to come?" Jeannette asked.

Sanura, eyes wide and shimmering in the torch light, shook her head. Her palm was pressed flat to the wall behind her, obscuring what appeared to be three individuals near the bottom of a larger mural. Jeannette tried to remember the painting in that corner, but her first visit to the tomb had been dusted with a thin coating of psychosis that had obscured the fine details. The scene merged together with the other images of that section of the wall: men farming, scribes sitting in lines taking down unknown records, hunters stalking waterfowl with spears and nets. But it wasn't a picture showing some duty or activity. Jeannette stepped forward; Sanura shifted, lowered her hand to uncover the scene, and dropped down on her heels.

The intimate scene painted in the corner almost looked smuggled into the surrounding picture like a last minute addition. Jeannette's eyes roamed over the painting: Osiris faced Bast, who stood a head taller than the mummified god. Behind Bast was painted an Egyptian woman in a white *kalasiris* with a jug at her feet and her hair pulled back into a ponytail—a style Jeannette had never seen in any of her previous research.

Jeannette couldn't take her eyes off it. The clay pot at the woman's feet was of the same flask shape as the ones she brewed beer in.

"That woman," Jeannette pointed at the scene shadowed in the poor light, "the one with Bast and Osiris. That seems familiar, but unusual. Have you ever seen someone painted like that? With her hair . . . ?" Jeannette self-consciously reached up and brushed down the length of her own ponytail.

"That is not Osiris." Sanura's normally lyrical voice sank like a stone to the floor of the small room. "He does not wear the crown, nor wield the crook and flail."

Abayomi reached out and ran his fingers along the image, caressing the bandaged arms and legs, the flat palette the man held in his crossed arms along with a long brush. "His skin is not green."

A golden archway waited behind them, the lack of proper perspective in Egyptian art making it appear to hover over the figures' heads. A giant snake curled up at the base of it. And flapping between the back of Bast's head and the woman's face was a small falcon, feathers colored vibrant blue, with the head of a man. A *ba*.

Running his fingers from the mummy to the arch, Abayomi said, "That must be the way to the Hall of Ma'at."

"No, I bet it's that gate, to the doorway back to my world." Jeannette had already reached her own conclusions, excitement causing her to spout the topmost thing on her mind. Just like the oracle had said: In Abayomi's tomb would be the gate to take her back home. She paused, her hand hanging in mid-reach for the gate. Or maybe it was the mirror to capture Sanura's true reflection. "Come on, let's all touch it at once."

"Jeannette, I do not think it will be so simple," Sanura said, though she did touch the two-dimensional passage with her small hand. Jeannette grabbed Abayomi's hand and forced it against the golden gate, letting her own fingers find their place within the small opening.

Nothing happened.

179

She dropped Abayomi's hand, staring at the images, trying to force inspiration with the sheer power of her glare. Her throat closed off.

"No, the oracle said something about naming our enemy. We must name our enemy to open the gate. Is that giant snake the enemy? Like Apophis or something?"

Abayomi shook his head. "Apep."

The giant snake's coils seemed to shift, the lighting causing the snakeskin to slide and shimmer. Jeannette's breath caught and she leaned forward, pulled forward by anticipation.

The torch flickered, then the snake went still.

"There are *still* two portions of your prophecy," Sanura said gently. "I was afraid you would see this and take such action prematurely. I was worried it would dispirit you."

Jeannette looked away, then nodded. It was a stupid idea. There were still Abayomi's and Sanura's missions to complete. Stupid and selfish.

She sniffed and then sighed. At least her promise to compensate Nekhebu wouldn't be another false jumble of words. Turning back to Sanura, she smiled. "Well, at least we know where to come back to, right? When we have finished the other two jobs." She tried to chuckle, but her throat was too dry. "It's us, isn't it?" She nodded towards the three painted people. "That's a painting of us."

"It would appear so," Abayomi said. "And my *ba*. That must be my *ba*."

Jeannette patted him on the shoulder, and then a scuffing noise behind her tore her attention away. She twisted around; a dance of flame-light fought with the splash of light from the torches lining the stairway.

"Someone's coming," Sanura said. "Perhaps it is your family, Abayomi."

A voice boomed from the top of the stairs. "You! Slave thief!" Bursting from the meager light like a cavalry commander on charge, the Slave Master stormed forward, a jackal-headed guard on either side of him. "Take the woman and the child of Bast. Do not let them escape!"

Part 3: The Ishvara

A Beautiful Thing is Never Perfect

Chapter 20

THE *MI-NETHER* GUARDS PROWLED into the sarcophagus chamber. The torch flame glimmered off the bronze leaves plating their leather tunics, giving them a sense of shifting movement. Elongated teeth flashed in the uneven light and their long ears were pulled back—dogs on the hunt— while the fat slaver blocked any escape at the top of the stairs. Three against three.

She knew—vaguely—these dark passages within Abayomi's family mastaba. She'd been lost here once before, and after a person had lost herself in a place once, it was always easier to navigate the second time around. It was practically a law of nature.

Jeannette grabbed Sanura's wrist, her cry of "Come on!" to Abayomi reverberating off the tomb walls as she pulled the girl around the open sarcophagus and down the passage that led into the depths of the tomb. She tossed away the torch, leaving the sputtering light behind. Blindness set upon her, but at least the guards no longer had a beacon to follow.

"Please. This is my tomb. I do not mind them there." Abayomi's voice faded as she ditched the scene like the guilty.

"One is property, the other the thief—" The fat slaver's voice disappeared under foot stomps pounding against the floor. They echoed within the empty chambers, chased them around each corner, down every hall, even as her own feet barely made a noise. Sanura, beside her, was a silent spirit.

Abayomi was trying to save them. Before, back when she'd freed Sanura, he'd proven himself quite the efficient fellow. Maybe he'd deliver them from this hairy situation too. Maybe. To be sure, she wasn't going to sit back and wait for divine intervention. No easy target: that was her motto. If the mini-gods couldn't catch them, all the better. Unfortunately, instinct insisted that the slaver wouldn't be so easily duped a second time, and mastabas weren't built with back doors.

One hand trailing along the wall, Jeannette wove deeper into the warren of sun dried mud blocks. Rough walls scraped against her fingertips, catching on her jagged nails, giving way whenever they reached a recess or side passage. Stubborn and frightened and desperate, Jeannette refused to face that she only prolonged the dark inevitable. If luck smiled its happy face upon her, she could possibly hide in one dead end, have them pass by and backtrack the way they'd come. But the slave master . . . could even she and Abayomi together overpower him? Perhaps Jeannette could hide Sanura in an empty sarcophagus and have them chase her. She'd be alone, but at least Sanura wouldn't be captured, subjugated, humiliated.

She couldn't hear Abayomi behind them and she wasn't sure if he was even there.

Her breaths came fast—not from exertion alone. Darting around one corner, Jeannette halted along the wall, pushing Sanura behind her, away from the door. Both of them molded themselves against the wall, flat and motionless like geckos under the shadow of a passing falcon. Jeannette turned her face toward the door, ready, eyes night-blind-wide and ears straining at the nothing surrounding her.

She couldn't catch her breath; holding one hand over her mouth and nose, she attempted to stifle the sound. Thunder rampaged through her head, hammered within her ears. The animal-headed men charged through the slim hallways, raging lions set loose in the Coliseum, not even attempting stealth. Unfortunately, she couldn't quite place them within any mental map of the place. And admittedly, she was just as lost on that same incomplete, mental topography.

"You cannot hide within the tomb, thief! There is no other way out." The words were followed by a sharp, yipping laughter. Filthy jackals. "You smell of the docks!"

Sanura gripped Jeannette's shirt, wrapping the fabric up within her small hands. Jeannette gently touched her head, right between the ears.

A faint glow highlighted the opening of the chamber they hid in; the light grew in strength.

She squeezed Sanura's hand and whispered, "Ready?"

Sanura squeezed in response.

Like approaching headlights on a deserted forest highway, the torchlight filled the small hallway. The two guards jogged past, their pace unhurried. The rumble of double stomping faded with the light as they traveled down the hallway. When the light turned feeble, Jeannette darted out into the passage, sprinting back towards her memory of the entrance.

"There they are!" came the cry from behind. With a glance over her shoulder she saw a *mi-nether* halfway down the hall, nose in the air, the other just returning around a corner. Damn. Her silly, simple, stupid ruse hadn't worked. It would have worked on television, she thought stubbornly. But things were never that easy in the real world.

183

THREE GREAT LIES

Before they had run more than six steps, a guard snatched up Sanura, the girl's piercing wail ripping Jeannette's bitter frustration into tattered shreds of panic. The girl slapped at the guard, fingers curled into a claw. Yowl after yowl rained spit on the jackal's snout, open and laughing with scornful amusement. Then the other guard grabbed Sanura by the middle and wrapped her tight into a single-armed hold. She writhed like a snake, twisting and turning like only the young and cat-spined can. Teeth bared, she looked mad, a frenzied beast.

All this Jeannette absorbed in seconds. The capture, the jackal's open-mouthed laugh, her friend's struggle. No bright ideas lit the way. No hero swooped in. So Jeannette charged the *mi-nether* guard. Shoulder leading her way, she rammed the less protected gap under his arm. The light swam as his torch dropped to the ground and he oofed out his breath. Sanura twisted and for one magical instant Jeannette felt her heart lift, the girl would get free, then the guard grasped Sanura with both arms as the other lackey scooped up Jeannette. Jerking, using all her weight, Jeannette tried to tug away. Her hair came loose from the deteriorating rubber band, blinding her with shifting chains of brown. The guard wrenched her back into his grasp. With a twist and a dip—a sadistic dance of foes—he yanked her arm and locked it behind her back. A shocking spike, sharp and burning, pierced her shoulder. Swinging around her other arm, she clawed at his eyes, small targets on his canine face, but he grabbed her and ground her wrist bones together. She couldn't stop the scream, couldn't stop the panic. Gasping, long strands of her hair sucked into her mouth, down her throat, forcing her over as she gagged; heart racing, she failed to quell the tears.

All sensation now filtered through her ears, Jeannette heard Sanura hiss, heard her curse and call down the wrath of her mother. Jeannette flicked her tongue along the roof of her mouth, trying to dislodge her hair. She could hear their sandals scraping against the floor, the collective breathing, the raging desperation. The girl, half the size of the adult men, attacked them with her bare hands while Jeannette fused her feet into the ground—a dead weight—and struggled to spit out hair.

"Please, just let us go." She panted for breath, swallowed down air and bombarded them with pitiful pleas. "I've been working hard. At a brewery. I'm making the beer better. Its texture and flavor. People love it." Long, slick strands of wet hair clung to her cheeks. "They buy it by the jar full. I can pay . . ." she gasped, ". . . for Sanura. She can pay, too." In sucked another breath. "She's been working in a laundry. Just let us go.

184

We'll work hard for your Master. He'll be a richer man for our cooperation . . ."

The *mi-nether* guard grabbed Jeannette by her traitorous hair and drew her head back. In one swift motion, he slapped her across the cheek. She stared at him, shocked into silence. The sting soaked into the entire left side of her face and she could taste the tang of blood.

"Hold your tongue, woman. We are tomb guards. You've trespassed within the inner chambers and desecrated the sanctity of this resting place." His canines gleamed yellow in the sputtering torchlight.

Bull. She knew they were the Master Slaver's lackeys. She opened her mouth to challenge his lie, but his raised hand cowed her and she dropped her gaze to catch her mutated reflection on the bronze scales. "But Abayomi didn't mind. We were with him!"

The two guards man-handled the women through the passages of Abayomi's tomb; Sanura continued her writhing struggle while Jeannette slumped along like a defeated soldier. The beautiful paintings flowed by her, the stories they told no longer catching her eye. A doorway approached and Jeannette wrapped her fingers around the passage's edge, feeling the coarse texture of the bricks; her fingers had gone feeble and the effort proved pointless. She desperately tried to come up with a getaway plan. Everything involved superpowers, a Colt .45, or a small, personal militia. She'd never been good with reasonable solutions on the fly. The slavers had them, possibly a less disastrous situation than being caught by the tomb robbers. With the slavers she was a commodity. Her skin had gone clammy and the guard had to readjust his control of her arm. At least she'd been able to swat the hair off her face, though it kept dropping in her eyes like misbehaving vines, or perhaps her hair was being merciful, veiling her from her failure. The burning in her shoulder had smoldered to a low ache. Jeannette couldn't look at his face, that leering, canine grin taking her back to those wicked childhood nursery stories. My, what big teeth you have. The better to chew your arm from your body if you try to break free, my dear.

At the entrance of the tomb, a huge black shadow waited.

"You've retrieved my merchandise," the man offered a low chuckle, and goosebumps flooded Jeannette's arms, "and the thief. I thank you."

"Of course, Master. It is our duty as tomb guardians," said the wicked jackal-headed man holding Sanura.

"Still," the man stepped outside, and the two women were pushed after him onto the open street, "you will be richly compensated." The sun

185

no longer ruled the sky, but the air roasted them like popcorn compared to the cool inner tomb.

The jackal-headed man who held Jeannette nodded once. His teeth and tongue were showing; Jeannette wondered if that was a smile, if the man was pleased with himself for his filthy deed.

"Where's Abayomi?" Jeannette asked, looking around for her dead friend. "What did you do to him?"

"He moved on once I told him he held no power to protect either of you. I do recognize the sanctity of his house of rest," the Master Slaver dipped his head, "and so, we shall all move on from the mortuary hill. And put right this matter of your crime." A self-satisfied smile twisted his lips into a leer and his black eyes fixed on Jeannette as though she were a ripe fruit to pluck.

"You're stupid and you're wrong." Jeannette's whine barely pierced the noise of the street.

The Master Slaver laughed again, a deep, amused sound that came straight from the barrel of his gut.

"I uphold the rules of Pharaoh, little woman, and the Gods. It is you, you and your foreign ways and thoughtless actions, who are wrong." He jerked his layers of chins at the guards. "Take her to the jail to be judged and the daughter of Bast to the pens."

"No!" Jeannette screamed, pulling her already raw and abused arm. "You capture us, simple visitors to a tomb, but you let thieves inside to take the things from Abayomi's mastaba." She lifted her heel and slammed it into the shin of the guard holding her.

"Filthy swineherd!" A hard punch smashed into her kidney and she crumbled under the force of the guard's blow. "Your dog's tail will never straighten." Here, in the great land of the pharaoh, her body had become a punching bag.

Really and truly, she held no power.

In action shows people got pummeled and still stood on their own two feet, unfaltering under the onslaught of blows. Jeannette wanted to cry foul and demand realism. Her side ached, her shoulder ached, her face ached, fear clogged her throat and a snake-sized worm of panic cinched her breaths into shallow, frantic things. She didn't want to struggle anymore, to force the man to hit her again. This didn't happen on Friday night dramas. A single blow felled nobody on television.

With little fight left in either of them, she and Sanura were dragged through the streets by the two jackal-headed guards. Once off the mortuary hill, slipping into the hubbub of the city, watchful eyes from a cornucopia of faces followed them as she scrambled to keep up with the pace of her captor. Men and women, human and *mi-nether*. She was a side show. Jeannette wanted to scream out, to beg these silent witnesses to help, but she knew freedom would not be found from these people who believed wholly in the law of the pharaoh. This place wasn't her home. She didn't belong and each one of them knew it.

Hiding her face with the veil of her hair, she watched her feet. Just another woman being dragged away by *mi-nether* guards. She wanted to avoid the detection of those other guards, the ones willing to risk their souls for profit. They could buy her, or steal her, then kill her for her silence. Slavery or death. It wasn't an equal equation. She could always run away from slavery.

Death was the last grand finale.

She glanced around, searching the crowd. Unless you were a mummified man, then perhaps you got an encore.

Without an obvious rescue pending from Abayomi, she realized she had to wait, and when the moment came, act quickly and silently.

One guard took Sanura down a wide side road, and Jeannette refused to stop calling out to her, Sanura's name only dying on her lips once the girl disappeared within the shifting crowd.

Where had Abayomi gone? People everywhere, and not one mummy amidst the crowd.

Soon, stripped of her pack and dignity, Jeannette was tossed into a small, brick cell through a door so low a dwarf would have whacked his head entering it. She stumbled with the force of the guard's push, dropping to the floor and skinning her palms and a knee on the uneven, stone slab floor. A flash of pain shot up her arm to her shoulder. A sob threatened to dam her throat. The cell was smaller than the bathroom in her apartment back home and had no ceiling. Short bars of smooth wood covered the hole above her head and made up the door that aimed towards a central walkway lined with similar little cells. The guard pushed the door closed and slipped a rectangular crossbar through two mounts on either side of the door. He left without another word.

Nobody else wandered the grounds of the jail. Everyone was locked away.

Sanura was gone; the other guard had taken her, probably to the slaver's market. Jeannette's imagination supplied her with a thousand possible abuses the girl could be going through at that moment. Her fear for herself dried up on the vine; instead, inside she seethed.

Wrapping her hands around the vertical wooden poles, she frantically jerked this way and that, like a tweaker at a rave club trapped within some repetitive beat. "Let me out!" she screamed in frustration.

"Stop your yelling. Your fate has been written, live with it," said a tired voice from someone nearby.

"Bull," she muttered, trying to slide the crossbar off whatever fixed it in place and monumentally failing. It held firmly. She only managed to break off a fingernail, tearing into the flesh of her finger. A drop of pain that lost itself in an ocean of it. The bar must be anchored to the wall somehow, she thought, her mind working itself into a froth. On the opposite cell, she could see the ends of that crossbar completely enclosed by gray brick. She took a breath and scanned everything, examining her miniscule world for that one clue that would ignite her brain into finding an escape route.

In the cell across from hers sat caged a bald man with blue skin and heavy eyeliner. Though striped by the overhead bar's shadows, his color came through as truly blue, not the kind of hypothermia-blue old men fishing on frozen lakes tended to develop, but bright blue like the egg of a robin. A man-sized Smurf. His legs were crossed into a pretzel only yoga masters could attain, and he sat with his back straight and features relaxed. In the air before him he held up one hand, the thumb and forefinger circled together to form a window between them. He appeared to be meditating with his eyes open just a crack.

Definitely weird. Maybe he was touched by the gods. Or maybe he aspired to be just like Violet, the world-record gum chewer who found the golden ticket.

She needed a golden ticket out of this place.

"Hey, you." She leaned into the wooden bars. "I really need to get out of here. You see, I didn't do anything wrong. Do you know a way out? Which guards to bribe? My friend needs me."

"She does indeed," the man said. Or didn't. Jeannette wasn't sure because his lips did not move.

Nearby a donkey brayed.

Was this another of those weird fever dreams? Her cell *was* stiflingly hot. The voice of an oracle? But no incense filled the air or muddled her mind.

Jeannette stared at the man. Before, she'd never believed in horoscopes or palm reading or the significance of the pattern of the stars at her birth. They were just a twist of supposed wisdom that could either be brushed aside without a single thought, or could tell you exactly what you wanted to hear. She wasn't a fool; she didn't like to be duped. Most people's considerations anchored only onto themselves, and if telling a little lie padded their pockets with some extra cash, then no sweat. Today is March fifth and if you wear red you'll find love, have success in business, and by the way, your grandmother's ring is trapped in the bathroom drain. They'd tell you anything.

From early on Jeannette knew what was in store for her: school, a job, buying a little house on Tulip Lane with a pointed, shingled roof. If luck struck her, she'd find someone to spend her days with. If she was even luckier, her existence would matter. But in this place, this riverside of magic and gods and lunacy, she was beginning to understand that these prophecies did have power. Things here were different and not everything came out false. All those secrets somehow decipherable from the creases in her skin or the riddles from the mouths of baboons, maybe they *could* reveal what Fate had planned for her, or worse, somehow show her what might have been.

And now another mouth spoke, or didn't, and Jeannette had had enough experience with oracles to recognize the heavy tone to the blue man's words.

"Are you another oracle?"

The man didn't move. "The final one."

She'd never imagined there were only three of them in the desert land of Kemet. Or maybe she only got three, like three wishes from a Genie lamp.

"Be wise in your questions, for time does not stretch out forever in the west."

Jeannette glanced up and down the walkway between cages. Did the Smurf know if the guards were coming? Her number of questions contested the grains of sand along the River Nile, but she'd start with the important ones. "So, yes, Sanura needs my help." Jeannette pressed her face and hands harder into the wooden bars; maybe the strength of will alone could fade her away and allow her to walk right through the bars like a ghost. "I need help, too, though." The wood smelled faintly of the tree it once had been. Dust coated the inside of her nose. "To get out. So I can help her."

The man didn't move; his posture remained prim—like a British house marm's—with his hand lifted before him. She wondered how long

189

he'd been sitting like that and if his arm wasn't burning with fatigue. "Can you help me?"

The man's eyes crinkled at the edges. "I cannot help you." Again, his lips did not move. It was creepy, but not as creepy as changing Abayomi's wrappings, so she wagered it a fair deal if she got any information out of him. "But they can." He paused.

Great. More helpful answers full of specificity and detail. Maybe he wasn't really an oracle. Maybe he truly was a charlatan. "Why are you jailed here?" Maybe he'd told the Master Slaver if he didn't lose fifty pounds he'd die of congestive heart failure. Even Jeannette could see that one coming.

His eyes shifted, his lids widened, and he looked right at her. Into her. The heavy kohl of his eyes added an intensity unattained by even the locals of class. "I am here because I choose to be here. Why are you here?"

Why are you here? The words hung in the air.

She sat back from the barred door and looked up through the open ceiling into the clear sky. Sweat trickled down her temples. "You choose to be here? What are you, masochistic?"

"You did not answer my question."

She shifted to the opposite side of her cell to sit in a growing patch of shade and glared at him—her best I'm-not-amused glower. He did nothing but watch her. In fact, he didn't even blink. She counted in her head, staring him down. Minutes passed. He still held up his hand, unwavering. She couldn't even tell if his chest rose and fell; he could be a garishly painted statue. No guards passed her way.

"I'm here because I got captured." She glanced away. "I'm here because I was slow and stupid."

"Do you await a just judgment from the priests?"

She snorted. "Just? What are the chances of that?" That snake of panic squeezed around her diaphragm.

"You do not expect the wise ruling of Anubis?" His voice was soft and strikingly compassionate, his accent melodic.

Jeannette swallowed. Her throat was dry; they had taken her water bottle when they'd confiscated her backpack. "Obviously," she said under her breath. "I expect nothing from these people, the wisdom of Anubis or Yoda or whoever. Someone like me—I just am not going to get fair treatment."

"Lie not down under injustice, even when the roar of the lion

190

cannot be heard for the barking hyenas."

Injustice. Was there any other lord of this land?

"I just want out of here so I can help my friends."

"Then, by your will, leave."

"Huh? I can't! In case you didn't notice the barred door, I'm locked up." She rattled the bars; they held solidly in their moorings. If she had a knife, or even a hard stick ... She peered at him. "Do you know something I don't?"

"I know many things you do not." His eyes squinted in unvoiced laughter. The ground gathered up her sweat.

Why did all oracles and prophecy wielders insist on toying with her?

Then his mouth opened, his pale blue lips rose and fell but she heard no words. Frustrated almost to tears, she yelled and lashed out against the center bar with her heel.

It shifted.

For an instant everything went pale, froze in that tiny space between one second and the next. She held her breath. Then the world snapped back into sharp focus.

The bar had shifted.

With renewed effort she kicked at the bar with her rope thick sandal. The bar wriggled around in its base. She dropped to her knees and began working at the bar, twisting it, tugging it. Her sweaty hands slipped against the smooth surface of the wood. She wiped them on her button down and kept working at the barricade; slowly, it gave up its hold. She judged that if she could remove this bar and just one more she could probably squeeze through the hole. She wasn't a big woman and during her time in Kemet her American padding had disappeared.

She had to find Sanura, let the girl know she wasn't alone. Nothing felt worse than being afraid and alone.

With persistent twisting and tugging, that ranged from frantic to that of the gentlest touch, she worked out one bar. She began on the second. The mysterious blue man watched as she started with the kicking and moved onto the full body heaving of the stubborn second pole. Even in the cooling evening, sweat landed onto the uneven floor, soaking into the stone and dirt almost on impact. Dizziness swam through her head.

"Be aware," said the blue man.

Jeannette stopped her work and looked at him. Then she heard it, the soft steps of someone within the quiet settlement of slave cells. For a moment, she was caught like a child with her finger covered in cake batter, staring at the man sitting across from her in his own small cell. Then she grabbed the bar she'd removed and pushed it back into its hole, piling the loosened dirt and clay around the bottom to keep it in place. She slumped against the wall, willing her breathing and heart to slow.

A man in a short kilt patrolled the jail, looking into her neighbor's cell, then glancing into her own. She didn't meet his eyes. Instead she picked at her sandal; a loose strand of leather needed replacing already, and the woven reed sole was flatted where she'd used it as a cudgel. Shoddy construction. Her finger bled a little where she'd ripped off her nail. The jagged wound stung, clogged with abrasive sand. She sucked on it. After the guard passed, she waited another few minutes, posing with an air of abandoned hope. When she felt reasonably safe that he wasn't coming back, she ripped out the second bar from its foundation and tossed it against the rear wall, pulled free the lose one and dove for the hole. She had to worm her way through the empty space between the bars, contorting her body to get her shoulders through and scrunching her chest against the other bar so tightly that it hurt. But in moments she stood in the center aisle of a long line of other cells, panting heavily.

The place was devoid of guards.

"Hey. You got out?" a male voice said from her left.

"Let me out!" another screamed. "Quick. Release me too."

A long line of cells full of a long line of trapped and desperate people suddenly came to life. A few began yanking at their own door bars.

"Now you are free." She looked at the sitting blue man who spoke at her with soundless words. "Is that your wish?"

She drew her shoulders back. "My wish—" she scowled at him and the world he existed in "—is to get the hell out of here and return to a life where I don't constantly feel helpless and in danger." This place was getting aged-cheese old and she longed for somewhere she actually belonged. Constantly tired and frustrated, she just wanted to feel normal again.

"Perhaps such normality is one of the three great lies."

Stunned, she stared at the man. He'd lowered his hand and had it cupped in his lap. His eyelids were shuttered closed.

China Palace. The fortune cookie. The little slip of paper tucked away in her wallet.

"What did you say?" she asked. He said nothing. "What did you just say?" she demanded, her voice carrying over the sounds of the near rioting prisoners.

"Get me out, too," one demanded while another begged, "Please, don't leave me here."

"I've got money. I can give you money."

"I did nothing wrong! They're going to kill me!"

Jeannette's ears rang. The man didn't move, didn't even appear affected by the pleading people. Her flight instinct nearly drove her from the jail, but she had to know. "Damn it. How did you know about that?"

It had only been last year. She and her co-workers frequented this Chinese place for lunch with the uninspired name of China Palace. Done up in fake jade and gold lanterns with red tassels, the restaurant had a fish tank bigger than a chest freezer in the front with a constantly rotating colony of koi. The food wasn't that great, but it was cheap, and she could stuff her face pretty easily on ten bucks and still have left overs for the next night.

One waitress, a waspish woman way past retirement age, took vile joy in shorting them on fortune cookies, usually bringing one less than the number of their group. Jeannette would immediately snatch the closest cookie on the plate, and it had become a gag with her co-workers that Jeannette's fate was wrapped up in a cookie.

Last Christmas she'd gone to China Palace with a couple scientists from India who didn't care much about baby Jesus, and that same waitress joylessly took their order. Jeannette used to go to Christmas dinner at Gabby's family's, but she and Ricky were already on the outs and Jeannette didn't want to deal with that melodrama. Traditions never held much sway with her. She'd offered to show the visiting scientists a true American tradition and took them to Chinese. Kung pao chicken, beef and broccoli, and stir fry were certainly the dishes of the season, and at the end of the meal she snagged her cookie before she was left without. Her dinner companions ignored the remaining cookies on the plate, watching her with unsure amusement. "They're cookies," she told them, and popped hers open, dropping some of the stale cookie into her mouth as she read the little strip of white paper.

It had read: You will be visited by three great lies.

She hadn't gone back since that night. Had almost obsessed over that little slip of paper that still rested in a small pocket of her wallet back in Spokane, tucked next to a folded, pink heart Ricky had given her before he'd moved on to Gabby. It had been a Valentine, handmade, gaudy, and sweet. She had kept both pieces of paper together as a testament to truth and broken promises.

And now that line, that stupid fortune, emerged from her past to haunt her.

"Help me!" a woman begged in a harsh whisper.

The blue man's explanation never came and the noise prodded Jeannette to get going. She would get nothing else out of this third oracle and she couldn't help these people. "Thanks for the help," she tossed out as she scurried down the aisle. A few rows over a guard yelled for quiet. Meeting nobody's gaze, she left the jail. To her right, under a lit torch near a garbage pile, she nearly landed on two others. Marching intently toward the desperate noise, the guards didn't see her in the dark corner she cowered in. She turned right and hunch-trotted through a row of cells, these mostly empty. She had to find Sanura and Abayomi. People who wouldn't fail her, who spoke with honesty. Between them she had promises—unspoken, but still made—and those she intended to keep.

She tried to laugh as she dodged sharp glares and harsh condemnation.

"Guards, a woman, she's escaping."

Jeannette growled and picked up her pace. What did that stupid Smurf know anyway? Normal was the gold metal standard Jeannette strove for. Someday, somewhere, she would live *normal* once again.

She ran low between the cells, taking lefts and rights, blocking out the cries for help, dodging the guards prowling the jail.

"What's this about, by the Nine Gods!" a commanding voice boomed. The voice came from behind her, somewhere in the plantation of jail cells.

"A woman escaped. If you release me, oh honored guard, I shall tell you—"

"Over there. She went south." That voice was familiar, it almost echoed in her mind. She thought as loudly as one can think a thought in thanks to the blue man as she trotted north.

"Gather the guards. We've got an escape."

A low wall cut off her getaway, and she hopped over it, first one leg, then the other, catching her sandal's toe with her trailing leg. She cursed her clumsiness as she hit the ground, re-scraping her already abused knee.

Bent over, she jogged quietly away.

"Over there!"

The street population jumped as guards and rubber-neckers sought out the escaped prisoner.

Her thighs began to ache—how she wished for a reprieve from

pain—as Jeannette moved quickly to the left, using the expanding night as coverage. Her knee screamed at her, her palms hurt, and a pressure filled her chest. Panic. Always on the edge of panic. She wanted Abayomi by her side. To give her strength. To take away her fear.

By now, torches were illuminating the streets and the city's slumber jacked back into wakefulness. Approaching footsteps, the determined pounding of guards at chase, sent her down alleys and up stairways to watch from above like a superhero, eyeing the city from building roofs. After trotting another two streets forward and one street to the right, she recognized some shops and discovered the slave market without having traveled in too many circles.

Torches still flickered strongly in the market; apparently you could examine the slaves at your leisure, a shop forever open, like grabbing a snack from a 7-Eleven after a Nightmare on Elm Street marathon.

She stopped skulking about and stood upright, checking herself over for presentability. No Wall Street lawyer, no leopard skinned authority. She could do nothing about her foreign clothing—her backpack was back at the jail—or the cannery smell, so she refused to worry about it. Tidying her loose hair, she walked to a nearby well and washed her face and hands in the bucket. After sluicing the streets with the water, she crossed the street, taking long, sure strides. She nodded at the few people who looked at her. Some of them nodded back. A slaver guard glanced at her, she didn't look away. He had a huge mole on his chin that broke the surface of his skin like an island. She kept her eyes on the monstrous blemish. Without so much as a pause, he looked on, checking out the next person to enter the slaver's pens. A few men and women still wandered the aisles, pointing at the huddling slaves and discussing their value. Jeannette continued, pausing at each cell long enough to appear like she was appraising the merchandise, but she really only looked for one person. A pre-teen girl with a cat head.

In the third cell, Jeannette found Sanura amidst a group of five other women. Their eyes met.

Sanura's ears were drawn back, her brow creased in what looked like sorrow. Her eyes, huge and shimmering, looked like they were drowning in it. The girl walked over to Jeannette. A burning sting crawled across Jeannette's eyeballs. Sanura curled one finger around a wooden bar.

Try as she might, Jeannette wasn't the consoling type. Try as she might, she could only come up with hollow words.

"It will be alright," she said quietly.

195

Sanura sniffed, then nodded.

"I will be back."

Sanura blinked at her. "Okay," she said.

"I will, and I will get you out of here."

Two finely dressed men passed behind Jeannette and she stepped away from Sanura, lifted her chin and dropped her arm to her side.

The men nodded at Jeannette as they approached the cage, then stopped, one awing in delight.

"A *mi-nether*. What a find."

"And a young one at that. I shall have to assure my attendance at the sale tomorrow."

This was all stupid. She was tired of running, tired of being afraid. This place had no understandable rules. Somehow, without her quite realizing it, her life had moved onto the next chapter and the story she'd been living was turning out completely different from what she'd ever expected. It was time to write her own chapter. First, she had to find Abayomi; they were all meant to journey this adventure together. Then, she needed to face the Slave Master and do anything she could to save her friend.

Jeannette ground her teeth, and with one last nod to Sanura, she turned and left.

Chapter 21

SANURA WATCHED JEANNETTE LEAVE, committed to memory the frown of her lips, the wrinkles along her hairless brow before the woman turned away. Her friend slipped through the onlookers and, like a ghost, slowly disappeared. A soft mew fell from Sanura's lips. Why was she left behind? Her mother had promised to watch over Sanura always, but right now nobody stood by her side in this filthy cage of forgotten lives.

Deserted by her mother. Deserted by her friends.

She kept to herself until night fell and the cool air forced her nearer the other women. They'd all been watchful of her before, a fallen *minether*. The pot she had had to urinate in overflowed with filth and her mouth tasted like foot. Within her lungs an infection of helplessness festered. Through the overhead bars she saw the dark sky awash with splattered milk. Out there, somewhere, were her siblings and her mother. Her brothers and sisters were all safe back at the temple, doing what the matron told them to, learning about their duties. They weren't alone. They weren't afraid. She prayed to her mother to deliver her, and to help Abayomi and Jeannette.

Her mother had sent her *out here* to be caught by the slaver, to find the strange woman and the man blessed with Anubis' gift. Her mother had explained those two were so lost that they needed Sanura more than Sanura needed her litter. Sanura, heart aching with fear, had agreed to help. Sometimes that fear would fill her like a miasma and her stomach would cramp. Sometimes she cried at night for her mother and litter mates. It was always so cold.

But she'd been given her duty: to help Abayomi and Jeannette do what they must do. Only then would Sanura know exactly why she'd been chosen. It seemed backwards to her, but then she was young and had been taught that experience led the way to understanding.

Eyelids growing heavy, Sanura struggled to trace the stars in the sky. With a sniff, she tried to shrug off her despair. The stars watched over her, her mother watched over her, and each in their own way, Abayomi and Jeannette watched over her as well.

She was not deserted. Alone, maybe, but not abandoned. It was a hope she must cling to.

She remembered a spell the matron used to whisper to the litter when they were all new to the world. Sanura released a single sob, then uttered, "I need the beneficial strength of my brothers and sisters. I banish all that wishes me harm."

She wrapped her arms tight around herself and squeezed, tempted to turn into her feline form and slip out, sneak away to find Abayomi or Jeannette, but her mother had forbidden it and so she did the only thing she could, she held on tight. She didn't want to walk this world alone.

"Mother. I'm lost. I'm so, so lost. Please, show me the way."

* * *

Jeannette wandered the city through the night seeking out Abayomi.

Night brought with it a chill she could do nothing about and her entire body burned with a constant ache. Her legs—especially her banged up knees—her shoulder, her finger that stung every time she bumped it on anything: all high points in her landscape of pain. She examined the fingernail, a paper thin strip jutted beyond the quick catching the hem of her shirt in unconscious moments. The first aid kit was beyond reach; again she cursed the loss of her backpack at the jail. She wondered if she should go to Montu's Temple, be blessed by the healing sniff of the magical bull, but she had nothing to offer the priestess.

That damned mummy was probably two steps behind her, nose to the ground like a hound on a scent trail. He'd proven he had a knack for hunting her down. She stopped walking, dropped her head back and stared up into the stars. Her entire body felt compressed, pressed flat under the weight of a thousand worries. Her smartest action would be to stop looking for him, sit tight and wait. It was the number one survival rule they talked about on outdoors shows: if you're lost, stay put.

A whiff of beer caught her nose and like a bloodhound, she followed it to a small brewery. Morning waited just around the corner, so she sat against the wall, rested her head on her arms, and snoozed until a woman with a beaded collar and thick wig stepped out and began opening her shop. Jeannette lumbered to her feet, unsteady and still exhausted. With a lightheadedness brought on by low blood sugar, she leaned against the white-washed plaster wall until her head ceased its whirlwind spin. In a yawn, she asked for some drink.

The Egyptian brewer handed her a jug with a rounded handle without even looking at her. Jeannette lifted the jug to the brewer and drank down four long swallows without pausing for a breath. She'd never been this good even in college.

"A bit thick." She licked her chapped lips.

The brewer was younger than Jeannette's own master, probably recently having inherited the brewery from a dead relative. Or she was an apprentice. Either way, she was surely no master. Her *kalasiris* was far too clean.

"Beer is a meal," the woman stated, voice level and eyes narrowed.

"I've heard of this master in Thebes who has beer like no other. No straw is needed. It's almost as pure as water." Which wasn't exactly true, but how was this woman all the way down the river to know that.

The brewer squinted at Jeannette. "No such thing."

"And there are different flavors. Mint, grape, date." Jeannette casually looked around. Many Egyptians, Nubians and even Canaanites walked by in the brightening streets. A woman with the head of a hawk passed by the shop, sharp eyes eating up her surroundings. No mummies.

The brewer turned to face Jeannette, who held out the empty red-clay jug dangling from one finger. The brewer took it and set it down to be reused.

"You should rinse that out, to remove any impurities. Even better, boil it." Jeannette nodded helpfully.

Looking her up and down, the woman scowled. "What do you know about beer?"

Jeannette almost laughed and pulled herself up to her full five foot five. "I'm a master's apprentice," she said with pride. "Our customers find the thin beer a delight. The beer is filtered through fresh linen. We clean all of our pots and boil our water to make the flavor richer." And to kill bacteria, but she wouldn't understand that. The fermentation process did a pretty good job of that anyway.

"You should abide the words of this woman," came a voice from behind.

Jeannette jumped. And then smiled. With an air of casual interest, she turned. Behind her stood her mummy.

"Abayomi!" She almost threw herself into his arms, then caught herself and ran her uplifted hand down her loose hair instead. A bubbling laugh possessed her for a good five seconds before she could catch her breath. She wiped away at the moisture gathering at the corners of her eyes. "I'm so happy to see you."

"It is apparently so," Abayomi said, his voice warm. Once upon a time he'd been wrapped leather and bones, now she could see brown flesh

199

at the gaps around his eyes and mouth. "Where is Sanura?"

Jeannette's smile dropped. "With the slavers. Not for long, though. I've an idea. The Master Slaver seems fairly keen on the pharaoh's laws; maybe I can play on that. Force him to work with us. Maybe, we can make a trade."

"Master Slaver?" the brewer said, the title sounding hollow.

Abayomi tilted his head. "You know, Sanura hates being alone."

The image of Sanura's eyes watching her as she deserted the girl in the pens floated to the forefront of Jeannette's memories. An uncomfortable sourness settled in her stomach. "Yeah."

"And, though I am sure your plan is terribly complicated, I want to point out that you have nothing of which to trade the master."

"How about information, about the tomb robbers?"

"You know little about them."

"Tomb robbers?" questioned the brewer, taking a step back into her building.

"But," Jeannette lifted up her finger to make her point, "we need to track them down anyway, since they most likely have your scarab. Maybe he'll unwittingly help us. Two birds, one stone."

His mouth dropped into a curious frown. "You are armed with stones?"

Jeannette sighed. "Just listen to my plan." She grabbed Abayomi's arm and led him towards the slave market. The muscle beneath flexed. It didn't feel at all creepy.

"Oh." Jeannette turned back to the brewer who watched them with mouth ajar. She had nothing to pay the woman with, so instead she offered a blessing. "May your beer never sour."

* * *

"Excuse me, Master?"

The Master Slaver, sitting at a low table, looked up from a long scroll. Recordkeeping from the day's negotiations should never rest until the next day, unless his lovely wife and daughter wished for his early return to discuss a befitting suitor. Rolls of papyrus lined a series of shelves along the graying walls of his office, and a writing pallet filled with red and black ink rested on one edge of the table. It was early, still dark within, so a small pool of oil filled the bottom of a lotus lamp. The lamp, carved of alabaster, was a gift from a priest of Isis' temple. With its light, he sought a path out of this time of lawlessness and chaos. He cherished it above most of his possessions. The rest of the room held few accoutrements.

"Yes, Senbi?"

His assistant cleared his throat, his arms held stiffly by his sides pressed against the linen of his *shendyt*. The Master Slaver knew he was not going to approve of this disturbance. "Someone here to speak to you. About the *mi-nether* we have in the cells."

The master wetted his writing reed. "Tell him she will be presented at the morning sale." He continued writing out the list of buyers for yesterday and whom they had bought at what price. He recorded everything by his own hand.

Senbi didn't leave. He hovered in the doorway, filling up space like a swarm of gnats. The master put down his reed and looked at the man, whose face twisted in anxiety.

"Well, she claims she's the girl's original buyer."

The flame of the lamp's wick flared up, then gentled once again to a steady glow.

"Is she pale skinned?" the master asked. "Without wig?"

Senbi nodded. "I do believe she is the thief you spoke about?" It came out a question.

"Send her in. And find some guards."

The Master Slaver sat back on his stool and scratched his belly. His duty waited for him and instead this foreign thief, who he had incarcerated, kept him from it. He scanned the scroll; he'd almost finished. Putting his writing tools away, he waited as Senbi ushered in the pale devil and a mummy. The Master Slaver raised an eyebrow. The mummy had poor choice in friends. They both smelled of fish.

The woman tried to smile, but it wilted.

"Hi," she said. Her hands were gripped before her and her thin hair hung limply around her face. "I was hoping we could work something out."

"How did you leave the jail?" He hadn't heard what the judges had decided, and it was too soon for any decision anyway. He'd had her jailed just the previous day.

"Oh, uhh, they just let me go. I walked out."

A lie. The woman came in here and flagrantly lied to him. He would throw her in the slave pens.

"Senbi, take this woman—"

Her eyes grew wide. "Okay, honestly—" she lifted her hands before

201

her defensively— "I escaped. I even left my things behind. You see, I can't sit in some jail, I've things I need to do." Her face lit up with haughty irritation, and she continued to babble her glut of excuses. "My friend had his tomb robbed, right here in this city, and I know about some tomb robbers in Thebes, too. He's missing his heart scarab and . . ."

Tomb robbers. The master scowled and stopped listening to her inelegant speech. He knew they'd breached his city, but hadn't been able to catch them. He and others of honor and power within the city would see these wretches pierced by a pike. His hand fisted against his thigh.

"What do you know about the tomb robbers?" he interrupted.

She stopped talking. He waited. She twisted her hands around each other, eyes bulging as if she might begin to cry. "They tried to kill me." Her voice had gone a pitch high. "Some of the guards are in on it."

The Master Slaver was a good judge of a person. He knew when someone lied; he knew when someone held on by their last dram of will. He knew fear and desperation, and this woman oozed both. But she kept those at bay with something entirely different.

"Do you know names, faces?"

She shook her head. "Not any names, but I do know faces. I think they're in this town because—"

"They are." His friend the scribe had given him the proof. Enough information to begin an investigation, but the guards he'd sent to incarcerate the thieves had come back with nothing. Not even someone to torture the truth from. "So, one thief turns on another."

The woman's face blanked, then twisted in anger, her worry discarded in her indignation. "I'm no thief!"

"You did not pay for the young slave," he reminded her.

Taking one step forward, she thrust her finger towards him in fiery accusation. Senbi reached out to catch her attack. "I am no thief! I tried to pay." He pushed her hand down, and she let it drop with a tossed glare. "Anyway, I was saving one girl. A person's freedom. It's completely different and you don't—"

He gripped the edge of his desk and pulled himself to standing, staring down at the woman. The mummy, who'd not said a thing since they entered the master's office, shifted his body to angle himself between the Master Slaver and the annoying woman, raising a hand to quiet her.

"Need I remind you that I've no obligation to answer for any of my actions to you? To the pharaoh and the Gods, yes. You are nowhere in that line of command. She is a *slave*," the Master Slaver said with such force the woman flinched. "If people cannot care for themselves or pay their debts, they are sent into slavery. If they are captured by our great pharaoh in times of war, they are put into slavery, as is their fate. Do not decry fate, stupid woman. And when you steal my slaves, you undermine the livelihood of me and my family, my wife and daughters. You undermine the livelihood of all of the people working for the market. And you think *you* are in the right. You know nothing of the proper ways."

"You're wrong. I know all about your *proper* ways and I know they aren't right. Aren't humane. You people are barbaric. You have no morality, no kindness in you."

The mummy grabbed her arm before Senbi could act. "Jeannette." Just her name, but the Master Slaver could hear the unspoken reproof. She looked to the mummy and pressed her lips shut into a thin line.

"Why do you not continue this explanation of your plan." The mummy gestured towards the Master Slaver with a nod of his head.

The master lifted his eyebrows and waited. He would hear the woman out before he made his final verdict. This wasn't about the small ordeal of one stolen slave. This concerned the pharaoh's passage to the afterlife and the very rise and fall of the sun.

The Master Slaver crossed his arms over his belly.

"Fine," the woman said petulantly.

The Master Slaver snorted. This mummy sure picked a hard woman to cast his fortune with.

She swallowed; her eyes roamed the walls of his office and seemed to mire themselves in the far corner of the ceiling. "Well," she paused, then added, "sir," in a suitably humble manner. "I overheard some men talking about selling items taken from a tomb at the workers compound. I think the vizier's tomb. At the Peak, by Thebes." She looked at him. Of course he knew the place and nodded for her to continue. "I take beer out there to the men—guards mainly. We make the best beer and they request it often. Anyway," she stared down at her hands, and mumbled, "I told a guard out there about what I heard—" The master sighed. She sucked in a breath, glared at him, but continued. "He tried to kill me!" Her long bangs danced with her venomous accusation.

Then she filled the room with a self-depreciating laugh and looked hard at the master, as if facing him meant facing the guard all over again. Such women of common stock were rare in Kemet. A hard life burned their spirit away at an early age. Merit, his own wife, breathed fire like this

203

devil. Her throat bobbed when she swallowed, and he heard the dry click of it.

He waited.

"They found me, at the brewery where I worked. Found me and the guard hounded my street. I left the city, running for my life with Abayomi and Sanura. Both of whom were vital in getting this knowledge to you."

They stood for a long time in his scroll lined office, the flicker of his dying lamp the only sign of life as everyone remained motionless. Two guards waited in the doorway, ready to jump at the master's orders.

The Master Slaver pondered what she told him. Some of the men, guards no less, in the tomb robbing circle knew her face.

"Master . . ." The Slave Master looked up to see the woman take in a deep breath and meet his eyes. "I am sure we can help find these thieves. The pharaoh must be respected because without respect for him, the whole land is sick. I would like to propose a deal."

He frowned at her audacity. "What makes you feel you have the right to propose such a thing? Your duty is to tell me what you know."

She ignored him and continued. "You let Sanura free, free from slavery, give me the opportunity to pay for her through my aid to this great land if you insist on payment." His chest filled with a shocked breath. "No hunting us down anymore. No more slave auctions. She and I, and," she gestured to her companion, "Abayomi will help find these tomb thieves. These desecrators of the dead." Her voice had gained a hard edge to it. "But we must be free to do it." She gripped her hands into fists. "While I take my duty to the pharaoh deeply to heart, I cannot focus on this most honorable of tasks if I were to worry for myself and my friend."

"Any plot against the pharaoh's tomb is a plot against the pharaoh, and any plot against the pharaoh is a plot against his people."

The woman nodded; he found her desire to agree with him annoying.

"Of course it is. I have this idea," she said. "And I know it will work. It's been proven in my land to be an excellent plan."

"Speak, then."

"Well, you see, I really need Sanura here to help." She looked hard at him. A no-nonsense stare down few would ever attempt with someone of his status. "I need her here with me."

Silence stretched brittle between them. The mummy rested his hand on the woman's shoulder, but she didn't release her challenge.

"What is she to you?" he finally asked.

"She's my friend. No . . ." the woman shook her head, "she is my family."

* * *

"Sanura!"

Sanura ripped her eyes from where they gripped onto her filthy feet to see Jeannette and Abayomi together with the master of the slave market. The room was dimly lit, but the low light posed little obstruction for her. Jeannette, showing off her straight, white teeth, waved a fast, welcoming greeting. Beside her, Abayomi smiled.

"Jeannette! Abayomi!"

She pulled away from the guard's hold and threw herself across the small room into Jeannette's engulfing embrace. Two guards had hauled her from a fitful sleep, and Sanura had feared it was her end. It could have been a priest of Seth; it could have been a brothel; it could have been the crocodile man. Any and all an imminent possibility. Any and all a looming terror. Jeannette brushed her cheek along the top of Sanura's head whispering, "I'm so glad you're safe. I'm so happy." Sanura squeezed Jeannette hard, blinking against a sting in her eyes.

She wanted to say "Thank you," and "You didn't leave me," and "I love you, I love you, I love you," but it seemed impossible to allot any of her breath to speaking.

"Now you've had your happy reunion, we must discuss this plan of yours," the Master Slaver said, sending Sanura's heart into a rabbit race again.

Though her freedom had to have been issued from the rotund master, he didn't appear happy. Sanura held tight to Jeannette, but the woman gently pushed her toward Abayomi and nodded to the man.

"Fine," Jeannette said, without the proper deference the master deserved. Sanura looked from one to the other, then finally turned to Abayomi.

He shrugged, then leaned forward and said with just a breath, "She is charmed, protected by the Gods."

Sanura smiled. Relaxed. It must be true.

As Jeannette paced the small office, her hands flicking through the air fast enough to catch flies, she spoke about confusing things to the Master Slaver. Sitting on the floor, Sanura curled up next to Abayomi's side and let him hold her. His arms were warm and comforting around her body, like a tightly wound pile of kittens. The master's guard had filled the lamp and left, leaving behind a pitcher of fruit juice that the small gathering had passed around. Though exhausted and famished, Sanura fell to neither of these urges; she couldn't tear her eyes away from Jeannette.

Her friend almost glowed.

Though she acted brashly and lacked proper respect, the Master Slaver listened to what Jeannette said. A flush darkened her pale face as she talked endlessly, only pausing in her lecture to wet her mouth from a mug of sweet juice.

"Wait." The master raised a hand. Jeannette held her cup in the air, stalled just before her lips. "Are you ill in the head? Are you're suggesting to pose as one of these swine-mating thieves and join their wicked business?"

Sanura blinked, yawning as she pushed herself to full wakefulness.

Shrugging, Jeannette nodded. "It's a tried and true method of finding out someone else's dirty little secrets. Pretend to be their ally. To really have it work, it will take some time. They must completely trust me, not just let me do the heavy lifting." She shook her head. "They've got to include me."

"They will not trust you. You're a foreign demon."

Jeannette laughed. Sanura couldn't help smiling at the sound. "They will, trust me," she said firmly, "because of that very fact." She punctuated the last two words with a thrusting finger at the master. Sanura flicked her ear, wondering if the master would take offense. "I don't believe in your gods with the same conviction you do." She included all of them in a wave of her arm. "I've had constant run ins with you," she pointed to the master again, "and therefore we obviously have no love for each other. I'm a perfect candidate for recruitment. Plus," Jeannette paused and took in a deep breath, head bowed, "I've a friend in the workers compound at the Peak. I could use her to get to know some of the locals. Though," she stared into her mug, "that doesn't seem very noble."

She turned toward Sanura. "Sanura will come with me. And Abayomi will help. He is very sly." She smiled fondly at Abayomi, a certain kind of joy on her face that Sanura hadn't seen before.

"Well," said the Master Slaver. "It sounds awfully implausible and overly dramatic. But, I've not met my own success."

"So, we have a deal then?" Jeannette held out her hand and the master squinted at it. She dropped it to her side.

The man's lips were pressed thin and then he laughed. Sanura glanced from man to woman, confused. "Such a simple woman. I will agree to your plan, and to let you and the *mi-nether* free, because I choose to. And because whoever I sold you to would be returning you within the fullness of the moon. No other reason."

Abayomi chuckled, the sound entirely amused.

Sanura looked up at him, holding her ears back.

He leaned forward and spoke the barest whisper in her ear. "Isis guides her way. Jeannette is quite the deal maker when she wants to be. She cares nothing for these thieves. She does this all to free you and find my scarab."

Sanura twitched her ear, trying to dislodge the tickle that had set in when Abayomi's breath brushed against her sensitive fur. As Abayomi watched Jeannette, he smiled. This knowledge pleased him, that was evident. Sanura knew exactly how he felt. To free her from the master's influence, Jeannette would help the Master Slaver with his own cause.

She did this all for them.

Closing her eyes and snuggling close to the mummified man, Sanura catnapped under the protection of this shared comfort. Before the morning was complete, she felt herself lifted up in Abayomi's strong arms and she sensed herself being carried somewhere more than harboring any actual awareness of the movement. Like back in the nursery, when the matron would watch over them and bear them in her mouth, Sanura felt completely safe.

Chapter 22

JEANNETTE'S STOMACH RUMBLED. The morning rampaged on, and through it all they discussed tactics and outcomes and not once did that damned slaver offer them a nip of food. Sure, he'd given them pulpy juice, but that only whetted her appetite. Now she wanted stew, or maybe shepherd's pie, something salty and hearty that could fill a girl's stomach to near bursting. Yeasty bread, with rosemary and maybe coarse salt without the brutal sand.

He'd put them up in a standard traveler's dormitory for the rest of the day, currently housing a small contingent of traders from Canaan. If only she'd known about such extravagant digs when she'd first tumbled into this world. Jeannette rummaged together some food and beer with her slim wealth as Abayomi took care of an exhausted Sanura. The poor girl, she had gone through so much.

The traders kept to one end of the long building, and once night set, they huddled around a warming fire in a bronze pot, while she, Sanura and Abayomi made their home in the other end. The group consisted entirely of men and a few cast hooded glances their way. The kind of glances you'd find on weary travelers who haven't seen civilization in an age, or women. Jeannette found herself migrating towards Abayomi each time she caught the foreigners' eyes, until she noticed her own behavior and flounced herself on her sleeping pallet in self-annoyance.

She did not need a man to protect her from other men. She blew out their candle instead, submerging her and her friends in darkness, hidden from those she wouldn't willingly associate with.

Still, she didn't mind being close to Abayomi, just talking. While discussing their plans, Sanura had curled up in a little ball on the pallet stuffed in the corner, still drained from the last two days. Soft murmurs, surprisingly similar to Archie's purr, filled the empty spaces between their conversation. This entire ordeal seemed to have destroyed Sanura's soul little by little. Jeannette wished there was something she could do to make it all better—what band-aid would heal this wound?

Exhausted, ignoring the glances cast from the illuminated end of the dorm, Jeannette and Abayomi sat in the dark, thighs touching, on the sleeping pallet that he would never sleep on. Never sleeping, never eating. A life devoid of pleasures, though he never seemed dissatisfied. He never complained, anyway. She often wondered what it would feel like to be content like that. Be satisfied with life in general. To come home from work and make dinner and watch her television shows and get up at seven the next morning and go to work and come home and . . .

She used to think that was what made people happy, because so many chose that drone lifestyle. But, was that what she wanted? To come home from work and watch TV or read some history or science mag? Wash, rinse, repeat?

Because, in a sick way—even though she was hurting and tired and starving and smelled ripe like bloated fish—right now, at that moment, she felt pretty damned satisfied. She'd convinced the Master Slaver to go along with her plan, half-cocked and only completely fathomable by someone who owned an entire collection of thriller flicks. He'd even released her from jail and relieved Sanura from her burden of slavery. She had a scheme, albeit a mushy one, for fulfilling the oracle's requirements. She had friends who seemed to want to be with her, truly so, not just playing along out of some sense of duty or boredom.

"Jeannette." Abayomi tripped up her thoughts in mid-charge. "Tell me about your world. I know it is much different than mine, but you rarely speak of it."

She watched the Canaanites ready themselves for bed, pondering what to say, what to tell him that would bring her world to life. He could never fully comprehend computers or space ships or cell phones, let alone the concepts of freedom and the American dream.

She thought about Spokane: the giant fir tree decked out every year in Christmas regalia at the mall, the trails all over the mountains, her lab full of glass and chemicals, walls painted all in white. She remembered the annual grass burning and the resulting haze smothering the valley every fall. She had friends—happy hour pioneers. She hadn't spoken to her father in months and her mother, whom she'd adored, was long dead. Is that what he wanted to hear about?

Is that what she wanted to talk about?

She cleared her throat. "Well, we had all this technology to make our lives easier. From preschool on we're taught to play fair, that everyone was equal, and everyone's opinion was right." In their dark corner, she could just see Abayomi's silhouette tilt its head, his typical curious dog pose. She knew she was being too vague. "Our chariots were faster than a diving falcon and our barques flew through the air. Water spread across the land and the desert constantly bloomed." She heard him gasp.

"Everyone had food to eat.

"But our cities ate the countryside and our spirits shriveled up. Our gods became money and entertainment, our pride a casualty of apathy and desire." She shrugged. "I guess that can happen anywhere, in any time." When she put it that way, it sounded like a terrible place.

"Diseases were conquered; most babies born lived." She was quiet for a moment. "Every corner of the land was accessible to those who wished to visit it. For a price.

"Then, I fell into this life, and it's nothing I ever imagined I'd want to live. Half nightmare, and half dream." Her voice barely dusted the silence of their secret world, her words unearthed from the root of her uncertainty.

Abayomi placed his hand on her leg. She squinted at it, each snugly wrapped finger a pale worm in the darkness. His rough wrappings scratched her skin even through her light pants. "Maybe that is not true, maybe you just never recognized your own wishes."

"You sound like a damned oracle." She forced a chuckle.

He patted her thigh and pulled his hand away. The vacated spot felt cold.

"It's just that . . . for so long, I felt so lost." She couldn't see his eyes in the darkness. What she saw were dark recesses embedded within an expressionless white mask. Talking in the dark, it was easier this way.

"Maybe," he said in the same low voice, "you did not wish to be found."

Jeannette struggled for a moment before replying: "Sometimes, Abayomi, I felt like I'd been living a pointless life. Everything I did, every opinion I had, just something I puked up to fulfill some expectation other people had of me." And that was it. She'd never been her own person, instead living for others' approval. "God, I'm such a lap dog." She laughed bitterly, knocking the back of her head against the hard, brick wall. Those programmed years at college, following her friend to the lab, even watching Gabby and Ricky slowly gravitate towards each other and not doing a damned thing about it. Throughout her entire life, she'd been a spectator, let things happen *to* her. She hadn't *lived*.

His hand rested on her leg again, patted awkwardly then slipped away in a rush. He'd never touched her so much. "Oh, Jeannette, I cannot imagine you would ever sit by idly and let others dictate life to you."

"I think that is exactly how I was." She paused, really thinking over her previous life, those memories oddly detached. Sanura snuffled in her sleep and the men at the other end doused their fire, dropping the entire length of the long building into shades of blended darkness. The smothered pot set off a harsh scent of smoke, nearly masking the sour odor of fish. The strongest impressions of her past were simply feelings, deeply seated in the center of her chest: loneliness, hurt, longing. "I don't think I was ever really me."

"I think you are you now." Abayomi chuckled quietly. "Ferociously. Vibrantly. Stubbornly you."

She rolled her head against the wall to look blindly in his direction. Though she felt buoyed by those words, Jeannette wished she could see his face, his features, read what was truly being said by those eyes.

"I want to be me," she whispered, hardening each word with steel. She pushed her head off the bricks. "I want to live my life. Even if all I have is one moment, I want to live it for myself. Not live it to fit in. Not live it to please others." One moment of truth was worth a lifetime of living in sedated complacency. She wasn't some fattened cow walking toward the butcher. She would be wild, running through forests, heart pounding, breath gasping until one fatal moment ended it all. No longer would she live this half-life.

Abayomi cleared his throat. "Then, I would like to live it with you."

Jeannette felt her heart contract once, then jump into a thrilling tattoo, and for a moment, eternity seemed to focus itself into this one pinprick of time: sitting together with Abayomi, bound in utter darkness, legs touching, his warmth spreading into her, and like the final drop of a reagent hitting an unknown solution, everything changed.

"If you will allow it," he added tentatively.

"Yes," she said. "I would like that."

* * *

When the noise of the morning's activity woke Jeannette, it seemed mere minutes had passed since she'd laid her head down on the straw mat. Though most of the previous day swam through her brain like a school of drunken minnows, she distinctly remembered her vow to live, and those promising words Abayomi had said. He wanted to be with her. *He* chose *her*. She wondered what it all would amount to, and allowed herself the hope that it hadn't all been misconstrued. But she'd known him only a short time. Should she choose him? A dead man?

211

THREE GREAT LIES

Someone walked past her, quiet footsteps, and she knew it was Sanura. Jeannette sat up; the straw crinkled under her as a mighty yawn disabled her ability to speak.

"Look!" Sanura lifted up Jeannette's backpack, the one she'd had to relinquish back at the jail. "It was here when I woke."

"Good morning," Jeannette finally managed, rubbing at her eyes. Their half-candle burned steadily, casting the girl's face in stark relief. "That's great. Any idea who brought it?" Jeannette searched through the pack to make sure none of her irreplaceable, and mostly useless, things were missing.

Abayomi, sitting on his pallet with his back resting against the wall, was watching Jeannette. She smiled at him; he smiled back. Her smile broadened and she had to look away.

She wished her camera hadn't died. She'd like to take a picture of him now.

"The Master Slaver's assistant brought it in not too long ago," he said. "And he told us to prepare to leave soon." He held out a jug of water and some dried fruit to Jeannette. "I wanted to let you rest as long as you needed."

Jeannette took the fruit and bit into the tough flesh with her molars. She noticed the merchants had gone, leaving them alone in their temporary squat. Sanura munched on some dried fish, sitting cross-legged on her pallet. Both of the women scarfed their food down in some tacit challenge, laughing with full mouths and gulping down water in between swallows.

"Disgusting," Abayomi said, watching them. Jeannette couldn't help it, she laughed even harder, nearly choking on a clump of mushed dates and joy.

After washing it all down with a swig of cool water, she asked, "Do you think we have time to clean up?"

Shaking his head in amusement, Abayomi shrugged. "Senbi only said the plan would begin soon. If you wish to clean yourself, I suggest you take the opportunity."

She grabbed Sanura and tossed a warm smile over her shoulder at Abayomi as they exited the dormitory to a small secluded washing room next door. His laughter followed them to the dorm's vacant washing area, where the two women stripped down.

She knew that such luxuries—even considering the cold water—might go the way of the dodo bird. Before she'd even know it, the Master

212

Slaver—a man who abided all laws, even those that were plainly wrong—would put their plan into action and the next time she'd be able to wash, or even sleep, was a great unknown. The man's dedication to his king was nothing short of fanatic. Creepy, in some rabid fanboy kind of way. She'd never felt that way about anything, couldn't even imagine it.

Three clay troughs of water nearly filled the small bathing room, whose damp floor had a stone-lined ditch running down the center. The water level of two of the troughs reached halfway up the container's side; one nearly overflowed. She tied her hair back with a long length of white string and scrubbed herself with rabid, superficial stokes that would never have flown at the lab. She remembered, with a kind of fond frustration, the hoops of cleanliness they'd had to jump through, the five minutes of sudsy soap under hot water. Her hands had usually been dry back then, but now—she stared down at her wet palms—they were a parched landscape.

From her backpack she grabbed her clean *kalasiris*, overjoyed by the lack of fish scent on her dress. Sanura tugged her own dress over her head. Too big for her, it gave the girl the impression of swimming in a rice sack.

"You ready?" she asked, feeling along her loosely cinched hair for any wayward poofy bits.

Sanura scrunched up her face and frowned. "I don't know the entire plan. I fell asleep."

Jeannette knelt down before the young *mi-nether* and ran her hands along the crudely spun fabric of the girl's dress. "That's not a problem. We're going to be chased out of the city, but it's all a game. Okay?" Sanura squinted her eyes. She didn't look okay. "It has to look like we're in trouble, but really we're not. Just follow my lead."

Like a butterfly, a smile flittered across the stoic landscape of Sanura's features and she delivered Jeannette one sharp nod.

They returned to the interior of the dorm and gathered Abayomi, who patiently awaited their return. As they left the dormitory, he held Jeannette's elbow, as if supporting her in case she might fall in such terrible footing. She found it kind of sweet. She found the rapid beating of her heart kind of pathetic.

"What do we do now?" Sanura picked at a rough weave on her dress.

"We go to Thebes." Abayomi looked down at Sanura as they began walking towards the river. "Keep your eyes open, the guards will be looking for us."

213

Sanura's eyes grew narrow. "But why do they chase us?" She looked to Jeannette. "We were freed."

Stopping under a sparse, olive green tree, Jeannette dropped her hand on Sanura's shoulder. "It's part of the game, remember? The Master Slaver can't let us just go. And he's supposed to be your enemy. It's better if we act in trouble, so if any of the tomb thieves catch wind of our chase from this city, they'll have more reason to know we don't love the law. Just pretend to be scared and run to the river."

"Pretend?" Sanura's ears pressed hard against her skull as she hugged herself tight.

Abayomi squatted next to her, the bandages at his knees sagging already, and wrapped his arms around Sanura's small body. "It will be fine, Sanura. We will be by your side the entire time. Nothing will separate you from us."

Jeannette watched him reassure Sanura, his fatherly actions disarming. This role of guardian that he'd slipped into somewhere along their journey fit him so naturally. It seemed strange to Jeannette, because even though she was older than him, he came out as the mature one. It didn't seem quite fair.

"There they are! By the acacia tree."

The fat lady sang, shattering the moment as two human guards ran for them from across the street.

"Here we go." Jeannette grabbed onto Sanura's free hand, the other already clutched in Abayomi's. The three sprinted down the street, trying to dodge those they could, but just plowing through the men and women too slow to scramble out of the way when someone yelled "Coming through."

Jeannette couldn't help but laugh breathlessly at finding herself, once again, running from the law. And it probably wouldn't be her last mad escape from some two-kit town along the *Iteru*. She'd never been in trouble with the police before her excursion to Kemet; the murky waters must bring out her inner rebel. With the threat only a phantom, she found herself enjoying the race down the busy main street of the town, the guards pursuing them like Hell's own hounds.

They tore off toward the Montu Temple and residential precinct, hoping to ditch their pursuers. Though her heart wasn't racing from danger, it had certainly hit the stress point from exertion. While scrubbing her body at the dorm, she'd faced the uncomfortable conundrum of getting down the river; she doubted she could trick a

214

crocodile to ferry them along this time, for the price of the cat *or* the pharaoh's coffers. They hid silently in a small garden behind a sizable house and waited as the guards ran by, cursing the narrow streets and endless passages. A fragrant bush filled the courtyard, churning up memories of lazy spring days in her childhood backyard.

Her pulse skipped along, nothing like a lazy spring day.

From beyond the walls they heard, "You go towards the bank, I'll continue downriver." The beating of feet bounced off the high, brick walls.

And finally, everything went quiet.

Within the garden, grape vines overran a trellis and a small alcove within the thick wall housed a foot-tall statue of Bast. Sanura trotted silently to the clay statue. Breathing slowly and letting her heart find a more manageable pace, Jeannette pressed her back into the wall's rough surface and watched the girl, taking in deep lungfuls of the floral perfume. The ache in her shoulder demanded a rub, and she reached back to sooth her injury. Abayomi came up next to her, his bandaged arm brushing hers he stood so close.

Sanura reached out and traced her fingers along the statue's base, then dropped her arm to her side. Something in her posture struck Jeannette as different, changed. Sanura's shoulders were pulled back, her ears upright. She looked ready, confident. Sure.

"Do you think she'll be okay? Out here in this world?" Jeannette asked. It must have been nice to have so many siblings, so many people who had to love her. "I'm not sure that she's going to be going back, to her litter I mean."

"I think she is stronger than she wishes to allow herself to be. I think, like all of us, she trapped herself into a mold that did not fit her true self," Abayomi said.

Jeannette turned to look at the mummy, his brown eyes thoughtful. "You, too, Abayomi?" He always seemed so certain of himself, even when he'd been a dried up husk inside linens.

Abayomi reached out for Jeannette; a rainbow shimmer danced across his palm. He hid it behind his back with a self-conscious smirk. Fish would forever haunt them.

"Yes. Even I have suffered a moment of self-uncertainty. I know, difficult to envision, is it not?" he asked with wry amusement.

Sanura returned, silently passing through the small garden. "Are they gone?" she whispered.

Jeannette raised her eyebrows and offered a shrug. "I don't hear them." She skidded down the wall and wrapped her arms around her legs. Quietly, they waited.

The sun breached the garden's wall and Jeannette shared the last of her protein bars—those things had the shelf-life of a stone—and passed the water bottle to Sanura, disinfected her scrubbed out scrapes, bandaged her torn fingernail, and popped two painkillers. Three left. She tried not to dwell on her various injuries of the past two days, though her shoulder reminded her of the spastic two-year old of pains, eager and always wanting attention.

"I think we can probably go," Jeannette said. "Or did we want to stay here until the lady of the house sics her dogs on us?"

Sanura pulled her ears back at that, turning to Abayomi without offering her own suggestion.

"I think it is now safe, but let us go quietly and discretely to the fishermen again, and have Jeannette find us passage to Thebes." He smiled at her, flashing his teeth.

"Me?"

"We need no help from the sons of Sobek!" Sanura almost spit out the name.

Jeannette raised her hands in surrender. "Fine, I won't hire any crocodiles for the river ride. We'll find another way to Thebes, even if we have to walk," she said as innocently as she could. The other two didn't look amused.

By joint concession, they evacuated their quiet sanctuary and slipped back into the alleys between the high walls. The heat of the day hammered against her eyes and exposed skin; Jeannette fanned out her hair to let it shade her shoulders. Even with her base tan, the sun still burned her nose and shoulders and she'd long ago used up her travel-sized tube of SPF 30.

She pushed her bangs out of her face, squinting into the sun. "I need a haircut," she mumbled.

"But your hair is so lovely." Sanura reached out and ran her small hand over it. "It is so light and soft."

Honestly, it was unsalvageable, with an eternal rubber band kink running through it like a tectonic upheaval. She smiled anyway. "Thank you. But I think your hair's much softer." She reached out and petted the top of Sanura's furred head.

Sanura broke into the delighted giggles of innocent joy.

At that moment, something inside of Jeannette bubbled up through her chest, unfettered and weightless. She rubbed Sanura's furry head, repeating 'noogie noogie' over and over again. With that same purifying power, Sanura's laughter filled the narrow alley and charged towards the busy streets; Jeannette's chased after it. She couldn't stomp out her delight; even if the guards ran up to them in that instant, she'd still laugh in their faces. When she hadn't been paying attention, life had turned on a dime: had turned from some dried up landscape into this fertile soil for happiness. She leaned against the mud brick wall, head tilted back and just gave into it. Sanura collapsed against her side, swallowing down hiccups.

Abayomi's stared from one of the women to the other, keeping his distance.

"Oh my." Jeannette tried to catch her breath, scrubbing away at her tears with the heel of her hand. Maybe she'd truly gone insane. "It's just . . ." She tried to explain, but one look at Abayomi, head tilted to the side, hands on his hips, totally sent her airborne again.

Swallowing down her next breath, she grabbed Sanura's hand and then, with no hesitation, grabbed Abayomi's.

"Come on. Let's go find a boat and blow this 'burb."

Though she tried to run for full speed, she only reached full limp. The hold on her friends twisted her wrist awkwardly, so she dropped their hands, unafraid that they would fall behind. Sanura, at her right elbow, giggled high and breathlessly, a carefree noise Jeannette expected from all pre-teen girls. Abayomi, a silent partner in their flight from the city, wasn't far behind. Glancing over her shoulder Jeannette saw him, his swaddled legs and arms slicing through the air.

The organized layout of the residential precinct dumped them into an area sprouting with businesses and market stalls. The market precinct's staunch formality collapsed in the wake of the laughing, racing girls. Jeannette and Sanura ducked around the corner of a dried fish merchant. Unsurprisingly, the merchant yelled out at them, shooing them with her hand in an international gesture of banishment. With a skipping twirl, Jeannette spun around and waved at the merchant, watching Abayomi slow to apologize and then speed up to join them.

Slipping through another courtyard-side alley, the girls came upon a half-a-haystack high pile of discarded bed straw.

They exchanged a look. Arched eyebrows met a grinning mouth.

As Abayomi ran toward them, charging forward without any

217

indication of stopping, they scooped up handfuls of straw and peppered him with the dried and broken sticks. Then quickly reloaded.

"What are you . . . ?" Abayomi ran his hands over his bandaged head and shoulders, brushing away the brittle straw and dust.

Jeannette snorted, then covered her grin with the back of her hand. Little bits of straw clung to the bleached hairs on her forearms.

Together, the women tossed double handfuls at the unprepared man. He roared at them, shaking his head to dislodge a clump that had caught in a fold of his linens.

Abayomi, chin dipped low, looked up at them from hooded eyes. He leaned over at the waist, and scooped up a clump of straw from the detritus at his feet. He held it out in his open palm as if to say: "You see this bedding? *This* is what I will destroy you with."

Sanura exchanged a glance with Jeannette, and the two began giggling again.

Sounding professorial, Abayomi said, "The wages of such a miscalculation are doom."

They ducked as straw hurled towards them, but it had been an unnecessary defense instinct since the already crumbled handful lost its form and caught in the air, falling harmlessly to the ground. Abayomi scowled, then charged towards them, catching one girl in each arm and landing them all in the pile.

A few merchants poked their heads around the corner, and unsurprisingly none of them joined in as the three friends rolled around in the large pile of discarded bedding. Jeannette couldn't swallow enough air, she was laughing so hard. Her jaw hurt; her teeth would surely shatter under the force of her grin. She wanted to savor this moment of blissful camaraderie, trap it in a jar to bring out later in more lonely times.

* * *

"You've got a . . ." Sanura picked another stem from Jeannette's hair.

"Right back atcha, babe." Jeannette flicked away bits of crumbled straw from the nape of Sanura's neck. They stood on the edge of the *Iteru*, downriver from the main docks they'd used on their last escape from the city.

Sanura smiled. "You speak in such riddles." The girl shook her head, not letting Jeannette's riddles ground her mood.

Jeannette scanned the bank for predators and didn't see anything obviously ready to eat her. She walked through clumps of reeds—heads heavy with red tubular flowers—into the river, her feet sinking into the muck and her dress sucking up half the water. Dunking herself, she tried to rinse away the scratchy dust, scrubbing hard at her face and arms. The mud sucked onto her feet, and her passage released the ripe odor of decomposing marsh. Small, tweeting birds darted away, flitting from reed clump to reed clump. Sanura dipped into the water next to her, sending out delicate ripples. Little bits of golden straw floated along the surface down towards the sea. Abayomi stood frozen on the dry riverbank.

"Don't want to dip yourself?" Jeannette asked.

Abayomi shook his head, eyes wide and focused on the great river.

"Are you itchy?"

He shrugged. "Not with great irritation."

With a dramatic sigh, Jeannette pulled her shirt from her pack. Squatting next to a vast clump of reeds, she trailed the polyester in the shallow water, letting it fluttered along the river surface like tan grass blades. She returned to Abayomi, carrying her dripping shirt before her like a blessed raiment. "May I?" she asked. Water droplets dangled from her lashes. At his nod, she delicately began to run it along the surface of his body, trying to gather as many itchy stems as she could.

Eyes closed, his chest rose and fell in a slow cadence.

"We could re-wrap you. Use new linens."

He shook his head, and his breathing deepened, turning into a hum.

"You're purring." Jeannette smiled to herself.

He shook his head in denial again, but didn't open his eyes.

"It's okay," she told him.

He smiled a crooked smile and opened up his eyes. Suddenly, she wondered what he would look like now. Wished she'd looked before. Was his face handsome? She wanted to reach out and touch him with her fingers, instead she ran her damp shirt along his arm.

"Look," Sanura said.

Jeannette, needing some excuse to wrench her hands away, turned to look out to where Sanura pointed. A wooden riverboat slugged its way through the water, heading towards the docks not far upriver. In between the sailors and rowers straining to keep the boat on course, Jeannette could see a huge block of stone taking up the middle. About the length of ten men high, one end of the vessel curved up out of the water in a graceful arc, the other ended bluntly. A rectangular sail hung flaccid in the stagnant air. Though she'd seen bigger, the boat dwarfed the others

219

floating on the river.

"They are missing rowers," Abayomi pointed out, and Sanura nodded.

"Yes. At least two on this side." Sanura twisted her body to look up at the adults. "Maybe we can find out where they're going and offer to row."

Jeannette groaned, glanced down at her hands, calloused from stirring beer, and groaned again.

Unhappy with the decision but mind made up, Jeannette waded out into the river, waving her hands high above her head.

"Hey!" she called out to the front man wielding a long pole. "Where are you headed? Do you need rowers?"

Chapter 23

"PUT YOUR BODY INTO IT. Come now! Row!"

Though no whips snapped through the air to urge them into a rowing frenzy, Jeannette still felt trapped in a late '50s historical melodrama. Only in this instance all the extras were truly North Africans, not Europeans packaged up in atrocious make-up and dismal wigs. She'd never rowed anything substantial before in her life. Back in junior high she'd rented a four-man canoe with some classmates and paddled down the Spokane with no destination or goal. The girls had splashed each other more than actually traveled in the wobbly thing.

"Shift west," the sailor stationed at the front wielding a long pole called out. "Shoal coming on."

Planted on hard benches on the deck of the boat, the river filled Jeannette's left-side view as she leaned forward and pulled back hard on her oar.

"Row!"

The call was incessant, and a little grating. Far away, down the river, she'd been knee deep in the water begging for a ride. A direct window into her past.

The riverboat held a huge stone obelisk excavated from a quarry seaward. As she rowed—Jeannette's arms already screaming with fatigue from the upriver struggle—she distracted her litanies of "ow" by counting the evenly spaced divots along the side of the monument. It wasn't the diversion jackpot she'd hoped for; a callus gained from brewing had already sloughed off and counting the pain sparks in her shoulder seemed an easier task. Instead, she watched the river unfold and the metallic-tinted swallows dart across the surface as if catching the diamond sparkles of sunlight.

The ship's master had stationed Abayomi on the opposite side of the ship, while Sanura sat right in front of Jeannette. The poor girl skipped the edge of her oar along the surface more often than not, and Jeannette could see the shift and strain of the muscles in her shoulders and upper back. She felt sure that Abayomi did the work of the two of them and added an extra heave to her own pull to not be complete baggage. There were still empty seats. By the expressions on the other rowers' faces, Jeannette and her friends were definitely part of the 'out' crowd, even

221

amongst the low men on the Egyptian totem pole. She didn't blame them, really. She and her friends were each a purple snowflake on a sea of sand. Not much more they could do to stand out. The ship's master had been desperate to pick them up after Jeannette told him of their vast experience rowing such a vessel. They had trotted to the docks upriver to be picked up—their conscription to the ship so quick, she doubted even a guard stationed to watch for them would have noticed their passage—and were unceremoniously plunked onto a seat and told "Row." Easy as pie. Though, Jeannette didn't really think pie was all that easy. Certainly, neither was rowing.

The man at the front of the ship, the one wielding the long pole he poked into the river, called out, "Crocodile!"

Jeannette twisted in her seat and leaned over the edge of the boat, scanning the waters at the bow. Coming from the riverside, its ridged tail breaking the surface of the river, swam a huge, green reptile. Over her shoulder, Sanura hissed.

With its beady eyes, the great man-killer pierced Jeannette, and she *knew*, knew with every prey instinct a human could have, that this was the Riverman, the same crocodile she'd duped not so long ago. She waited for the inevitable tick-tock accompaniment and choked out a strained, manic kind of laugh. No limbs would be lost to this beast, she, Sanura and Abayomi were safe from those bone-cracking jaws.

She couldn't take her eyes off the beast as its tail sliced through the water, propelling it towards the boat's hull. The Riverman extended its mouth, a wide yawn flaunting its sharp teeth as if saying, "Look at me human woman. Look at me and know your fear." Jeannette knew her fear, no arguing that.

The pilot began to lift his pole from the water when, in a burst of speed—surely supercharged by some prehistoric radioactive meltdown—the crocodile snatched the pole from his hands and snapped it in two. The crack echoed in the cloud of silent awe that had curled around the boat and all its crew.

Mr. Jawbones looked at Jeannette. Stared at her. Yellowed teeth on display. Jeannette's skin broke into a cold sweat even as she blinked away a sting set in by the hot wind. The words the crocodile had said exploded in her mind like a bomb. *The stone of nature is shown in the tooth.* She definitely saw his teeth.

Then the crew of sailors broke into a cacophony of chattering, awed at the great demonstration; the pilot ordered another pole and a lackey

222

quickly materialized one. Jeannette shared a secret moment with Abayomi and Sanura.

A great splash drew her focus back to the water; Mr. Jawbones had disappeared. Jeannette scanned the water all along the riverside, looking for those huge nostrils or protruding eye ridges and didn't see anything but a flock of geese congregating in the reeds. Running her eyes up and down the bank she almost missed the crocodile's next move, but the squawk of the geese yanked her attention back. Within the circle of waterfowl, now spreading out like oil on water, floated the crocodile, bolting down a bundle of feathers. One webbed foot jutted out from the left side of its long snout, and then, with a gulp, it all disappeared.

Mr. Jawbones' beady eyes tracked her the entire time.

* * *

The rest of their day was no less nerve-wracking. The shipmaster had taken the ship up a series of canals that brought the obelisk as close to the workers compound as possible. Since the powers that be constructed the village at the base of the Theban Cliffs, a tractor-trailer's worth of manual labor was still necessary to drag the block of stone the final leg of its journey. Coming to terms with the new mess of work that haunted their near future, Jeannette gathered up her small group.

"We promised to row, not lug a stone monument around," she whispered, and they casually walked away while the ship master barked out orders to those who waited for some form of paycheck at the end of their day.

Avoiding the Thebian market areas, and anyplace Jeannette might be recognized, they followed their noses and found some food merchants. Not surprisingly, nobody sold fried chicken, roast baby potatoes with rosemary, or ice cream; instead she bought sandy bread, cooked fish, and some grains. What she would give for fresh peas, though her hunger was monster enough she'd probably eat fried cow feet. Sanura was happy enough with her fish meat.

Jeannette mournfully jiggled her dwindling store of debens and kits. She'd given most to Nekhebu, though it was peanuts compared to what he'd done for her. Embarking with scant savings, a coin here or there amounted to a depressing lack. While dealing with the Master Slaver's duty, she would have to get a job. She closed her eyes and sighed. Did this work never end?

"Are you troubled, Jeannette?"

Jeannette looked at Abayomi and offered him a smile. Ripping some grainy bread off the whole, she handed it to him. "Want some?"

He tilted his head—his pondering pose—reached out, and took the bread. "It has been a long time since I have partaken of food; I have forgotten the flavor."

He opened his mouth, pink inside, no longer an obscene cavern of desiccated body parts reminiscent of Discovery Channel horrors, and bit into the bread. Jeannette and Sanura watched him, mesmerized by the grinding of his teeth, the flex of his jaw under his gauze.

Jeannette offered her water bottle.

"Water?"

He nodded, chasing down the chewed mass with a swig. He returned the bottle with a smile.

"More?" she asked.

Abayomi shook his head. "I am sated, thank you."

After that, Jeannette couldn't take her eyes off him.

Sanura led them back to the riverside where they killed time throwing dirt clods into the water until the night sent the men and women of the river to their homes. Any cats in the area quietly scrammed through the reeds, seeking out mice, locusts or other disgusting, yet obviously tasty prey. Sanura pouted when they didn't come and say hello, and secretly darted disappointed looks Jeannette's way.

Jeannette found a flat stone and rubbed her thumb across the slick grain of it. Soapstone, maybe. She bounced it in her palm as she watched the waves ripple down the river.

"Did you know," she asked to distract herself from her uncertain future half-buried in hopeful, yet untested, plans, "that in some cultures they believe that after you die, your spirit—your *ba*—gets reborn into another body?"

Sanura, nearer the *Iteru's* edge, had dug her feet into the bank of the river; the mud oozed up her shins. In the slanted, evening light, her dark skin appeared to be a reflection of the dark soil brought in by the river of life.

"I do not know about such a treacherous thing," Abayomi said from where he sat by her side.

"Treacherous?" she asked. With a flick of her wrist, she chucked her stone into the river attempting to skip it across the surface, but the river wasn't the smooth plane it could be in the morning and the stone plunked into the water, never to be seen again. Eat that, Mr. Jawbones.

"When you have worked hard in your life to live well by the Gods, you should earn your rewards. Do you not think?"

Jeannette shrugged, letting her hands seek out another flat stone as she stared out across the water. She wanted to believe in their fairytale afterlives, but that kind of belief took a lot of energy. Abayomi was dead. A mummy. But his state of non-life didn't prove an afterlife. He existed in a body suspended somewhere between this world and the next. Maybe that *next* was a paradise, maybe nothingness; maybe it simply amounted to some realm mere mortals could not comprehend.

She put her money down on the latter. Probably, there was simply nothing.

Though reincarnation wasn't a bad plan. If she were reincarnated, Jeannette wanted to be somewhere where life made a little more sense. Where being a good person really did matter, and boyfriends weren't stolen by selfish best friends for an amusing interlude. Where gods weren't force-fed to the masses and no one was ruled by fear. Where people didn't own each other, and each person was truly measured by their actions, not a silver tongue or daddy's influence.

Where she felt well and truly cared for.

"I guess," she told Abayomi, pulling her fingers out of the wet soil, stone-less. She rolled her shoulder, the pain less defined and more of an all-over ache. Her muscles felt heavy on her bones. "I definitely agree with going to a place of peace and happiness." Though it all sounded like a trite daydream. Death was death. Still . . .

"I think when we die, we do go to that kind of place, Jeannette." Sanura twisted around at the waist to look at them. "I believe in the love of my mother, and that she would not abandon me."

Jeannette looked at Sanura, really looked. Somehow, though the girl sounded certain, she also sounded a little sad.

"Aren't you immortal or something?"

Sanura snorted, the sound reminiscent of ripped paper. "Nothing lives forever."

Jeannette brushed her hands against each other, trying to dislodge the sticky soil. Sanura was exactly right. Even in Egyptian mythologies the gods found their end.

"It's pretty dark. We should go find some jugs."

"I do not like this plan of taking jugs for our own use without properly compensating those we take them from." Abayomi gained his

225

feet and offered Jeannette an arm. Jeannette took it and let him hoist her up. Sanura kicked her way through the water, rinsing off her legs.

"It isn't for our own use. We're helping the pharaoh. Maybe just a few . . . okay, just two, from the laundry. They had a ton of them."

Though Jeannette hated the idea of taking something, anything, from the working man, she didn't have the money to pay for them herself and still make sure she had cash for food. The three entered the laundry, the building dark and empty as the bowels of Abayomi's mastaba.

Sanura lit a torch. Everything looked a little different now, with a new, daunting task hanging over her shoulders. She wished all she needed to do was wash a dead man's body, instead of ripping off the place and somehow undoing a tomb robber ring. She and Sanura found two smaller jugs of the proper shape and some wax to seal the lids. Abayomi paced the length of the building, agitated and active. She wondered if he'd pull out one of his treasures from inside his linens to leave behind, but she should have known better. That gold was for the gods.

"Abayomi. I'll pay them back later. Would that be okay?" When she spoke the words out loud, her own tension lessened. "We'll come back and give them new jugs."

He looked at her, the torch light creating deep shadows over his white-wrapped face. With his head tilted to one side, his shoulders heaved once as he took in a deep breath. "Yes. I think that would be a fair recompense. Maybe we should return three jugs."

Jeannette laughed, then she rolled her eyes. "Fine, Abayomi. Three jugs. And maybe some of my amazing beer."

They sought out the crooked shack Sanura and Abayomi had been staying in during their search for Jeannette and found it still empty. The sleeping mats were fairly thin and musty, but the weariness weighing down her bones didn't seem to mind. Sanura cuddled up next to Jeannette. Jeannette wrapped her arm around the girl's waist. At her back she felt the press of Abayomi against her.

* * *

Haggling for breakfast, the ruckus of the morning market swept away all conversation the three might have attempted. A small boy, maybe three, a force of nature actually, ran around Abayomi's legs screaming about grandpa and pulling on the loose ends of his gauze. Then, with a spasm of ancient break-dancing, knocked Sanura's fish out of her hand.

226

"Stupid brat!" Jeannette secretly tried to trip the kid with her hiking boot. "If you keep that up, Osiris will kick your butt out of Heaven!" The child gave her the evil eye, but eventually his mother came to collect him, with three other children in tow. The woman offered no apology as Sanura gathered up her breakfast from the ground. Dark bags swam under the mother's eyes and she looked half sucked dry.

Sanura watched the family with a kind of horror bulging from her eyes.

"Surely that child is possessed. That woman should take him to my mother's shrine to throw out the evil spirits."

"Just think," Jeannette shifted the jug she carried on her hip, "you were almost a midwife. You'd have to deal with kids day in and day out."

Sanura looked stricken.

"I'm sorry! You can . . ." Jeannette broke off. Whenever Jeannette saw a pack of kids, she wanted to escape into the crowd. They were little terrors. "You can maybe just deal with the pregnant women," she finally said, glancing between Abayomi and Sanura. Both still watched the tiny demon child—wailing as his mother dragged him away by the arm—as if waiting for him to shed his human skin and reveal his true form.

She didn't even wonder how they'd handle the modern kids jumped up on energy drinks and video games. Something about hard work and duty at a young age seemed to beat out the annoying habits of most children here.

With food in their bellies, Abayomi's bandage ends tucked safely away from violating fingers, and a full bottle of water, the three made their way up the pathway to the Theban Cliffs. Jeannette constantly maneuvered her jug from one hip to the next. She missed Ass. Abayomi, ever stoic, trudged along without once readjusting his jug. A flock of dark ibis flew against the tan hills; the cliff-side leg of their flying V about half as long as the near one. Once high enough up the cliffs, the three could see the fertile green strip of ground around the *Iteru* stretch on endlessly, but Jeannette understood its inherent fragility. A bad flood year could unbalance it all. No wonder everyone here prayed to Hapi, the breasted god of the Nile and abundance. They prayed so much Jeannette had learned some of the words through aural osmosis. Standing to the side of the trail so the other travels could pass easily, Jeannette studied the river and its valley.

"Come to nourish Kemet, Oh Hapi. Overflow your shores, Oh Hapi. We sacrifice for you, our oxen, our beer. We repay your bounty.

227

Nourish all who thirst in this waterless desert. Oh joy when you come, Oh Hapi." As she spoke the prayer, Abayomi joined in. A few of the words didn't match, and Abayomi's had far more 'joy's in it, but the general sentiment was the same.

Sanura beamed at them.

Jeannette turned away, swallowing down a gallon of self-consciousness, and re-joined the procession through the dry, windswept hills. A haze of dust followed the line of people and Jeannette's heavy boots became encased in a thin veneer of dirt that held shimmering flecks of quartzite. She couldn't wait to put her sandals back on, but the boots didn't fit well in her pack. High above, the cliffs blocked out half the sky as they made their way to the workers village. The path climbed brutally, and though she had no donkey to drag this time, she did have the jug to carry and she was panting by the time they queued up to enter the compound. After giving Sanura her fill, Jeannette guzzled down the rest from her water bottle while noting each and every guard.

Trotting along the line of milling tradesmen, all waiting their inspection to pass beyond the brick walls surrounding the village, were the ever present jackals. Sanura reached out to pet one, but it shied away after it stole a good sniff of her legs, huge ears pressed to its head like a misbehaving dog. Jeannette's palms grew clammy, and she rubbed them along her dress. As the line whittled down person by person, she rehearsed what she'd say to the guards once her turn arrived. The bottom edge of the jug bit into her hip, a part of her that had little cushioning. She shifted from one leg to the other, marching forward inmate-style, short steps, head down.

Their turn snuck up before she'd stumbled through her half-formed speech. Suddenly, face to face with an unknown guard, all practiced phrasings conveniently went the way of the water from her bottle. His mouth moved, and out came a garbled rendition of the Gettysburg Address, or so it sounded. Something sharp poked her in her kidney. She swung around to glare; Abayomi delivered two sharp nods at the guard. "Pass, Jeannette. You did not forget our pass, did you?"

The pass. She'd decided not to repay kindness with misery by swiping the Master Brewer's pass. Knowing they would ask for it, she'd tried to mold a fake early that morning, but she knew it wouldn't meet muster even if she'd had more time. Now, facing the guard, bad counterfeit, still damp, in her bag, panic tethered her wayward mind firmly to reality. "Oh, of course. I have it here . . ." She smiled at the guard—she'd hoped for a familiar face—as she set down her jug. "Sorry, it's here somewhere." She dropped her pack and rifled through it; the rough edge of her home-made pass scraped her sore finger.

No ticket in to this exclusive club.

"I'm sorry." She offered an apologetic smile. The man's eyebrows drew together and Jeannette's slim hope began to wither on the vine. She knew five of the gate guards by face, just her luck that she got someone unknown. "I seem to have lost it. Listen, I just have to drop off this beer—"

"Jeannette?"

Jeannette looked up from her fumbling and saw—

"Tabiry!" Jeannette waved excitedly at her friend. "My God, you're here."

The woman, still radiant with otherworldly, inner joy, had a worn edge to her smile, new lines around her eyes. No adornment graced her slender neck, though she still had her black hair beautifully plaited, the ends sparkling with copper beads. Life must be hard as one of the country's top artists, Jeannette thought, though not unkindly.

As Tabiry joined them, Sanura stepped away, giving the two women room for their reunion. Jeannette apologized again to the guard. "I'm really sorry; I must have dropped it—"

Tabiry lifted her hand. Jeannette waited, acid burning the back of her throat.

"Dutiful guard." Tabiry's voice reverberated with a deep nobility. "This is my friend, an apprentice to a master brewer in Thebes. His beer is the most sought after drink in the entire compound, and she delivers it regularly." She lowered her gaze; lashes, long enough to be extensions, dipped, framing her dark eyes. "She has been through here many times, ask the other guards. Look at the jugs she carries, heavy with beer. I think the loss of one pass should not bar her entry to deliver her most vaunted product." She shook her head, sending the copper-tipped ends of her braids into a tinkling melody.

The guard stood straighter, shifting his gaze from one woman to the other. Jeannette held her breath, biting her lip to keep her smile from blooming into something manic. Another entrance guard approached, poking through bundles exiting the village.

"You know this one?" the guard asked. Jeannette's pulse jumped, she knew the black guard that approached and relaxed at the spark of recognition in his eyes.

"The brewer, of course." He walked over to join them. "You willing to share some of that beer with us today?" he asked. Lines of sweat channeled down his temples. "This is thirsty business."

Jeannette let herself grin. "You know this beer is meant for others. My master would not allow me an additional jug today for you to quench your thirst. I must pray your forgiveness." She dipped her head.

"You never give in." The guard shifted his pointed stick from one hand to the other. "Where is your donkey today?"

"Died."

His eyes grew wide. "Oh. Unfortunate."

Jeannette shrugged, it was the first lie that had come to her mind. "Luckily I have smaller jugs today and this man here to help."

Abayomi said nothing.

"Dropped on his head," Jeannette offered, chills threading through her body at each lie. "Isn't good for much but lugging things around." A lump clogged her throat.

The Nubian laughed at Abayomi, then gestured for them to come forward. "She's fine, Khay. Just let her through."

Khay stood aside, head rolling in an eager nod, obviously happy someone else had made the decision on what to do with the foreign woman without her pass. The familiar guard waved them on, then went back to poking and searching the outgoing people and their goods.

Safely within the workers compound, Jeannette released her burden of worry with an allover body shiver. Then she set her jug down and hugged Tabiry in relief.

"It's wonderful to see you again. Last time I was here, I couldn't find you anywhere." And I ran through half the village, Jeannette finished to herself.

Tabiry laughed and returned the hug, if a little less enthusiastically than Jeannette.

"The Hidden One smiles upon us this day, Jeannette. I see you have deliveries. If you have time, please share a meal with me. And I have another message to my old master, if it's no trouble."

"No, no trouble at all." Jeannette beamed, happy to return the favor. "Food sounds wonderful. So does beer." Grit deposits ground between her teeth and her throat felt just as arid as the outer dunes. "After I deliver these jars, I would love to sit and talk," Jeannette said. "Where can I meet you?"

"There is this bread baker who blends honey with his flat bread. It

230

is up the main road, past the temple of Ma'at."

"I'll meet you there soon."

Jeannette hugged her friend one more time, then left to find someplace to dump the decoy jugs, water-filled and not up to any intense scrutiny.

"That was close." Jeannette led the others down a small alley. "I had hoped we'd get a friendly guard. I know half of them by now." It had been the squishy part of this stage of her plan. Of a mostly squishy plan, if she were to be honest.

"Dropped on my head?" Abayomi complained. "I could just be your silent assistant. I did not have to be deficient."

"Sorry, Abayomi." Jeannette spotted a refuse pile and plunked her jar along the edge of it. Someone would scavenge them for reuse. "Next time I'll tout you as the strong man who speaks only upon the deeper matters of the gods and the afterlife." She turned to him and forced herself to meet his eyes.

"I am to leave now," he said.

Jeannette nodded.

Sanura's ears went back. Annoyance smoldered off of her more violently now than when they'd devised this stage of the plan. "I don't like it. You shouldn't leave." She grabbed Abayomi's hand, implanting her fingers within his. "Why do you have to go?"

Jeannette squatted next to Sanura. "Because he's the silent type, and very, very sly." Jeannette smiled, but didn't feel it inside. She could tell Sanura didn't buy it, either. "He'll be in the shadows learning important things while I act the loud, brash fool."

Abayomi placed his hand on the girl's shoulder. "I will be gone not long." He nodded stoically. "I never am." He hugged her, a rough, not quite comfortable kind of hug.

Sanura practically choked him in her grip. "I don't want you to go," she said into his neck. "What if you don't come back this time?"

"I will."

"But what if you don't?" Sanura's voice cracked.

Jeannette inhaled roughly, and looked away.

"I promise. Your mother watches over me, Sanura. And you. We will all find each other again before you even become aware of my absence. It is written in the great texts. It is talked about by the Gods." He stood, rubbing his palm over the top of the girl's head, right between her ears. "It is a vow I make upon my honor and my pride. I will seek

231

you out in a few days."

"No."

Jeannette blinked at the steel in that one word.

"There is no reason for you to leave. We all stick together." Sanura's ears were pressed to her head, with her legs firmly planted giving her the stance of a readied boxer determined to never go down.

"But—" Jeannette looked over at Abayomi. They'd not discussed his leaving in any detail, but they'd both agreed he should remove himself from the girls to avoid any future association to give their infiltration plan more pathways to success.

"No," Sanura repeated. "We can separate for the day, we can avoid each other in public, but we have to meet for the evening meal." She growled. "Promise me, Abayomi. You will find us at meal time and you will share our supper with us."

Abayomi, eyes wide, alarmed almost, nodded. He leaned down and Sanura hugged him, tightly, desperately, arms wrapped around his neck in such a vise that if he had had to breathe, Jeannette would worry for his continued existence.

Then Abayomi hugged her too. She shot down the urge to cling to him like Sanura had, to hold onto him just as desperately until the sun set and the days spun by in an endless river of time. But she didn't. She hugged his flesh and strength, let him go, watched him walk away, wondered if the heart beat she'd felt had been hers or his.

Chapter 24

FROM ONE HISTORY BOOK—a reference volume with a weight overshadowing even that of her long-haired cat—Jeannette had read that most tombs were robbed by the same people who carved them out of the limestone cliffs, often with help from local officials and priests. It wasn't the job of roaming, homeless boys raised by jackals or godless heathens who spurned the divine order of things. Gangs of up to a dozen thieves would break into a sealed tomb, uncaring of the curses laid upon it, and smash and steal. Sometimes the very embalmers would pocket a golden trinket without so much as batting an eye.

At least she'd guessed no eyes were batted when she'd read the sanitized descriptions from the glossy pages of the coffee table book. Few individuals, no matter what era or belief system, would think twice when riches were so easily in their grasp. Do not tempt the morally mushy, for they cannot overlook the low hanging fruit.

Though Jeannette knew the guards were in on this crime ring, other facts were as fuzzy as a bacteria culture stored in a boiler room. Though boastful when confronting the Master Slaver, she hesitated on her next step now that she'd put her plan in motion. Get to the workers compound. Check. Find the thieves and convince them of her desire to join their ranks, thwart the establishment, and take what would not be freely given to her. Not so check.

She hoped that Tabiry would introduce her to the other workers. Unfortunately, even if hanging onto the skirts of the popular girls had ever been Jeannette's modus operandi, she couldn't come out and ask Tabiry for anything. Right now, if she were to sculpt out her emotional landmark from the cradling limestone cliffs, barren and unscalable, those men deserving Dante's inner circle would be waiting, staring down at her from the top. Et tu, Jeannette? But Tabiry didn't need to know her true motives. She only needed to inform folks that Jeannette was okay, trustworthy and a friendly type, and she would do the rest on her own. It wouldn't be instantaneous; it could take weeks, months. She expected that a few precise words dropped within earshot of the right people would spread through the cloistered society like dandelion seeds on a windy day, only to settle to earth and sprout a weed that took over every neglected lawn. Eventually someone would make a move on her. Hours of spy movies couldn't be wrong.

She just hoped it wouldn't be that guard, the one who'd as soon have his forceful way with her and then see her head on a pike.

Sanura, in a sour mood, trudged along beside Jeannette like any recalcitrant teen who hadn't gotten her own way. Though, to Jeannette's view of things, she'd gotten just that. They passed the temple of Ma'at in bitter silence; the rich scent of baked bread and honey swimming through the still air did nothing to break the girl's mood. Climbing up the temple's columns like living things were painted vines in rich greens, and the feathery heads of papyrus plants seemed poised to sway in the wind. From the cool inner chambers of the temple, beyond the cedar doors, priests recited a toneless liturgy. It was pretty much the same in every faith: God protect me. God help me. God give me the things I need.

While Jeannette bought them beer and bread from the baker, she watched Sanura, mopey since Abayomi had taken his leave. "You know, I didn't want him to go, either." In a wash of guilt, Jeannette hoped that Sanura's attitude didn't sour Tabiry's opinion of her.

"You didn't talk to me. Include me in the decision," Sanura said, and Jeannette acknowledged to herself that the girl had a point. "He better come back," she continued, lip curled.

"He will!" Jeannette raised her arms in surrender. "He promised, didn't he?"

In the rear garden attached to the bakery, a few short tables mingled with potted vines and palms, fragrant blossoms and small trees with bright red fruits. The sun's reflection glinted along the iridescent wings of a dragonfly that danced across the calm surface of a rectangular pool. Papyrus lined the pool, shading a corner from the persistent sun. All the reeds needed were red stems and they'd be the unmistakable cousins of Seuss' Thing 1 and Thing 2. Other patrons were also enjoying the calm of the garden in the late afternoon. The lazy buzz of insects filled the spaces between spoken words.

Tabiry sat near the pool, a red clay mug on the table before her as she cast her attention to the dragonfly. Jeannette took a moment to study her friend, beautiful and elegant in profile. She wondered if the woman practiced such a pose, or if that kind of grace came naturally to some people.

Sanura slammed to a halt beside her. Jeannette sighed, wondering if counting to ten really helped. Composing a more lengthy apology she thought unnecessary, Jeannette turned to Sanura, but halted at the apprehensive angle to her ears.

"What is it?" Jeannette coaxed, following Sanura's focus, seeing only Tabiry and a few diners in the path of her gaze.

"Jeannette!" Tabiry called from the table.

Jeannette glanced at her friend, who was offering a welcoming smile and motioning for Jeannette and Sanura to join her. Facing Sanura again, she noticed the girl had composed herself, but her ears were still cocked at her uncertain angle and her chin dipped toward her chest, setting her gaze forward.

"Are you okay?" Jeannette asked.

Sanura looked into Jeannette's face and frowned. "I don't think so." Her gaze dropped from Jeannette's face.

"Do you want to go sit?"

Sanura looked over at the table where Tabiry waited, ears still pulled back in an expression of uncertainty. "I suppose."

They approached the table and Jeannette slapped on a smile. "Hello, Tabiry," she said, keeping half an eye on Sanura. She placed her mug and bread down, and squatted on a short stool. Sanura, silent as a spirit, sat next to her and lost herself in the pool.

"And hello to you, too," Tabiry greeted. Sitting with Tabiry, eating real food and drinking thick beer, Jeannette assumed she'd find some contentment and ease of wariness. Instead she kept casting searching glances at Sanura, who kept her hands in her lap and head bowed. That straight jacket of tension encasing Jeannette's nerves took on the density of lead. Guilt trip mastery came easily to the young.

Their conversation bounced upon lighter subjects such as the weather, a local festival for Horus, and good clothing merchants until she steered it into that dark recess she'd not been looking forward to. "I was thinking of trying to get work in this compound." Jeannette forced her features into lax neutrality. Her jaw tightened and she forced herself to relax.

"What of your apprenticeship at the brewery . . ."

"Today was my last run; I need something else."

"Why, what did you do?"

Jeannette flinched at the edge to Tabiry's words; the unspoken word *wrong* dangling from the end of the sentence. The woman's model-perfect face lost its radiance under the displeased twist to her mouth. For a moment, she looked like a completely different person. Jeannette turned her face away, unseeing eyes aimed toward the pond. The dragonfly had left for better hunting grounds; nothing stirred the surface. She hated that look, that how-could-you-fail-at-something-so-simple look. In her previous life, such a glance would have stirred up instant feelings of shame.

Jeannette swallowed, but continued with her plan, a little less guilty about using her friend to introduce her to the compound's inhabitants.

"I had a run in with a Slave Master." Jeannette jerked her chin towards Sanura. "I didn't much like the idea of Sanura being sold for a man's uses. His guards were chasing us constantly, so we had to leave the city."

"Oh," Tabiry's voice softened considerably, "I see." Jeannette chanced a look at her. That dark cloud of disappointment had gone, and in its place settled an expression of amused endearment. Jeannette didn't think it much better.

"Sorry, I can't be your postal girl anymore," Jeanette said. Tabiry lifted her eyebrows and Jeannette waved the question away. "Taking messages to your old master. Anyway," Jeannette continued, "I'm very skilled at brewing now, as you know. I just can't be too visible. I've no idea how far the slaver's power reaches. I'd like to avoid the guards and just make some money to feed myself and Sanura." She hummed in thought. "And eventually save enough to get out of here all together. Maybe go to the Delta. I just . . ." She stared hard into Tabiry's eyes. "I hate that slaver. Fat pig." She looked away, wiped some spit from her lips. Really, she did hate his ideas, though he didn't seem such a bad sort if you looked at things from his side. His side, her side, Sanura's side. How many sides could be examined before you trapped yourself in inaction? She slurped her beer, and then set the mug down precisely in its damp ring fading in the heat. "I know that a good artist can make a solid wage here, and I was hoping a brewer could make a little more, too."

Tabiry's eyes lingered on Jeannette's face.

"You wish to find another master to work under?"

Jeannette shrugged, but her inner cheerleader whooped and chanted war cries. "If possible. I need to ask around, find out who's open to an apprentice."

"I know a few people who might need you," Tabiry said with her typical gracious smile, but something about it didn't seem as approachable as it used to. "Please, follow me to my home and I will find a place for you and your friend to rest and maybe tomorrow we can find someone you can apprentice with again."

236

"Really? Well, I—Thanks."

After that, Jeannette scarfed down the rest of her bread, ready to jump to action, but Tabiry ate her small meal at a leisurely pace. Sanura, quiet as a statue and not using her mouth for anything but eating and pouting, had finished her meal long ago.

Jeannette shifted in her seat. A strawberry tree grew nearby and she wondered how it would taste compared to an actual strawberry. She rolled the nylon strap of her backpack into a spiral, let it unfurl, rolled it up again. The air felt heavy, useless weight tacking her to the ground, but Jeannette refused to deflate it by saying something inane. She didn't want to be that kind of person. Attempting to relax on her stool, she stretched out her legs and waited until Tabiry finished, stood with that familiar, sweet smile, and led them from the bakery.

"So, how's business?" Jeannette asked as they walked through the workers compound. Built for a purpose, the place was run with efficiency. The refuse piles were all out of the way and absent were the ubiquitous streams of waste sluicing down other city's streets.

"Very well, thank you." As Jeannette trudged along in her hiking boots, Tabiry glided along on a cloud. Her white robes flowed behind her in such a way Jeannette wondered if magic wasn't somehow involved. Forever an earth-bound angel. "We're always busy with the decoration of vases and cups. Right now we are crafting amulets for the dead, though our supply of red jasper has met its end and we await another shipment to complete that task."

Only about five minutes passed before Jeannette could smell their approach to the smithy followed closely by a gray haze that sunk everything into an industrial, dreamlike quality.

"Doesn't this smell bother you?" Jeannette rubbed at her nose briefly, then abandoned the attempt at stifling the smell. The taste coated the roof of her mouth. Metallic, like blood.

Her pace unchanging as she wound her way deeper into the metal crafters ward, Tabiry shook her head. "The scent of metal working becomes a comfort after a time." She nodded to those they passed, her hair beads tinkling at each dip of her chin, and many lifted a hand in greeting as they worked their bellows or fed wood to a fire. Through every section they passed, the locals watched them.

"Do you have many breweries here?"

Tabiry glanced over her shoulder at Jeannette. "I'm afraid not. We do have two, but they are well staffed." An old woman on the street offered Tabiry a linen bag fat with something light weight. "Thank you," she said to the woman, then to Jeannette, "Can you carve, or make pottery?"

Jeannette lingered on her childhood, back at camp the summer before junior high. It had been her first time at camp, a secular outdoors institution surrounded by fir and alder that most of the girls had attended for the past four years. Jeannette knew nobody. She'd put her hand to whittling, to give herself something to do when the other girls of her cabin planned out and performed skirmishes against the boys camp a mile up the road. The knife the director had given her was duller than a banana, and the pony she'd tried to create looked exactly like a stick hacked to death with a butter knife.

"Honestly, no. Probably something else would be better."

Following behind Tabiry, Sanura's hand held in her own, the two would exchange squeezes, a kind of companionable communication. Maybe Jeannette would be forgiven eventually; maybe she already was.

As her feet swept her along, she studied everything around her, trying to imprint the lay of this city into her brain like a mental GPS. Though she'd been here before, her previous business dictated a seek and destroy tactic of getting in, doing her business, seeing Tabiry if convenient, and getting the hell away from that handsy guard. Now, she needed to know it all.

They didn't speak much as they followed Tabiry through a uniform neighborhood, each house a mirror of its neighbor except for the various colors the brick walls had been painted. They did not speak of the weather, nor did they speak of Tabiry's homeland, how she came to Kemet, where she learned her skills with gilding. Truly ignorant of nearly everything but the superficial, Jeannette felt unable to ask anything personal due to the woman's own armor of silence and focus.

The friendly bridge that had once connected them had twisted apart under the breath of her lie, unknown, but perhaps sensed. Jeannette didn't know. She couldn't read this woman without imprinting on Tabiry her own expectations.

Tabiry ended their game of Follow the Leader, and with a smooth swing, pushed open the door to a mud-brick home, two stories with high windows, washed in the color of pale reeds. "This is my home. Please, come in with peace in your heart." On the home altar squatted a traditional statue of Bes. However, next to Bes was another statue unexpected for a home altar: Sekhmet, the lion-headed goddess.

238

Jeannette dropped a bit of bread she'd tucked away for a snack on the altar.

"You worship the Kemet Gods?" Tabiry asked, no emotion in her voice.

"It is the custom of these parts." Jeannette studied her friend. "I meant no disrespect."

"But do you believe?" She asked so pointedly Jeannette couldn't dodge the argument.

She gently shook her head and readied herself to say, "I don't believe in anything," but that no longer resembled her truth. Her denial turned into a shrug and she dropped her gaze to the floor. "I think, maybe, there's something out there." Was it a god? Was it all powerful? Probably not.

Tabiry dropped her gaze, her long lashes dipping to shade her eyes. "I have my own Gods, from my own land, but I too speak to these local Gods." She returned her attention to Jeannette, her eyes having gone hard with her jaw clenched. "In public."

Few other adornments decorated the main room: a fine linen hanging with a painted scene of fields of grain, a gazelle captured in mid-leap carved of white alabaster rested on a table, a fan of woven reeds propped up against the wall. Something about these sparse items—the altar, the fan, the carving of non-Kemet origin—seemed to say more about Tabiry than any words the woman had voiced.

"You may stay on the extra sleeping pallet for the night." Tabiry began puttering around, scooping out dried beans to soak, wiping the ever present dust from the surfaces.

With an intense desire to not share the afternoon in unpleasant silence, Jeannette grabbed Sanura's hand. "Thank you. We'll find some other place soon. Right now we've got some errands, but we'll be back before nightfall. I'll grab some things for the night meal, too."

Tabiry looked up and smiled, but the effervescent happiness that had always danced in those eyes didn't spark that positive glow. The smile was forced, and it seemed Tabiry just didn't have it in her to offer anything more.

"I'll have some dinner waiting then," she said as they left. The door quietly closed behind them.

"Dourness is spreading," Jeannette said while looking at Sanura, their feet leading them away.

Sanura stared at Jeannette, a kind of worried hunch to her shoulders and an off-kilter angle to her ears.

"Out with it. What's wrong?"

Sanura shook her head. "I don't know. I just—" She looked back over her shoulder in the direction they'd come from, toward Tabiry's house. Her chin dropped. "She feels funny," came the tiny words. "I just don't know."

"Feels funny?" Jeannette asked, but Sanura wouldn't say anything more.

The early evening of canvasing the local craftsmen and merchants directed her to a typical, two-story building washed in light blue. "Herit needs a helpmate," an old woman had said. She'd had a mouth full of horse teeth and a crop of whiskers any donkey would have been proud of. "She's a brewer of sorts." The old woman laughed, and the comparison with an equine didn't end with the teeth.

The metallic smell of the metal workers had been mouthwatering compared to the cloying scent of Herit's business: a perfumery. The flowery odors assaulted her nose and Sanura fell into a spasm of sneezes. The poor girl's eyes oozed with tears and she mewled pitifully.

"The air is bad." Sanura held the corner of her dress over her nose. "Like rancid almonds and too many flowers." Unshed tears shimmered in her huge eyes.

Jeannette leaned down and asked, "Do you think you could get used to it?"

Sanura shook her head vehemently.

Jeannette inhaled and puckered her lips in the exhale. This was going to be a challenge.

"Well, Sanura. I haven't much choice. Nobody else knew of anyone looking for help." No kiosk in the center of town had been plastered with Help Wanted signs. "Do you want to wait out here?"

Sanura nodded and Jeannette entered the perfumery.

The woman's face, presumably Herit's, twisted tight with objection. She looked Jeannette up and down only to mutter, "More foreigners, overwhelming the native people." Then, louder, she said, "What experience do you have?"

"I was an apprentice brewer, and my beer was enjoyed by people throughout Thebes." She didn't want to mention the foreman of the guards, Raia. She had no idea which guards had been bought and paid for. "Though, I am proud of my beer, all of my successes I must attribute to Tenenit, who guides my hand. Through my body, the goddess acts. I'm but a vessel for her art."

Herit squinted at her, the wrinkles around her eyes and lips multiplying. "You are from the north?"

Jeannette nodded. "From a distant land." She gestured roughly, indicating a place on the other side of the stars. "Will you take me on?"

Herit shrugged, not looking all that impressed. "I need someone strong to stir." She grabbed Jeannette's bicep, which was no lab worker's arm anymore.

Jeannette flexed, and then laughed as Herit nodded once.

Once outside, Jeannette nearly stumbled over Sanura, squatting on the ground, nose stuffed in her armpit.

* * *

"There are at least two separate groups involved in this scheme."

"Two?" Jeannette asked.

Abayomi nodded. "The Pharaoh's own men are involved. I recognized one as a vizier's aid."

He'd found them not that evening like he'd promised, but two days after their parting at a well near the metal worker's precinct, approaching them like some next door neighbor on his daily stroll. He only needed a small wagging dog on a leash and a tweed jacket to fulfill the image. Sanura almost leapt from her own skin, she'd been so excited to see him. Now, a few days later, the three huddled in a squat on the flat roof of a home she now resided in and Jeannette couldn't tear her eyes away from Abayomi's own—brown and warm and comforting. His return look was almost tangible.

"It breaks my pride in my countrymen. They are filth." He spat. The moist spittle splat against the plaster.

They'd found their current digs—the furnished hut of an unmarried weaver named Werel—by bothering everyone who'd stop to listen to their pleas. Werel didn't seem bothered by Jeannette's smell, but Jeannette had to admit she'd never smelled quite so foul as she currently did, all lilies and myrrh. Sanura kept scowling at her, keeping Abayomi between them as if he could block the odor molecules with some not yet discovered mummy magic. It had to be worse than the overly floral, girly scents of pampered harem girls. Or what she imagined pampered harem girls would smell like. Her hands and wrists were as soft as velvet, though, having been overly coated with balanos oil. Her lips no longer sloughed off a blizzard of dry skin flakes. She'd secretly coated her feet with the oil as well. Her own unspoken form of rebellion.

The precious, rare perfumery ingredients imported into the village in a single day could have been liquidated and fed Nekhebu and his family for a year. Or more. She wasn't quite sure just how precious the Biblical resins and imported flowers were. Not to mention the fine containers: vials and little jars intricately crafted from clay, or those beauties coaxed into graceful curves from pure alabaster. Mostly, Jeannette worked with cobalt glass, the same shade she could find at the local hippie shop that sold Oregon Grape Root and Echinacea extract for those ailments people were too embarrassed to go to their regular doctor for.

"Jeannette and I found them packaging some items for travel late at night. We followed, but couldn't get too close. They have guards," Sanura said from where she sat at Abayomi's feet.

Jeannette gave them her same old line. "Maybe we can bribe one of the guards?"

She prepared herself for Abayomi to shake his head at her suggestion. Again. "They will all die at the hands of the pharaoh's loyal men if caught. They know their lives are forfeit. What do you suggest we could give them that is worth more than their lives, or the items they currently sell?"

Truthfully, they had nothing. "Maybe we could threaten them with some monster gobbling up their soul for their evil deeds."

Abayomi shook his head in a slow, sorrowful arc. "They well know they will wander through the wastelands for all eternity for this unforgivable crime. Ammut will have her fill in the Hall of Two Truths on their weighing day."

"Why am I not surprised?"

A short, obscure note had been sent to the Master Slaver with another brewer Jeannette knew, suggesting they were hot on the trail of the thieves, braying hounds after the frightened fox. The thieves could not avoid the sharpened blade of Damocles.

Jeannette stared down on the street, watching for anyone paying them too much attention. They garnered a few stray glances, but these people were far too busy to worry about folks chatting on the roof of a linen weaver's home.

"Sometimes the hunger of Sobek fills the hollow people and they cannot deny this appetite for the prizes of this material world," Sanura said sadly. "If only they knew of the pain of wandering."

Jeannette mumbled "Yeah" at the same time Abayomi nodded his own agreement. Like those dogs roaming El-Balyana streets, they were all strays, and only the smart ones survived. She would survive, and so would Sanura and Abayomi. She bit the fleshy part of her hand, thinking.

Chatter from home-bound workers crossing at a nearby intersection mingled with Jeannette's unsettled thoughts, muddling them into a murky wretchedness. Even though she'd explained that her ploy to infiltrate the thieves would take some time, secretly she'd hoped her clever plan would come together like a jigsaw puzzle. Unfortunately she couldn't even find a corner piece to begin. It had been nearly a week of spying on the culprits, and she found herself no closer to being accepted into their folds than she had been straight out of Abayomi's tomb. Beside her, the mummy sat frozen in profile in the early evening light, and Sanura's only movement was a random flick of her ear.

"Well, we aren't going to get much done sitting here, lost in space," Jeannette said. "What do you want for dinner? We've some boiled beef, a fresh cucumber. And the fruit woman had peaches for sale." She patted her backpack. "And I've got nut bread." She hummed in delight. "I love nut bread."

Sanura giggled and hugged her knees to her chest. Jeannette grinned, her chest expanding with warmth.

"I would think you were enjoying your time here, Jeannette." Abayomi rose to his feet. "Loving nut bread. You have practically become a citizen of the great pharaoh's."

"I'm just tired; it's been a long day."

"Hail to Isis, the day is done," Abayomi chanted.

"The night has come." It was an automatic response to his invocation.

"Daughter of the Word, end this day of light," Sanura finished.

Jeannette stood. "Okay, let's eat."

* * *

On a working day during week three in the workers compound, she finally stumbled on that corner piece. The morning opened with a stiff neck and added an aching hip free of charge; her pallet needed fresh stuffing but such worries were luxuries she couldn't ante up. As the sky outside lightened, she remained an immobile, bed-trauma victim, day-dreaming about Sunday mornings on a mattress, wrapped within soft, cotton sheets freshly laundered, the cool feel of the fabric against her skin, a soft pillow to cradle her head. No weather man predicted a cloudless, hot day, but she knew she'd need no sweater to keep warm. That was how her day started, missing things she'd never feel again.

The small house she, Sanura, and Abayomi shared with the enterprising weaver had a cellar and the typical rooftop landing. A four roomed replica of the house to their right and the house to their left, lined up like disciplined toy soldiers, each painted with either a red or yellow door. Jeannette's had a jaunty, red door, of which she grinned at daily, finding it somehow a little brazen.

At the small altar near the front of their house Werel had placed statue of Ra. Sanura had rummaged up a statue of Bast, a very pretty piece of red pottery. Jeannette, in a mercurial mood one day, put a mud brick on the altar explaining, "I worship all my ancestors and those who will come after me, which at some point will have all emerged from this same soil." Sanura had given Jeannette that I'm-unsure-if-you're-pulling-my-leg look, but had allowed her the worship of the brick.

At full dawn, she shuffled her way to the perfumery and stirred pots. Her parents would so be proud of where her state education had gotten her. Though the work was as challenging as that at the brewery, at least the Master Brewer had let her play. He'd give her the chance to experiment with the brewing process, adding flavors, filtering and such. Herit struck Jeannette with a pinky-thick stick every time Jeannette even asked to try something beyond the limited recipes traditional perfume making incorporated. Welt ghosts lined her forearms.

Once finished with her morning chores for Herit, Jeannette could enjoy her siesta. However, instead of relaxing during the heat of the day like the sane, she'd wander the city, munching on a portable fish snack. Though the city became as close a friend as her old stomping grounds in Thebes had, it meant she got no respite. The alleys between dormitories, hidden exits through the walls, which houses were empty and could be put to use as a hide-out: all of it, she watched.

She hadn't seen Tabiry in days; the woman was always absent when Jeannette stopped by her home. It took no time at all before she realized Tabiry would not be her key to meeting the wannabe-rich and soul-daring.

Even if she had no idea how to go about enlisting with the thieves, she couldn't waste time napping. So every day she cruised the precinct, watching the scribes record the artists' supplies and the men weigh their bronze chisels under the demand of the guards. She had seen the

244

contrails of some activity, but it was late at night and the faces had all been masked by shadows. It wasn't that she expected the thieves to announce their new profession by wearing purple feathers in their hair or having a special hand signal or anything. Well, maybe a special hand signal. Jeannette secretly tried to catch someone flashing some hand sign.

Her time with Sanura and Abayomi had nearly gone the way of the cathode ray tube. Evenings were sacrosanct and they always met for dinner, but following the final swallow of juice, they each went their separate ways. Sanura and Abayomi did their own scouting, each of them bringing in scraps of information. Her life had become uncomfortably similar to that of her time in Spokane. Go to work, grab some lunch, come home, eat dinner. Rewind. Replay. Ever since Gabby and Ricky had married, and even after their divorce, Jeannette had lived a fairly solitary life, her rigid schedule only broken by her weekly jaunts to the theater. One pop, one bag of popcorn. One ticket to entry.

On the roof of a half-finished house, tucked between the western wall and a garbage heap, the river breeze rambled from the floodplain casting aside the stench. Snug between piles of mud bricks, she had a good view of the side road and its tributaries, so rarely traveled that the likelihood of anyone spotting her balanced within an acceptable range of risk. Munching on a fish cake, she instead watched the wild cats scrabble over leavings that their not so delicate palates deemed edible. The cats on the hillside seemed oblivious to Jeannette's previous infraction against their kind, and some even mounted the roof, begging for scraps of fish. The motley browns and yellows, even striped tabbies, swarmed her once she gave one kitty a strip of fish.

"I've not enough for all of you." She tossed down more fish. So much for her hiding place.

None of them were long haired, like Archy was. Too hot, she guessed. How many years until a long haired cat developed? Did the felines have to mass migrate to more northern climates to trigger the gene? Gabby was hopefully feeding Archy well. He liked his tuna.

How about a long haired daughter of Bast?

Jeannette snorted; the cats scattered. Which was probably good, since she'd run out of fish and didn't want these felines to hold a grudge too.

High noon came and went, and as the sun's trajectory tilted toward the great desert to the west, the people once again put their noses to the grindstone. From her high perch she heard talking and movement on the

245

invisible, nearby streets, the sound of hammers clanking from the smithies. Time to return to her mentally demanding task of stirring. She flexed her fingers; her joints popped.

And that was when she'd noticed.

Below her on the street, a man of average build and average height walked at the pace of the hunting benu bird, scanning each side passage. A braided cord, of the type some of the craftsmen wore, encircled his waist. Various wooden instruments that looked suited to a kitchen dangled from the cord, but Jeannette knew they were used by a potter.

She'd seen him in this area before, and something instinctual froze her in place as he glanced in her direction. A gray cat leapt from the pile of bricks and dashed toward the man, keeping a safe distance separating them as it yarled for food. Another joined it.

"Beware little felines, or you may be made as sacrifices for Bast," the man said. He absently rubbed his fingers along the braided material, his movement slow and methodical. Then he seemed to shake himself from his thoughts and continued on in his surveillance.

Everything had gone sharp. The brown on the man's fingers. The tans and grays of the cats. The faded blue sky. The air's flavor caressing the back of her throat. Each breath she took filled her, and the expansion of her lungs and diaphragm felt monumental, the air rushing over her tongue a marvel. The gray cat sat and licked its hind leg, then looked up at Jeannette, leg pointing to the sky.

With mumbled profanity, Jeannette crawled silently down the ramp of bricks that got her to the roof and tiptoe-ran to the edge of the building blocking the way the man had gone.

The man had paused at an intersection and looked down the left side, then the right, then stepped down the right alley and was gone.

Slipping off her sandals, she trotted on the bare balls of her feet until a sharp command had her silent and still. Focused on her hearing, she listened—nothing but a harsh mumble. Taking mouse steps, she reached the edge of the building; voices argued in a hush.

". . . You don't have to listen to me, but I think it a wise choice," said a man.

"We need to finish up and move the things downriver. Thethi is no help," another said, rough with frustration. "The guards watch him too closely. One on Yuia's tomb claimed he'd been slicing off slivers of his chisel. The idiot."

"Was it that *mi-nether* of Thoth?" the first man asked.

A woman hmmed in affirmation.

The second man grunted. "I think so. Damned keen eyes on that one."

"We need another watcher. Without Thethi, there would be only seven."

You've got to see, Jeannette. You've got to look. Pulling her ponytail tight, it brushed against her mostly bare shoulders. She bopped her head around the corner of the building.

There, three stood in a guarded bunch so close to her she could almost reach out and touch them. The two men she didn't know, though the one she'd seen before, but the woman was very familiar to her.

She must have made some gasp, some noise she herself didn't even notice, because the woman looked up and met her eyes. Dismay sunk Jeannette's tattered heart as the woman, beautiful and elegant, sunk into a shadow of herself, her shoulders dropped, her perpetual smile a faded memory and in its place a frightful grimace.

Too late to back out now, Jeannette still wished she could slink off and have time to think everything through. Instead she took a step towards them and nodded in greeting.

"Hello, Tabiry."

Chapter 25

TABIRY'S EYEBROWS LIFTED, her nostrils flaring like a frightened animal.

"Jeannette." Only Jeannette's name, but it held a well's worth of despair and sorrow.

Jeannette stood as stiff as one of the many statues that decorated the very tombs this village had been founded to build. At the sight of her, the unknown man brandished a gnarly walking stick, while the potter took a step back, fists raised before him.

She had to do this. She couldn't hide her head in the sand.

In a defensive rush, she shot her hands up in surrender, palms facing the three. "Hold on, hold on. I just want to talk. No baseball with my head today, please."

"What did you hear? What did you just hear, woman?" the man with the deeper voice said, poising his stick to strike her. Dressed in the worn clothing of a laborer, she could only guess at how much he squirreled away for his family. Waylaying the useless, yet priceless trinkets from their delivery to the tombs wasn't done to pad his wardrobe. He readjusted his grip on the twisted stick, taking an awkward step to steady himself. His foot was a knotted mass at the end of his leg.

"I heard enough." She spoke directly to Tabiry. Her friend's chin rose defiantly. Jeannette clenched her jaw. "I want in."

A heavy quiet filled the air, then smashed into a cacophony of protests from the two men.

"Why would we allow you—?"

"Let's just kill her. She'll tell the guards."

"I know some of the guards. They like me," Jeannette cut in. Unhappy expressions from the men turned even more volatile. "I can help to keep them out of your business—for a cut." She turned to Tabiry. "Tabiry, you know me. You know I know many guards." She tried to look her most earnest, tried to mask her face with sincerity as she pleaded with her friend. Her friend, the tomb robber. "You also know I wouldn't tell them anything. I've known about your activities for a while, and I told none of the guards."

The men looked to Tabiry, and Jeannette held herself still. For a moment, the strain seemed to stretch everything to just about breaking, but then Tabiry's body relaxed and that dangerous almost-teeter into violence tipped back toward sanity. Jeannette felt herself release a breath.

"Jeannette. It is apparent we have much to discuss." The woman's black eyes, usually so expressive with amusement and warmth, now revealed nothing. "I will find you later." Tabiry turned to leave.

"Tabiry," Jeannette called out. "I've no love for the pharaoh." She couldn't lose this now.

"This I do know," she said as she walked off, the two men going their own way.

Alone, Jeannette brushed her bangs from her forehead; they landed in a heavy clump against the clamminess of her skin. She needed to cut her hair; it was forever poking her in the eyes.

Tabiry.

Jeannette could not believe it. Tabiry was one of the bad guys. One of the people she had to turn in to the guards. And, if she did, her friend would surely die.

* * *

The night sky sprawled forever into the east. Jeannette pointed at a spattering of stars shaped like a doughnut. "That's the Tutu Constellation." Then she saw another pattern of bright and pale stars in a spiral pattern. "And that one is called Fibonacci." Where she and her friends sat on the roof, the breeze caught up the sweltering air and tossed it over the walls of the village.

Sitting to her right, Sanura sighed in awe at the stars. Abayomi, on Sanura's other side, examined another portion of the sky. "Right there," he held up his hand at arm's length, fingers splayed wide, "is the Mummy's Hand." He looked down at Sanura. "See it, Sanura? The fingers?" He wiggled his wrapped fingers.

The young girl giggled, lifting up her own hand to lay it over the pattern in the sky. Jeannette didn't see a hand herself. Maybe a palm tree if she tilted her head just right. "Oh yeah," she lied.

She popped a piece of goat into her mouth and ground her molars into the tough meat. The thieves—she had a hard time thinking 'Tabiry and her friends'—had been talking about the priest Yuia's tomb. Though Jeannette didn't know where that tomb was planted, she knew she could find out.

"That looks like a benu beak," Sanura added to their re-creation of the sky.

"That long curve, near Sopdet."

The brightest star above them twinkled at her, the light of Isis and Anubis in the sky. One of the closest star systems, Jeannette knew that the Sirius System was probably more reachable to her right now than of her own place of origin.

"He who is on the mountain watches over us," Abayomi said in reflexive prayer to the star.

"*You* maybe," Jeannette said. Anubis protected the dead and the underworld, not aimless travelers. "I think I want Isis on my side. She's one goddess I can totally respect. All her magic and power—"

"What about my mother?" Sanura's words tumbled over each other. Her eyes glimmered in the depths of the night, illuminated reflections of her soul. Or, maybe, it was Jeannette's.

"Of course! Bast is one of the greatest." Jeannette smiled and grabbed Sanura's hand. "But you see, I've already got her in my corner." She squeezed that hand firmly, and Sanura squeezed back. "She sent you to us, didn't she?" Sanura's whole face lit up, her canines showing in her predatory cat smile, and as explosive as a champagne cork, she said one word: "Yes!"

One final squeeze and she released Sanura's hand to lean back onto the reed mat, cushioning her head on her crossed arms. After a few deep breaths, she finally told them what she'd stumbled upon that afternoon. They didn't interrupt her, didn't even make a noise—except for dismayed sigh from Sanura—as she laid out how she'd found the thieves. About Tabiry.

Even after the short rendering of the facts, they remained silent. Then Sanura laid her head on Jeannette's chest and hugged her. Abayomi stood up, grabbed his mat, stepped over the girls, and repositioned himself Indian style by her other side. They surrounded her, their presence offering a support she'd only recently allowed herself to accept.

"Thanks guys; I'm okay." She took a deep breath. "Well, a bit dazed I guess. I just never imagined." She swallowed, then continued in her smallest voice. "I don't think I can turn her in." Though, a no nonsense part of her wondered exactly what was written on those notes she had delivered for Tabiry during her previous visits.

Abayomi hunched forward, elbows propped against his thighs; Sanura slid off Jeannette's torso and curled up close to her side as if the comfortable air held an actual chill. A fly crawled across Jeannette's thigh, and she shooed it away with a flick of her hand. The three of them observed the earth's slow rotation as the stars crept across the black sea above.

"There is reason enough for her to involve herself with the thieves," Abayomi said, breaking their silent vigil. "She does not hold our same reverence for the dead—she is not of Kemet."

Jeannette bolted upright. "Neither am I, but you don't see me stealing." She tried to keep her words low but her attempt only turned them into a growl.

"No, Jeannette. That is because your sense of the proper way to live is different from that of anyone I have ever met."

He nipped her budding annoyance with his words, and she wondered if she was really that easy to manipulate. "Fine." She relaxed her body back down. Sanura stared at her, ears half-erect. The *mi-nether* opened her mouth, as if to add her own measure of words, but then closed it shut. "I'm weird, someone who I thought was really nice is a lawless villain, and you've got it all figured out," she listed off. Abayomi grinned at her. Inexplicably, she remembered that he had dimples under all those layers of white. "Of course I do."

"Abayomi is very smart," Sanura announced like some grand proclamation.

"Of course he is," Jeannette agreed. "He should totally figure out what to do next."

A shooting star streaked across the sky, low on the horizon. Its string of light burned away.

"You should convince Tabiry to include you in her group."

She really wanted to say, "Duh," but kept her opinions to herself. Instead, she said, "And?"

Abayomi rolled his head toward hers. The wrappings still held tightly to his cheekbones, chin and nose. She'd done a good job gauzing him up without really looking at him. "And you find out their members, their schedules, their routes of dispersal of the treasures . . ."

"And I just turn Tabiry in with the rest of the rats?"

"Well, she is a thief of the dead," Sanura said as if speaking to the slowest kid in class. "There is something wrong with her."

Jeannette wanted to poke her. Hard. "But she's no rat. She's my friend." Jeannette found it nearly impossible to view this entire situation in blacks and whites. Tabiry had helped her out when Jeannette had had nobody. She didn't want her to go to jail, to be skewered on a pike or thrown in some cage until her flesh sloughed off from starvation. She felt the scales teeter precariously with this new information: Tabiry's life against Abayomi's scarab, and her and Sanura's freedom. Her *life*.

"She chose her path." Sanura wouldn't look at Jeannette, though her tone held no forgiveness.

It was a bitter pill, one she'd rather not take without a mouthful of strong drink, and a mouthful of the local beer certainly wouldn't cut it. She knew in her next update to the Master Slaver there would be no mention of a beautiful woman from Kush amongst the numbers of the damned.

"Well, they didn't solve the construction of the pyramids in one night." At the moment, even a movie solution escaped her. She climbed to her feet and Sanura took her offered hand. "I'll get them to accept me and deal with Tabiry's sticky problem when the time comes."

The moon had set by the time they climbed down the stairs from the roof. With a last look at the sky she saw another shooting star. She turned away, not bothering with a wish.

* * *

According to her fingers measured against the horizon, Jeannette had another hour of stirring until she could ditch the most boring job on earth. Herit checked up on Jeannette under some random schedule, set down by a calculation considering the proper stars in certain positions and the height of the *Iteru* divided by the patterns derived from scattered goose bones. It was nothing Jeannette could anticipate. Old Herit, dedicated sergeant to all things strict and full of toil, disapproved of straying from her ancient recipes and other time wasting activities like talking to Jeannette.

A few days ago, Jeannette had attempted a little creative straying from the path of a thousand year old perfume mix and added a little of this and a dash of that. Jeannette had no chance to hide her trial jars before the woman had approached Jeannette's small experimental pot and sniffed.

The woman's eyebrows drew together, nose wrinkled aggressively, and without a word she stood there until Jeannette dumped the entire thing out in the street.

Her wages were still being garnished for that adventure.

The sun met the tip of a hill far off in the western horizon and she began cleaning up. When she'd met with Tabiry after throwing her lot with the thieves, her friend had been distant, so unlike her previous self overflowing with affection and charm. She wanted to drop to her knees and beg Tabiry to tell her why she'd ally herself with people in the *wrong*. But Jeannette ripped up those words before they could even take form and tossed them to the winds. She had a role to play now.

"I wish this hadn't happened," Tabiry had said. "I worry for you. Some of these men . . ."

Jeannette worried for herself as well. Unfortunately the actors were in place, the director had called action and Jeannette hoped this tale wouldn't be told by an idiot. She'd always felt happy endings a bit trite before: everything neatly wrapped up in a bow, no loose ends and everyone getting what they wanted—especially if they didn't realize what it was they wanted from the start—but this time she had her fingers crossed for nothing but.

Tonight Jeannette would meet with Tabiry's gang. She'd eaten nothing all day—her stomach hadn't much approved of breakfast. With her tiresome duties as a perfumery peon, she could only occupy her mind with Tabiry and the convincing trap she had to set. She'd practiced speeches, one after the other, only to toss them aside as corny or completely unbelievable. She ran her face through various facial expressions: happy to be with the thieves, scared of the Master Slaver, sad to have nothing. And of course sincere.

She could do sincere. If she really put her mind to it.

Forcing down some cured goose meat and dates, she went to the meeting house on the other side of the village. In a covert conference by the smithy, Tabiry had told her the tenth house in the row, and sure enough the clay pot with blue flowers decorated the stoop. Sucking the salt from her thumb, she was yanked through the door into the house two seconds after she'd laid down her first sturdy knock.

"Oof! Let me go, that hurts." She tugged her arm free from a man's grip. Behind her the door thumped shut, and before her watched a gathering of luckless peons sheltering in the cramped room.

"Who the hell are you?" one man demanded, a no-man-zone around him that no others crossed. His voice chilled her marrow. The look in his narrowed eyes was hard. Jeannette wondered how many bodies he'd buried. And she didn't mean properly, as in the tombs. He'd seen many difficult years here in Kemet, his missing two fingers a testament to that. Due to the good ten inches he had on her, plus his broad shoulders, she categorized him as a Mafia goon.

Jeannette glanced at Tabiry, who stood in the back of the living area with another woman. She wore an impervious, stone mask offering no support.

Tabiry had to have told them her story, so no reason repeating the heartbreaking tale of her sad state. So, they must want to measure her sincerity, just how far into damnation she'd be willing to go. Jeannette let her features twist to reveal her bitterness and anger, and she looked away from those eyes, hiding the fear by pressing her hands to her thighs, shunning the erratic pace of her heart. "Jeannette. But you know that." She gestured at Tabiry with a nod. "I'm just like you." Her words burst from her, a solemn pledge. "A slave for the pharaoh who wants more."

She attempted an easy shrug, but her body kind of jerked under her will and she abandoned the false sureness she'd tried to display. Her ears burned; the air in the room smoldered. Nobody moved.

The man, certainly the leader of this criminal group, frowned, his eyes reduced to slits. She didn't think this was going so well.

"I'd like to point out that I've known about your actions for weeks and I haven't told any guards." It was technically the truth. "And I don't intend to." Did her nose just grow an inch? She ran her tongue across the roof of her mouth, trying to entice some saliva to do its job.

"How did you find us?" the leader demanded.

She straightened, landing her hands on her hips. "All I had to do was keep my eyes open. I stumbled on some of your men in Thebes, not very smart." She tapped her temple even as she counted the five men and three women she could see, plus another who'd shut the door behind her. She wasn't about to just jump out of there if things went south. Unbidden thoughts of Abayomi and Sanura constricted her throat; she wished she wasn't here alone.

The man hid none of his disgust. Jeannette dropped her chin, but forced herself to maintain eye contact with him through a shield of her loose bangs. "Why do you want to join with us?" he asked. The others kept quiet as she tried to negotiate for her life. "To steal from the tombs brings the anger of the Gods." His voice had grown quiet, calm. She could smell his fetid breath and her knees grew weak. She felt small, and only wished to be smaller.

She glanced at Tabiry, who nodded once. Latching her eyes onto the man, Jeannette shook her head. "They're not my gods. I don't worry about the gods from Kemet. I just need to be free of this place. The Master Slaver has his eyes on me and I just want to go north. I need money to do that. I'm so tired of stirring vats of perfume." Nobody said a thing. "Look, I am an excellent spotter and I know the guards and their schedules."

The leader looked unimpressed.

What would it take to win this hardass over? Then, she remembered.

She dropped her pack to the ground and squatted next to it to unzip the main compartment. The unseen man behind her wrenched her arms into a knot behind her back. With a yank to her hair, he forced her to face the leader. A snarl had taken over his face; Jeannette's legs gave and she dropped to her knees. Ineffectually she struggled against his grip, then like a dead fish on land, went still. "Just . . . let me show you . . ." She pointed her chin toward her bag. She could hear her heartbeat booming louder than a live rock concert in her ears, steady, like the war drums of a native tribe. The leader nodded once and she was released, pushed forward to catch herself with her hands. Slowly, she looked over her shoulder to glare at the goon behind her. It was Club Foot, from when she'd first discovered Tabiry. He grinned, a vilely disgusting show of stained teeth. Turning away, she stared at her hands on the floor, fingers splayed to hold herself up. Her backpack lay half opened below her. The dark recess of the pack caught her attention, something to focus on, something to do. She pushed herself back into a squat and pulled out her money belt. The veil of her hair surrounded her face. The edges of her vision had gone fuzzy; all she could concentrate on was the money belt as she fumbled to unzip the inner pouch. The zipper wouldn't slide, and she tugged on it, twisting the teeth. Hands shaking, she almost dropped the entire thing onto the ground, but managed to jam three fingers into the opening. As the silent crowd waited, Jeannette's fingers found what she wanted, and she slipped out the ankh necklace that had put her on the lam so many months ago.

Someone murmured at the rear of the gathering; another grunted acknowledgment. The leader looked at the ankh and nodded.

Jeannette wet her lips. She didn't want to sound frightened. "See, I can be useful. I just want a cut."

* * *

Sanura gripped Jeannette's arm before she could grab the door's handle. "Before you go, I wanted to do a prayer for you. To give you Bast's protection."

255

"I'm not a pregnant woman," she groused, "or a baby." Jeannette's nerves brought about a mood akin to a pharmaceutical junky without his next handful of codeine. The dinner she'd tried to eat remained in her bowl, cold and destined for the slop pile. Tonight was her first night 'on the job'. Starting at the lab hadn't sent her into such fits, and she'd been green back then.

"Bast protects all." The cat-headed girl's ears edged back. "Please, let me do this."

Catching Abayomi's nod, Jeannette succumbed. If it made Sanura happy— "Fine. If you want to." The butterflies crammed into her stomach struggled to break free.

"I do. The blessing will give you strength against the darkness. Please, sit here, Jeannette." Sanura gestured to Jeannette's fluffy cushion, deformed by the indent of her butt, near the hearth. Jeannette slipped her backpack off her shoulder and dropped it to the ground, then plopped onto the cushion. The hem of her *kalasiris* hitched up to her thighs and she tugged it down over her knees.

"Do you mind if Abayomi helps me?" Sanura asked.

Jeannette shrugged.

"Lie down, then. And close your eyes."

Realizing this wouldn't be a quick Hail Mary followed by an Our Father, Jeannette wiggled her body forward along the floor until she could rest her head on the cushion. With one last glance at Sanura's orange eyes, she closed her own. She could feel her friends on either side of her. Slowing her breathing and keeping it at a steady pace, she tried to relax. Sanura began a low chant, the words soft, barely audible, and completely incomprehensible. Maybe it was the special Bast language, or something only mini-gods knew. Either way, it filled her ears with a species of music she only ever remembered hearing when out in the pastures and open places of eastern Washington, away from cities and people. Birdsong and wind.

The chant continued and with time Abayomi added his own voice, low and rough. He spoke no words, just added to the sound with nonsensical syllables. Their mixed tones began quiet and consistent, like a hymn at a cathedral hummed in the background as the priest rang the virtues of cleanliness and daily devotion. The hymn seemed to touch upon the nerve endings in her earlobes, the tips of her nose, fingers and toes. She felt it in the base of her skull and in the beat of her heart.

Like slipping into a doze after a hard day stirring, she sank into a heavy relaxation. The chant continued: the soft female purr and the deeper male voice weaving together in an array of benediction.

At first she just felt sleepy, then a deep-seated exhaustion settled into her bones with chemical swiftness. Akin to that thick haze when she'd met with the baboon woman, the edge of sickness like she'd drunk too much cheap liquor pooled in the well of her gut. Her fingers went numb and she floated for a moment, forgetting everything.

Which was just fine, because nothing really much mattered.

Slowly, in small increments, the lethargy and intoxication faded away, from her arms, legs, then her chest and head. When her awareness bobbed to the surface, the chanting had burrowed to the underside of her cognizance. As easily ignorable and persistent as the buzzing of insects on hot summer days.

Maybe due to feeling mentally fuzzy, Jeannette wasn't terribly surprised to notice she no longer sat in her dark hut with Sanura and Abayomi chanting over her like dedicated monks. Instead, she sat in a palm tree-lined courtyard with a pool and a tiny patch of manicured lawn surrounded by the lush overgrowth of tall grasses, reeds and leafy plants probably available in the local nursery back home for a price. Above the courtyard, the moon hovered like a half chewed-on cookie and a mixture of night-blooming blossoms celebrated their fertility with delicate scents that Jeannette couldn't stop inhaling. A dark obelisk stood guard over a horde of little black kittens, mewling and crawling over each other in childish play. A steady rattle bundled in beats of three filled the air as Jeannette got to her feet.

A tall, cat-headed *mi-nether* woman was sitting on the stone edge of the pool holding a nursing kitten to her bare breast. Low on her hips hung a white, linen skirt—her only clothing—and around her neck was a torque of bronze. Upon her head sat a uraeus, the centerpiece a rearing cobra. Reaching up from the pool, lotus blossoms and their broad seed heads framed the woman. The kitten, black from the tips of its ears to the end of its tail, was kneading her flesh with eager paws. Slowly, she ran one long nailed finger down the back of its head, over and over in a caress as she smiled upon it.

Tall columns, each mounted with a flickering torch, circled the courtyard, supporting the roofs of the surrounding buildings. Between two of them stood another cat-headed woman, this one dressed in the long, gauzy gown of a priestess. Clutched in her hand she rattled a sistrum. Shake shake shake. Shake shake shake. The priestess dipped her

257

head at Jeannette and then faced the woman nursing the kitten. Her rattle never faltered.

With the kitten nestled against her ribs, the nursing lady now had her eyes on Jeannette. They were brilliant orange. The lady blinked and those eyes gleamed, lit by the very reflection of the overhead moon setting the night sky in partial glow. In that instant Jeannette felt small. Incredibly small. The ant crawling along the palm leaf's serrated edge loomed larger than even she. Desperation flooded her chest; she wanted to turn away, to slink away, unseen, and hope she would be forgiven this appalling trespass.

Her arms crossed her stomach and she pressed her damp palms into her sides. Gaze dropping from those soul-knowing eyes, she mortared her feet to the paving stones. Sanura had sent her here, so this must be where she was supposed to be. Even in the evening's warm sigh, a shiver tickled over her limbs.

The lady blinked again and Jeannette sucked in a breath, shuddering, the air now thin. She let her shoulders droop. The priestess between the columns continued to shake the horseshoe shaped instrument. Ching. Ching. Ching. Like clockwork.

Jeannette waited, attempting to appear patient and polite. With her placid face, the one she used for annual performance reviews and irrational people, she hoped to draw no ire. Neither of the women said anything, the only noise that of the sistrum and the random meow or hiss as the kittens tussled. Finally, Jeannette released an unsure noise, a kind of 'uhh' that, to Jeannette's assessment, admitted some weakness. The cat-headed woman sitting on the fountain's edge turned up the corners of her lips in a feline smile.

"Ah, hello?" Jeannette immediately wished she'd kept her mouth shut. She shifted her weight onto her left leg. The sistrum rattled on. A little black kitten noticed her, then sprang away, tumbling on the paving stones.

"Are you Sanura's mother?" Jeannette decided to ask, sounding a little less like a dolt in the prime of her doltishness.

With a lazy blink of her orange eyes, the woman nodded and looked back down at the kitten suckling away. She scratched the kitten on the back and slowly pulled it away from her nipple. It cried out in protest.

"Mom! I'm still hungry."

Jeannette blinked. Talking kittens, the latest addition to her long list of weird. But really, such things didn't hold that much weird-weight anymore.

"Not now, son. I must share words with this woman."

Jeannette's brows crinkled. The words seemed to bypass her ears and go directly to her soul. This was Bast. Sanura's mother. The goddess. Jeannette wasn't exactly sure what this meant, meeting face-to-face with a mythical deity: protectoress and poster child for the '60s sexual revolution.

"Mom, she's funny looking. What is she?"

By now the other kittens had ceased their play and stared at Jeannette, some with ears half-pulled back, teeth bared, as if she was an unheard of horror, a furless monster sent to eat them, tails and all. It was a slight relief that she'd worn her Egyptian dress instead of her pants and button top. They'd probably scamper away, hissing their little hearts out if she had.

One kitten—a brave, tiny thing—tottered over to her, its hind end going one way when its front end wanted to forge a path toward the unknown intruder. Jeannette couldn't help but giggle. Kittens and puppies always had that effect on her.

"Aren't you cute?" She squatted down to the kitten's level. The little kitty stopped, puffing out into a fuzzy ball twice its original size. A furred puffer fish. Jeannette laughed louder and held out her hand, palm down, fingers lax. The kitten took a step forward, lifting its feet up high as if it walked through a puddle, and when it drew near enough, it sniffed her.

Then it spun around and scampered back to a small circle of other young black cats.

"Did you see that? Did you?" The other young cats all nodded. "I got so close."

"We saw," a few said, upright ears and half-puffed tails.

"I sniffed it," the brave kitten continued.

"What's it smell like?"

The little kitten licked its lips. "Fish," it licked again, "and flowers."

Jeannette feared she would have the fish smell in her pores until her dying days.

"Hello, Jeannette," Bast finally said, her words reverberating, somehow inflated, as if the whole of the courtyard couldn't contain them. The goddess set the kitten down and it tottered to the others. The entire mass of kittens watched them intently, ears perked up and barely a blink amongst them. If they'd had a television they could pop in a DVD of darting birds, or maybe a fish tank, and set the lot of them before the screen and have a bit of privacy, but as it was, such luxuries were not for them.

"Hello," Jeannette said again and did a little bow. Should she have curtseyed?

"Is Sanura well?" The woman rose from the ledge of the pool and walked toward Jeannette, placing one foot before the other just like a cat would. Her hips swayed in a lascivious manner that Jeannette hadn't realized was even possible.

"Yes," came Jeannette's automatic response, wanting to appease, but then Jeannette remembered Sanura's sleepless nights and sad talk of not belonging, of her fear of being separated from Abayomi. "Though, she misses you, and," she looked around the garden, the grasses and pool, at the apt kitten faces, "being here." Jeannette wondered if this was the exact place that Sanura had come from, this block of kittens running around the green lawn, playing in this pool and chasing each other's tails. Were there other gardens? Thousands of them? One for each star in the sky? For each grain of sand? Were they just up the river from the workers village, or were they floating up on invisible clouds or in a temple on some mighty mountain that no man could climb where all the gods resided, just beyond reach?

"I know." The woman looked down at her empty hands. Though Jeannette couldn't really see it in her features, Bast's words were laced with longing. The same tone Sanura often slipped into in those quiet moments when internal reflection snuck upon her with ease. *"But she is the one to do what only she can."*

"And what is that?"

Bast brought her eyes up to touch on Jeannette's. *"Oh, sweet human child, that is for her to find out. You can help her find the answer, but she cannot be told."*

"One of those life lessons?" Jeannette asked, her tone hollow and disappointed. It was a beat-to-death scheme parents often used—packaging up information with hindsight value into a 'life lesson'—so they didn't have to bother explaining a thing. Parents and men of God and best friends who pretended to be above everyone.

Bast's eyes flashed with that five-hundred watt glare and Jeannette felt trapped in a drawn out second. *"Exactly. Everyone must experience life to learn the truth behind the meaning of their own existence. It is not something that can be mastered by taking in others' choice words."*

Then that second ended, and like a taut rubber band, Jeannette was snapped loose. She had the sense that Bast wasn't just talking about Sanura and she bristled. What did Bast know, bestowing her existential wisdom from on high in her make-believe world away from conflict and poverty and betrayal?

The goddess turned away, reaching out and holding a lotus seed head in her palm. *"My child is lonely, I know this. I can hear her crying out for me. But as unjust as it is, she is not for the path of my other children, and all children eventually leave their litter behind."* She glanced at the bundle of kittens, half staring at her adoringly, the others watching Jeannette with that revered distrust of all isolated peoples.

The woman's gentleness intimidated her. "But why, why is she not like the others? She doesn't understand why she's been sent away."

Bast half-closed her eyes, allowing only a slit of orange to peek through. *"As it sometimes occurs, her ba is of a central course of the river. There is more strength in her. There is more passion. She bathed in the waters and took to the challenges of the current."*

Jeannette waited, but the goddess said nothing more. "So, she's different than—" Jeannette waved her hand towards to the litter.

Eyes downcast, Bast gently dipped her head.

"She's doing a blessing on me." Jeannette swallowed, holding back the press of words that wanted to fill the silence.

"Yes."

"So . . . are you going to? To bless me?"

"Bold, aren't you, young human?"

Jeannette half-shook her head. She'd never really thought so.

"Is she happy?" Bast asked. Jeannette blinked and tried to reprogram her brain to keep track of the goddess' train of thought and forget her own agenda for the moment.

"Sanura?" Jeannette glanced down at her feet. Under her sandal straps, pale lines crisscrossed over her skin revealing strips of her northern ancestry. Sand ground under her toes as she curled them up. "No. I really can't say that she's happy." Sanura wasn't miserable; she wasn't afraid anymore. She loved Abayomi, and probably even Jeannette. But a whole chunk of her life was missing. That was a question Jeannette pondered and still couldn't answer: how can you be un-whole and still achieve happiness?

Bast said nothing, didn't even look at Jeannette. The sistrum clattered on. A kitten rampaged across the grass and tackled its sibling, filling the warm evening air with hisses and meows as they tumbled, all tails and teeth. Some had piled up for an evening nap, a pocket-sized mountain of black fur. The night blossoms' perfume filled Jeannette's

261

nose, sweet and clean and a little melancholy.

She shifted, her knees having been locked, and now she glanced at the pool edge next to Bast, wondering if it would be rude to sit without an offer. Bast didn't move, only the kittens—perpetual motion machines until they collapsed from fatigue. Finally, after another few minutes of rattle-rattle-rattle-hiss, she gave in. "I think she's happy when she's with Abayomi. He's like a father to her."

Bast chuckled a half sigh. *"A father? That's unexpected."*

Jeannette's eyebrows furrowed.

"They are birthed from me alone," Bast explained as she sat primly down on the pool's edge. One minute seductress, the next a lady in waiting.

"What? But you need a mixture of DNA or they would just be clones—" Bast turned her attention to Jeannette, and Jeannette snapped her mouth shut.

"Yes, but your world is not as ours."

Obviously.

And then it dawned on Jeannette—of all the oracles and wise people she could have within arm's reach to ask, right here was someone of potential power and knowledge. Bast could tell her how to return to her home.

"And before you ask me," Bast said, *"think about why you hadn't thought to ask this of me before."*

Jeannette stared at the cat-headed woman. She'd read Jeannette's mind. Just swooped in and sucked out her thoughts. Bast reached out and stroked a passing kitten.

"Don't trap yourself within the inconsequentials," she said. *"You radiate your thoughts enough that the deaf can hear you. Just consider my words."*

Jeannette glared at the side of the woman's head. After a few moments of being ignored, she turned her attention to what Bast had said. Of course she wanted to go home, back to the world of science and proper soap. But her absence amounted to many months. Unless some Star Trek space-time anomaly thing moved time here at a different pace than in reality, she'd long ago been pronounced missing or deceased, and some deadbeat straight out of junior college was probably doing the monkey work of her job at half the pay. She wouldn't fool herself anymore: her life, when she got home, would be totally topsy-turvy and that wasn't exactly a pleasing idea. However, so much had happened that she'd dropped her focus from returning—temporarily—to helping her friends. She knew once Sanura and Abayomi were sitting pretty, the Sky

Watcher said she could go home. Help them, then return to Abayomi's tomb. So, it wasn't like she had forgotten anything, she was only doing what she'd been instructed to do. "I was thinking about that blessing you haven't given me yet," Jeannette ended up saying. She scratched at her arm. With the knowledge that the woman saw her thoughts, she added, "Anyway, I am doing what the Sky Watcher told me to do. Should I be doing something else?"

Bast finally faced Jeannette, abdicating those simple glances from the corners of her eyes. Jeannette felt she'd scored some point in a game in which she had no comprehension of the rules. The goddess' eyes were half-squinted like a content cat's. Maybe this wasn't Jeannette's point after all.

"Perhaps you are on the proper path, but you need to strengthen your ka to meet your success."

Jeannette studied the woman. She'd learned to distinguish some cat-featured emotion from her time with Sanura. Guile held no prominence on Bast's face, though her words seemed snide.

"*Ba?*" Abayomi whined about that all the time, like it was his immortal soul and he'd been Hitler in a past life and was weighed down with all that to atone for.

"No, ka. The force of your spirit. Separate from your ba. *You need to feed your spirit to sustain yourself for the trials to come."*

Hadn't Jeannette had enough trials already?

"So, this blessing will feed my spirit?" Jeannette wondered how powerful Bast's blessing was compared to the Pope's. Gabby's grandmother had shelled out a chunk of her pension to travel to Rome and attend mass with the Catholic leader. Already older than dirt, the woman did last another five years after that trip. Though Jeannette paid no money for *this* blessing, she still felt the cost was much higher.

"It feeds the spirit in one way. Another is as simple as reinforcing your body. You must build your strength, for you enter the desert lands."

"No, I'm not. I'm just infiltrating a group of thieves."

Bast paused a moment, blinked once, a slow drop of her lids. *"And isn't that a wild, unknown place?"*

"I guess." Jeannette scooped up a kitten barely within arm's reach. It wriggled about in her arms attempting an escape until she began to rub its neck, just above the shoulders. Archy loved a neck massage. "But this whole world is unknown," she said to the back of the kitten's head. "I'm completely lost. Half the time I'm frantically running around like my hair's on fire, without any confidence that what I'm doing is what needs to be done." The kitten's nails dug into her arm as it began kneading, purring steadily. "I need to return to Spokane. I had a job and a cat. There's the Slave Master I have to help so he won't hound Sanura, and then Abayomi needs to find his heart scarab so he can go to *Yaaru*. Then there is Sanura . . . facing her reflection. I'm really only struggling to keep afloat. Find the thieves and stop them. Stop my friend. Is that the right thing to do? I know they're stealing from the dead," she tickled the kitten's belly and it giggled, "but the dead don't need much. It's like I have this list of things to do, but I've really no idea where it's taking me."

If she succeeded in her current path, Tabiry would have her head violently removed from her body. All of the thieves would. Every last one. Did they, men like Nekhebu who had nothing under the harsh caste system, deserve to die for wanting more? With a life as hard as the typical Egyptian's, perhaps death was a reasonable risk, and in fact, not necessarily something these people feared. After all, they had created this entire religion around preserving themselves for some self-made, idyllic afterlife. Sounded familiar. Still, Jeannette didn't like it. Maybe death wasn't a horror, but she'd prefer it be delivered by a less brutal avenue. She felt sick just thinking about sending them all to the chopping block.

And what would happen after she helped Sanura and the slaver threat no longer hung over her head, or when Abayomi had his scarab and moved on to his afterlife? Jeannette would be a lone soldier, standing amidst a battlefield she had no sense fighting in. This wasn't her world.

A sharp hiss drew Jeannette's attention to Bast. The goddess was standing, teeth bared and orange, almond-shaped eyes scorching holes into Jeannette.

Jeannette's heart stopped its life-long march. The sistrum chimed.

The kitten jumped from her limp hands and galloped over to its littermates. Bast watched her child scamper away, eyes narrow. A gripping pain bloomed from the center of Jeannette's chest, invading the reach of each of her limbs, sliding over the surface of her skin. The goddess' slivered eyes burned as they landed once more on Jeannette.

She couldn't breathe, not even one breath.

"You have a tongue that needs tending too, Jeannette. And hands that should not sully that which is pure." The ruby eyes of the uraeus' cobra flashed in the torchlight.

Then the flame left Bast's eyes. Jeannette's heart jumped. Beat. She stumbled away, pressing her palm into her chest, slipping upon the stone-lined floor. Beat. Adrenaline shot through her body. Beat. There was no fight to her autonomic response, only flight.

"Okay . . . if you could just send me back now," Jeannette begged from a quiet shadow, her voice a hint of a whisper.

Bast settled back onto the lip of the pool edge. *"What of your blessing?"* The words were teasing, a hint of vindictive feline to them.

Never with the Sky Watcher, or her brief exchanges with the cow oracle and the oversized Smurf, had Jeannette felt panic's cold hold. She tried to steady her breathing, but couldn't stop the hitch that crept in as those orange eyes measured her worth. Pressure filled her bladder and she hoped she hadn't wet herself. She took a step back, another. A jitter had set in her limbs, but she had nowhere to run to. No weapon to grip.

Those eyes.

"Listen, mortal." Jeannette stiffened under Bast's proclamation. *"You do not know what the dead do or do not need. Stealing from the dead is vile. It is an affront to Ma'at, Osiris, Anubis and all Gods. The universe is more complicated than you can imagine, small thing. You are not the center of it, nor the most important aspect within it."*

Sweat coated her body and Jeannette really needed to use the toilet. Her knees had gone soft and only the pillar behind her held her up.

"Do you understand?"

Jeannette nodded, the agreement not so much directed by her opinion but by the deep seated need to appease this woman, this god.

"Remember this, human child." As Bast spoke, her voice softened, no longer hitting the inner hollow of Jeannette's soul. *"There are many paths to walk; all may be the wrong way. All may be the right way. It depends on the state of one's ba and intent as to where one truly ends up. And often enough, the ending you arrive at is not the ending you initially perceived."*

Pulse still racing, Jeannette kept her mouth tightly clamped. She preferred solid answers like the square root of sixty-four was eight and the atomic weight of carbon was twelve, but wasn't about to say anything remotely insolent. But she couldn't help but ask in her weak voice, "Are you saying that nothing is right and nothing is wrong?" The sickness that had been boiling in her lower esophagus gurgled. She wanted to leave this garden. Leave this cat-headed woman with the glowing orange eyes.

"What do you think?"

Frustration poked up its tiny head within the taiga of her fear. "I'm unsure, Lady. That is why I am asking you. You're the divine god. As you pointed out, I'm just one woman, bumbling along with my friends,

265

hoping we figure it all out."

Bast smiled; Jeannette felt emotional whiplash attempting to keep pace with the goddess' moods, but that fear, that terrible, near-death fear, had gone. *"I'm glad you are going to help my daughter. She is such a sweet girl."*

Jeannette's shoulders slumped, the energy pumped into her body fizzling away like a dud firecracker. "Yes, she is. So, we figure it out as we go with no help from you." It wasn't a question.

"I will help you when I can, but as I said, life is something you must experience or the experience amounts to little but sand and stones."

"Sure, fine." The kittens had all piled together for a nap, though the half-moon hung in the exact same position, marking no passage of time. No longer drenched in fear, Jeannette was simply tired. Tired of standing. Tired of Sanura's crazy mother. One last time she asked, "About this blessing, then?"

Bast laughed, a sultry, low sound reminiscent of a femme fetale from those old black and white noir flicks. *"That you have always had, my sweet child."* Jeannette stifled an obstinate grunt. *"You travel this journey together, remember this. Each of you carries the breath of Bast within you."*

Jeannette pressed her lips together, sighed through her nose. "Well, if that's the case, why does Sanura think that I need to have another one?"

The woman stood and took a step toward Jeannette. Her breasts were perky and full, causing Jeannette to look awkwardly away. Another step closer, and Jeannette knew she had nowhere to run to. When Bast was an arm's length away from Jeannette, the goddess pulled off the circlet of bronze from around her neck.

"Take this, Jeannette. I give you this talisman that will bring to you insight when you need it most."

She stared at the torque. Bronze and some other metal, silver maybe, spiraled together until they formed a stylized cat head at each end. With a nod from Bast, Jeannette took it. Forcing the ends open, she tugged the torque on around her neck. It fit snuggly, and still held the warmth from Bast's own body.

"Tha—Thank you."

Bast dipped her chin just a fraction, her eyes in a half-squint. Jeannette sighed, and found herself smiling. She struggled to find that memory of her fear of this woman, but she had lost it somehow, a washed-out recollection that might not have been true memory at all. *"It is time for your return."*

Now, Jeannette didn't want to leave. The warm, open courtyard with the green grass, the cool pool of water, the hordes of kittens all watching her: it seemed like a place she could rest forever. With awe-wide eyes she gazed into Bast's brilliantly orange ones. Opening her mouth, she prepared to ask to stay. To beg, if she had to. But before she could, Bast's eyes flashed as she gently shook her head.

And then everything began to go the pale of colors scorched by a daily dose of the desert's brilliant sun. Jeannette's head spun. She reached out to steady herself, but there was nothing around to grab. Nothing but deep darkness with gemstones of light. In her mind she heard, *"You cannot stay. This is not your home. Tell my daughter I love her."*

Chapter 26

NIGHT STILL HELD DOMINION when Jeannette reached the high priest's tomb. Since tomb construction was as eternal as the *Iteru*, it took no sweat to conceptualize how pilfering objects created for and stashed within these tombs could be a lucrative business.

She had been in the goddess' realm for an irreconcilable time. Now, off to the east, the sky was a deep purple and the stars were fading. In the emerging dawn, the cliffs were dark shadows piercing the sky like lumbering dinosaurs. Within them rested the dead. The Necropolis. All this time and effort spent toward dead people when the living were starving and working themselves into miserable exhaustion. A totally misplaced obsession.

Back in her house only an hour or so ago, she'd awakened from her trance to the soft voice of Sanura mixed with the lower tones of Abayomi. Though she couldn't remember everything from her visit with Bast, odd emotions and nostalgia clung to Jeannette like dissipating mist. A circlet was wrapped snugly around her neck, warm and comforting. Her fingers migrated to the adornment as often as they'd aim to scratch a mosquito bite, a thoughtless and automatic gesture.

Trying to keep to the darker recesses, she strolled by each tomb entrance, counting the night guards. Some of the tombs, pathways and staging areas weren't watched, and she noted them for future intel to pass onto the gang, though she guessed a good thief would already be aware of the empty spots in security.

She was new to the casing business, so she had to do her best.

When she'd passed on Bast's message of the love of her daughter, Sanura had almost cried. Jeannette could see it in the girl's quivering lip. Jeannette had added, "She's very proud of you," and Sanura trapped her lip between her teeth and nodded. After that, Jeannette had lost her words.

She'd showed them the torque. Fingers brushed against Jeannette's skin as the two reverently touched the warm metal from the goddess.

Abayomi had been rapt, jumping on her every word. What was the goddess like? How beautiful was her palace? Did she bless Jeannette? The questions took a half hour to end—finally cut short by Jeannette's pleas. Jeannette had tried to answer them all to the best of her memory, but how could she contain a goddess in mere words?

"I'm sorry guys, but it's all fading," she'd told them. "I remember she was a lot like Sanura, only bigger and half naked."

"We'd always run around unclothed in my mother's garden," Sanura had said, a glint of amusement sparkled in her gaze and a memory of flashing orange eyes had sent a bolt of fear piercing Jeannette's heart. "Your sense of modesty is amusing."

When Jeannette had prepared to leave, backpack packed and goddess blessed, Sanura had thrown herself into her arms. "Be safe." With a fierce protectiveness, Jeannette had nearly crushed the mini-god, burying her nose into the soft fur covering Sanura's head. Inhaling her scent, Jeannette pressed it between the pages of her memory. On her other side Abayomi had nearly encircled them both, leaning his forehead against her temple.

"Yes, be safe, Jeannette." His grip tightened around them.

It had been oddly emotional, like she was saying her farewells for some long, dangerous trip. Really, the tombs were only up the cliff face, a few minutes' walk away.

Then she'd pulled away. "I'll talk to you all soon, once I do my thiefly duty. Don't worry about me," she added with a smile. "I'll be fine."

Abayomi had reached out to her, hand hanging in the air as if asking permission. Jeannette grabbed it, squeezed, and then left them waiting in the dark doorway of their hut.

Later, in the meeting with the gang of robbers, Funsai—the grizzled leader of Tabiry's group—had spoken in the blunt cadence of a drill sergeant. "We'll try you out. You will be a scout; watch the streets. We do the delicate work." Jeannette had been ready to drop down and give him twenty if he barked the command. "I hope that doesn't bother you," he'd said insincerely. She'd shaken her head. "Meet Tabiry at the Den of Men." He gave her directions. "Tell her what you find nightly, at the cusp of day, but for now, get out of my sight."

Now, Jeannette distanced herself from the tombs, a shadow in the night passing meager feet away from men napping on duty and the watchful gaze of painted gods. She stood before a weather-beaten door amidst similar doors, most of which stored grain. The Den of Men. A place Funsai had told her she would fit right in. She tapped the door with her knuckles and when it opened, a man behind it squinted at her. "What'dya want?" He was chewing on a long stem of grass, the head dipping under the heavy weight of grain.

"I'm new on the shift." Her voice barely trespassed on the night's cradle of silence. "Funsai told me to meet Tabiry here. At dawn."

"Eh? Tabiry? She ain't here." His breath had the force of a tidal wave, and Jeannette had to turn her face away and scrunch up her nose. He squinted out into the dark streets, carving out heavy wrinkles around his eyes. Jeannette sighed. Too damned early. "Well, get yer butt in. Don't get many women squatting in the dirt with us."

Jeannette slipped through the cracked door, clutching her pack to her chest as she scanned the jumble of people in the shack. About fifteen pairs of eyebrows rose as she entered. Most of the men were older and crafted from the mold of a man that clean clothing never seemed to touch. A few even leered. She considered scowling at those, but realized her spirit had been trampled under her exhaustion, so kept her eyes off any faces.

The old door man waved toward a spot in the corner that wasn't covered by a body. "You can stay there 'til Tabiry arrives, yeah?" A good many teeth were missing and his words were born a mumble.

"Yeah, thanks." She made her way to the corner, stepping over bed mats and men's legs.

"Beautiful, I've got space here," one man said and his fellows chuckled.

Jeannette plastered on a smile that hurt her jaw. "Sorry, Funsai told me no fraternizing with the help."

The man reached for her leg, but she hopped over him, easily out of his reach, and made her way to sit in her spot. With her pack in her lap, she trapped it between her knees and her chest, wrapping her arms around her legs. She didn't move, didn't look at anyone. After a few minutes, they turned back to whatever they had been doing before a woman had joined their numbers.

These men, old and broken, no longer filled a vital societal role. Did Funsai give them a large enough cut to make their lives better? Here, no angel called Government Assistance allowed for a life of idleness, a respite when times were tough. Each one wore a ragged kilt, little to no adornments. Their linen was the gray of too many washings, not the white of a proper citizen. These people were castaways, simply struggling to eke out a lifestyle in the only manner offered them: following the demands of a smarter castaway who knew the good haunts where one could scrape together some dough, with a quiet place to sleep safe from harassment.

They were all strays. Trying to avoid the boot of the establishment. And Jeannette was sitting here among them.

She curled her fingers around her torque, tracing the entwined metals of the circlet. It was still warm. None of the men had seemed at all impressed by her jewelry. Now that she was a tomb bandit too, was that like a shield against being robbed? Honor amongst thieves, and all that? It had grown quiet in the hut; a few men were talking, others played some game with carved beads. The soft chatter lulled her into a fitful doze.

* * *

"Jeannette." A kind voice danced across the edges of the void. "Jeannette, wake up." Jeannette groaned and realized she'd fallen asleep sitting upright. Her neck ached, and as she pried her eyes open, she saw Tabiry sitting by her side.

"So, I did not need to get a bucket of water." She smiled, and her voice was warm, and Jeannette felt the grip on her heart relax just a bit. This seemed more like the Tabiry she'd remembered.

Jeannette grabbed the top of her head and pulled, stretching the muscles along her shoulder and upper spine. Then she twisted her neck, eliciting a series of popping that telegraphed down her backbone. "Yeah, I'm awake. Is it dawn yet?" She drank some water from her bottle and then gained her feet, using the wall as a support. Still half asleep, she felt dizzy.

"Yes. I am sorry to have arrived late. Can we go somewhere to talk?"

Jeannette blinked again, fighting away the blur that had invaded her vision. She hoped the unrelenting sun of the land of Kemet hadn't scorched her retinas. She bet the local optometrist wouldn't quite meet her expectations.

She nodded at Tabiry. The two crossed the shack to the door, stepping around each man's sleeping form like a deserted island, too small to sustain any life on its own.

With a gentle nudge of her hip, Tabiry pushed open the door. The sky, the gray-blue of almost-day, still held no visible sun, keeping the narrow footpaths between buildings in morning shadow. The birds had begun their prattle, a recipe of tweets and caws punctuated by a piercing skree here and there. The chorus had always been on its tail end by the time it rallied Jeannette to rise and face a day of stirring. Few people in the village were out, though Jeannette paid little attention as she struggled against the last hold of exhaustion. Fatigue pulled at her arms and legs. Tabiry walked before her as if she rode on a cloud, her white *kalasiris* almost glowing against her skin, the copper beads releasing a soft melody every time they clicked together. The entire morning was a song.

"Please, come in with peace in your heart." Tabiry's voice was flat in the open space of her home. The statue of Sekhmet once again caught Jeannette's attention.

"Why Sekhmet?" she asked.

"That is not the goddess." Tabiry walked up and poured water from a clay pitcher into an alabaster offering table at the foot of the lion god on the altar. The water splashed within the small, square indent, staining the stone. "This is Apedemak, the great lion of my people. The Lord of Royal Power."

Jeannette leaned forward and examined the god. "I haven't heard of him." Then, so as not to be rude, "But he looks strong and wise."

Tabiry smiled sadly, facing her altar. "Apedemak *is* strong and wise. He guards the royal family, but the pharaoh's might was too much for him. For us." She closed her eyes. "I come from a conquered people."

Of course Jeannette had known that—intellectually. But hearing Tabiry admit it so bluntly, with such emptiness branding her words, dislodged some of Jeannette's ill will towards her friend turned thief.

"We are proud, but pride brings us no bread. Pride brings us no peace. We will dry up in the desert, with nothing to drink but our pride, and pride sustains nothing under the harsh eye of Re.

"I've no love for the pharaoh." Tabiry curled her hands into fists. "He destroyed my family; he destroyed my temple; he destroyed my world. I've no loyalty to him who would end my people, and crush my city, and steal away my pride." An angry blush burned over her high cheekbones. So alive in her fury. Then she looked at Jeannette, met her eyes and the rage melted away leaving only defeat. She released her fists, holding her open hands away from her body in a form of supplication. "I am an empty woman, Jeannette. Watered down by the endless river. Washed clean of my people."

This poor woman, whom Jeannette had thought had everything, was more alone than even she. Jeannette nodded, clearing her throat. "This place—" she began, but stopped and shook her head. Her hand moved to touch her torque without any direction from her mind. "You strap on your sandals and march on. Nothing else you can do."

Tabiry's face smoothed into a reflection of calm. "No, you see I *can* do something. I can dismantle the altars and take away the precious offerings. I can outwit the guards and undermine the temple priests. I can disrupt the passage of the pharaoh's *ba* through the gates. You see, Jeannette. I am far from helpless."

She stared at Tabiry—who only had pride and anger to fill her heart—and Jeannette desperately wished to be home, sharing beer and bread with her friends.

Gritting her jaw, Jeannette grabbed Tabiry's shoulders. She was the inside man, here. She couldn't flee. Every angle, she would use every angle to get what she needed. She'd sold her soul along this road of subterfuge and betrayal, and backing down now was not only impossible, but stupid. "They deserve your scorn, Tabiry. The things they did to you, to your people, were terrible. The pharaoh is nothing but a tyrant, this system unfair. Everyone's trapped. We're all stuck." She felt her eyes begin to burn. "I'll help you. If I could bring back your family, your city and people, I would. If I could make it all better, I would." She sniffed, struggling to keep her emotion inside. "I understand what it's like to have nobody."

She was the inside man. She had no choice.

Tabiry wrapped Jeannette up in her arms, pulled her tight to her chest. "Thank you, Jeannette. Thank you so much." She pulled away and poured them some beer. "So, tell me about what you saw tonight."

* * *

Trickles of perspiration streamed down Jeannette's temples and between her breasts in the humid air hanging torpidly over the wide-mouthed jug. The sweet scent of fruited beer and the earthly essence of charcoal worked to alleviate the vicious atmosphere still roosting in her mind. She missed brewing. When she entered her home that afternoon following the morning at the perfumery, the charcoal had been laid out and water filled half the brewing jug. Clean, filtered water, like she'd taught the Master Brewer. Neither Sanura nor Abayomi had been there. She'd thank them with some beer. Unfortunately, she couldn't brew all day. With a ten day work week and nights filled with double agent duties, her free time had been allotted for sleep.

273

THREE GREAT LIES

Jeannette flaked some more bread into the mix, watching the pieces slowly disintegrate in the water. Ah, what was she thinking? Sleep was for the weak. She needed a gallon of coffee to inject straight into her blood stream. Temporary energy with hypodermic infusion.

Tabiry had listened, nodded, listened, nodded some more. It had taken Jeannette back to those office meetings where she tried to look attentive and display actual interest. She'd slipped away as soon as the recitation was completed. On her return home she passed through an area that looked familiar, and it hadn't clicked with her until she'd passed by that guard, the one with the spear, the one who'd incited Jeannette's exodus from Thebes. He'd scowled; she'd scurried away. At least he hadn't tried to skewer her.

The guards knew—at least the ones on the take—that she was one of *them*.

Jeannette brushed the sweat from her forehead. Soon, she'd have to return to Herit the Perfume Nazi and she hadn't even eaten any lunch. Scrounging up something to eat was too daunting. Even her heart felt tired. Wrung thin. Half-heartedly, she bit a chunk from the loaf.

The door opened and Sanura bounded inside.

"You're brewing! I love the smell of your beer, Jeannette." The girl wrapped her arms around Jeannette's waist. Jeannette returned the hug with an awkward one-armed embrace, squeezing with a vengeance.

"Did you do this for me?" Jeannette gestured toward the pot with the bread. She gathered up the ladle and dipped it into the vat, slowly stirring the young beer.

Sanura nodded, ears perked up. "I had Abayomi help me get the ladles and pot and everything, though."

After her conversation with Tabiry that morning and the reunion with the wicked guard, Jeannette had been drained empty. Now, chatting with Sanura, she felt revived. It was hard to explain, maybe even harder for Jeannette to understand, how she could go from forlorn to uplifted in the span of a hug. Maybe she was trying too hard, and it was actually too simple for her modern mind to accept. With Sanura, and Abayomi, perhaps she could let her brain give up a bit of its control. Perhaps she could give up her worry.

"Well, I have to get back to Herit the Stern. Would you mind stirring until the charcoal dies?"

Sanura shook her head. "Of course not. How was your first night?"

How was your first night as a spy? Jeannette heard.

Jeannette tapped the ladle against the brim of the clay pot and laid it across the mouth. "I didn't do much. They don't trust me yet, but at least I'm in, right?" Her smile felt like a grimace. "Look, tonight we shall drink three jugs of beer and eat all the remaining bread and fill our empty places with dates. How does that sound?"

Sanura smiled at her, but didn't offer the giggle Jeannette had been hoping for. The smile faded.

"Be careful." Sanura displayed no hint of amusement in her voice. "Don't let the guards catch you and don't anger the thieves." The girl's eyes dropped to the brewing jug, strangely focused and unwavering. "And be aware of those who appear too kind."

Jeannette tried to laugh, but the chuckle was dry. Nobody was too kind. "I won't. I'm always careful." She smiled at Sanura, but she couldn't seem to appease Sanura's unease. "Come on, I can talk my way out of anything. And your mom gave me this." She laid her hand on a cat-head end of the circlet.

Sanura hugged her, brushing along the circlet of her mother's, and then waited behind in the street as Jeannette walked to the perfumery.

* * *

The job was sucking the life out of her with the fevered intensity of a swarm of ticks. The *jobs*. Like a house of persistent orphans, each one wanted its share of time, gripping onto her apron strings, whining at her, "Feed me. Play with me. Me. Me. Me."

Work, the curse of the brewing class.

Morning full of stirring, followed by a lunch break of more stirring—only this version of her own choice—and worthless tomb stalking. Back to the perfumery and the Woman of Displeasure. If she lucked out, she got some dinner, a nap, time with Sanura and Abayomi. Once night swathed the land in darkness, out she went to the mortuary hill, wandering the same shadows, discovering the same holes in security, then heading home for another few hours of sleep before she met with Tabiry.

"God, kill me now," she mumbled to herself, adding a little myrrh to the pot.

Luckily, Abayomi and Sanura were forgiving of her absences and helpful around the house. She wondered when Werel would petition to be placed in another home, but so far her home life was the sweet life. She just needed more of it.

"What did you say?" Herit asked, her frown extending.

"Nothing, ma'am. Just thinking about my shopping list." Jeannette tossed her a brilliant smile, then turned back to stirring, the smile already a casualty of her frustration. Though her skin's softness could be compared to that of a baby's butt, the calluses could have been a testament to years spent on a chain gang. Speaking of shopping list, she needed some extra linen to strain the beer. It was ready. Her entire house had been saturated by the pungent odor of fermentation.

Her roommate was a weaver, but as a small business practitioner, Jeannette doubted she'd have extras just lying around. Werel didn't seem too excited about the amount of space the make-shift brewery ate up, nor the smell, but Jeannette promised her a good share of her famous beer, blessed by Tenenet herself.

"Well, if that is true," Werel had said, hands on her hips, "I want four jugs." Jeannette had readily agreed.

If she gave her mind time to measure out these things, her biggest frustration, of the vast array she'd collected like trading cards, was Funsai. When would the thieves actually pull her into the fold? Jeannette paused, then reworded her question. *Why* would the thieves pull her in? She had to offer them something they needed.

After leaving the perfumery, Jeannette dragged herself to the tombs, carrying water up the street once there. It had turned into one of those unnecessary things she made herself do to have a legitimate excuse to skulk there regularly. A village guard sauntered toward the warehouses in his usual slouching gait. Though his gait might have been usual, his position near the warehouse wasn't. His station had been near the smithies, weighing out tools. The building he slouched by held the art pieces ready to be moved into the tomb. The thieves never touched anything in these holding zones, so there was no need to worry about them getting caught. But still, it was unusual for this guard to be here at this time.

She watched him go inside, then come out a few minutes later, casual as could be. Standing in the shade beside a one-legged man shouting out prices for his plain bread, Jeannette realized she knew nothing. Maybe the thieves did have a finger or two dipping into the warehouse. If they got caught now, without Jeannette offering more than a spit of an idea about their sea of crime, would the Master Slaver be appeased?

"Bread?" the one-legged man asked.

Jeannette glanced at the guard walking away. "Yes, please."

Giving the man some water from her jug, she took his bread with a nod and went to the nearby weavers to collect some linen remnants, half convincing herself to return to the warehouse later that night.

"I only need a square chunk—" Jeannette opened her arms about three feet wide before her "—about this size. Nothing special. No dye." She shook her head.

As the woman tossed a couple of thin, cloth strips to the side, Jeannette considered teaching Sanura the art of brewing. It could be something fun for both of them—she seemed interested enough to set up the brewery in their home. The idea struck her as odd, almost desperate in her desire to maintain the status quo. The weaver held out a scrap of undyed linen about the right size. Jeannette paid with the simple bread and some extra fish and left for home.

On her way to the housing district, she passed by two bird-headed *mi-nether*. Their long, ibis beaks clicked as she strolled by, but neither said a thing to her. Of all the mini-gods, the sons and daughters of Thoth were by far the most unnerving, with their tiny necks coming out of human shoulders, stretched thin like a piece of silly putty. Governing the heart, Thoth was wise and intelligent. Jeannette wondered if the sons could see into her own heart and find the truths she'd hidden there even from herself.

Leaving them behind she walked by two bread stalls, a beer seller, and someone selling a hearty-smelling stew. She added salt and dates to her grocery list. Mundane tasks helped keep her from worry. Still she crinkled the edges of the cloth up in her tightening grip. Her mind might be able to ignore the elephant, but her body knew better.

She was on the expressway to nowhere with the thieves.

A naked girl ran up to Jeannette, a bundle in her arms. "Temple offerings. Only a deben."

Jeannette stared at the oblong mummy the girl was holding. "A deben? That must be a rare offering indeed."

The girl, face streaked with a week's worth of dirt, nodded violently. Jeannette worried she'd give herself whiplash if she continued much longer. "Yes. A very special cat mummy." She lifted up the offering. White linen, indeed, wrapped around something vaguely cat-shaped. It even had ears and a painted face.

"A mummified cat?" Jeannette scanned the crowd for Sanura. "You can't be mummifying cats! They're sacred to Bast." She touched her torque.

The girl's eyebrows jumped up her forehead. "Yes, they are. You can appeal to Bast and offer her a cat. Only a deben."

Shaking her head, Jeannette pushed past the girl. "I'll not participate in the slaughter of cats for offerings."

"Jeannette!"

Jeannette looked up; Abayomi was practically jogging towards her, short legs striding for all they were worth. Streamers of gauze trailed behind him, making him appear almost festive. A sudden injection of adrenaline had her on edge. She scanned the area, looking for threats: guards, thieves, angry crocodiles, then realized—Sanura was not with him. When he reached her, her demands dropped from her mouth until the most important landed in air.

"Is Sanura okay?"

He tilted his head. "Sanura is fine. I must speak to you. Now." His eye caught the cat in the peddler's arms; he frowned. "What is that?"

The girl stared at the mummy. "It's a cat. I mummified it myself. Do you want to buy it? Only a deben."

Abayomi reached out and traced along a painted line the length of the cat mummy. "How did it die?"

The girl shrugged. "Old age. Lost her teeth and couldn't eat." She wiped her nose along her arm, and stared at them with bored, brown eyes. Jeannette stared at Abayomi.

"We don't need any mummified cats, thanks all the same," Jeannette said. She grabbed Abayomi's arm and walked him away from the girl, who'd moved on to another to hawk her mummy.

"Do you need an offering?" the girl said to a craftsman. "One deben."

"Did you see that, Jeannette?" Abayomi asked. "She had cats. Mummified cats."

Jeannette nodded and kept leading Abayomi away, not releasing his arm. "Yes. She is selling them as an offering to Bast. What is wrong? What's gotten all your linens in a twist?"

Abayomi watched the girl over his shoulder. "I have long wondered why I appear to be the only mummy in this land. Then I see mummified cats. Why do they not walk as I do?" Jeannette guided him around a couple of old men both badly in need of walkers but making do with a double set of canes.

"I've no idea. Maybe they weren't given the proper rituals, nobody spoke the right spells." She'd long ago taken it for granted that Abayomi was the only walking, talking mummy in Kemet, like she was the only woman who'd ridden in from the future on a rickety motorcycle across a highway of potholes.

They walked the short distance to their subdivision in silence. Abayomi refused to tell her anything until they returned to their home. "It is not for the ears of the city," he said. But as he took in a breath, looked at her, then let it out, she'd sped up their forced march. Out of the edge of her vision, she watched him. Finding out what was bothering him tugged on her nerves. Maybe it was that cat that dumped him in this mood. Being the only living mummy must be a lonely existence.

When Jeannette and Abayomi arrived at their home, Sanura opened the door wide, welcoming them with the scent of fresh bread and honey.

"Honey." Jeannette took the offering, letting the sweet flavor linger on her tongue. "Where did you get this?" Abayomi did not take any to eat.

"Tabiry came by." Sanura's ears drew back as she grunted out a low growl. "She said she would return later to speak to you, and left the honey here."

Glancing between Abayomi—abuzz with his news—and Sanura—growling about Tabiry—Jeannette chose to focus on Abayomi. Unfortunately, he wouldn't meet her eyes, wouldn't speak. Jeannette sighed. "Well, why don't we strain the beer while we wait for her." And let Abayomi find his words, she finished internally.

As Jeannette explained the straining process, Abayomi interrupted. "Jeannette."

Her name, heavy with implied importance, ceased her tutorial.

"What is it?" she asked steadily, already steeled for the worst.

"Today I found something," he began, then halted. The words seem to have been swimming in his brain and he had to reach out and catch them one at a time. "I think . . . Well, I am certain. These thieves, they *are* the ones who desecrated my tomb."

Chapter 27

THE TWO WOMEN GAWKED AT ABAYOMI, then Jeannette's curiosity kicked in like a fifth shot of gin. "What? How do you know?"

For over an hour, words hastened out of Abayomi's lips, explaining what he'd dredged up the previous night. His words began timid as mice, peeking their heads out of the tight vice of his lips, then gained strength and momentum as he warmed to his indignation. The beer was forgotten. The women sat around him intimately on cushions, nibbling on dates and listening intently, no questions, no comments, just attempting to keep up.

Abayomi told them he'd been lurking around the older tombs in the desert beyond the worker's complex, not the areas recently constructed where Jeannette had been conscripted. There, he played the amazingly challenging role of a dead man in a coffin, somebody else's desecrated coffin—how nasty was that?—and was able to eavesdrop on the simple-minded who expected dead men to have deaf ears.

"So, they totally spilled the beans with you just lying there nearby?"

Abayomi nodded. "They thought they had already looted me. Each of the cities, each of the mortuary hills. It is a long list. My tomb was just one of many." He swallowed and Jeannette watched the bob of muscle and bone under his wrappings. "The biggest challenge was just getting into and out of this village. I found a low point in the eastern wall that I could climb over without much damage to my wrappings, but sometimes the guards would patrol that section, so I had to hide and wait."

Jeannette laughed loudly, and leaned toward Abayomi, wrapping him up in her arms. It didn't matter how girlish it was. Nobody here would judge. Looking over her shoulder at Sanura, she said, "See, I told you he was sly."

Abayomi's arm encircled her shoulders and gave a little squeeze. Sanura's lids slowly closed over her eyes and a little fang poked out from under her upper lip. That content expression ignited something bold within Jeannette, and though she still felt shy and silly, she looked directly into Abayomi's eyes and smiled. "You're awesome, you know?"

"Awesome?" His hold tightened.

She nodded. His body felt warm next to hers. And solid. "Awe inspiring. It's a good thing."

280

He kept staring at her; the air zinged, as if alive with bees. Then the careless fun cartwheeled into something awkward. Her muscles grew stiff. Jeannette looked away.

Abayomi truly was awesome, but he was still a mummy. Still encased in linen. Untouchable.

But, he was *Abayomi*. Strong, loyal, sometimes goofy, Abayomi. Plus, she'd never remembered Ricky smiling at her like that. Did it matter that she'd never really looked at his living face? Did it matter that they'd never be able to kiss, or do any of that fun stuff she'd been denied for years? Celibate since Ricky. Would it be such a trial to continue her nun-like lifestyle as long as Abayomi was with her, supporting her, laughing with her?

At least until he walked on to the Afterlife.

In the next breath, Abayomi released his hold, sliding his entire arm length against her back. His elbow then wrist, and finally his fingertips lost contact. Jeannette shivered, though her body had grown warm. Sanura's satisfied joy turned into an amused grin, and Jeannette let loose her best expression of 'whatever'. Internally, she was screaming "What do I do now?" She needed to run along the city's wall, work off her sudden jitters.

Instead, she rocked back and forth on her cushion, brushing away the gauzy spider webs of unpleasantness that she'd let bed down between them with an easy toss of her head. "I'm just glad they didn't find you laying there helpless and do something nasty to you."

Abayomi leveled her a look. "I am not helpless, Jeannette." Then he chuckled, resuming his good-natured ease. "I wanted to tell you sooner, but until tonight I was not certain. Tonight, the loud one talked about the tombs along the mortuary hill down the river, my mortuary hill from his description. How those valuables taken seasons ago would now need to be categorized. He suggested that those items were here, in this village." Abayomi's eyes were bright, giving away his excitement. He leaned towards Jeannette. "My scarab. It might be here. My *ba*."

Golden flecks dotted the dark brown of his eyes. She'd never noticed that before. Jeannette wondered if he saw life differently with his flesh eyes. She wondered if he could shed tears. As often as she looked at him, how could she not have noticed the gold? Forgetting her previous trek into inelegant indecision, she reached out and squeezed his hand. "I hope so. If it is, we'll find it."

A delicate knock on the door shepherded the three into silence.

281

Jeannette jumped to her feet and opened the door.

"Hello, Jeannette," Tabiry said. Jeannette returned Tabiry's smile.

"Tabiry, please come in." Jeannette stood back, holding the door wide as Tabiry almost floated through the opening, her *kalasiris* apparently made from something akin to thistle down. In her hand she held a finely-crafted clay jug, its handle a slim construct that looked too delicate for actual use.

After she dipped her head to Sanura and Abayomi, causing a raindrop tinkle from her beads, she turned to Jeannette. "I hope you do not mind my coming to your home, but I had some extra olive oil from the north and wanted to share it with you."

"Thank you. And for the honey too. Would you like some bread with some of the honey?"

Tabiry shook her head, the tinkle hanging in the air. "No thank you. I'm just here for a moment." She glanced at Jeannette's friends through her thick lashes.

Not often a hostess, Jeannette jumped to introductions. "Tabiry, you've met Sanura." Sanura looked at the newcomer and twitched an ear. She'd never been friendly to Tabiry since she'd told Jeannette the Nubian made her feel odd, and Jeannette wondered if the girl harbored childish jealousy. Jeannette scowled at her from behind Tabiry's back, and finally Sanura greeted her with a little wave. "And this is Abayomi. He's . . . ah . . . a mummy. A scribe."

"Hello Tabiry, thank you for helping out Jeannette, and may Amun guide your steps along the path of truth." Abayomi bowed his head.

Jeannette relaxed. Trust Abayomi to be genial, if philosophical, when the need arose.

"And may Re light your way," Tabiry replied. Then she handed Jeannette the jug of oil.

"Tabiry, if you have a moment, I would like to—" Jeannette didn't finish. She looked at her friends and forced a smile. Running her hand along her ponytail, she tugged it at the end.

"Of course."

Gesturing for Tabiry to go first, they left the house.

"I'll be quick," Jeannette said. "I saw one of the guards, the lazy one. You know, he walks like his legs have to be coaxed for each step?" Tabiry nodded. "He was checking out the buildings up the street from the three bread bakers, where some—" Jeannette glanced up and down the alley, then lowered her voice, "—where they hold onto things before they are

282

put into the tombs. He went in and out." She watched Tabiry's face, seeking out any little sign. "I know it's not a place we go, but I thought I'd pass on his aberrant behavior."

Tabiry's eyebrows bunched, a thin line drew between them. "It is probably nothing to worry about, Jeannette." She touched Jeannette's arm and nodded gently with a smile. "But it's good you told me of your observation. It might prove useful."

Though Jeannette's detective education amounted to watching old black and white film classics in her film studies class as a sophomore—the recent detective movies just didn't compare—her gut told her this news held more importance than Tabiry let on. Tabiry was good. A high stakes shark in this game of thievery.

* * *

She could have avoided the building of thiefly loafers that night, exhausted as she was, but she didn't. Like the eternal optimist she had never been, she showed up at the overly crowded squat and hoped someone would give her something to do.

The Den of Men was blacked out, but if she stood outside the door and held her breath she could hear the low drone of conversation. The loudest, a steady cadence of command, seemed to have compelled all other speakers to take vows of silence while he spoke.

Jeannette tapped on the door and whispered her name, watching the streets for anyone passing under the low light of the quarter moon. An unfamiliar man, bald with a pointy nose, answered; Jeannette offered her best long-time-no-see grin.

The man stood back, his hang-dog posture making him look a thousand years old. Jeannette slipped in as Funsai continued speaking. He didn't even glance over at her interruption.

"Mensah, you fetch those jars over the wall, through the wall, under the wall. The route's your trouble. But do not draw any eyes. Questions?"

Nobody said a thing. Each face held a measure of shock, determination, or even fear. Like the President, he delivered his State of the Union address full of enough doom to guarantee their attention, but with a heap of his own personal solutions to seize everyone's support. Funsai's back was straight, his body of the build a New Year's Resolutionist hoped to attain in three months or less. But his muscle was

283

carved from the same stone as the tombs; men took years bullying them from the hills.

He turned to Jeannette and frowned. She lifted her chin and waited. Her teeth felt fit to shatter.

Not looking away from her he said to the group, "You fish still squatting? Was I unclear?"

The men in the hut jerked to action, half lining up to leave, the other half stuck on some minute task, looking busy.

The first man left as Funsai pulled her aside.

"Why tell Tabiry about the guard at the upper warehouse?"

Jeannette furrowed her brow. Another man slipped from the hut; cool air curled into the building before the door shut again. "Because it was a break in routine. Breaks in routine are generally bad for us." She shifted her weight from her left leg to her right.

His frown deepened. "The decision was sharp. Heed the unusual."

"Really?" she blurted, then reflexively grinned. "Yeah, okay."

A third thief left, the crisp, night air only enhancing the stench of the place each time the door clicked closed. The men's weekly wash must have been a month overdue.

Funsai did not smile back. "You go with them."

Her eyes would not blink. Another man left. "Tonight?"

Funsai's black eyes pinched into a narrow line. "Go and do what they tell you." Each word was clipped.

She nodded, ponytail bumping against her shoulder blades, and turned around to join the departing line.

* * *

The men scattered and lost themselves in the network of streets. Jeannette followed one whose stench wasn't particularly overpowering. Though she'd followed him without so much as a do-you-mind, he didn't try to lose her, for which Jeannette was grateful. Even though she knew exactly where she was, she had no idea where she was going. Slinking from one shadow to the next—in a ninja role action heroes would have been envious of—she and her chosen guide made their way to the wall.

The man, Poarma or Paruma, maybe Padma, pressed his back to the wall and lowered himself to sit on his heels. Casting searching glances around the vicinity, Jeannette saw they were secluded from anyone out for a midnight stroll.

The man's hands dangled between his knees, elbows braced against his thighs. "We wait."

Jeannette huddled next to him. "Are we crossing the wall?"

He waved his hand at her in a shushing motion. If she wasn't trying to stay in the thieves' good graces, and not get caught by any guards, she'd sing the Star Spangled Banner just to spite the librarian wannabe.

Instead she nodded and followed Poarma's lead, dropping her butt to the sun baked dirt. Shifting her shoulders, she felt oddly naked without her backpack. Dark splotches against the sky darted this way and that; Jeannette shivered. Bats and bugs and beetles. The Triple Crown of Creep.

If she'd had her watch, she would have checked it compulsively, but it'd died at 3:27 some days ago and now amounted to nothing but memories of a better world. All she knew was that the stars didn't budge much by the time Purma stood and stepped into the black between building and wall. Jeannette followed, stepping lightly into the obsidian shadows as if she were descending into Hades itself. It reminded her too much of Abayomi's tomb, on the real world side, and though she logically knew she wouldn't fall down any holes and crack her skull, she couldn't help hating the unknown.

With time, her eyes adjusted to catch the shade of difference between the buildings and the sky above, a kind of inky blue instead of the nothing surrounding her. Inching along, palms flat against the wall, she strained for any sound. Her next cautious step brought her colliding into her companion's back.

"Sorry."

The man released an *oof*. "Watch it. Through here," came his whispered voice. He grabbed her forearm and pulled her down. Reflexively she pulled away. His breath came too loudly.

"Where are we going?"

"It's a tunnel. You want to try on your own, or you want me to lead you?"

Great. The blind leading the blind. Literally.

"You know your way?"

"Sure. Done this plenty."

She reached out and landed her palm against the man's body. His fingers wrapped around her arm again and he pulled in a down direction. She lowered herself and let him lead her forward.

"Keep your head down." His words were loud; they must have

285

entered a confined space. It made her think of those news stories about miners, trapped underground for weeks. Madness would have hounded her every hour of every day. Small space with a limited supply of air and too many people stealing it from her own lungs. She couldn't tolerate such captivity.

She scuttled along on hands and feet in an unruly frog walk, head ducked down and chin pressed to her chest, following Poarma's scuffled steps. Before the cramp in her thigh really set in, a gap of lighter darkness peeked ahead of her. She hurried, neck already annoyed at its abuse, and stumbled to her feet once she burst free from the crawlway through the wall.

"Come on." Her fellow thief jogged across the open desert towards the tombs and Jeannette chased after, her feet sinking into the thick sand. Appearing to rest on the hilltops, the partial moon beamed down spotlight-bright. Not accustomed to running in any form, let alone with loose sandals, her steps soon turned into clomps as her legs tired out. The sand ate away their footprints and the desert wind would smudge away their passage in by the sun's morning rise. She stopped and looked back. A few torches at irregular intervals lit the village below like fireflies. Her companion stopped too.

"Sure is a long way," she whispered, afraid to put any force into her speech. "Couldn't we have come straight here, instead of running around the lower hills?"

"We have to take precautions."

She swallowed her breath, nodding. A tacky film of dried saliva varnished the roof of her mouth. "Yeah, okay."

He led her a little farther up the hillside until they reached a series of mastabas that must have seen a millennium already.

"Why are these tombs in such bad shape?" she asked him as they crossed the gently sloped ground to the entrance.

"An evil family was buried here. Montu flew down and cried his piercing *kree*, his voice crushing the bricks to dirt again. Then he flapped his wings, emptying the tombs of the dead's *ba*. It is no longer a place of the dead."

Eyes wide, Jeannette looked from the man to the moonlit tombs. Nothing decorated the front but fragments of pottery. No Memorial Day fake plastic plants to honor these dead.

"I thought Montu was a bull." She raised her hand, the one the bull healed a lifetime ago. The list of injuries to it was long and mostly forgotten, but she remembered that first hurt well, soothed by the cool breath of the purple bull.

Padma squinted into Jeannette's face. "He is."

"Yeah, but aren't you worried that he'll retaliate if more people enter these cursed tombs?"

The man turned away and began walking towards the burial tomb. "Cursed men walk cursed paths. The Gods know of these things we do. They have already abandoned us."

And I walk these paths along with you, she thought. Curses in this ancient land were easier to pick up than ticks in the scrub oak of the eastern Cascades. Not that she believed in curses. But whether they were real or not, they had a corrosive effect.

They entered the old tomb along a path worn smooth by countless feet. Guards must avoid this place like the fleeing *ba*, or the outfit would have been discovered long ago.

The man's back muscles shifted with the swing of his arms. "What's your name?" she asked him.

The passage before them grew lighter. "Not important."

"I'm Jeannette."

"I know." He glanced over his shoulder and tossed out his name. "I'm Piourma"

Piourma. She'd been close.

As they turned a corner, a torch cast a halo of light along the mastaba wall. The depictions of the afterlife were all faded, worn away by the careless years. The tomb looked like a relic from her era, not one of the fresh burial chambers she imagined lined the Theban Cliffs in this one.

Below the lit torch, others, unlit, were piled on the floor like a jumble of pick-up sticks. Piourma grabbed one and set it alight before he began walking deeper into the tomb.

"We carved out larger sections of the tombs here, to do our work," he explained. She followed closely, checking out the small rooms spurring off the sides. They were all empty, dust coated and desolate. A smell bloomed its fetid flower as they continued towards the dull murmur of activity. Finally, their next steps landed them in a man-made cavern, oversized and overflowing. It probably once harbored the sarcophagi of a prominent family and now boomed with pirate plunder, stuffed with urns, jugs and boxes, and crawling with people she recognized from the Den of Men. Scant ventilation aired the place out and the torches left a gray haze that transformed even the gold peeking out of one sack into a lusterless yellow metal. Even compared to the rest of Egyptian working standards, this place would still whisk up a local OSHA agent into a fevered froth of ire.

She pressed the back of her wrist to her nose and scanned the room. A series of pots were pushed into the corner that, by the smell of them, had been converted into a privy and hadn't been emptied since the operation began. Bile licked at the back of her throat. She struggled to keep it down. Piourma's nose wrinkled and Jeannette felt slightly vindicated.

Men, and a few women, settled themselves in disarray throughout the room, hands constantly busy in whatever task they were engaged with. A bundle of three she knew laughed at something and Jeannette realized she'd never seen them so carefree.

From the noise, one conversation jumped out at Jeannette, drawing her attention in as sharply as a diving hawk.

". . . and he already owes the priests. Serves him right for trying to rat on us." Jeannette's gaze unfocused as she struggled to hear more as Piourma led her through the hall.

"His brother already paid the price. I hear he's taken in all those kids. You would think Nekhebu would keep his accusations close to his heart, not shout them out for the Gods to hear."

Nekhebu? The fisherman who's brother was accused—wrongly, according to Nekhebu—of tomb robbing? Were there more Nekhebus?

Piourma gestured to a tunnel that led off from the cavern. "Just go to the lower storage room, I guess. Ottah will tell you what to do. Don't get lost, stick to the main passage. The old passages are no longer safe."

Mind occupied with what she'd just heard, Jeannette nodded and plodded toward the tunnel. They needed some fans, or at least little holes for air. Jeannette tried not to dwell on how much this was going to suck: bad air, no friends, no water, pissing in an already filled pot. With witnesses.

And realizing that those men knew something about Nekhebu and his brother.

A few other tunnels—some so low she wouldn't have been tempted to explore them even in clear air—branched off from the main one. Before long, the tunnel dropped quickly onto a short, rough staircase. Nearly twisting her ankle on the mis-sized steps, they tossed her into another hazy room. The smoke of the torch fire took little time to scorch away her ability to smell anything, but she was fairly certain a lower privy was happily absent.

A sitting man, scowly with one eye bulging and the other pressed in a squint, glared in her direction.

"Ottah?" She approached him, trying on a friendly smile. He wasn't a man from the hut.

"Who are you?" If he'd been munching on chaw, a smattering of brown would have textured the ground before him.

Jeannette's eyes narrowed. She hated that tone of voice. "I'm Jeannette. I've been told to come and help you." His twisted feet caught her attention. One ankle sickled inward, huge growths bubbling under his flesh like braided bread. Patches of skin, darker in the light of the torches, spread across his legs; the rest of him was pale for an Egyptian. From a birth defect, or an accident, Jeannette didn't know, but she guessed this guy was in pain every day of his life.

"Who told ya?"

After a shallow sip of unhealthy air, she frowned and said in a flat voice. "Funsai."

"Don't need any help." Ottah grumbled, then gestured to a spot some distance from him surrounded by wide-mouthed jugs. "Sort out those."

On closer inspection, the containers held stolen censers, figurines and other small objects. Combs and bracelets and jewelry, all things meant to be used in the afterlife, instead waylaid to be sent to Arabia, Syria and places farther afield. Like the wilds of Scandinavia. Someday to be trapped within glass cases in almost every nation of the world.

"Sort those into separate baskets. One for gold, the other for gems."

She nodded, planted a torch in a sconce above her head and began to sift through the items.

The first bracelet she grabbed from the jug looked dull and she had to squint in the low light to get any detail. It might be copper, it might be gold. With her fingers, she felt some carved design in the metal. The stone could be green, maybe black. She glanced up at Ottah; his back was to her. He tossed one item into the right pile, and with barely at glance at the next, laid it onto the pile to his left.

Bringing the bracelet closer to her face, she counted the stones—one, two, three . . . ten, eleven, twelve—and mentally compared that to how much gold might be in the ornament. She rubbed the bracelet against her side, squinted at it again. Were twelve gems, if they were gems, enough to put them in the gem pile, or if this was made out of pure enough gold, should it go in the gold pile? She studied one basket of cups and collars and other smooth metallic items, then the next, holding smaller items of a bit more sparkle, and laid the jewelry in that one.

This was going to take forever.

Other than the sound of metal jingling against metal, the two worked in silence for a mind-numbing length of time. So long, and so boring. She was sure she'd seen her hair grow. Constantly, she had to push her bangs up her sweaty forehead, hoping the sweat would gel it out of her eyes. She needed to slice her bangs off again, but the cut never ended up clean.

Every time she came across a scarab piece she would touch the circle around her neck, waiting for some sign. Like she would hear "Yes" in her head, or it would grow hot or there would be a spark, or something, anything. But there was nothing. Only figurines of gods and kings, and jewelry to adorn the dead in the afterlife. Small trinkets in a variety of shapes carved from stones indiscernible in the abominable light. All priceless. And here she was, tossing them from one pile to the next. She grabbed a figurine of Bast, and the torque around her neck grew warm.

She stopped everything, waiting for more information.

Ottah's piles grew; nothing stirred on Jeannette's side.

"I wish this was more than a you're-getting-warm kind of game, Bast," Jeannette mumbled. Ottah looked over, eyes as wide as his open-mouthed frown. Jeannette ignored him in favor of the statue.

"Am I close to something?" she whispered. "Is someone coming; this a warning?" She shook the statue. "What are you trying to say?" The metal against her skin became uncomfortably hot, and then cooled down to its typical warm.

Was that a no?

"Work or leave." Ottah was glowering at her. She set the statue near her thigh and continued, wondering what Bast was trying to get across to her.

Her solitary assembly line processed ruby-eyed animal sculptures of gold that went in the gold pile. A lapis lazuli facing of some artwork that would have lined a wall—that went in the gemstone pile. Some of the items had an unbalanced size to weight ratio, and she figured they were some other metal and only coated in gold. Those, Ottah told her, got sent back to another storeroom, same with the ivory.

Without her pack, she had no water, no snacks. Dry swallowing had become a nervous tic. Ottah worked on like a robot, his gears never once winding down. At least she didn't have to pee. Her left leg had gone numb. Unbending it, she bounced it against the ground. The statue hadn't turned her circlet on again, though she'd touched it with the propensity of a developing OCD habit.

Get up and walk out, she told herself. Stop being an indecisive chicken. Tell them you're after water, they'll understand.

But what if they didn't, her thoughts continued. What if they think I'm trying to desert, that I'm too weak for this job and they kick me off it.

And then her gut dropped. They could consider her a threat and try to kill her, spear between the shoulder blades as she guzzled from a trough like a water-starved pack mule.

Every few minutes, after a disturbingly hard swallow, she ran through her logic again, telling herself she'd get up and leave, find a water bucket and, no matter how nasty it was, at least wet her mouth. She coughed, a spontaneous event triggered naturally by her body trying to expel its lungs of all the crud in the air. She looked up, stared at Ottah for a few minutes as he unceasingly increased his piles of stolen holy items.

Rubbing her hands clean of the dust against her *kalasiris* only split the skin. So much for soft and supple. The webbing between her thumb and forefinger cracked and her cuticles were something for which Gabby would have disowned her. If it weren't for the days at the perfumery, she'd probably shed layers of skin like a molting lizard. Dust coated everything, even blinking no longer dislodged the film from her eyeballs. She could understand how mummies and parchment lasted the ages in this moisture starved environment.

She looked at Ottah, again. Still working. The torches flickered and suddenly she just couldn't breathe. The room had somehow grown smaller between her last breath and the next. She needed fresh air. Scrambling to her feet drew the unwavering frown of Ottah the perpetual motion machine. Did anyone in this guild of thieves do anything but look displeased?

"I need a break," she said. "I'm thirsty."

"No breaks, not until they come get us." In the dim flicker of the torch, his frown lessened. With a decisive swipe, he slid his palms down his own filthy kilt and turned back to his task. "We only have a little time left."

The skin over her arms prickled, glistening with her last ounce of body moisture. Measuring his Everest pile to her mole hill only whipped her heart into a faster pace. She grabbed a trinket from a basket and tossed it in a pile. Then a handful more. Bast's statue landed in the gem pile. What if she didn't do fast enough work? A gem studded pectoral glittered from the gold pile, and she grabbed it, stabbing herself in the palm with a thin, loose wire as she threw it violently into the gem pile. She'd never finish. Blinking against the smoky miasma of air, the basket barely looked fuller. Was she in some hell space where she had to continuously sort out piles of cursed objects until she could no longer breathe, her body shriveled up by the thirsty Egyptian air? She was trapped down here, underground with—

"Jeannette."

Jeannette looked up, her breathing fast. One of her neat piles of gem encrusted cups tumbled over in a clatter. Ottah was hunched over his piles, motionless, staring at her, eyebrows high on his forehead in silent judgment.

After a frozen moment, she rubbed her palms down the front of her dress. "Did you say something?"

Ottah shook his head and returned to sorting.

Looking around the chamber revealed nobody else sharing the space with them. She examined the dark corners farthest from the torches, the doorway, even the ceiling in case the owner of the voice could somehow climb up the walls. Nobody was there. Nobody else to call her name.

In the gem pile the half buried face of the Bast figure watched her, eyes sparkling in the low torchlight.

She took a breath; the circlet had a warm tingle to it. A gentle heat flooded her neck and shoulders, arms, her entire body. Leaning her head back and closing her eyes, she imagined she was standing outside in the wheat fields south of Spokane, a breeze whispering through the heads of the grain. Warm sun and fresh air. Wide open spaces. She'd go south on Fridays after work sometimes, to get away from her personal expectations of life that always fell short when dealing with other people.

"You two can git now."

Jeannette popped her eyes open, dashing away the clean air and warm sun. A man stood in the doorway, nodded at each and continued down the passage. With a glance at her piles she counted no less than seven misplaced items. One was a bug figurine, shiny with green and gold flakes of gems, veins of gold filigree. Such fine work for such primitive technology.

"Hey, Ottah."

The man had struggled to his feet, swiping dust off his butt. "What now?"

"These little things," she lifted the brightly colored beetle, "are these those heart scarab things that people use to house their *ba*?"

"Stupid swamp walker. Change of conscience now?" His eyes darted from the scarab to Jeannette's face, back to her hand.

"No," she said with a sneer. "I was just wondering. Is there a *ba* in here?" The piece sat easily in the scooped palm of her hand. The idea of a soul in this thing caused her gut to flip over. Was such a thing so impossible? After everything else she'd seen in Kemet? And if there was, surely these people must be stopped.

Ottah stood there, jaw muscles flexing. Then his face fell, all the glower and spite evaporating like spit and tears in the selfish desert tomb. He nodded, looked away. "Yes. Someone will forever wander now because of our greed."

Jeannette wrapped her fingers around the beetle.

"You can't back down now, you're in this with us!" Ottah practically yelled, lumbering toward the door on his deformed leg. "You too will be eaten by the demon in the Hall of Two Truths for the possession of costly woods and fine products from the east. You made your choice; you made the pact."

Flinching at his venom, she gripped the heart scarab in her hand. It didn't feel like a human soul filled the empty space within. Though, maybe a soul didn't need much room. The space between molecules a pleasant enough crash pad. "I know. I didn't say I was backing out." She scowled, and to his back she asked, "How many souls do you think we have here, trapped?"

He whirled around on her, face pale, teeth bared. "Stop asking such stupid questions, woman!" He stumbled a few steps toward her, shoulders hunched over in pure primate fashion, almost kicking a bronze bowl out of his way in his race to wrap his hands around her throat— which he didn't do, though she surely expected him to. "*They* are heart scarabs, you stupid foreigner." He thrust his finger at a tiny baboon carving. "Scarab." Then at a beetle. "Scarab." With an open hand he gestured at a jumble of some of the smallest trinkets: scarabs, baboons, ankhs, scythes, all tiny and intricate and some of the best artwork of the bunch.

"What?" The word scratched against her dry throat. "All of these?"

Ottah didn't stick around to chat, he charged from the room like a demon was on his tail. And if the world could be viewed through an

Egyptian kaleidoscope, there probably was, distorted from the everyday into something terrifying.

Jeannette brushed her fingers along the circlet, shocked at the piles of soul containers carelessly piled into a heap, categorized by the value they could bring in simply for the materials they were constructed from.

She waited for the heat of hellfire and the scent of brimstone, instead she only wanted water and to ditch this oppressive cave and see the Tutu Constellation and the torches of the city below. The room felt small, and slowly growing smaller without Ottah's sturdy busyness cluttering up the quiet. With a skip and a near tragic tumble to the ground, she escaped the room, burdened by thoughts of gods and heart scarabs and if, at some point that evening, her fingers hadn't probed Abayomi's soul with a complete lack of veneration.

Chapter 28

THE RETURN HOME PASSED IN A BLURRY HAZE of men coated in dust and an impossible, eternal need to swallow. Those things didn't matter, though, because all she could think about was that menagerie of heart scarabs and the mummies that must have been torn apart to harvest the damning metal and gems. Her feet, directed by automatic impulses, took her from one stumble to the next, down the hill under a moonless sky into the walled village. She took a different route this time, led by two light-skinned men from the west; their long braided beards bobbed against their chests when they agreed to let her follow them. Piourma hadn't sought her out, and Jeannette would have only had the sense of mind to find him after two Valium and an hour of deep breathing exercises. Instead, after her near body cavity search by the thieves, she'd clung to these men, foreigners yet less alien than herself, begging their aid after drinking from a jug of water that had already been licked and slobbered on by a legion of thieves. Dignity, thy death be desperation.

As porous as a sieve, the village's hidden entrances kept nobody out except for those willing to follow the law. Jeannette had never realized just how trivial the guarded gates and pottery passes were until that night when at least twenty individuals in groups of two and three snuck in through separate, secret access points all within a thirty minute span.

Walking under a weight of exhaustion, Jeannette found her way home barely before sunrise.

"Where have you been?" The words were out before Abayomi could even gain his feet.

"I went to the tombs. They let me in." She landed on a pillow. "I'm in." She should have sounded excited, or proud, or something. Instead, she sounded empty of everything.

"How was it?" Abayomi asked as Sanura offered her some beer. The girl had sprung awake when Jeannette walked through the door. Werel was probably chasing fuzzy goats through dreamland—the woman could sleep through a stampede of water buffalo. Jeannette took the mug and guzzled it down, thrusting out the cup in a mute demand for more. Sanura obliged.

"Fine, I guess," she finally said. She held up her hands and examined the creases and cracks that branched across her skin like the baked surface of a desert lake in late August. Wordlessly, Sanura began rubbing a greasy concoction into her skin. She could smell myrrh; probably something from the cache of pilfered products from her day job. Jeannette sat there like a loose noodle, thinking back to the pile of pilfered souls, Spokane and her job, the daily habit of showering, and finally her mind settled on China Palace's fortune cookie. Sanura gently rubbed the palms of her hands, each finger and the knot of muscle at the heel. "My hands are a little chapped."

"I can see. Here, drink some more." Jeannette took the offered mug and did what she was told.

Abayomi stood over them like a vigilant guard. Or maybe a stereotypical grandmother, the kind she'd never had. With every twitch, every aborted move to touch her, he revealed his anxiety. Every question he tucked away for a better time. He was so active now, like a real, living man. She looked at him, at his brown eyes, the fleshy lips settled into a worried frown. This man, this mummy, was without his heart scarab. Without his soul.

Hell, did we really have ourselves duped, she thought. Caught up in a world of self-imposed limitations for fear of the unknown. Be good and brush your teeth before bed and eat an apple a day and say your prayers because there might be a God and you might have a soul and it's better to play the game *just in case.*

Maybe *that* was one of the promised lies. That damned fortune cookie haunted her thoughts. If the theory held, Abayomi was a soulless monster. Obviously, even suggesting he was without his soul, he was a good and thoughtful person. A man to trust and look up to. Jeannette closed her eyes and sighed heavily. Could the essence of a person be trapped in a token ornament, so easily separated from the individual? With her American upbringing, it seemed such a hard story to sell. And being here beside one of the soulless right now, a loving person who understood right from wrong and strove to do well by his pharaoh, well, it became a right damn impossible journey. But if it was true—and maybe it was in this world of animal-headed *mi-nether* and gods made flesh— Abayomi did not fall into the same category. That was the only explanation. He was as much a visitor to this place as she. He could not be soulless. Those rules did not apply.

She finished the mug of beer, her fevered thirst tempered.

"How are you now?" Abayomi asked, a hand lightly resting on her shoulder.

296

"Better."

And if that was the truth, if his essence wasn't trapped in a piece of jewelry, how in the world could she convince him of that? That he could drop the worn, linen wrappings and step out into the bright day and find a new path, a new life, that had nothing to do with his search for ancient lies. How could she convince him that the past was dead, and the future would unfurl at its own pace, and that he had to live each moment before it fell away like dust?

Such an insurmountable task. She sighed. It was all crap.

Through the overhead window, a purple wash to the night's blackness announced the coming dawn. The daunting fact that in a few hours she would have to play guard dog again and smile and pretend that this was the life she'd chosen for herself didn't help her spirits.

Nothing she did was of her own choice. College and losing Ricky and her job: all events shaped by momentum. Stumbling into this land of magic and myth, also an accident. She brushed at her eyes. She needed sleep.

What she needed was to finally make a choice.

She set down the mug and glanced from one friend to the next. "We need to send a message to the Master Slaver. It's got to end now." She could only think of that pile of heart scarabs, the mauled mummies . . . Even if the scarab wasn't necessary, it was still abhorrent.

"The time of your realization has finally come. This is good." Abayomi reached out and patted her, a smile dancing on his lips. Her heart twisted like a long strip of licorice. "We were worried about you."

"I needed *some* proof." She curled her fingers into her palm and shook her head. "I just—those people trust me." And now they would die. She swallowed down the self-loathing, bitter as a mouthful of rancid milk.

Sanura caught her eyes. "There are things you cannot walk away from, not if you want to live with yourself afterward."

She forced a weak smile. The loss of souls, or the loss of life. "Abayomi, can you please write the letter?"

Abayomi remained silent for a moment, thoughtful, and then his head listed to the right, his posture a mix of curiosity and disbelief, his expression saying, "You are not fine, my friend, but I will let you hold your secrets close." She struggled to not look away, to keep her face as inscrutable as the sphinx. With a shrug, he pulled out his writing tablet, his movements methodical, the actions of a body going through well-

297

learned motions. Sanura boiled the water while Abayomi honed the edges of the reeds, and when all was ready, little pots and tooled reeds covered the surface of the small table.

Without papyrus or clay shards, he painted his words on a strip of his own linen, harvested by Jeannette's practiced hands from a thicker layer on his lower back. A neat bow now decorated his left hip: a loosely wrapped gift. On a table, small vessels of grain weighed down the edges of the cloth strip and Sanura pulled it even tighter to give Abayomi a smooth writing surface. Jeannette watched as he prepared a message from the scrounged writing implements. Even without a professional writing tablet he still performed beautiful artwork. It wasn't the hieroglyphs made famous by eternal monuments, but another form of writing in a flowing cursive that bloomed under his brush. She watched Abayomi write, the words forming backwards from English: right to left.

When he finished, he turned to her and demanded, "Now is a good time for you to tell me what ails your mind."

"Abayomi." In the strained silence, his name boomed from her lips. "I found some heart scarabs." The pile of scarabs and ankhs and feathers doubled in her depressed reflection, turning into a dragon's horde grand enough to fill the Osireion. "I've no idea how to find your scarab. It might be lost . . ." she watched him blink, his eyebrows bunch together, ". . . forever. I'm so sorry."

He looked up at her, his dark eyes capturing hers. "Why is that? You tried."

I'm sorry for the loss of your wife. Because you're as out of time and place as I am. Because I feel guilty about giving up, even though the task is an impossible one. She thought all those things, but voiced only: "Because your scarab had been taken."

His Adam's apple bobbed under the layer of linen and he looked away, nodding.

She grabbed his hand, pulled it into her lap. "Look at me. Please."

In a slow swing of his head, he did. She could lose herself in those eyes. "You are no less a man, Abayomi. Can't you sense it? Can you say you are empty of a soul? You're already complete, even if you may not think so. You are no less than Sanura or I."

Abayomi's gauzed expression was frozen in time. She could stare at it for ages and still be a thousand years distant. "Thank you, Jeannette." He gently pulled his hand away; she let it slip from her grasp. The corners of her eyes stung. The two women watched him stand and leave their home.

For a moment she felt that same dumfounded paralysis that had infected her the night Ricky had taken her to a fancy dinner only to tell her that he'd decided to leave her for Gabby—the feeling that the only thing to do next was to step away, leave that slice of time behind and come back later when sensibility reasserted itself on the world.

Abayomi. She'd hurt him. Profoundly. She'd given up when he'd relied on her so thoroughly.

Jeannette buried her face in her hands. "I can't find it, Sanura. It's gone."

"The *ba* is not so easily lost." Sanura's voice was thoughtful as she continued to watch the closed door. "It seeks its return."

Jeannette stood, linen message going damp in her sweaty grip. "I've got to pass this message on. I'll be back." She left the house, closing the door behind her with a grinding click.

When she returned, the hut was empty except for Werel, who squatted on a low stool and worked her spindle, a basket of fibers next to her on the floor. With nothing more than a nod, Jeannette passed by the woman to her own sleeping chambers and dropped into the tenth circle of sleep with the closure of her eyes.

Her dreams took her back to Spokane, where she talked to a cat with a woven metal collar who kept telling her the answers were always with her. She took to the streets on donkey-back, trotting under the downtown skywalks, waving at people as she went. Most ignored her, others threw fruit.

Then she was in Egypt—teleported there as only dreams can do— the real Egypt, and that smiling mongrel dog kept smiling at her, laughing almost like he knew everything, saw everything and the entire situation amused him.

She woke to a nudge at her shoulder and Sanura looking worried.

"You were whimpering." She patted Jeannette's forehead with a damp cloth. "And tossing."

Jeannette laid her arm across her eyes, letting the cool soothe her heated skin. "It was just a dream."

"Something about the tricks played on you," came Abayomi's voice from behind her. "You were very vocal."

Jeannette groaned, and rolled over onto her side, taking an age to sit up and face her friends. The off-white gauze wrapped Abayomi's expression in an inscrutable mask.

"You okay?"

He blinked at her, then nodded. "I am what I am. The King of the Living is my only guide to *Yaaru*," he said in a level voice. "If not tomorrow, if not in the years ahead, someday I shall live upon everything good and pure."

Oddly optimistic, Jeannette wondered if she was misinterpreting his words. Sanura drew her ears back and studied Abayomi, seeing something there that Jeannette was blind to. She wished for the clear vision of the oracles, but realized they were all cursed to speak only in riddles, and unsharable truth was as useful to her now as a wool sweater.

The rude call of a benu bird brought Jeannette's attention to the bright day outside. She jumped to her feet.

"Ah, damn. I overslept."

She rose, washed her face and drank some beer, wishing for a shot of espresso to get her gears cranking. Beer did nothing for the exhaustion in her long muscles; nothing would help the frustration in her heart. She stuffed her full water bottle into her backpack and pulled it on. Behind closed lids that dog smiled, and in moments of distraction the cat told her she already had the answers; Jeannette felt helpless.

But she also felt angry.

"Can I walk with you?" Sanura asked, head tilted in a good imitation of Abayomi. She'd absorbed his mannerisms like a sponge and Jeannette wondered what, if anything, the girl had adopted from herself. On a stool near the brewing equipment, Abayomi sat quietly, motionless, lost in his own headspace.

"Of course," Jeannette said, but her concern stayed with the mummy.

As they walked through the morning streets of the workers compound towards the perfumery, alive with intention and determination, Jeannette couldn't help but watch out for the guards. The man she'd given the note to was gone already, which was good. They passed by a fruit seller, and Jeannette bought a melon and some fish for Sanura from another stall.

"I'm worried about him," she said to the girl. Sanura bit into her fish, a portion of the tail poking from her lip as she nodded her agreement.

"You must not give up your hunt," Sanura said. "I hope you know that you cannot abandon him."

The melon went sour in her stomach. "I know," she said grudgingly. "I just don't think the scarab is necessary."

Sanura studied her. "Of course it is."

Jeannette tried again. "Though he doesn't have his scarab, I can't think he's without his *ba*," she said, as if correcting bad trivia rather than arguing about the state of one's soul.

Though her heart still danced with depression's less brutal little sister, she knew she couldn't quit the spy business yet. It wasn't only about Abayomi's heart scarab. Though she'd be delighted if she found it, she also knew he wasn't a half-person without it. Mainly she had to return because, though the circle of thieves might attribute her immediate disappearance with someone who just couldn't handle it, she knew they could also see it as a betrayal. Their retaliation could come in many forms, least of all would be to double the watches, pay off more guards. And she still needed to speak with Tabiry. Eyes were everywhere.

Maybe, once the thieves were caught, Abayomi could sift through all those scarabs on his own, his body immediately being drawn to the spirit within the ornament—if it was really there. Maybe, he could complete himself, even when Jeannette could not.

As they walked in silence, Jeannette observed the guards do their usual thing. Nothing out of the ordinary, nothing suspicious, though one of them watched her a bit too closely. He was a thin character with a harelip that cast his expression into perpetual censure.

She grabbed Sanura's hand and they ditched the main road for another street heading toward a cluster of temples.

"That guard wasn't your friend . . ." Sanura noted, trotting along behind Jeannette.

"Not mine, though I'm not sure if he prays to the gods of spirit or the gods of gold."

Coming from a minor road to a busy arterial, they slowed their pace to cross the busy intersection. Across the street a cluster of women with jugs on their hips surrounded a well. Jeannette knew of this well, though it wasn't near her own little house and she'd never used it. The water, they said, was sweet and cool, tapped from a different source than the other wells lower down the hill toward the *Iteru*. Many of the women, on closer look, were girls, bare-chested with low hanging skirts that reached to the ground. It wasn't their bareness that caught Jeannette off guard. It wasn't even the fact that it was one of the largest collections of a single animal type of *mi-nether* she'd seen since entering Kemet. It was the yank on her shoulder when Sanura suddenly stopped dead. It was the look on the girl's face: shock so striking Jeannette dropped to a squat to run her hands over the girl, seeking some injury.

THREE GREAT LIES

"Sanura. Are you okay?"

Sanura stared at the women, eyes wide, mouth popped open revealing her sharp, feline teeth.

Jeannette looked again, assessing the situation, categorizing the things of note, those little items out of place. And it hit her. The small group of young women was just like Sanura. Each one a daughter of Bast.

From a young age Jeannette had cultivated a watchful eye for disapproval to the exclusion of all else. Then, the *Trick* happened. Her best friend and boyfriend had a lengthy affair to the point that they were engaged without her notice, causing a recalibration of her radar. Now she sought, instead of disapproval, the lies that laced every tongue.

So, it was to Jeannette's credit that she recognized the fragile, glassy veil over Sanura's eyes. Her expression was pure loss, the exact color of sun streaks dividing the river's surface following a later afternoon sandstorm. It was as if the sight of her sisters, pre-pubescent and energetic, faces open to the wonders of a city outside of the cloistered temple walls, reminded her of her own state: independent and without a purpose.

"Did you want to go talk to them?" Jeannette asked, words as gentle as if speaking to a frightened rabbit in a trap.

Stuck in emotional tar, Sanura didn't move. Just stared. Jeannette wavered, then decided. A woman on a mission, she stalked up to the girls, gripping her pack straps. If only she had experience with pre-teens, then maybe she'd know what to say, like those moms who forced fifteen different activities upon their kids. From ballet to soccer to pottery, they ran them around in a beige SUV: they had kid skills.

Having no distinct plan, Jeannette opened with, "Hey, girls."

Eight pairs of orange eyes turned on Jeannette, lips pressed tight together, ears half erect. Their movement was so simultaneous it could have been choreographed. A wide collar of entwined metal with an image of Bast rested against each of their collarbones. An aged daughter of Bast turned from the well and faced Jeannette. Gray frosted the fur around her muzzle. She measured up Jeannette, her body language expressing disinterest, until her eyes landed on Jeannette's circlet.

"You."

"Me?"

"You, the chosen of Bast."

Jeannette touched her torque. "Bast gave this to me."

All of the girls began talking at once.

"Mother gave that to you?"

"Did she task you with a great duty?"

"You? She picked you of all non-God children?" That wasn't said with any malice, just open awe.

"Ah, I guess. And yeah, I've a task—" the faces lit up, "—but I can't tell you." She didn't think it something to gossip about. "So, ah, do you know my friend?" Jeannette gestured for Sanura to come closer, but instead of looking excited to see her family, she looked ready to bolt. "Come on, Sanura."

Awkwardness and embarrassment seasoned the atmosphere.

"Ah, okay then." Jeannette added a little excitement to her voice like the friendly server at China Palace whenever a gaggle of soccer kids entered the banquet room. "I'm Jeannette, what are your names?"

Sanura stared at her like she'd just asked how much for the lot of them for a night of debauchery. The girls all shared a glance with each other that by now Jeannette had learned to interpret as uncertainty.

One of the girls, the one who'd asked about Jeannette's great duty, dipped her chin, eyebrows bunched together.

"We are daughters of Bast," another said.

Jeannette folded her hands together before her, shifting her weight onto her left leg. "Yeah, I know that. But, what is your name?"

The older woman stepped through the muddle of girls. "We are Bast's children, we are not given names."

Jeannette glanced at Sanura. She wondered where exactly her lines had gotten crossed.

The girls began whispering to themselves. The older woman shushed them. "We are not given names. We simply do the works of Bast, happily, without any distinction." Jeannette couldn't tell if the tone of disapproval was actually there, or Jeannette was somehow projecting it from the woman's words.

"Forgive me, Matron," came Sanura's voice from just behind Jeannette. "I hope Re's light forever shines upon you."

"And you, my sister," said the matron.

With all parties now close enough for comparison, Jeannette could tell these girls were younger than Sanura. And of course their inexperience kept them even more immature than their years. Jeannette remembered when Sanura had such gawking mannerisms, even if she never gawked. That seemed a lifetime ago.

THREE GREAT LIES

The girls asked Sanura and Jeannette questions. Jeannette began to lose track of which little Bast clone spoke, they all looked exactly the same, like Gabby's Pomeranian puppies. Except Sanura. Not only was the girl older, dressed in roughly made clothes of undyed linen, but she held herself differently. Ready. Watchful. Confident. The girls kept asking Sanura what she was doing on her mission beyond the cloister walls. Sanura spoke in riddles to Jeannette's ears, but the other *mi-nether* seemed content with her explanations. Then, Sanura asked about her litter mates.

"They are in training for their duties now."

The circlet around Jeannette's neck warmed pleasantly against her skin, as if the sun's heat it had soaked up throughout the weeks had developed a slow leak. In that moment, watching Sanura talk to her sisters—each standing on opposite sides of an expanse built of an entirely different set of experiences—Jeannette saw the essence of the young woman spelled out in automatic understanding. Here was a girl who her entire life, up until her mother had cast her out, wanted only to be useful. Then, by some random event as slight as the beat of a butterfly's wings, the girl was expelled, walking a road of isolation.

"Do they wonder about me?" Sanura asked.

The matron smiled, the edges of her lips lifting. The smile hinted at things more gloomy than simple happiness. "Some do. It is good to see you are well, my sister. Re's light guide your path."

That sounded like avoidance and a dismissal if Jeannette had ever heard one.

Sanura nodded, a wounded heart, and the two turned from the well and walked away, the girl following in Jeannette's slow wake.

Jeannette had put Abayomi's heart scarab at the top of her to-do list, a chore with a tangible goal. But she saw now that it might have been her greatest mistake here in Kemet. There were things you couldn't turn away from, not if you wanted to be able to look back on your actions with anything like pride.

From behind her Jeannette heard, "Am I to be alone forever?" Jeannette nearly stumbled; her throat closed as she turned towards the girl behind her. The pain and aching radiated from Sanura and seeped into Jeannette's bones.

She fell to her knees, looking up into Sanura's downturned face. She reached out and dabbed her fingers along Sanura's arm, afraid a firm touch might shatter her on the spot. "Never. You'll never be alone, Sanura. I'll be by your side. So will Abayomi."

304

Sanura said nothing for a moment, then she smiled, a grimace in disguise, and met Jeannette's gaze. "But you will return to the land you came from. Abayomi seeks his pleasures in the Hidden Fields with He who Faces West." Sanura dropped her farce, ears pulled back in sour anger. "I'll be the only one left."

Jeannette wondered how she'd gotten so old, so fast. Were heart to heart talks easier for other people, or were they just better at faking it, of devising the right choice words?

"I should have stayed a slave. Then when you were gone, I'd have something to do. Somewhere I belonged. They can have my freedom; it's the only thing left for anyone to take."

On Jeannette's tongue were poised words like "Everything will be okay," and, "It's not as bad as you think," but right then okay seemed a faraway concept.

She had no idea how to varnish her words into something acceptable. Into something that would pierce Sanura's armor of anger. She knew how Noah felt in that pinnacle moment, stranded on an isolated mountain with an ocean rising up to swallow him whole. Instead of an ocean of rain, Jeannette was threatened by a sea of unshedable tears, and she didn't have one inkling on how to pull the plug and have it all drain away.

So she hugged the girl, wrapped Sanura up and held her to her chest. A hug was medicine in and of itself.

The small body contracted to board stiffness, then the rigid muscles softened, a rippling relaxation that fluttered through her body from her shoulders down to her feet. Sanura's head fell against Jeannette's chest, rested there as if drained of all strength after the eternal struggle to keep upright. Using gentle strokes, Jeannette petted her smooth fur.

She couldn't fail Sanura. *Couldn't.* A presumptuous part of her believed she was charmed. The gods and oracles supported her success. Bast had even given her personal attention and a gift. The goddess was this girl's mother; certainly she'd beam into Jeannette's brain the right and proper thing to say to bring Sanura around. Divine inspiration. It was going to happen any second now.

To be honest, Jeannette had never amounted to much. Never meant anything to anybody. This girl, small, yet strong, valued Jeannette, and to Jeannette, Sanura was one of the most important people alive. This person, she did not want to fail.

"Sanura," Jeannette whispered into Sanura's ear, "I think we can't really know what's going to happen. We can't expect everything to unfold as we planned. You were sent out here with a purpose, a purpose your mother had given you. Sometimes it's not the goal you need to accomplish, but the steps you take to complete that goal that are the important things." She squeezed the small body. Sanura sniffled, hugging her back. "I don't think you'll ever be alone. You're a strong, loving young woman, with an open heart. You will not end up alone."

Ditching work that she was already late for, she took Sanura to a bakery where they sat on short stools in the inner courtyard. She tapped her toe against the fading fabric of her backpack resting at her feet. At least the salesman's promise hadn't been false; this pack sure held up to quite the beating. No pool was available for Jeannette to lose herself in, no acacia trees shaded them from the afternoon heat, just the building's shadow and a holey, reed awning. Jeannette was no smooth talker, but she'd learned how uplifting it could be to just know that someone was by your side.

Of course in order to deliver such assurances, Jeannette would have to offer up more than words. Jeannette would have to stay in Kemet.

Chapter 29

SANURA DID NOT WANT THE FISH. Had no desire to sit there in the half-sun with Jeannette's flexible, furless face twisted in worry. Her sisters had treated her as if she'd mastered the birthing chant after hearing only one repetition. Had treated her as a daughter of Anubis, and not one of Bast. Someone unknown, to keep at a distance. They didn't welcome her like one of their own. The place at her siblings' side was no longer hers. Thinking back to her early days in the birthing chamber, the warm mound of her brothers and sisters surrounding her on every side, Sanura missed everything. Her family, the sanctuary, the lessons. Her life had grown still, like a hunting crocodile, and she'd accomplished not a thing since she'd left them.

Jeannette tapped her fingers along the side of her mug, a fast drumbeat of a pattern Sanura didn't know from any of the chants she'd learned. This woman, the one who'd saved her from a man who dealt in flesh, did not want her anymore. Sanura had nowhere and nobody, only the promise of the long river and the final gate at its end.

That's what she had to look forward to. Loneliness before the final pleasures.

But, that was what every person had. She wasn't anyone special.

Her eyes focused on Jeannette's pursed mouth that frowned, then drew tight, whitening her skin. Sanura stopped meeting her eyes. Her selfish outbreak embarrassed her, but she would not apologize for what she'd said. Sanura knew the truth. Had known it for some time. Jeannette would be gone and Abayomi would move on to *Yaaru* and they would forget her, just like her sisters had done.

Jeannette pulled on her tail of hair. The woman's attention hopped from one thing to the next, never finding a comfortable place to rest. Regret stirred with the lonely foreboding in Sanura's chest.

In time all would fade to death and dust. It was the way of the desert; it could not be refuted. Maybe it wouldn't be this day, or the next, but soon. However, to be honest to that child part still inside of her, she didn't want to sit helplessly and wait for that tomorrow.

But she didn't know what else to do.

Jeannette wiped the back of her hand across her brow. "Back home, we had air-conditioning. It made the hot weather tolerable. Here, we only have shade." She said it with a laugh, but the laugh was forced. Sanura didn't say a thing.

"You know, I don't want to give up on Abayomi's scarab." Jeannette balanced her mug along its bottom edge, let it go and watched it wobble to stillness. Sanura watched Jeannette. "And I understand how important the heart scarab and *ba* and everything are, but I just can't think that he's some body walking around without his soul. Can't you see that?"

Sometimes, when Jeannette tried to convince Sanura of the superiority of her world, Sanura wondered if her friend wasn't trying to convince herself.

"It's more like," Jeannette said, looking up into the sky, "he's really a soul, trapped in a body that's trying to heal itself. His body's the piece that's not healthy, not his *ba*."

Sanura hissed her disbelief, then flicked her ear in thought. No, that couldn't work. It didn't work like that. But she'd left the teachings so early . . . Still, the *ba* rested within the heart scarab of the dead. There was nothing you could argue to prove otherwise. Sanura shook her head.

Jeannette sighed. "Don't worry. I'll go back and look some more." She propped her chin on her hand. "You know," she said softly, finally meeting Sanura's eyes. "I don't want to leave you." That wandering gaze dropped down to her mug. "I just don't belong here. Nothing's consistent with my own sense of reality."

"But you've made a life for yourself here," Sanura said.

Jeannette barked out a humorless laugh. "Yeah. I have a great life. Herit is the kindest, best boss and I've got the most prestigious job stirring . . . all day." Jeannette's grin turned mad. "And when I get home, I eat bread full of sand and water that's generally unclean and instead of sleeping on a hard floor, which I would rather do, I leave to pretend my loyalty to bastards that I'll eventually betray. Peachy life. Really, it's what I always dreamed of."

Sanura didn't like Jeannette's tone, her arrogance. Didn't like that she seemed to measure up to nothing on Jeannette's scales.

"What is it you want to return to?" Sanura asked, her own voice hollow. She swallowed hard, nearly choking on the burning in her throat.

With a tired voice, Jeannette said, "It's my home. It's where I belong, Sanura."

"Is it? So, yes, your trade is not what you dreamed; we all must work with what is given us. And the deception with the thieves will meet its end soon. In your land you don't even have Gods. You don't have family."

Jeannette opened her mouth, then closed it. Her skin had darkened under the sun, darker than the wood of the acacia tree, but nowhere as earthy as the soil of the *Iteru*. She was still a foreigner in a land of strangers. Sanura again regretted her words. Her friend must make her choices and Sanura should not coerce her with anger or snake language.

Picking up the fish, she bit off a chunk and chewed. Her fingers picked at a scab on her knee. They didn't talk. Sanura felt selfish, and panicked about her upcoming solitude. Jeannette looked confused and frustrated. Nothing useful would be done this day. She might as well do her laundry.

"You must go, Jeannette. You are already late for the perfumery."

Jeannette needed constant reminding at times when her *ka* appeared to be traveling. Sanura worried that she'd have no guide on the day it wandered the river's edge in the land of her origin.

The heat had settled on the hillside village; the power of Re could always be felt more strongly here than at either the riverside or her childhood temple. She watched Jeannette walk away, her steps heavy; her bag, strapped to her shoulders and arms, seemed to add more weight than its contents alluded to.

When Sanura reached their home, Abayomi stood in the doorway, arms crossed, a strip of linen dangling limply from his wrist. Her approach had him stepping aside to let her in. They sat together for a long time.

"Abayomi . . ." The rest of her words dried up on her tongue, though she was certain she had more to say than just his name.

"Yes?"

The desire to go to him, crawl in his lap and have him hold her, was stalking her. She didn't, though; that was a child's action. She wasn't a mewling kitten who needed to be warmed by the body heat of her siblings. The day was hot enough.

"What will . . . ?" No, that wasn't what she wanted to know. "How will you feel when Jeannette returns to her land?"

The mummified man sat lifeless, his already depleted activity banished further by the question. When he spoke, only his lips moved. "I will mourn her loss. I had hoped . . ." He turned his head away. "No, such things are selfish. She must live the life that Khnum's breath instilled within her."

Sanura frowned. What a pose, she thought, like a kitten with arched back and fluffed up fur. Right then, she couldn't find a grain of respect for this man that she loved.

"I'm going for a walk. I'll return later." She brushed past him.

Was nobody willing to fight for what they wanted? Well, Jeannette would, but she obviously didn't want the right thing.

In a sour mood, Sanura hiked to the workers' tombs carved into the reclining cliff face just north of the royal tombs. In the hot afternoon, she scurried from one shaded recess to the next, each meager and struggling for life. Scaling the rock face with fingertips and bare toes, she reached her destination: an outcropping above a small chapel topped by a pyramid. She worked herself into a crack within the stone and waited.

She knew they would come, many men and women, tattered but determined. Once Sanura figured out their pattern, she would wait under the vigilant tip of the Peak, its height almost dizzying, and observe. On those days when Abayomi and Jeannette were gone—most days lately—or when boredom's presence pressed her heart flat, or she needed to think, she simply watched and listened. Though the thieves were cursed by Anubis and Horus and Re, they still left offerings at this temple, perhaps hoping for leniency for their crimes. Sanura knew the Devourer awaited them.

Little time passed before a group of four entered the rock-cut chapel and mere minutes later left. Then a family entered, stayed a few minutes, and they too returned the way they'd come. Sanura counted thirty people entering and leaving within the time it took for the shadows to grow less than the width of her finger. Not once since she'd been attending to the pyramid topped tomb had she seen such behavior. There had never been such significant prayers to the Gods and ancestors before. Never such traffic to this one temple the cursed men attended above all others.

Instinctively, Sanura knew something had upset their routine.

She crawled out of her hole, half her body visible to an accidental glance. Fortunately, or perhaps unfortunately, nobody was down there anymore.

Before she'd become aware of it, they had all gone.

* * *

The courtyard of the chapel was empty. Sanura entered cautiously, holding her foot in the air, listening, before she placed it down within the prints of other feet in the dust. The wall paintings passed by her, unnoticed as she entered the vestibule, where she paused again, waiting. Still, no sound.

The chapel's ceiling towered high over her head. She passed through the open chamber like a whisper until she reached the offering hall. From within, she could hear the telltale sounds of men moving things, their actions muffled by care. She squatted in a dark corner until the beating of her heart no longer echoed in her ears.

Broken fragments of hushed urgency drifted up from the rear chambers. Sanura needed to see, needed to know more, but a shake had taken over her body and she didn't want to go back there.

". . . the road of the river . . ."

". . . up from the docks. Four barques of . . ."

". . . clear the warehouse. Everyone is gone. No one . . ."

". . . hurry. Curse the guards. Curse Funsai's greed."

"Curse the Gods."

Words and curses and the continued sound of movement, of something heavy dragging against the stones, filled her ears. The men were moving. The thieves were on the run. They knew, somehow—she didn't know how—somehow they knew the guards were coming.

Sanura crept out of the chapel and, once certain no watchful men stood guard, sprinted toward the town. The hem of her dress caught on her bent knees, constricting her stride, so she hiked it up to her thighs. Her speed stirred up a wind to flick her whiskers, sending false messages to her body. She wondered what she should do. Go tell Jeannette, because wasn't she in danger? Or go for Abayomi, because he would tell her what was best?

No. Sanura wasn't an empty duplicate, like her siblings. She wasn't a crude effigy of her mother, similar in likeness, but without her own convictions. Her mother had told her she had a task to do, a job only for her. To do that, she had to act, not do as she was told. It wasn't difficult to recognize the best course of action: above all else, the Master Slaver's men must be told.

Through her labored breath, Sanura said her own curse, and changed direction to the long, steep road that would take her down to the river.

* * *

The heat rising up from the hillside hung lazily in the stagnant air, baking him and his men like rolls of bread in an oven. The woman had her final message delivered as Khepri pushed the sun into the sky. It had taken her so long, the Master Slaver had been tempted to incarcerate them all for failing to protect the pharaoh's property. It had crossed his mind to make the foreign cur wait, show her that she did not dictate his actions. But that would only bring harm to the dead and the pharaoh. Nothing was worth that. Instead, he'd hastened to gather his men and they crossed the great river. The joy he would have gotten from making the foreign woman wait was nowhere near the joy he would gain from doing the work of the Gods and stopping those who undermined Pharaoh's rule.

The main roadway from the docks to the village of artisans would surely be watched, so he forced his guards of men and *mi-nether* to take the less-traveled, winding road to the south. It snaked around small hills that cut off their visibly, so two of his men trotted ahead and pulled them forward little by little. Their progress inched in agonizing slowness, and he ground his teeth at the necessary delay. He could taste the moment when he would end the accursed circle of men who thought nothing of the pharaoh's laws passed down from the Gods. It tasted sweet.

He scratched at the scar on his cheek. Sitting high on his litter, the view of the river breaking between the protruding hills caused him immense pride in his pharaoh. The land was fertile, green and vast. He could not see the edges of the domain, not even from this height on the shoulders of six men. Soon, Khnum would take over the sun's rule and tip it over to the west and the desert would be plunged into darkness. He wiped his damp forehead with a cloth and looked over into the western sky. Soon, justice would prevail.

* * *

The docks on the western shore of the *Iteru* were smothered with fishermen and women selling bread, spices and dried fish. One lady, her skin deeply creased, pushed some linen into Sanura's tired face.

"Your dress is all ripped up, daughter," the old woman wheezed. "Patch the rip with my linen."

Sanura ignored the split she'd ripped to allow her legs their stride. "Were there—" she broke off to gasp for more air, "—men here? Guards?"

The long tresses of the woman's ill-fitting wig bumped against her shoulders as she scanned Sanura up and down. "One of the girls said she saw several boats moor downriver. Just after we came out after the day's heat." She pointed to the south; Sanura couldn't see anything but the line of the river and the tall reeds. "I can sell you some linen to replace your dress. Fine, undyed linen. Just a few kit."

Sanura's arms, neck and back wore a skin of sweat, and she was tired of running around blind. Why had they landed so far away?

"That way?" She lifted up her arm, a heavy, lifeless weight, and waved vaguely to the south. "Did they come this way? By Re's light, did they pass this way at all?"

The linen seller gave Sanura a scolding look. "Daughter, such bluster."

Sanura muttered an apology.

"No, they must still be at their boats, or moved south I would guess. I wouldn't miss such a collection of men if I was sitting here fast asleep. They must be upriver."

"Thank you," Sanura said, then began another sprint, arms and legs pumping. The men must have taken another road into the village. She knew of another path, she'd explored it early on, but it was long, without any water, and nobody ever traveled it.

At least the road wasn't as steep as the main way, and though she had to stop to walk a few times, she finally came upon a band of armed men surrounding the rotund master on a litter hoisted by six. The sun had descended and cooled the dry air, but it hadn't cooled her annoyance at her river-and-back race.

"I've been looking for you!" Sanura yelled up at the Master Slaver, his face a picture of wilted determination. "Taking this road meant nothing but wasted time. It is evening and they already seek out their path to escape!"

The master's jowls shook. "Here, set me down."

The litter carriers lowered the bulk of the Master Slaver and helped the man gain his feet.

Sanura wanted to shy away, avoid his direct gaze, but she knew Jeannette would be in trouble, and perhaps only the power of this man could help her. Standing up staller, she breathed in strength.

"Tell me," he demanded.

Sanura stared at the line carved down the man's face, not looking into his eyes. She licked her lips and swallowed, her dry tongue gaining some moisture from the movement. "I said, sir," she began in a milder tone, "that the thieves know of your approach and, as we speak, are escaping your true justice." Her ears flexed, holding themselves to her head.

He stared at her; she remained still.

"If it is as you say, you must direct us now." He turned to settle himself onto the cushioned seat of his litter.

"I can't." Her voice shook. "I must tell Jeannette, catch her before she returns to the tomb. She's pretending to still work for them so they don't suspect their justice is soon to be met."

And she needed to make sure that the woman of dark skin, who had the malnourished *ka*, would do nothing harmful to her friend.

Nostrils flaring, the Master Slaver said, "We came across no individual along our path, young daughter. We did not even land at the docks."

"It matters not, Master. Either they saw you, or the guard Jeannette used to handle the message told someone or was caught. It matters that they know you are coming. They have many locations where they hide the stolen treasures. There are warehouses near the smelters, and the chapel of the workers' tombs is a place that they meet. A hut in the temporary settlement near the valley of tombs. Older mastaba with tunnels carved into the hills. I would suggest going to those tombs north of the valley, the ones that have been abandoned. There, they have been working day and night. That is where Jeannette will be come nightfall, and that is where I am going now." Sanura could not redirect her imagination from the things they would do to Jeannette if they knew of her deception. "Please, do not waste your time, Master." She dropped down to her knees. "Send the men ahead and do not hold them back."

"Your directions are too vague, girl. You must escort us." The command in his voice almost forced Sanura to task, but it wasn't just about capturing the thieves and finding her freedom, it was about helping her friend.

She growled—the low hanging sun took on the orange glow of evening—and lifted her eyes to look at the man. "Your man can follow me, and he can come back for you." Then she popped to her feet and rushed off. Behind her came a shout and the delayed pounding of feet in a run; she didn't bother to look. First, she would go and get Abayomi, she would need him and he wasn't that far out of her way. Then they would go to the abandoned tomb Jeannette had struggled in the previous night and take her away from those cursed men.

* * *

Jeannette trudged up the long path to the old tomb alone that night, flinching each time she revisited her confrontation with Sanura. She couldn't stop questioning what enticed her to return to her world. The world of reason, the world of the mundane laws of normality. Comfort. Of her solitude.

Simply, it was where she belonged. This world was constructed from fairytale and the one she had come from was solid and real. Though, that place she'd come from, the *real* one, had—before she'd even noticed—begun to fade away like shadows. She wanted to jump up on the highest point, climb to the Peak, and scream. Scream at the top of her lungs, yell at the oracles and the gods—all of them. "I'm standing right here," she would yell at them. "I'm right here, come down and tell me what the hell this is all about!"

And now, she knew she would expect some kind of answer.

Damn, how she'd fallen.

She scoffed at herself. Well, she prided herself on honesty. In an alien land, far, far away from home, she couldn't afford to be dishonest to the most important person: herself. She'd not fallen ... she'd adapted. She'd reacted to empirical, eye-witnessed evidence in a rational manner. Gods existed, well, at least Bast did.

She shook her head a bit, her bangs bouncing against her forehead. Her hair grew so long so fast, and the jagged trim job looked like a rat chewed on it. Maybe she should let it grow out. Maybe she would shave it all off and do the wig thing like the locals.

Did she trade this new life, with people who really cared for her, for the memory of a place she could lose herself in? Her instinct told her to let that memory live and die alone, like she probably would if she returned.

As she approached the tomb, the change alarmed her. People came and went, their regard for secrecy apparently dashed away by some unknown impetus. A knot of bile pressed hard into her esophagus. They must know.

A woman hunched under a heavy sack on her shoulders passed by and Jeannette grabbed her arm. "What's going on?" she asked.

The woman stopped to catch her breath before she said anything. "We're removing everything. We're almost done. The bottom levels are all that are left."

"Why? Did something happen?" Jeannette's thoughts galloped through her mind. She had to find Tabiry. She had to find Abayomi's scarab, and somehow, she had to find where they were taking everything.

THREE GREAT LIES

The Master Slaver's men were coming, but she had no idea how long it would take his S.W.A.T. team to land and mobilize.

A man passed by, carrying a jug a donkey would have been burdened under. He followed a line of five other men; she could find them easily, later. She only had to follow the ruts in the earth.

"I'm sure," said the woman, "but I don't know what. The guards must be coming, no other reason for moving everything." The woman sneezed. "Go grab some jugs and help," she said before she walked off. "They've already sent some gold to be melted down."

Melted?

She rushed into the derelict tomb, pushing by people flooding out as if from a burning barn, grabbing everything they could before it all crashed down into smoldering coals. Everyone was carrying something. So many people; she'd had no idea. Hopping down the broken steps three at a time, she bounced into the depths of the tomb. One torch lit the Scarab Room—as she'd dubbed it in her head. Ottah wasn't there. Half of his piles of artifacts weren't there. Gone, all those scarabs gone to be liquefied into their base elements.

The sight of her two wide-mouthed jugs and baskets punched adrenaline into her system.

It had to be in her collection of baskets and jugs. Her collar from Bast had gotten hot. Maybe it was there and she'd just not recognized it yesterday.

Above, someone shouted a wordless command. Her collection, they would take these and the remains of Ottah's piles next.

Rushing to her corner, she fell to her knees and plunged her hands into a basket of heart scarabs, touching as many as she could, brushing her fingers over every one, chanting in her head "which one, which one" until she'd upended the basket and rifled through the contents three times over. Frantically, in a parody of Isis' search for her husband's rent body, Jeannette sought out Abayomi's scarab. None of them were warm, or gave her a buzzy feeling, or pinged something in her head to make her know, *know*, that this was Abayomi, her friend whom she knew so well, whom she'd grown to love. Not one gave any sensation, any feeling, of the mummy.

"Damn!" She snatched up an ivory jackal figure and hurled it against the wall. "Where the hell is it?"

"You're here? Can't believe you came back to show your crocodile smile." Ottah lumbered up behind Jeannette, towering and looming and pouring off waves of animosity. Twisting around, she dropped to her butt, scooting across the sandy floor to put distance between her and the utterly pissed off man. Her back hit the wall. Rolling to her side, she tried to get beyond his reach, but though he wasn't fast on his misshapen feet, his hand snapped out like a viper's strike. With a vice-like hold on her ponytail, he jerked her head back, throat exposed to his bared teeth.

"You were the one, you serpent-tongued get of Ammut." He slammed her into the wall, smacking her head against the jagged brick. Her teeth slid through the tough muscle of her tongue. "You betrayed us all!"

"I didn't do anything," she slurred; blood tickled up bile with each micro-swallow.

"You think we're stupid? That our guards don't know who funds their sarcophagi?" He pulled his fist back and Jeannette caught the feral gleam in his bulging eye. She tacked her chin to her chest, wrapping her arms around her neck to cushion his blow. The strike came fast and hard, and knocked away all coherent thought other than: he'd hit her. She'd narked him out, and in retaliation he'd hit her. She shouldn't have been shocked, but as the next blow came down, and the next, while she curled up and cried for him to stop, she still couldn't believe that this was her life, being beaten up with nowhere to run.

Her legs kicked out, scattering the heart scarabs all over the floor. The beetles and ankhs and crooks skipped across the room. One of them could be Abayomi's.

He jerked her to her feet; she buried her face into the bend of her elbows, caught in a contest of tug-of-war with her ponytail. Single fisted blows fell in a steady cadence: her shoulder, her head, her back. Some were cushioned by her backpack, but its protection was no suit of armor.

"I know just what to do with you. Filthy traitor."

She'd never been hit before her detour into this heartless place. Never got into any fights with the other girls. God knew she'd never have put up with an abusive boyfriend, however few and far between men in her life had been. It was such an alien thing, something from sensationalized television documenting the lives of people she'd never come in contact with.

She struggled, and not some wimpy, feeble girl-squirm; she kicked and bit at Ottah, but then another man came, and another, and as if dragging women up crumbling stairs and down darkened halls provided great sport, they laughed the entire way.

THREE GREAT LIES

Fight, she thought to herself. Don't stop, fight them. But she was getting tired, and they held her arms at odd angles. The pain in her shoulder and head was sinking everything into a dull and fuzzy mire. Someone behind carried a single torch that sputtered, casting the hall in shadows of ghosts. Fight, the ghosts whispered in her ears. Fight, said the silent darkness.

"Let me go!" She twisted, and a hand crushed her wrist, pulling from her a high-pitched scream she had no sense to be ashamed about. Sweat slicked up her arm, but even after several fitful yanks, she could not free herself.

The men half-carried, half-dragged her. "We've got the best place for a woman like you." And then there was a push followed by falling, and for a moment she wondered if this would take her back, take her home, but she didn't want to leave Sanura and Abayomi. Didn't want to leave them. She opened her mouth and screamed, "No!" defying everything that was happening to her with the force of her breath and the strength of her will.

She didn't fall far, and when she landed there was no blackout, only blackness, and an odd metallic chittering she'd only ever heard before in horror films and nightmares.

The first bite stung, the second burned.

The third made her scream.

Chapter 30

UNDER THE BARRAGE OF UNHESITATING BITES, the pain scorched up from her feet to her legs. Birthed as a tiny prickling sensation scuttling up her ankle, it quickly redefined itself into something encompassing, smothering. She hopped about, thrashing out her legs in a flailing dance of survival, desperate to toss off whatever assailed her in the dark.

Something scrambled up her leg. With no restraint she screamed.

"Get off me. Get off me. Get off!" She swiped the hard, little things off her feet and legs, the noise of their bodies hitting together invading her reason, amplifying her fear. Behind her, a hard wall impeded her backwards momentum. She turned to it, ran her hands over the surface of stone, seeking cracks large enough to jam her fingers into. Her backpack shifted, the heavy bottle of water taking over the left corner. Something scraped her calf. She spun around, pressing herself into the solid wall of her cage, her coffin.

"Help. Help me!"

But she knew better. Nobody here would help her. She'd essentially delivered them a death sentence. But I'm important, she wanted to say out loud. But not anymore. She'd failed Abayomi, and had little idea how to help Sanura. As the scratching, ceaseless noise drove the thoughts from her mind, Jeannette ripped off her pack and jerked on the zipper. It'd been forever since she'd gone through the contents blind. Maybe she could devise something to help, anything to fend off the inevitable.

Her feet and ankles had turned into a mat of swollen skin. She wanted to fall to the ground and cry. Give up. How the hell did she end up in the dark, dancing amongst horrors that bit and stung and thirsted for her blood? Jeannette let loose a sick little laugh, a counterfeit tinged with insanity. She entered this world in the dark, it only followed that she'd leave it in the same manner. But she wouldn't go down without a fight. She would never roll over again and give up what was hers, and right now, she was very attached to her life. No vindictive men would be the end of her. She may be a vagrant to Kemet, with little support, but she was smart and feisty and she would *not give up*.

The first thing she tore from her pack was the first aid kit. As she rubbed her sandal sole against her opposite leg, she mentally categorized its contents: astringent, band-aids. No more painkillers. Unless the little demons had an aversion to latex and alcohol, that wouldn't help her much. Swiss army knife: she highly doubted her blind-fighting knife skills. Matches: she bounced those around in her hand, maybe . . . She kicked again, dancing away from the unfaltering monsters. Like an acid burn, the sting spread wide and deep. A jug of beer. Some leather straps. And then, as her foot became noticeably numb, her hand landed on her money belt.

The only thing worth anything in that artifact out of time was the ankh pendant, the breath of life.

The metal around her neck got hot, instantly, uncomfortably hot.

Jeannette tensed, her breath trapped in her calcified lungs, afraid she'd unknowingly jinx whatever message Bast was trying to send her. Breaking her petrification, she fumbled with the zip to the money belt and dipped her fingers inside, seeking out the pendant she'd bought in an open air market back when life meant nothing. As she summoned to mind that ride through the desert—how crazy had she been?—her fingers nudged the cool stone of the ornament, and between middle finger and pointer finger, she gently pulled it out. In that sidecar she'd taken an insane risk. It had dropped her into this unbelievable world, and now she knew she didn't want it to end. She had people now and they would mourn her, and she didn't want to put them through such heartache.

As she lifted the ankh, the metal torque cooled to simply warm and soft, and a blue luminance glowed from the pendant, filling the hole and revealing the nightmare before her. Jeannette gasped and licked her dry lips.

Beetles. They were everywhere. Filling the hole. Filling her vision.

The light swayed from her shaking hand. The horde of beetles swarmed over each other, seeming to materialize from the dark corners the ankh's light couldn't reach. Two, three deep, the mass of them undulated in waves that surged toward her. Squealing, she thrashed out her feet, kicking away bugs large enough to face down any sane cat.

Where she had come from, nobody believed in curses of the dead. But Jeannette knew now that belief didn't matter. You desecrate the dead, no matter your intentions, and there would be a price to pay. She screamed, and with it she heard the echo of her dying reason.

A scorching tear dripped onto her cheek.

Eaten alive by bugs.

But they didn't charge for her, pinchers raised, venom dripping from their eager mouths. Instead, the scarab beetles receded to the edges of the ankh's light. They moved with an ordered precision that was nowhere near natural. A long line of them faced her, as inanimate as the *ba* containers back in the Scarab Room. The light caught on the exoskeletons, giving off metallic blacks and deep blues, some even rusty oranges or greens. As she watched them, unable to take her eyes away, her numbness began to fade. With steeled nerves, she glanced at her legs. No chunks of flesh were missing, no scrapes or scratches slashed her dry, cracked skin. A flash of a page from a college text book reminded her that these beetles didn't even bite. A quiver rattled through her body and she forced down slow, deep breaths, lowering her arm to rest her elbow against her side. The pendant swung pendulum-style at the end of its chain. The beetles marched forward to the edge of her light.

"I can't die now," she whispered to the bugs. "The star baboon woman and that funky cow gave me something to do. Sorry bugs—" she sucked in a breath, "—but you can't have me." A breathy giggle trickled up through her throat. "You can't break prophecy." She raised her eyes into the black above her and wrapped her fingers around the torque. "Bast?" She didn't know what to say. "God?" She felt like that girl from the pre-teen coming of age book everybody snickered over in grade school. But she wasn't after advice, and she knew there was no point in making deals with gods. "I know I'm not the most pious or anything, but please . . . Help me get out of here. I'm not done yet. I've finally found where I belong and I'm just not done."

Time: a river stretching from point A to point B, from mountains thousands of miles away to the Delta at the sea. It flowed one way; you could remember the past and you could guess at the future, but you were still trapped in the current. But not Jeannette. Somehow she'd stepped sideways, jumped into a past that had never existed. Time, she realized, was unknowable and all she could count on was this one moment. And she wanted to make every moment count.

She squeezed her eyes shut. "I want to live." It came as a confession.

"That is good, Jeannette, because our desire for you to live is strong as well."

Jeannette flipped around and lifted up her ankh, washing everything in the competing light of the blue ankh and the yellow of an approaching torch. Then out of the gloom emerged her friends' faces, relieved, peering over the lip of her near personal tomb.

Her eyes burned, but the laughter won out, and Jeannette thought it greatly ironic that all the transitions in her life seemed to take her into the dark.

"You're here," she said between joyful sobs. "You guys came for me."

Sanura jammed her torch into a sconce loosely attached to the wall. "Of course we did," she said as she lowered a rope. "The knowledge should be strong in you that you can count on us."

Until that moment, Jeannette hadn't truly accepted that, and it gave her an odd kind of stomach pang.

Awkwardly she climbed up the thick rope, necklace chain wrapped around one wrist to assure the ankh still cast its light on the beetles below, keeping them at bay. It wasn't too far to the rim of the pit she'd been tossed in, but the stress of the last few days had exsanguinated her body of most of its energy. Once she neared the top, Abayomi grabbed her hand and hauled her the remaining distance, her feet scrambling to keep contact with the jagged wall.

As she breached the edge, Abayomi pulled her to his side. The tenderness of the gesture brought a smile to her bruised face. For a moment, she leaned into him, absorbing strength from his presence.

"Thanks—" she began to say, but the look on Abayomi's face coaxed her to a halt. His mouth had dropped open, his eyes bulged. She wondered if she'd missed some injury, and checked herself over one more time. Nothing but her bruises to be seen, so she inspected his hidden face once again. Mouth ajar and eyes intense. Then she realized, the drop of his jaw wasn't due to fear, but awe. His eyes weren't wide because of some horror, but in surprise. Following his gaze he wasn't mesmerized by her, but the pendant in her hand. The lapis lazuli ankh with a little bug design in the center.

"You found it . . . My heart scarab."

Jeannette stared at the dangling pendant and quickly cradled it in the palm of her other hand. "Really?" The blue glow was warm and comforting, like Abayomi himself. "This is it? I—I've had it this whole time," she said in a quiet voice, lowering the pendant from its chain into Abayomi's shaking right hand. The chain pooled around the ankh with the soft slither of fine metalwork brushing against itself.

He marveled at what rested in his palm. This close to the torchlight the pendant's glow dwindled, though the brilliant blue of the stone stood out against the silver casing. Once Jeannette had confused the ankh with a cross, the top branch replaced by a loop, some twisted form of Christian piety. That wasn't the case. This symbol spanned ages. The three were caught in the ankh's spell, entranced by the beautiful work of art. And it wasn't just the craftsmanship or the expensive materials, it was the essence, this subtle feeling that *was* Abayomi. She hadn't taken notice of it, because it'd been with her for so long.

"Abayomi," she said. "I think your *ba* has always been with you."

Sanura laughed.

They peered at the girl. With erect ears and a flash of canine teeth, Jeannette could see the *mi-nether* was just as elated as she was.

Sanura nodded at Jeannette. "I told you long ago, Jeannette, that you had magic in you."

Jeannette held up her hands, spread her fingers wide and remembered that tingle in her fingertips the day she'd replaced Abayomi's linens. She looked back up at Sanura and caught the delight in her orange eyes, feline pupils wide in the low light.

Abayomi stared down into his open palm, his attention enthralled with the artifact cradled there. This whole time he'd never needed the scarab, he just needed something to have faith in.

A grin touched his lips as he ran a finger over the silver scarab tracing in the center. In that moment she wanted him to look up at her and smile. Wanted him to look at her, to acknowledge her and maybe make some decision she herself had only just made. It was all very childish, but she still needed to know.

He looked at her. Those eyes, always so murky, deep, were crinkled at the edges.

"Thank you. Now my heart cannot stand witness against me."

Jeannette nodded, blinked repeatedly, swallowed. In his eyes lay the proof that not everything in her life had been a mistake.

"I'm sorry it took me so long," she said, meaning so many different things.

He laughed, so warm and full. "Better to have happened now than to happen after the Sun-Disc sets."

A cry echoed down the passage and the three turned as one to look into the impenetrable darkness. "We should go," Sanura said. "The guards would have arrived not long after we did."

"I have to find Tabiry." Jeannette looked down into the dark pit, the sound of exoskeleton on exoskeleton eerily gone.

Sanura's ears went back. "She can watch after herself."

Abayomi tucked the ankh into the wrappings over his chest,

unheeding Sanura's harsh tone. The girl blocked the way out of the tunnel, ears hugging the curve of her skull. "She robbed from the dead; destroyed *ba* for her own benefit."

A sick sensation dropped out the bottom of Jeannette's stomach. "But she helped me, Sanura."

Sanura closed her eyes and shook her head. When she opened them again, she stepped out of the way. "Your compassion is incomparable to anybody else, Jeannette. You are different from all in this world."

Jeannette stiffened. "Then why am I here?"

Abayomi set his hand on her shoulder. "Maybe Kemet needs your compassion. Needs you." He dropped his hand and pulled himself to his full height. "Let us find your friend, but first . . ." Abayomi's joints ratcheted into a stiffer and stiffer disposition until his entire body readied itself to disassemble into its baser parts from the stress, ". . . who did this cursed beating to you?"

Jeannette experienced the most overwhelming pang of gratitude and love and shock, all wound together into a tight knot at the base of her throat, blocking her ability to take in breath for a few, intense seconds.

She shook her head. "Don't worry about it. The guards will get them all anyway."

"Jeannette. Tell me."

She ran her hands over her face, flinched as she touched the sore spots and bruised muscles that spoke up in the simple act of movement. Souvenirs of her adventures as a spy. "Some guy named Ottah. I don't know the others." She laughed, mock amusement debased by bitterness. "He's a cripple, but he still overtook me."

"Well, he is a man." Abayomi stalked towards the exit. Jeannette scowled at his linen-wrapped back. "Crippled how?" he asked.

Sanura retrieved her torch and the three trotted single file through the small passage she'd been dragged through earlier in a blind panic.

"Bad leg. All twisted. He couldn't walk well. But he had help," she rushed to say. "It wasn't just one crippled guy I couldn't defend myself against."

"Are you hurting badly?" Sanura asked. Put between the two adults, her torchlight lit the way for both of them. Soon, more light ahead illuminated the tunnel and the noise of people moving very quickly announced more than anything that their time was limited.

"Just bruises. Nothing broken." She didn't want to tell them that those phantom beetle bites had been akin to boiling alive in oil and that a

324

few fists to the shoulders couldn't even compare. "I'll be fine, thank you though. So . . . Tabiry." She glanced at the drop to Sanura's ears. "I don't think she was in this tomb. But I'm not sure. I'd never seen her here."

"Well, we can ask for her, and maybe someone will let us know. And maybe we can find this Ottah as well," Abayomi said, spine straight, marching on with purpose.

By the time they'd hit the main passage, only a few stragglers continued their exodus and the three joined the fleeing thieves. All the riotous noise thundered ahead of them, funneled by the tight tomb tunnels. Then they landed in the lap of chaos. Guards with spears fought the thieves who wielded clay pots and weak sticks. Jeannette grabbed a man; he whirled around, a bronze statue of Hathor's human form in his hand ready to pound into Jeannette's head. Abayomi seized his arm, delaying the strike.

"You," the man said. Jeannette studied him in the dusty lighting. "We threw you in the pit."

"*You* threw her in the pit?" Abayomi said, his words a feral promise of retribution. He grabbed the man's arm, yanking him forward.

A nearby woman, a thief Jeannette only knew by face, ducked her head and rushed to the exit.

"By the power of Re and the Pharaoh," came a booming voice from the main room, "this place shall be purged of your villainous blood."

"Tabiry told us to!" Jeannette's attacker babbled, eyes drawn toward the only way out. Even twisting his arm, the man couldn't disengage the mummy's grip. "It wasn't me. Not my idea."

Abayomi slammed the man against the tomb wall, driving out all his breath. "Tabiry did?"

Sanura growled.

Jeannette was certain the goddess' statue had struck her. Struck her deaf and dumb and delirious. "What?" That couldn't be right.

The snarl of a demon transformed the thief's face. "She said you spoke against us." Quick as a striking snake, he kicked out at Abayomi's legs. Abayomi grunted, stumbling back, then lunged forward, bracing his forearm against the man's throat.

Screams filled the rooms, the hallways, the tomb, drowning Jeannette's repeated thought, tainted with fear and denial: Tabiry did this?

"Woman of flapping tongue," the man said through gasps of gurgling air. "Curses on you." He spat at Jeannette.

"Where is she?" Sanura demanded. "Where is Tabiry now?"

THREE GREAT LIES

Using his shoulders, the thief pushed against the wall, only to have Abayomi's full weight lock him against the unforgiving brick.

"Where is Tabiry?" Sanura demanded, her voice filling the passage, defeating the bedlam quaking at the exit as guards overcame the thieves.

Someone within hearing distance called out, "Tabiry? I think she's in the Den. Please, take care of her." A man from Kush blitzkrieged his way through the swelling blockage of guards, only to earn a spear through his gut for his daring. Dust and noise and pain crammed the tomb. The dust defeated by blood. Jeannette was numb to it all.

Sanura took hold of Jeannette's elbow. Abayomi pressed closely to her back as he maneuvered the thief towards the exit, pushing the bundle of flailing arms and legs right into a broad shouldered guard. The press of bodies was impossible to avoid, and feet stomped and elbows punched and Jeannette's collection of injuries soon became eligible for the world record. A guard appeared before them, spear slicing down toward Jeannette and her first instinct was to dodge to the side, but that would expose Abayomi to the flint blade. He was a living man, with a *ba* all along. She could not condemn him to death.

Still, Jeannette was no victim, and she swung her arm under the spear to deflect it into some other unsuspecting person. Sanura leapt forward. "No!" she cried out and the guard redirected his aim towards the tomb floor.

"Daughter," the guard said, heavy eyebrows raised in recognition. "Are these the people of your household?"

Sanura nodded. "Help us get out, please."

The guard turned, and with elbows wide and voice cracking through the pandemonium, charged a path through his fellow guards and the few desperate tomb robbers who had made it that far.

Once outside, the air tasted of liberation, and Jeannette breathed deeply.

"Thank you," Sanura said to the guard. The man nodded sharply, then rushed back into the tomb, spear point lifted above his head to defeat his fangless foes. "Come," the girl then said to Jeannette and Abayomi. "The guards will be at their work here for a while."

Sanura dragged Jeannette through the dark towards the wall of the village below them. Jeannette's legs moved unwillingly. Abayomi caught her as she nearly tripped and fell. Through a place of numb disbelief, where the truth was half-lost and sought some place to hide, she tried to reestablish a baseline from which to continue.

Betrayed. Again.

This was such bull.

Jeannette's resolve hardened, an unfamiliar fury energized her limbs. Sanura no longer needed to drag her downhill. The three skip-trotted over the rough landscape to a crumbling portion of wall near a soft hill of silty earth where they crossed, one at a time, not even attempting any fashion of secrecy. They charged forward like tiny sandstorms, hurling glares of slicing grains of sand in anyone's direction who dared look their way. Luckily for the residents of the workers compound, evening was in its infancy and the morning's duties were far way. They watched from their sleeping mats atop building roofs, safe from the trio's raging anger.

Frustrated, she ground her teeth. Hadn't she'd learned life's hard lessons? She'd sworn she'd never be duped again.

At the Den of Men the word must have spread that the tombs were being raided. Blood pounded in Jeannette's temples as she examined the few faces. Some she knew, but Tabiry was absent from the confusion of fleeing thieves and bystanders rubbernecking the midnight great escape.

"Tabiry, where is she?" Jeannette asked and a few men pointed into the warehouse, not even pausing in their flight.

Leaving behind the others, she slammed the door open with the heel of her hand. Tabiry's back was to her; she was speaking to a local woman, both laden down with bags slung over their shoulders messenger-bag style. Amidst the litter of daily lives tossed away in split second decisions of Necessary or Not Necessary, the two looked like the last survivors of a category five hurricane. The woman whom Jeannette had once thought of as a friend whirled around, ready to make her own escape—until she spotted Jeannette. Shock and panic branded her face, then those unforgiving expressions were shuttered away behind Tabiry's gentle, helpful smile.

Jeannette smiled in return. "Surprised to see me, Tabiry?"

"Yes, I had thought you were in the tombs. I'm glad you got away from there. Can you grab that bag? We've got little time before the guards discover this place."

Jeannette grabbed the bag, dangling it before her with both hands. "I *was* in the tombs."

Tabiry's worried expression almost made Jeannette sick. "Oh, did you witness the guards? I've heard it's just terrible. A slaughter by the pharaoh's guards." A look of calculation cracked Tabiry's mask of worry.

"Oh yes." The Kemet woman trudged out of the hut under her

327

heavy load, leaving Tabiry and Jeannette behind. "They were rounding everyone up. Some even threw themselves on the guards' weapons in an attempt to escape. Luckily, I got away."

Tabiry took a step towards the door, then snapped her gaze to Jeannette's face. Her white teeth flashed, a snarl as feral as the wild dogs of the desert. "You did this."

Jeannette clenched her jaw; she'd never again offer another fake smile. "I would have been here sooner to warn you, my friend," she said bitterly, "but I was delayed."

"Will you hand me over as you did the rest of our allies?" Tabiry laughed; madness peeked out from the whites of her eyes. "You wish to see my head laughing down at you from the point of a spear lining the road to the pharaoh's great palace? My people have already painted that road with their blood."

It was her fate: Jeannette would always be too trusting. Hadn't old Jawbones warned her, in a way, that the nature of a person was bone deep? She had to learn that she couldn't expect the lion to lay with the lamb. Or someone who'd resign the dead to endless wandering to have any compunctions about sending the living to the bugs.

"I trusted you."

"I trusted *you*." Tabiry sprayed the words with spit and venom. "I helped you. I brought you *in*. Gave you opportunity." Her face contorted as true pain twisted those perfect features.

"You were using me as a tool for your own vengeance!" Jeannette pressed her lips together, took two deep breaths. "I was coming to warn you," she said, then, more quietly, "I had to stop you from ruining the mummies."

Tabiry did not let up. "Ha. What do you care for mummies? What do you care for the laws of these local Gods? They are not your Gods. I thought I could trust you; I thought you would understand, being someone from a land of different Gods, like myself." She shook her head, the beads tinkling against each other, their sound dull against the power of her vehemence. "You promised your help, but you only commit curses with that mouth."

"I care about the mummies," Jeannette said firmly. "And I care about the people, some of them, and their gods. You came to this land with revenge in your heart, and I guess you earned that after what happened to your people. I came to this land because I fell through a hole." Jeannette turned her head away.

The door banged open, and two Kemet guards charged into the hut. Twin spear points had a direct line on the center of each of their chests; the torchlight reflected off their deadly-sharp points.

Jeannette dropped the bag and shot her hands up straight in the air.

"Hey! Don't kill me. I helped you guys find this place! It's me, Jeannette." Surely they knew her.

The guards shared a look. The taller of the two, whose hold on his weapon never wavered from Jeannette's body, squinted at her. "The foreign woman who helped the Master Slaver?"

"Yes!"

The tool of death lowered from its piercing pose, aiming now at her knees, scarred and knobby and equally vulnerable. "I know you." The tall man smiled. "The master says you're crafty. If you have an interest, I'm in need of a wife—"

Jeannette looked meaningfully at the honed point. "You're still aiming that at me." If her voice squeaked two octaves too high, nobody seemed to notice but her.

The man rested the spearhead on the ground, but the other guard kept his weapon on Tabiry, who remained still, watchful of Jeannette. "Oh, Rabiah, don't let the arrest of the desecrators hamper your pursuit of a wife," the guard said, tossing a quick glare at the tall guard.

Rabiah ignored his companion. "You don't look bad, if a bit roughly handled. And strong—" Rabiah continued, nodding his approval at Jeannette.

"I already have a man, thank you very much. And stop pointing that thing at her, too." Jeannette's heart thudded; she'd begun to find dancing on this edge of panic distasteful. All this over-stimulation had probably done lasting damage to her pulmonary system. Too young for a heart attack, maybe it was simple anxiety. A two week vacation from betrayal and life and death situations was just what her nerves needed. "She's with me."

The shorter guard studied Tabiry. "We were told one of the ringleaders was a Nubian princess."

Princess.

Tall, beautiful, proud. Bitter and brimming with hate. Though, now the woman's wild spite hid behind her guise of complacent innocence.

Jeannette had been blind to it. The truth. And now, she'd grease this grand machine and pull her own wool over these men's eyes, or maybe she'd be blinding them with mud, a better mud slinger than word wielder.

Jeannette sighed out her nose, breathing life into her very last lie.

"She's no princess. I'd asked her to help me. So, she was only helping the thieves like I was, to get more information. She's no ringleader."

Tabiry's eyes closed briefly, a cat-blink contrivance that Jeannette now recognized as a role the woman had slipped on for the new audience as skilled as any Broadway prima donna. Tabiry deserved a Tony Award.

The short man pulled his weapon off Tabiry, settling its butt against the floor with a listless thump. The death-warrant desire drained from his posture as he leaned to the side, using the spear for support.

"All the rest of the thieves have vacated this place." Jeannette scanned the empty building, once the sanctuary of desperate men, from one corner to the next. It looked smaller than she remembered, hollow and full of clutter. "But I would stick around, in case some come back and try to gather these last scraps." Lightly, she kicked a clay cup with the side of her foot. The four watched it roll once, then settle next to a discarded heap of cloth.

"I'm going now. Thank you for your hard work," Jeannette said to the guards.

Rabiah smiled and puffed up his chest. Jeannette resisted the amused smirk by clamping her teeth together. "I am stationed with the master here for the next few days," he paused, and then his face brightened as he continued with, "Jeannette. That is an odd name. Where are you from?"

Jeannette considered that. "Somewhere north of here. Nowhere important. May Re light your way."

"I'll be here if you want to share a meal," he called as she walked out, actually feeling a little better until she noticed Tabiry right behind her.

"Why did you do that?" Tabiry demanded. "I did not require your help."

With a half-turn of her head, Jeannette kept a wary eye on her once friend. "Yes, you did."

Silence from Tabiry. Then, "I will not let them win."

"Win what?" Jeannette wanted to yell, to pound the woman's head into the sand. "They've conquered your people. They've destroyed your plot. Think, what else can they take from you? Don't hand them your head on a platter, Tabiry." Why did people let their pride lead them to ruin? "The people of Kemet say that 'one foot isn't enough to walk with.'

330

You won't get far without a head, either. Keep moving. Throw away your vengeance and live, Tabiry. *Live.* If the guards find the truth, you are dead."

Tabiry's mouth pursed, and from the narrow silt of her eyes, Jeannette could just see the mental curse brewing, twisting, a dark storm in the night.

Jeannette lifted a shoulder, trapping the torque between her shoulder and neck, feeling the ridges of the woven metal mold to her skin. "Tabiry, if you work hard to travel somewhere, through deserts and packs of bandits and over mountains, and find you've ended up in a swamp rather than a paradise, the only way you can fix it is to just get walking and keep looking for that paradise." Dropping her shoulder, the metal band settled on her collar bones. "But the next time you seek your goal, at least you'll have strong walking legs to get you going faster and farther than you did before."

The woman blinked at her, her pinched expression softening just a bit.

Maybe Jeannette got it now, maybe not, but as Bast had tried to explain, you had to make the journey before you could really understand if that journey was right for you. And every journey taught you something, even if it didn't lead to the paradise you expected. All anyone amounted to was a collection of their experiences, and you had to walk those roads to find that place your *ba* really belonged.

Suddenly feeling light, Jeannette wanted to laugh. Maybe she did get it.

"Good luck," she said to Tabiry, the woman who would have seen her die a gruesome death. Without fully turning her back on the woman, Jeannette left her behind.

Abayomi and Sanura were waiting a few buildings down. She ran for them, arms open, and they collided together, desperate for the assurance of touch. For someone who'd always sat on the sidelines, Jeannette now understood completely: there were some things worth fighting for.

The three walked away, Jeannette and Abayomi on either side of Sanura. She never turned back to see if Tabiry had left the building or not. The guards came in like a tsunami. They would find little here, a few bags unclaimed, stinking mats of forsaken men. By now the word had slipped into every needful ear about the raid at the old tombs and the rest of the thieves would be long gone. She was surprised she'd even got to see Tabiry, but the woman's voraciousness blinded her common sense.

They wouldn't all be captured, which was good in a way—little justified a killing offense—but they certainly wouldn't be pilfering any more tombs. Or so her optimistic heart wanted to tell her.

"How did you know?" she asked Sanura. "About Tabiry?"

Sanura shook her head, eyebrows drawing together. "Her *ka* had gone fetid."

They walked in silence for a while until Jeannette asked, "Why didn't you tell me?"

Sanura's expression relaxed. "Would you have believed such a thing possible?"

Probably not. But she promised herself, she'd never disregard her friends again.

"Anyway, it's over. You did it, Jeannette," Sanura said with a squeeze to her hand.

Jeannette squeezed back and shook her head, negating any importance of what she'd done. "Anyone could have done it."

Abayomi looked over at her. "But nobody else would have."

And she realized that, in this land, he was probably right.

Chapter 31

THEY RETURNED TO THEIR HUT, not even attempting stealth for poor Werel's own slumber, and fell into the heavy coma of exhaustion. It was the first night Jeannette slept without visions of capture and dismemberment, or the anxiety of duty rampaging through her dreams like a drunken water buffalo. At dawn, long before she wanted to be awake, someone banged at her door, causing more ruckus than a one-man-band. She squeezed her eyes shut, hoping the sadist would find better doors to plague. Eventually Werel came into her room.

"There is a guard at the door for you."

Abayomi and Sanura had already risen, their sleeping pallets empty. Jeannette ran her fingers over the indents in the sheets, feeling the last traces of their warmth. A life without them: just the thought of it gave her a cold chill. She rolled over onto Abayomi's bed and let the fading heat seep into her skin.

A man bark-coughed from the doorway.

Werel and Jeannette shared a look of concern. Jeannette's duty was done, what did they want now? Without even bothering to pretty herself, hair hanging loose down her back in matted clumps, she went to the door.

A tall *mi-nether* with a jackal head waited outside. "The Master Slaver will speak with you."

"Why? I did what he asked; I thought we were even now." She sliced her hands horizontally through the air.

"Come." The mini-god turned and marched off, his long legs whisking him away, his golden kilt swaying with each stride. Dropping her head back, Jeannette released an exhausted sigh. Needing to shop anyway, she grabbed her pack, scooped up her sandals and followed after him, holding onto an ache in her side.

The walk passed with a steady flow of adrenalin pumping into her bloodstream. Though the sun had barely peeked over the eastern hills, sweat dripped down her temples and between her breasts as she finger-combed her hair. Men and women dashed by her, all busy, all seemingly infected by her own state of anxiety.

She followed him in a direct path to the Den of Men. Four human guards were stationed at the door, two on either side, standing tall like British Beefeaters with spears at their sides. They nodded to the son of

Anubis and Jeannette as the two entered the once dank and dark warehouse. Completely transformed now by flickering candles and torches, it was as if Re himself had blessed the place, washing it away of all its darkness. Not to mention the dazzling grin splitting the jowls of the Master Slaver. The fat man jumped to his feet, setting his bulk to rolling, and clapped his hands once. His spryness amazed Jeannette, not to mention the transformation of the hut. The sleeping rolls had all been tossed and a low table and stools filled the left side of the building. Though nowhere near as pleasant as Bast's inner garden, a good scrubbing had decimated the stench of unwashed bodies. Trust this man to subdue anything.

"Foreigner, may the Sun-Disc shine upon you from the horizon each day. I cannot tell you how pleased I am. I knew when I witnessed you squawking over that abandoned girl that you were a strange, yet effective woman."

Jeannette managed to flash her teeth in mimicry of the Master Slaver's unusual joy as she said, "She's not abandoned."

"Oh, of course not." He waved the air before him as he approached her, a laborious heaving that housed none of his earlier vigor. "That girl, she's a smart one. Found us on the north road and led us to the old tombs. Expedited the deliverance of Re's justice.

"My hope is that the one who gives food and provisions, who keeps away the serpents and rules the Two Lands, passes through the Fields with you and yours, Jeannette."

Then the master's smile dropped, and he grabbed her chin and turned her face to the left. Jeannette jerked her head away. "My, how did you earn that? You gain injuries as an ass gathers flies."

With a snort, Jeannette narrowed her eyes and stepped a couple feet away to deny him any more manhandling opportunities. "All in the line of duty."

Turning from Jeannette, the master gestured to the table and a letter he was writing. "I am informing the pharaoh's men of your great achievement. You shall be honored." Jeannette didn't roll her eyes, though she felt like it. The man nodded at her, as if satisfied at the gamble he'd made the day they'd cemented their deal. There was a little pride in that half-frown and appraisal-wide gaze, and with an uncomfortable stirring in her heart, she acknowledged this man was probably an excellent father.

"Thank you, Master. I want nothing more for myself. You know, I could have never succeeded on my own. If it would be no further bother to you, I would beg you to clear a falsely accused man's brother. This man is named Nekhebu, though I do not remember his brother's name. I overheard the thieves, that they masterminded the situation to place the blame on his brother." She swallowed, rubbed her palms against her hips. "His brother was taken."

The Master Slaver lowered his bulk on his stool, frowning. "I know of Nekhebu and his brother Seker. Seker was taken long ago for desecrating the tombs. His punishment has already been fulfilled."

Jeannette remembered Nekhebu's railing, his haunting words: "My brother, he is dead. His head cut from his body." Her skin tightened and gooseflesh popped up along her arms.

"Then you must do something for his family," she urged. "Seker had a wife and kids and now his brother, Nekhebu, a fisherman, is trying to feed them all. It's impossible. He was wrongly killed and so reparations should be made to Nekhebu. He shouldn't be punished for the mistake of the guards."

A dark shadow washed over the features of the Master Slaver, followed by the construction of an unimpressed scowl. Preparing for a full on rage, Jeannette tightened her stance and planted her feet on the ground, though her saner parts that hadn't dried up and been blown away by the desert winds wanted her to step down, thank the man for not smothering her small, insignificant life and leave. She had little power in Kemet, but maybe she'd earned enough street cred to help out someone who'd saved her bacon more than once.

"*You presume to dictate to me—*"

She nodded in contrition. "I'm sorry, but please, just listen." The *mi-nether* behind her growled a warning. "He's a good man and he played an invaluable role in helping me stop these thieves who were destroying mummies, hawking *ba* containers, and undermining the authority of our dear pharaoh. He is a hero of the land." She shook her arms in the air politician style. "It would cost you little to help him have a comfortable life, and show everyone on the river what an honorable and noble man you are." She had gone breathless—breathless from her speech and breathless from nervous anticipation. The master's eyes squinted as he studied her. Jeannette swallowed, an action she tried to abort but had no strength to. The Master Slaver snorted, his face in motion until it settled into a wry grin.

"You expect I cause an ebony coffin to be made for every simple man, don't you?"

Jeannette, forehead wrinkled, shook her head. "No, it's just that—"

"Fine, where is this Nekhebu."

"At the docks in Thebes. He has a little boat he fishes from daily. His brother's daughter is with him."

"You are ever the fishwife, foreign cur." He shook his head, a put-upon gesture if ever she'd seen one, and picked up his reed and poised it over a fresh sheet of pottery. "Though it is not ordained that such a thing be done, I will send someone to him and offer him compensation for the loss of his brother."

A sudden dizziness spun her in circles, causing her to blink. She sighed in relief. "That's great. Thank you." She bowed. Old habits didn't die. "Thank you so much."

The Master brushed her thanks aside with a slight shake of his head. "I am thankful for the victory to end this corruption of the pharaoh's land." He called for a messenger and sent the pottery proclamation off.

From near the door, the guard asked in his half growl, "How is it you knew so much about this conspiracy?"

A proud, yet small smile lit upon her lips. "I pretended to be one of them, infiltrating their numbers. I was a spy." It almost chilled her to give voice to these things, like she had done something stupid and deadly, but the guard nodded, his ears pricked up, appearing impressed.

"Devious, is it not? Only a woman could conceive of such a plan," the Master Slaver said with nodding satisfaction.

She rejected that completely. "No, only someone who thinks outside the box could come up with that. Someone who's seen as many movies as I have."

That shut them both up. Jeannette grinned at their shared glance, expecting the master to twirl his finger beside his temple suggesting she was loopy, but that was a gesture for another time and another world.

"I cannot talk the morning away. Work calls," the master said. Her spirits sank at the reminder. And then he informed her of her reward.

"Though, with your demands for your friend, I am considering our dealings concluded."

"I thought they were concluded, that now you'd leave us alone." She paused at his soured expression and changed her words. "Would allow for Sanura's and my freedom."

The Master Slaver shook his head, his jowls swaying like a king's pennons. "You are a smart woman, Jeannette. I want to give you an opportunity for more. Re knows few would marry you."

He chuckled at her scowl and proceeded to tell her about the gracious gift he would be giving her. Deserting her annoyance, she decided that morning she would quit the perfume business and divest herself of working for others.

With chin a little higher, back a little straighter, she left the Den of Men, hopefully for the last time. With her determination to be her own woman, leaving town became her first intention. Carried by strides of excitement, arms swinging pendulum arcs at her sides, she bounded through the door to her home to tell her friends. They were not on the main floor, nor in the basement. They probably had their own loose ends to cauterize. Though she doubted a two weeks' notice would be required, Jeannette figured it would at least be polite to go tell Herit she would be quitting. That battleax only hired her because Tabiry had asked her to.

A twinge twisted in her gut.

Herit frowned. "You're late."

The sky's steel gray was nearing blue. "Actually, ma'am, I'm early."

Jeannette didn't go to her pot of oil to stir as she typically did each morning. Herit's eyes narrowed.

"I will no longer be working for you, Perfumer."

They narrowed more. Jeannette wondered if the woman could even see through those tiny slits.

"Thank you for the job and teachings." Jeannette nodded, then turned to walk away.

"Why?"

Jeannette paused, considered the many possible answers, and simply said, "I've tired of stirring a pot not my own."

Never before had Jeannette felt so light. The air even smelled fresh as she walked away from the perfumery. Maybe she'd still develop an ulcer at a young age, but a rock fall no longer hung poised above her head ready to crush her under duty and terror and desperation. Well, not a large rock fall anyway. Family and friends of those she'd betrayed might know about her dealings and treachery. There still might be guards with spears hungry for her blood. The Master Slaver had told her, when he'd informed her of her reward of land and debens, he had influence in many cities and she could pick from the lot. Jeannette wondered if Abayomi and Sanura would go with her. She looked up into the cloudless sky, felt her lips move of their own accord, a silent wish. A hope. A prayer.

According to the oracle, she had to return to the start.

337

It felt slightly poetic.

The scent of baking bread caught her attention and her stomach rumbled. The last good meal she'd eaten was filed away under 'fond memories'. Today, she would cook something splendid for everyone.

"Baker, how about some beer for your bread?"

The two bartered until Jeannette was happy with the price. Then she took her time and picked out ripe fruits to juice from another merchant and considered cooking up some peas and beans, and probably some fish. Thinking of the fish made her remember Nekhebu and that she should tell him about the pardon and aid the Master Slaver would be sending him.

In mid-stride she changed directions and made her way to the gates. It was a long way back down to the river, but unburdened by anything but food, she expected the trip would be a quick one.

Trotting up to her, Sanura, with pert ears and a bit of fang showing, looked happier than her typical expressionless self. Jeannette understood the feeling. "There you are."

"Here I am," Jeannette said in a voice that sang out the 'am'. "I was just going to find Nekhebu. The Master Slaver has offered to help him, since his brother was wrongly executed." She was more than a little unnerved that she could say something so heavy with such a light heart.

"Really!" Sanura's ears swiveled forward. "I'm glad to hear it."

"Is that her?" came a gruff voice, nearby but still a part of the crowd noise around them.

"So, I was hoping to talk to you and Abayomi about ditching this village. If you guys don't mind. I kinda quit my—" She trailed off as she became aware of the excited voices and repeated word 'foreigner'.

"The foreigner, yes. I've seen her before."

Jeannette spun around to face the mass of men marching towards her. The tomb robbers' families. It must be the families. First to her left, then to her right she sought out a path to escape, already reaching behind to grab for Sanura, but the girl walked past Jeannette and began speaking to the men.

"Yes, this is her."

"It is amazing. We heard it was by her word that Nekhebu's got amends for his brother's life," said a man, older and weather worn. A man who obviously worked hard for his bread.

"Yes, I was just told," Sanura said.

"Nekhebu?" The fizzy panic threatening to send Jeannette into a fox frenzy went flat.

"Jeannette would not let a friend be treated so brutally," Sanura said. Jeannette shook her head in confusion. This mob—really only eight men, most in undyed kilts with little adornment—had come to thank her? "The Speaker of Truth set the words from Jeannette to the Master and made their meeting sweet."

Another of the men—judging by his upright stance and full accounting of limbs, possibly one of the Master Slaver's men—smiled at her and said, "It truly is a good thing you did, Jeannette."

Jeannette froze. She knew that voice.

The dark, coffee skin of the man who spoke was clean, as was his pleated, knee-length *shendyt*, the lines of fabric crossed in the front. With an upright posture allowing him a level look into Jeannette's eyes, he was an odd bird within this flock. She'd taken him for someone from the upper crust of society because his skin held no scars and looked soft, touchable, like Jeannette's was before the avariciously dry air of the tombs. Tight curls clung closely to his scalp. And his eyes, brown with smile wrinkles at the edges, were so familiar. She knew those eyes as intimately as that voice. Around his neck hung a lapis lazuli ankh on a fine chain. With no warning, she reached for his hand and pulled him towards her, muttering "get over here," as she wrapped her arms around his torso.

Chest to chest, he hugged her back.

"Abayomi," she said into the warm skin of his neck. "You're alive."

She could feel his chuckle more than hear it, his voice was quiet, a whisper only for her. "I am. I think my restoration began that first moment we met. You brought to me my *ba*. You restored me."

Not letting go, she pulled back a little to look at his face, into his eyes, see his smile. Blind to the rest of the world, she traced the ridges of his cheekbones and the line of his nose with tentative fingers. He tucked a loose strand of her hair behind her ear. He was handsome, and he was smiling at her with twin dimples, and they stood embracing each other in the warm, morning sun.

"How?" she asked, tearing her eyes away for a moment to look at Sanura. Delight filled the *mi-nether's* toothy grin.

One of the men muttered about young people and love, but Jeannette didn't pay them much attention as they stepped away.

"I told you, you had magic; you had his *ba*," Sanura said in the 'duh' tone of any American teenager.

Jeannette didn't know what to say. Had no words for anything. So, instead, she tightened her embrace and laughed, her entire body rocking under the force of it.

Abayomi's arms squeezed in response, and he leaned forward. He was going to kiss her, every sense in her body told her this, but then he pulled back, and she could almost see the mental fortitude involved in not performing such a lewd act in public.

Screw propriety.

It happened with gentle warning, so Abayomi could prepare himself if he chose to dodge the bullet. Jeannette moved to brush her mouth against his lips, freshly licked and parted for breath. With a giddy jolt their lips met, and they hung there in freeze frame until Abayomi pressed harder against her mouth. Jeannette's eyes slipped closed even as she opened her mouth, and right there before Sanura and a bunch of old men, and all of Kemet and the gods, the two kissed.

Jeannette had never felt so affected, so wanted by anyone she'd ever kissed before. Nothing had felt this full of promise, and certainly hadn't felt this right.

Forget Nekhebu. He already had his reward. She was due her own.

* * *

Sanura examined the table, eyes wide. "Where will we go?"

Jeannette set down another plate, this one holding a cooked fish, next to the others on the heavily laden table. This would be a feast, she'd promised. A good-bye feast.

Abayomi shrugged, looking at the young *mi-nether*. "Toward the Delta?"

"I was thinking, why not just cross the river again. The Master Slaver said he'd help us all find jobs that would fit our stations as heroes of the land." That wasn't exactly how he'd put it, but Jeannette wanted to add her own flair to their rewards. "Even you, Sanura. You can do whatever you want."

Sanura nodded happily, a loud purr coming from her upper chest.

"We'll be like a family," the girl said.

Jeannette almost choked, and had to stare at the ceiling for a moment. "Sanura," she said, slipping her gaze back to the girl's, "we already are."

All this time Jeannette had been worried about returning home, when she'd really been making her home here. All the mistakes, well, she guessed they might have been worth it. One thing she'd learned was that

340

she'd never again be crushed under the regret of the things she didn't say. "I don't care where we go, as long as I'm with you guys."

And by the looks on Sanura's and Abayomi's faces, they fully agreed.

She'd never had friends—true friends, she supposed. Gabby's tolerance and general dismissal certainly did not count. Ricky had been lust more than anything. Tabiry . . . well, that didn't end well. Friends let you do all the stupid things, even after warning you. They helped you out of the messes you got yourself into. And at the end of it all, they were still by your side, helping to glue together the pieces of your life into something stronger and more complete.

"I think we should go back to Abayomi's tomb."

Silence settled on the table. Then Sanura asked, "You still looking for the gate back to your world?"

"No." Jeannette reached across the table, displacing a mug of beer to take up Sanura's hand. This young woman, with the head of a cat, so odd, yet so much someone Jeannette did not want to do disappoint. With a glance to Abayomi, she felt a smile form on her face, rooted with a deep sense of rightness at the pit of her gut. For these people, she wanted to give her best. Be her best. "I want to be with you. I just think that there's something unfinished there. The Sky Watcher said that together we made up the key and that we needed to name our enemy to open the gate. I think she meant *our* enemy," she gestured to each of her friends, "not just mine. We need to go back to Abayomi's tomb, all of us, and find out exactly what she meant."

Sanura didn't seem fazed. "That is good." She squeezed Jeannette's hand. "Just as long as you no longer seek to leave us, because you belong with us now."

A herd of wild horses couldn't hold back Jeannette's smile.

* * *

She liked the sound of the wind across the desert landscape. She'd never paid it much mind before, because she'd either been dragging a donkey, or running for her life, or trying to be like the lizard, silent and scurrying from one hidey-hole to the next. The early afternoon sun brought out the real lizards, performing pushups on stones and dashing for the shadowed protection under rocks as they passed by. The hike down to Thebes felt like a kind of holy pilgrimage, like those folks did in Ireland, walking barefoot all the while, perhaps in penance to prove their worth to God. Only in this pilgrimage, Jeannette performed no penance, because she wanted to believe that God wished people to be happy. And happy she was.

Werel hadn't seemed too shocked at their exodus.

"Though I won't miss a brewery in my home, I will miss your beer." Werel bore Jeannette's hug with grace and their roommate stood outside the red door watching them as they walked off to the village gates.

They passed through Thebes on one of the main streets, as unobtrusive as the shadows of hawks flying overhead, the smell of wet soil and the offal of gutted fish hitting them before they even saw the water.

"It is Jeannette! Re always light your way." Nekhebu charged at them with arms held wide. After his eternal, bitter scowl from before, his joy was entirely disarming. Sunny and open and covered with honest adoration. It made Jeannette feel a little squirrely and she paused in her approach, letting the others get a step ahead of her. She couldn't help but feel amazed that underneath the weight of all the miseries she'd borne, this kind of good deed persevered.

"Nekhebu, it is good to see you happy," she said.

"I have been given a little land that the older children can work. It had already been planted. We will not starve, me and my brother's family." He gathered up a bundle of dried fish and shoved it at them. Abayomi took it with thanks. "Please, take this," Nekhebu said. "And if there is anything I can do . . ."

So much for never asking him for anything ever again.

"Well, we do need a ride down river," Sanura managed to slip in through his flood of thanks.

His face grew serious. "Let me find my friend. His boat is large and he will take you across if I ask this of him."

The alacrity of getting the boat and then being ferried down the river for free—"Oh no, I couldn't take your beer. You saved Nekhebu and freed his brother's soul"—was something Jeannette only ever expected to happen to local heroes or movie stars. Never for her. Especially in this land not her own.

They left the fisherman and his boat on the western bank of the *Iteru* and hand in hand, almost like preschoolers attempting to cross the road on their own, they hiked up the mortuary hill to Abayomi's tomb.

"Leather strips for sale," a salesman called as they trudged up the mortuary hill. None stopped to survey his merchandise. Nor the bread man's. Nor the linen stall's. They had someplace to be.

They fell behind two *mi-nether* of the ram variety as the hill began its steep climb to the tombs. All of them leaned into the hill; chatting dropped to stranded words between breaths.

"We return again," Abayomi said, "to where I once awaited the Guardian of the Veil. Each time, it feels more unsettling."

What an understatement, Jeannette thought. She'd probably be a little more freaked out if she was heading to the place of her own interment. Like old Scrooge landing his eyes on the headstone of his own grave site. What a dismal, yet inevitably true oracle of the future.

Though, Abayomi was a new man now. Once a dried up mummy wrapped in resin and linen and stuffed with sodium carbonate. Now he was alive, not just animated. His cheeks grew pink when she embarrassed him. He licked his lips and moisture caught on the skin. Sweat glistened on his shoulders when he stood in the afternoon sun, pulling forth the scent of sunshine, and beer, and the underlying essence of masculinity. She couldn't help but look at him differently now. She couldn't help but to look.

The columns stood guard at the entrance of the tomb as they had when they'd come here seeking the keyhole, as they had on that hot day back in Egypt when Jeannette had crawled out of the sidecar of an Egyptian kid whose name she'd never learned. Back then the columns had leaned inward at tired angles and she'd worn khakis and a beige shirt. Today she was wrapped in a well-washed white dress that licked at her calves as she walked.

"Are you ready?" Jeannette asked.

"You. Out of that tomb!"

The three turned and spotted the alligator-headed man charging towards them, neck bulging to support the weight of his head.

Sanura stepped forward, her small hand lifted as if she had the impressive power of negation and her simple declaration of "no" would mire him in mid-charge. "Son of Sobek," she said, "do not worry. We are not here to harm the dead, for it is this man's family's mastaba. We are only here to worship and pay homage to his blessed ancestors."

The *mi-nether* peered at them, a membranous eyelid flicking over his tiny eyes that appeared too small to even be of use. He growled low and a jackal came trotting up.

"Yes, Master?" the canine asked.

"Watch these three. They're up to something."

THREE GREAT LIES

The black jackal yipped and the *mi-nether* guardian walked off, each step a beating against the earth.

The jackal sat on his haunches and panted in the heat; Jeannette decided to ignore it.

"Well, here we go." Jeannette stepped in between her friends, swallowed up Sanura's small hand in hers and gripped Abayomi's firmly, to offer a lifeline if this return incapacitated him in any way. Their last visit had been harrowing and she didn't want her friend to feel so afloat in his own heart's wilderness. None of them were alone. They were a family, and so together they stepped into the tomb.

The torches were still lit, and she wished they'd had this version available in the thieves' hideout. All around her the images of men and women, gods and beasts, watched them. An ibis appeared to flap across the ceiling in the torches' rippling light. Before, those images might have seen desperation on their faces. Now there was only eager determination. They came upon Abayomi's sarcophagus chamber, the spreading wings of the unending phoenix vaulting over the ceiling. The sarcophagus remained open and empty, and they continued on to the corner in the west with the unusual tomb art addition.

The image had changed.

Abayomi, no longer in the guise of a tanned Osiris, stood full in the flesh beside Sanura. Jeannette stood on the other side of the girl, dressed in the very same clothing she wore that day.

The winged *ba* rested on Abayomi's shoulder like a falconer's favorite bird, poised to fly if required, but content to remain with its master.

"How did this happen?" Jeannette touched the image of herself.

"By the Gods' will?" Sanura pointed at the doorway above the three figures immortalized on the tomb wall. No snake waited at the base of the gate. A faint light emanated from the archway, increasing until it glowed with the strength of an early dawn.

Jeannette looked long and hard at the glowing gateway. "But I don't want to leave you." She calmly turned to face Abayomi and Sanura, shaking her head in denial. "I don't want to go back anymore." A world with Abayomi and Sanura, or a world with indoor plumbing. No contest. "It's just that . . . when I got here, I was so lost. For so long."

Her two friends nodded, awash in their own understanding.

"I thought I was the only outsider in this bizzaro world." But, in all honesty, she'd been more lost back there, in Spokane, at the lab, with nobody but her cat.

"As you said, I do not believe this gate is solely for you." Abayomi stared into her eyes. "It is truth—it is for all of us."

"All of us? Together?" Sanura's words were distant as she watched the doorway.

"Well, each of us comes from another place." He chuckled, the sound no longer the rustling of dry leaves dancing in a fall breeze. "Maybe this is only an island within the river, a place for us to stop and rest and find each other. The Montu Oracle told me the stagnant river would flow once the statues poured sweat. It confounded me initially. At one time I took it to mean once I had found my *ba*, I could move on to the Fields."

Jeannette's chest drew tight. "Is that where you will go?"

Abayomi shook his head. "It is for the Gods to know. But I think this is a journey for us together. I do not think our courses met unintentionally."

"Then, who are our enemies?" Sanura asked. "Are we to now name our enemies?"

Jeannette thought about that. It wasn't Apep, nor the Master Slaver. It wasn't even Tabiry.

"I don't think our enemies are people, or demons, or anything." Jeanette didn't think life was that simple, nor the words of oracles. She thought about what the Sky Watcher said about Sanura, about counting grains of sand or facing your own reflection. She thought about what had kept her in the desert.

"My stubborn independence," she said after some thought.

Abayomi's naming rode on the tail of hers. "My certainty that my next destination be the Promised Lands."

Sanura's face scrunched up a bit. "I think, it's that I wanted what every other kitten had, and that I was unhappy for so long by being forced down a separate path."

Jeannette nodded. "Destroyed your expectations."

Sanura nearly growled. "It wasn't fair!" Then her flash of fang disappeared. "But then I realized, I wasn't like the other kittens. I wore the same fur, but my insides were made of something . . . different. Independent."

The archway painting on the wall blossomed into the brilliance of day, sending out its illumination to fill the entire room. The metal circlet resting around Jeannette's neck ignited against her skin. Abayomi ducked his head, shielding his eyes with a hand.

THREE GREAT LIES

Jeannette wrapped her fingers around the metal and lifted it away from her flesh. "Okay, that's a little . . ." She almost said freaky, but realized it wasn't much out of line of normal for this mythical place of gods come to life and the restoration of lost souls.

"Where do you think it goes?" she asked her friends.

"Somewhere new," Sanura said.

Jeannette laughed. Oddly enough, the glowing archway in the wall didn't worry her, and she wasn't even scared about what was going to happen next. In this world she'd made choices. Here she was, with friends, in a tomb of the dead, and before her opened a gateway into the unknown. Not her world, not Abayomi's. Not this one, either. Not that it mattered much. With them at her side, she'd go anywhere. She began to grin. Was this what happiness was? Having people belong to you as much as you belonged to them?

When she was growing up she used to keep a list of all the things she'd missed that the other kids got to do. Pony parties and Disney trips. The first drive with dad, clutching the hard plastic driver's permit tightly in one hand. Not only things she never got the chance to do, but things that had lost their appeal. Dressing up for the prom. Cruising down Division playing loud music, honking at the cars full of boys. She'd felt like she'd missed so much and such failures had to be cataloged.

Kemet was her starting line for a new life void of lost opportunities. She was the one making stories to tell others. She was the one trekking across worlds, having adventures, *living*.

She would never get those years back. Months ago, before this fantastic adventure had begun, she would have molded mud and straw to build a tomb for all those lost dreams. Now she knew they were simply slices of a childhood that never suited her anyway, and that happiness could still be found if she opened her eyes and looked.

Her happiness had not failed to appear.

"So, are we going to step through the gate?" Abayomi asked, his voice rich, and his smile richer. Jeannette leaned into his shoulder and he pressed back. Had he always been so handsome? Had she ever smiled so much?

"What if we get separated?" Sanura asked, ears cocked back with uncertainty.

Abayomi took Sanura's hand in his own and entwined their fingers together. "Do not be concerned. I have you, and I will not let go. Only Atum can split the waters from the air."

"I've got you, too." Jeannette grabbed Sanura's other hand. She reached across the girl and took Abayomi's free hand in hers, forming a circle as they faced into the west. "We're a family, you know. Fat slavers and angry crocodiles and tomb thieves couldn't tear you from my hold."

The truth, she realized, was there were no great lies. She snorted, amused, that she'd been so caught up in seeking lies that she was blind to the things that mattered. With a calm certainty, she knew it was the same for everyone, each person just rambled along until they discovered what truth and love were all about and that each took their own pathway, however long and laborious it might be, to get to the same place.

Abayomi took in a deep breath. "Let us be on our way, then."

As one they stepped forward, wishing for peace in the beautiful west.

With a last impulse Jeannette glanced back. In the room, sitting next to the sarcophagus was the black jackal. Its sharp, dark eyes watched her. She smiled at it.

The jackal smiled back.

Acknowledgments

This book has marched a long road to get to where it is today. I have so many people to thank, but I want to specifically thank my own personal editors: Mark McCarron-Fraser, Joe Morreale, Kaleb Lynn Thomas, Walt Socha and especially Fonda Lee and Anne-Marie Gerber who dragged this work through the sands of Egypt to help polish it up. I want to thank Tait Anderson for the hours spent working his magic on formatting. Thanks to John St.Clair who offered up his fortune cookie, and therefore the title of this novel. (I know I've forgotten some major players here, please forgive me.) I'd also like to thank Professor Bob Brier Ph.D., from Long Island University and his Great Courses lectures that unknowingly helped bring truth to this novel. Most of all, thanks to Eric T. Reynolds of Hadley Rille; a greater champion for this book I couldn't have asked for.

About the Author

Photo credit: Natalia Kreitzer

Vanessa MacLellan was born and raised in the farmlands of eastern Washington, works as an environmental engineer, and is an avid birder, naturalist and runner living in Portland, Oregon. Her website is vanmaclellan.com.

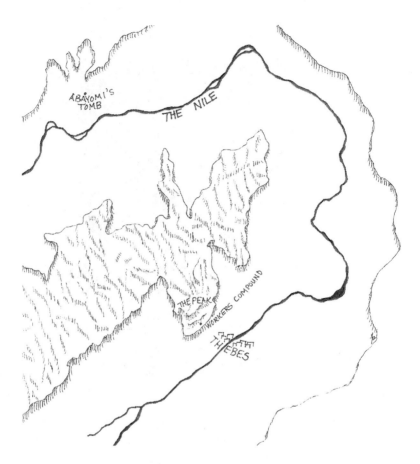

Sanura's Egypt

CPSIA information can be obtained at www.ICGtesting.com
Printed in the USA
LVOW11s1934011015

456528LV00007B/940/P